THE YALE EDITION OF THE
WORKS OF SAMUEL JOHNSON

VOLUME XV

A Voyage to Abyssinia

PREVIOUSLY PUBLISHED

VOLUME I, *Diaries, Prayers, and Annals*

Edited by E. L. McAdam, Jr., with Donald and Mary Hyde

VOLUME II, *The Idler and the Adventurer*

Edited by W. J. Bate, John M. Bullitt, and L. F. Powell

VOLUMES III, IV, and V, *The Rambler*

Edited by W. J. Bate and Albrecht B. Strauss

VOLUME VI, *Poems*

Edited by E. L. McAdam, Jr., with George Milne

VOLUMES VII and VIII, *Johnson on Shakespeare*

Edited by Arthur Sherbo, Introduction by Bertrand H. Bronson

VOLUME IX, *A Journey to the Western Islands of Scotland*

Edited by Mary Lascelles

VOLUME X, *Political Writings*

Edited by Donald J. Greene

VOLUME XIV, *Sermons*

Edited by Jean H. Hagstrum and James Gray

SAMUEL JOHNSON

A Voyage to Abyssinia

(Translated from the French)

EDITED BY JOEL J. GOLD

NEW HAVEN AND LONDON: YALE UNIVERSITY PRESS

1985

The preparation of this volume was made possible (in part) by a grant from the Program for Editions of the National Endowment for the Humanities, an independent federal agency.

Set in Monophoto Baskerville type by Asco Trade Typesetting Ltd., Hong Kong. Printed in the United States of America by Murray Printing Company, Westford, Mass.

Library of Congress catalog card number: 57–11918
International standard book number: 0–300–03003–7

The paper in this book meets the guidelines for permanence and durability of the Committee on Production Guidelines for Book Longevity of the Council on Library Resources.

EDITORIAL COMMITTEE

In Affectionate Memory of
James Lowry Clifford
1901–1978
Scholar, Biographer, Teacher, Friend,
Johnsonianissimus

PREFACE

This edition owes much to the help and encouragement of many individuals and the resources of many institutions.

Grants from the University of Kansas General Research Fund, the National Endowment for the Humanities, and the Newberry Library have provided support at key periods. Research libraries and the invariably helpful curators and librarians who staff them have allowed me to solve most of the puzzles presented by the text. I would acknowledge my debts to the Spencer Research Library (and especially Alexandra Mason) at the University of Kansas, the Beinecke Rare Book and Manuscript Library of Yale University, the Bibliothèque Nationale, the British Library, the Department of Rare Books and Special Collections (and especially Harriet C. Jameson) at the University of Michigan, the Henry E. Huntington Library, the Institute of Historical Research at the University of London, the Lilly Library of Indiana University, the Newberry Library, and the New York Public Library. Material from my essay on "Johnson's Translation of Lobo," *PMLA*, 80 (1965), 51–61, is reprinted by permission of the Modern Language Association of America.

"Lobistas" like Father M. Gonçalves da Costa, C. F. Beckingham, and Donald M. Lockhart have gone out of their way to provide needed guidance on Portuguese and African materials; Joseph Klaits has done the same with information about Joachim Le Grand. My colleague Oliver C. Phillips provided translations for long passages in Latin. Otis E. Fellows of Columbia University kindly modernized Le Grand's French for the annotations. Those who read and commented on various incarnations of the Introduction or the text have made this a better book. They are: O M Brack, Jr., Bertrand H. Bronson, the late James L. Clifford, Bertram H. Davis, James Gray, Jean H. Hagstrum, Robert Halsband, the late Allen T. Hazen, Benjamin B. Hoover, Gwin J. Kolb, Herman W. Liebert, and Howard D. Weinbrot; both J. D. Fleeman and Donald J. Greene deserve special thanks for generous and valuable suggestions. I appreciate as well the confidence of Robert W. Rogers, who first involved me in this edition. For various contributions,

I would express my gratitude to the following scholars at Kansas and at other institutions: Robert E. Anderson, Richard L. Eversole, Thomas Kaminski, Robert Karrow, Elizabeth Kuznesof, Norris J. Lacy, Carolyn Nelson, Edward L. Ruhe, Thomas R. Smith, Ronald W. Tobin, and Jon S. Vincent. Among the research assistants who have contributed are R. Barrie Walkley (USC), Sharon LeFevre, Richard Rabicoff, and Deborah Rogers (Columbia); those who have been extremely helpful to me at Kansas are Kim Bethea, Roger Bland, Karen Goodman, Theresa M. Towner, and Phyllis White.

I have a few special debts. One is to Philip B. Daghlian of Indiana University, who supervised a dissertation long ago on Johnson and Lobo. Another is to John H. Middendorf. Only he knows how very much I owe to him, but all my readers should know how much I appreciate his support, guidance, and general good humor through all the stages of this edition.

And finally what can I say about my gratitude to my wife Ellen, who has lived with the *Voyage to Abyssinia* almost as long as she has lived with me? It is my last best debt.

J. J. G.

The Editorial Committee wishes to express its sincere gratitude to all those individuals, institutions, and organizations whose generous contributions to the Friends of the Edition have helped to make possible the publication of this volume: John L. Abbott, Paul K. Alkon, American Motors Corporation, Donald K. Bain, Sheridan Baker, Lionel Basney, Emmett G. Bedford, Edwin J. Beinecke Trust, Edward and Lillian Bloom, Daniel G. Blum, O M Brack, Jr., Rev. Dr. Winthrop Brainerd, H. Brunnemann, W. Bliss Carnochan, Chester F. Chapin, Henry S. F. Cooper, Jr., Bertram H. Davis, Harry C. DeMuth, Tyson Dines III, East-Central American Society for Eighteenth-Century Studies (in memory of James L. Clifford), Robert T. Eberwein, Bernard Einbond, Elan Foundation, Archibald C. Elias, Jr., Alan H. Foster, Mrs. Forrest W. Frease, Paul Fussell, Jr., Joseph F. Gannon, Richard L. Greene (in memory of Allen T. Hazen), Robert Halsband, Raymond E. Hartz, Joyce Hemlow, C. Beecher Hogan, W. J. Holman, Jr., Mrs. Donald F. Hyde, Elise F. Knapp, Gwin and Ruth Kolb, Peter T. Koper, James M.

Kuist, James R. Lancaster, Louis A. Landa, Lichfield Johnson
Society, Herman W. Liebert, Irma S. Lustig, Paul D. McGlynn,
N. Floyd McGowin, Helen Louise McGuffie, Dr. Lawrence C.
McHenry, Jr., Carey McIntosh, Alan T. McKenzie, T. K.
Meier, John H. Middendorf, Henry Knight Miller, James B.
Misenheimer, Jr., *The New Yorker*, James S. Noel, J. Churchill
Owen, Catherine N. Parke, Stephen R. Parks, R. G. Peterson,
Richard R. Reynolds, Arthur G. Rippey, George S. Rousseau,
Charles A. Ryskamp, Roland J. Sawyer, Pamela and Jack
Schwandt, William R. Siebenschuh, Karl I. Sifferman,
Albrecht B. Strauss, Eugene J. Thomas, Jr., Edward Tomarken,
Mrs. Lila Tyng, Robert W. Uphaus, John A. Vance, Halsted B.
VanderPoel, Magdi Wahba, Marshall Waingrow, Howard D.
Weinbrot, Mrs. William K. Wimsatt, and anonymous donors.

The preparation of this volume was made possible in part by a
grant from the Program for Editions of the National Endowment for the Humanities. For this support the Editorial
Committee is sincerely grateful. The General Editor wishes also
to thank Maureen MacGrogan and Mary Alice Galligan, of the
Yale University Press, for seeing this volume through to com-
pletion with unfailing helpfulness, efficiency, and good sense.

Changes have occurred in the Editorial Committee since the
publication of the previous volume. We are pleased to announce
the appointment to the committee of Bertram H. Davis, Jean H.
Hagstrum, and Roger Lonsdale. But it is with deep sorrow that
we report the loss by death of James L. Clifford, whose energy
and enthusiasm helped to bring this edition into being, and
whose steady concern for its progress ensured its continuation.
As a sign of our admiration and affection, this volume is dedicated to Jim.

CONTENTS

A Voyage to Abyssinia.

* Printed at the end of the volume in 1735.

A Description of Abyssinia

The Sequel of the Account of Abyssinia

Dissertations Relating to the History of Abyssinia

ILLUSTRATIONS

SHORT TITLES

Beccari—Camillo Beccari, ed., *Rerum Aethiopicarum Scriptores Occidentales Inediti*, 15 vols., 1903–17.

Commentarius—Hiob Ludolf, *Commentarius ad suam Historiam Aethiopicam*, 1691.

Dictionary—Johnson's *Dictionary of the English Language*, 4th ed., 1773.

Gazetteer—Laurence Echard, *The Gazetteer's: Or Newsman's Interpreter*, 12th ed., 1724.

Itinerário—Jerónimo Lobo, *Itinerário E Outros Escritos Inéditos*, ed. M. Gonçalves da Costa, 1971.

Library—Donald Greene, *Samuel Johnson's Library: An Annotated Guide*, 1975.

Life—Boswell's *Life of Johnson*, ed. G. B. Hill, revised and enlarged by L. F. Powell, 6 vols. 1934–50; Vols. V—VI (2d ed.), 1964.

New History—Hiob Ludolf, *A New History of Ethiopia*, 1682 (translation of Ludolf's *Historia Aethiopica*, 1681).

Prester John—C. F. Beckingham and G. W. B. Huntingford, eds., *The Prester John of the Indies ... the Narrative of the Portuguese Embassy to Ethiopia in 1520 written by Father Francisco Alvares*, 2 vols., 1961.

Relation—Joachim Le Grand, *Relation historique d'Abissinie du R. P. Jerome Lobo*, 1728.

Sandys—John Edwin Sandys, *A History of Classical Scholarship*, 3 vols., 1906 (2d ed. Vol. I), 1908.

Telles—Balthasar Telles, *Historia Geral de Ethiopia a Alta*, 1660.

INTRODUCTION

Samuel Johnson's first book, *A Voyage to Abyssinia* (1735), was an English translation of Joachim Le Grand's French version of the manuscript account of the travels to Abyssinia of Father Jerónimo Lobo, a seventeenth-century Portuguese Jesuit missionary.

The *Relation historique d'Abissinie* (1728) contains Le Grand's translation of Lobo's Portuguese manuscript, or *Itinerário*, along with a series of dissertations written by Le Grand "on various subjects" concerned with Abyssinia. The first 136 pages, containing the translation of Lobo, cover the years 1621 to 1635, when the missionary was sent to Goa, on the west coast of India, made the dangerous journey to the empire of Abyssinia, labored long for the conversion of the natives, and finally returned to Portugal to seek help for the embattled missions. Le Grand follows this section with his own sequel to Lobo's travels as well as sixteen dissertations (pp. 177–357) on topics ranging from Abyssinian geography and history to church history and religious practices among the Abyssinian Christians. The final segment of Le Grand's book (pp. 359–514) consists of supporting documents—letters (e.g., from Sultan Segued on his conversion; from Rassela Christos, the emperor's brother; from a number of emissaries), memoirs or brief accounts (e.g., on Murat, the supposed envoy from Abyssinia; on the death of the Sieur du Roule), and even a papal brief of Urban VIII. Johnson did not translate these last 155 pages. "In the first part," he tells us in the Preface, "the greatest freedom has been used, in reducing the narration into a narrow compass, so that it is by no means a translation but an epitome" (p. 6). In the sequel and the dissertations by Le Grand he came somewhat closer to a full translation.

About six months before Joachim Le Grand's death in 1733, Samuel Johnson, unemployed and still living at home in Lichfield, was invited by his old school friend, Edmund Hector, to visit Birmingham. Consequently, from the end of 1732 until the middle of 1733 Johnson was a guest in Hector's apartment in the house of Thomas Warren, a bookseller and newspaper printer of Birmingham. Warren himself "was very attentive to

Johnson,"[1] perhaps because the younger man could be of use in a variety of literary ventures.

It is possible that Johnson contributed essays to Warren's short-lived *Birmingham Journal*, only one issue of which is known to exist. Joseph Hill, in his *Book Makers of Old Birmingham*, speculates on the likelihood of Johnson's having written the preface to one of Warren's publications, Edward Brodhurst's *Sermons*, but the lack of clear evidence makes such an attribution unconvincing.[2] Warren appears to have specialized in books of a religious nature, a fact which may throw some light on the publication of Lobo.

In June 1733, after six months as Hector's guest, Johnson took lodgings at the house of F. Jervis in Birmingham.[3] "Having mentioned," writes Boswell, "that he had read at Pembroke College a Voyage to Abyssinia, by Lobo, a Portuguese Jesuit, and that he thought an abridgement and translation of it from the French into English might be an useful and profitable publication, Mr. Warren and Mr. Hector joined in urging him to undertake it." But the book was not to be found in Birmingham, and so, according to Boswell's manuscript notes, "Hector borrowed it of the Library of Pembroke."[4] Johnson's terse note for the winter of 1733 reads: "Mensibus hibernis Iter ad Abisiniam Anglicè reddidi."[5]

But the characteristic inhibition of Johnson's later years was a problem even in 1733. As Boswell explains:

1. The details may be found in *Life*, 1. 85–87; Boswell was drawing on "Particulars of Dr. Johnson's Life communicated to me by Mr. Hector at Birmingham 1785," *The Correspondence and Other Papers of James Boswell Relating to the Making of the Life of Johnson*, ed. Marshall Waingrow, Boswell's Correspondence, Vol. 2, The Yale Editions of the Private Papers of James Boswell (Research Edition), [1969], pp. 85–91. Thomas Warren, according to A. L. Reade, was working in Birmingham from 1727 (*Johnsonian Gleanings*, v. 94). In February 1743 he is listed among the bankrupts in the *Gentleman's Magazine*.

2. See Allen T. Hazen, *Samuel Johnson's Prefaces & Dedications* (1937), pp. 246–47.

3. *Diaries, Prayers, and Annals*, ed. E. L. McAdam, Jr. with Donald and Mary Hyde (Vol. 1, Yale Edition of the Works of Samuel Johnson, 1958), p. 31.

4. Waingrow, ed., *Correspondence . . . Relating to the Making of the Life of Johnson*, p. 87; in the *Life*, however, Boswell writes that "he [SJ] borrowed it of Pembroke College" (1. 86). Dr. J. D. Fleeman, Librarian of Pembroke, informs me that although Hector might have been able to borrow a book for SJ by proxy (in 1733, he notes, *someone* had borrowed a copy of Politian "For ye Use of Mr Johnson"), there is no record of the Le Grand volume ever having been in the Pembroke College Library.

5. *Diaries, Prayers, and Annals*, p. 32.

A part of the work being very soon done, one Osborn, who was Mr. Warren's printer, was set to work with what was ready, and Johnson engaged to supply the press with copy as it should be wanted; but his constitutional indolence soon prevailed, and the work was at a stand. Mr. Hector, who knew that a motive of humanity would be the most prevailing argument with his friend, went to Johnson, and represented to him, that the printer could have no other employment till this undertaking was finished, and that the poor man and his family were suffering. Johnson upon this exerted the powers of his mind, though his body was relaxed. He lay in bed with the book, which was a quarto, before him, and dictated while Hector wrote. Mr. Hector carried the sheets to the press, and corrected almost all the proof sheets, very few of which were even seen by Johnson.[6]

For this work Johnson received five guineas.

Apparently after Johnson had exerted his mental powers and Osborn had finished setting the type, the sheets were run off and left to lie in Warren's shop for many months. J. D. Fleeman has brought to my attention the inscriptions in the copy Johnson gave to Hector (untraced) and suggests a publication date of perhaps December 1734: in addition to Johnson's note, "Sl. Johnson, Translator, 24 yrs.," there is Hector's inscription: "Donat Amici S. J. Authoris ad Ed. Hector 1734."[7] The book was certainly available early in 1735 (an anonymous review consisting mainly of paraphrases was published in the *Literary Magazine, or Select British Library* for March). A title page in black and red announced it as a London production, "Printed for A. Bettesworth, and C. Hitch at the Red-Lyon in Paternoster-Row." Evidently Warren had some kind of working arrangement with these two because the title page of Brodhurst's *Sermons*

6. *Life*, i. 86–87. The fact that the volume was a quarto does not appear in the "Particulars" Boswell took down from Hector; it is simply added to the account in the *Life*. One ambiguous sentence in the "Particulars" does not appear in the *Life*: "Hector wrote it over almost the whole of it ..." (Waingrow, *Correspondence*, p. 88). Close examination of the text does not reveal what Hector did or even the precise point at which he began taking dictation.

7. Dr. Fleeman notes the appearance of the volume in "the Meysey Thompson sale (Sotheby &c. 28 Apr. 1887, lot 750), in Tregaski's Catalogue 778 (March 1916), item 281 (illustrated), and ... the Henkels Bookshop of New York, Catalogue 1407 (3 Apr. 1928), item 455."

reads: "Birmingham: /Printed by T. Warren; / And sold at London by A. Bettesworth, and C. Hitch, in Pater-noster Row; R. Ford, and R. Hett in the Poultry."[8]

From the available bibliographical evidence Herman W. Liebert has demonstrated that the volume had only a limited sale. A new title page all in black was prefixed to the original sheets, which added a new bookseller: "J. and J. Marshall at the Bible in Newgate-Street"; and an advertisement appeared in the *London Evening-Post* for 17 and 19 June 1735 announcing the *Voyage*, reduced in price from five shillings to four, as that day "published, and printed and sold by J. Osborn at the Golden Ball in Paternoster-Row." Liebert sees this advertisement not as evidence of a new edition but rather as "a bookseller's effort . . . to push the book" and concludes that the entire enterprise was unsuccessful: "The reduction in price, the use of a cancel title with the same sheets, and the addition of other and smaller booksellers are all typical expedients to stimulate lagging sales."[9] In 1789, two years after Sir John Hawkins chose not to include the *Voyage to Abyssinia* in Johnson's collected *Works*, George Gleig, a future editor of the *Encyclopaedia Britannica*, published the second edition of the *Voyage* in a volume containing "various other tracts by the same author" and sharply criticized Hawkins for omitting it.[1]

Before Johnson's work on the *Voyage* can be fully appreciated, it is necessary to understand something of the history, especially the church history, of Abyssinia.

The Abyssinian Background

Situated in middle eastern Africa, bordering the lower part of the Red Sea, Abyssinia (or Ethiopia) is a mountainous region

8. Type peculiarities, wood-blocks, headings, and tailpieces found in Brodhurst's *Sermons* are found as well in the *Voyage*, which does not mention Warren or Birmingham (Joseph Hill, *Book Makers of Old Birmingham*, Birmingham, 1907, p. 43).
9. "Dr. Johnson's First Book," *Yale Univ. Library Gazette*, xxv (1950), 28.
1. "General Preface," *A Voyage to Abyssinia* (2d ed., 1789), pp. 1–2, 8–9. Hawkins had a very low opinion of the *Voyage*: "Were we to rest our judgment on internal evidence, Johnson's claim to the title of translator of this work would be disputable; it has scarce a feature resembling him: the language is as simple and unornamented as John Bunyan's; the style is far from elegant, and sometimes it is not even correct" (*The Life of Samuel Johnson, LL.D.* [1787], p. 22).

A VOYAGE
TO
ABYSSINIA.
BY
Father Jerome Lobo,
A PORTUGUESE JESUIT.
CONTAINING,

A Narrative of the Dangers he underwent in his first Attempt to pass from the *Indies* into *Abyssinia*; with a Description of the Coasts of the *Red-Sea.* An Account of the History, Laws, Customs, Religion, Habits, and Buildings of the *Abyssins*; with the Rivers, Air, Soil, Birds, Beasts, Fruits and other natural Productions of that remote and unfrequented Country.

A Relation of the Admission of the Jesuits into *Abyssinia* in 1625, and their Expulsion from thence in 1634.

An exact Description of the *Nile*, its Head, its Branches, the Course of its Waters, and the Cause of its Inundations.

With a Continuation of the History of *Abyssinia* down to the Beginning of the Eighteenth Century, and Fifteen Dissertations on various Subjects relating to the History, Antiquities, Government, Religion, Manners, and natural History of *Abyssinia*, and other Countries mention'd by Father *JEROME LOBO.*

By MR. LE GRAND.

From the FRENCH.

LONDON:
Printed for A. BETTESWORTH, and C. HITCH at the *Red-Lyon* in *Paternoster-Row.*
MDCCXXXV

A VOYAGE
TO
ABYSSINIA.
BY
Father Jerome Lobo,
A PORTUGUESE JESUIT.
CONTAINING,

A Narrative of the Dangers he underwent in his first Attempt to pass from the *Indies* into *Abyssinia*; with a Description of the Coasts of the *Red-Sea.* An Account of the History, Laws, Customs, Religion, Habits, and Buildings of the *Abyssins*; with the Rivers, Air, Soil, Birds, Beasts,

Fruits and other natural Productions of that remote and unfrequented Country.

A Relation of the Admission of the Jesuits into *Abyssinia* in 1625, and their Expulsion from thence in 1634.

An exact Description of the *Nile*, its Head, its Branches, the Course of its Waters, and the Cause of its Inundations.

With a Continuation of the History of *Abyssina*, down to the Beginning of the Eighteenth Century, and Fifteen Dissertations on various Subjects relating to the History, Antiquities, Government, Religion, Manners, and natural History of *Abyssinia*, and other Countries mention'd by Father *JEROME LOLO*

By Mr. LE GRAND.

From the FRENCH.

LONDON:
Printed for A. BETTESWORTH, and C. HITCH, at the *Red-Lyon* in *Paternoster-Row,* and sold by J. and J. MARSHALL at the *Bible* in *Newgate-Street.* MDCCXXXV.

Left: Titlepage of the first issue of the first edition of Johnson's translation, printed in black and red, with Bettesworth and Hitch in the imprint.

Right: Titlepage of the second issue, printed in black only, with J. and J. Marshall added in the imprint.

Reproduced by permission of the Beinecke Rare Book and Manuscript Library, Yale University.

with great plateaus thousands of feet above sea level.[2] Europeans familiar with the rumors of an isolated Christian kingdom ruled by Prester John had often speculated about Abyssinia, but the country was virtually unknown to western travellers before the arrival of the Portuguese in the early sixteenth century. From that time on, Europeans generally had information more reliable than the periodic rumors of a powerful Christian monarch in distant Asia and more detailed than could be gleaned from the sporadic meetings in the Holy Land of pilgrims from Abyssinia with pilgrims from Europe.[3]

A long-accepted legend among the Abyssinians traced their dynasty back to Menelik I, a son born to the Queen of Sheba and King Solomon following her visit to Solomon's court. According to Rufinus's *Historia Ecclesiastica*, the conversion of the Abyssinians occurred in the fourth century when Frumentius and Edesius of Tyre were taken as prisoners to the Abyssinian court. The two Christians were favored by the emperor and released, but Frumentius, after being consecrated by Athanasius at Alexandria, returned to convert Abyssinia to Christianity.[4] The Abyssinian Church later took the momentous step of rejecting the Council of Chalcedon (451) and its definition of the dual nature of Christ, and henceforth adhered to the monophysite doctrine, which postulated the belief that the human and divine in Christ constitute only one nature.

About the middle of the seventh century, increasing numbers of external enemies and the spread of Islam in surrounding nations served to isolate the Abyssinians in their mountain fastnesses. "Encompassed on all sides," wrote Gibbon, "the

---

2. The material in this section is drawn from a number of sources including J. Spencer Trimingham, *Islam in Ethiopia* (1952), Edward Ullendorff, *The Ethiopians: An Introduction to Country and People* (1960), and Tadesse Tamrat, *Church and State in Ethiopia 1270–1527* (1972). SJ and his contemporaries were likely to have gained their knowledge of the country from Hiob Ludolf's *Historia Aethiopica* (1681) or the English translation, *A New History of Ethiopia* (1682).

3. Some first-hand accounts of the quest for Prester John may be found in O. G. S. Crawford, *Ethiopian Itineraries, circa 1400–1524* (1958) and C. F. Beckingham and G. W. B. Huntingford, eds., *The Prester John of the Indies . . . the narrative of the Portuguese Embassy to Ethiopia in 1520 written by Father Francisco Alvares* (2 vols., 1961).

4. These stories are discussed fully at various points in the *Voyage*: the Queen of Sheba in the seventh dissertation (pp. 225–33); the conversion of the Abyssinians in the first chapter of the "Description of Abyssinia" (pp. 40–42) and the ninth dissertation (pp. 244–65).

Aethiopians slept near a thousand years, forgetful of the world, by whom they were forgotten."[5] This seclusion lasted from around 650 to 1270 and helped to produce a Christianity indigenous to Abyssinia. It included such pagan survivals as sacrifices and a belief in evil spirits as well as a cult of the Virgin Mary that saw her haunting "high mountains, springs, and sycamore trees, the former abodes of pre-Christian genii."[6] In addition, there were such Judaic survivals as observation of the Hebrew Sabbath, circumcision on the eighth day after birth, distinctions between clean and unclean animals, and a special reverence for the Ark of the Covenant housed at Aksum.[7] Distinctive Abyssinian practices relating to the sacraments are the subjects of many of Le Grand's dissertations.

Toward the middle of the twelfth century there were greater numbers of Abyssinian pilgrims in the Holy Land and increasing references to foreign ecclesiastics in Abyssinia, but little is known about the effects of this intercourse. After 1270, when the throne was regained by those who traced their lineage back to Solomon and Sheba, Christianity was strengthened, and there was "a prolonged series of wars and skirmishes against ... Muslim invaders."[8] The reign of Zara Yacob (1434–1468), a strong ruler and a zealous Christian, was important for the expanding empire and the flourishing church. With his death, however, the wide-ranging empire began to show signs of disintegration, and by the opening of the sixteenth century Muslim power had grown sufficiently to pose a threat. At this crucial moment the Abyssinians entered formal relations with Europe: at the suggestion of Pedro de Covilhã, who had been residing in Abyssinia for some time, they requested a Portuguese embassy, and one arrived in 1520, almost a hundred years before Lobo. The chaplain of that first expedition, Francisco Alvares, wrote an account of the six-year mission, the first European embassy to reach the Abyssinian court and to return safely.[9]

5. Edward Gibbon, *The History of the Decline and Fall of the Roman Empire* (7 vols., ed. J. B. Bury, 1909–14), v. 176.

6. Trimingham, p. 28.

7. Ullendorff (pp. 97–103) discusses these practices in some detail.

8. Ullendorff, p. 66; Trimingham (pp. 60–75) provides a fuller account of the conflicts between the Muslims and the Abyssinians.

9. Beckingham and Huntingford, eds., *The Prester John of the Indies*, regard Alvares's *Verdadera Informaçam das terras do Preste Joam das Indias* (1540) as a valuable source, "incomparably more detailed than any earlier account of Ethiopia that has survived" (I. 11–12).

Within a few years after the departure of this mission, the rising power of the Muslim leader Ahmad ibn Ibrahim al-Ghazi, called Grañ (or left-handed), pressed on the Abyssinian kingdom. Raids, invasions, and some serious defeats led Emperor Lebna Dengel to send a delegation to Portugal in search of assistance. This request, with its indication of a politic willingness to bring the Abyssinian Church under the jurisdiction of the Church of Rome, resulted in 1541 in the first substantial European expedition, when Cristovão da Gama, son of the explorer Vasco da Gama, landed four hundred men at Massawa. Despite damaging setbacks, including the loss of Cristovão da Gama and half of his force,[1] the Portuguese destroyed Grañ and his followers, and the supremacy of the Abyssinian emperor was assured. Although the Muslim threat was now over, the kingdom was severely weakened and a prey to the raids of the fierce, nomadic Galla tribes of the south and east.[2] Travellers into Abyssinia in the sixteenth and seventeenth centuries, including Jerónimo Lobo, frequently wrote about the dangerous Gallas, who controlled whole areas or states.

The Religious Struggles
in the Sixteenth and Seventeenth Centuries

When in 1540 a bull of Paul III approved the establishment of the Society of Jesus, the collision course was set for the Church of Rome and the Church of Abyssinia. A successor, Paul IV, decided to send a Jesuit mission to Abyssinia, and, at Ignatius Loyola's suggestion, a Portuguese, André de Oviedo, was named its head, with the title of patriarch. This mission reached Arkiko in 1557 and headed inland to begin the uneasy relationship of Jesuit and Abyssinian clergy that would culminate in the Jesuits' expulsion in 1632. During the remainder of the sixteenth century the Portuguese were occasionally drawn into (and sometimes appear to have entered freely) the intrigues, plots,

1. See Lobo's description of his recovery of Cristovão da Gama's relics (pp. 69–71).

2. Tamrat argues persuasively that "Christian Ethiopia was never the same again" after Grañ's wars. The frontier defences had been disrupted, and the pagan Gallas could not be kept out; the destruction of the royal prison had freed many of the princes whose ambitions led to "dynastic conflicts and political instability—particularly between 1559 and 1607." And he traces "the religious conflict with the Jesuit mission" to these "Muslim wars" because "direct European involvement in Ethiopia only started after the Portuguese military assistance in 1541" (pp. 301–302).

and counterplots of Abyssinian politics. For the most part, however, they were left to carry out their work as they wished at the mission house in Fremona, a few miles from the city of Aksum. But by the end of the sixteenth century all the missionaries had died, and there was for a brief period no resident priest at Fremona.

By 1603 one of the most astute outsiders to enter the Abyssinian realms, Pedro Paez, a Spanish Jesuit, had reached Fremona, where he immediately set about learning both the vernacular and the literary-liturgical language, Ge'ez. Moving slowly and diplomatically, Paez eventually translated a catechism into Ge'ez and opened a school for the Portuguese and for those Abyssinians who wished their children to be taught. Invited to the court of Susenyos (Sultan Segued), who ruled from 1607 to 1632, Paez impressed the emperor by delivering an eloquent sermon in Ge'ez.

The reign of Susenyos marked a period of successes for the Jesuit missions and helped prepare the way for Jerónimo Lobo's voyage to Abyssinia. Susenyos' cautious acceptance of Roman Catholicism and Paez's careful diplomacy resulted in real gains for the Jesuits: proselytizing was once again permitted, and observance of the Judaical Sabbath discouraged. The high point may have come in 1622 when Susenyos professed his Roman Catholic faith by accepting the doctrine affirmed by the Council of Chalcedon that Christ has two natures, not one, as taught in monophysitism.

But Jesuit influence soon showed signs of waning. By the time Lobo reached Fremona in June 1625, Pedro Paez had died and been replaced by a man whose temperament and methods were very different from those of the patient and scholarly Paez. Afonso Mendes, a Portuguese Jesuit appointed as patriarch, appears to have been somewhat narrow-minded and arrogant. Not content with accepting the emperor's oath of obedience to the Pope, the patriarch required still more, forcing Susenyos

> to link this personal act of submission with a general abjuration of monophysitism for his whole people. There followed an outcry, especially as [the patriarch] had tied this conversion to an abolition of the entire Ethiopian ritual: baptism, circumcision, fasts and feasts, ordination of deacons and priests, &c. The opposition was not confined to

the clergy, but included members of the Imperial family and, above all, the ordinary Abyssinian, who had no interest in, or knowledge of, doctrinal matters, yet whose life, in every phase, was deeply anchored in the national ethos of the monophysite Church and the expression it gave to the special character of people and country.[3]

The reaction was serious and unremitting, and in 1632 Susenyos reversed himself, revoked the empire's submission to Rome, and restored Abyssinia to the faith of its fathers. His abdication in the same year brought to the throne his son Fasiladas, who banished the Jesuits from the empire and, as Lobo informs us, meted out humiliation, punishment, and even death to them. According to Abba Gregory, the Abyssinian cleric who provided Hiob Ludolf with much of his information about the country, the expulsion of the Jesuits was the cause of rejoicing. Supposedly the people chanted in their own language a version of the following lines:

> At length the sheep of Ethiopia free'd
>   From the bold lyons of the west,
> Securely in their pastures feed.
> St. Mark and Cyril's doctrine have o'ercome
>   The folly's of the Church of Rome.
> Rejoyce, rejoyce, sing Hallelujahs all,
>   No more the western wolves
> Our Ethiopia shall enthrall.[4]

Because of the idiosyncratic nature of Abyssinian Christianity the Jesuits were in the awkward position of Christian missionaries in a Christian land, trying to reconvert the natives to the religion the Abyssinians thought they were following. The geographical isolation of the country, the hostile Islamic and Galla forces surrounding them, and the Abyssinians' firm belief in the Solomonic connection and in themselves as *dakika Esrael* (children of Israel) made them a particularly difficult people to proselytize. They had long been self-sufficient and resistant to outside pressures, and their Christianity had developed dif-

---

3. Ullendorff, p. 78.
4. Hiob Ludolf, *A New History of Ethiopia* (1682), pp. 357–58. The apparent bias of the German Lutheran scholar against Roman Catholicism was the source of much criticism from Catholic writers like Le Grand.

ferently from that of other monophysite churches. This was the Abyssinian religious scene when Lobo arrived.

The Portuguese Traveller

Jerónimo Lobo was born in Lisbon early in 1595, the third son of Francisco Lobo da Gama, Governor of Cape Verde, and Doña Maria Brandão de Vasconcelos.[5] On 1 May 1609 he entered the novitiate and began his study of the humanities in the College of Arts at Coimbra, where the Jesuits had been in charge of the College of Jesus since 1547 and the College of Arts since 1555. At the time of Lobo's attendance, there were in all of Portugal about 650 Jesuits, and in the College of Jesus, if all levels are taken together—priests, scholars, brothers, *coadjutores*, and novices—there were 220. In 1612 the class in eloquence produced three distinguished students; one of the three was Jerónimo Lobo.[6]

In 1617 Lobo left Coimbra for a two-year period of teaching Latin at Braga, in northern Portugal. He returned to Coimbra in 1619 to begin his studies in theology at the College of Jesus. By April 1621 his request to become a missionary had been granted by the Father Provincial, and that same month in Lisbon he was made a subdeacon by the Grand Inquisitor and then ordained a deacon and a priest. Lobo celebrated his first mass on 25 April in Lisbon, and by the twenty-ninth of that month he was on his way to the Indies. The French translator presents, but Johnson omits, an account of the ensuing five-month passage, which was so filled with misfortunes, dangers, sickness, and periods of exhaustion that it had to be aborted. The ill-fated voyagers finally reached Lisbon on 6 October 1621, and a few months later Lobo returned to Coimbra.

Although confined to bed for three months to recover from the harrowing effects of that failed attempt, Lobo was ready by March of the following year to try again. This second expedition

---

5. The fullest account of Jerónimo Lobo's life is to be found in the long and detailed Introduction which Father M. Gonçalves da Costa has included in his critical edition of Lobo's *Itinerário E Outros Escritos Inéditos* (Barcelos: Companhia Editora do Minho, 1971). Most of the material that follows in this section on Lobo is based on Gonçalves da Costa's Introduction and Lobo's writings themselves.

6. *Itinerário*, p. 9.

embarked from Lisbon on 18 March 1622 with a new Viceroy for Portuguese possessions in India, the Count of Vidigueira. It is at this point that Johnson begins his epitome of Lobo's story as translated by Joachim Le Grand. After rounding the Cape of Good Hope toward the end of May, the travellers reached Moçambique on the east coast of Africa on 23 July and left a month and a half later for the settlement of Goa, command post for the missions in India and eastern Africa.

Lobo remained at Goa studying theology from December 1622 until January 1624, when he sailed from India to the coast of what is now Somalia and attempted unsuccessfully to penetrate Abyssinia. Moving southward down the African coast, Lobo reached the island of Patta, just south of the equator, where a Jesuit mission had long been established. Learning there that the Patriarch Afonso Mendes, on his way from Portugal, had passed through Moçambique and was now in Goa, Lobo returned to India and at last, in January 1625, joined the patriarch. Three months later they set out together across the Arabian Sea, landed at the Red Sea port of Baylur (Beilul on modern maps), and started the arduous and dangerous journey inland.

By the third week in June 1625, some four years after Jerónimo Lobo had departed from Lisbon on his first unsuccessful voyage, he finally arrived at the Jesuit House in Fremona.

All of Lobo's experiences in this period of his life are carefully recorded in the *Itinerário*, and most of them are included in Le Grand's French version from which Johnson produced his English epitome. The next few years were taken up with the work of the mission, the teaching, the attempts at conversion, and the rebaptisms that engendered so much ill will toward the Jesuits. In October 1626 Lobo undertook the task that he describes at length, the search for the relics of Cristovão da Gama, murdered by Grañ almost a century before. The recovery took a month, but he returned with the precious bones. Two years later, he tells us, he was bitten by a cobra and was seriously ill for some time. In the following year, 1629, he journeyed to the province of Damot in order to examine the sources of the Nile. Six months after that, in July of the same year, he returned to the province of Tigre and went back to Goiama. At the end of the year he went by way of Natal to the annual Jesuit reunion in Dambia and afterwards returned to work at Fremona.

The missionaries continued their labors over the next two years with only occasional protests from the native clergy and from the people themselves. When the rule of the empire passed from Susenyos to Fasiladas in 1632, however, new problems and dangers began to confront the Jesuits. By 24 April 1633, the patriarch and his company had fled Tigre and taken shelter with Lobo at the Jesuit House in Fremona. It was only a matter of time before all the missionaries were banished from the territories of Abyssinia. Aided initially by friends among the local chiefs, they were subsequently betrayed and delivered to the Turks at Massawa and Suakin. Lobo and most of his companions were finally released from imprisonment after pledging a substantial ransom payment for the patriarch and another priest. They left Suakin aboard a Muslim trading vessel at the end of August 1634. The long, arduous journey eastward to Goa and from there westward to Portugal, begun in February 1635, was interrupted by shipwreck, capture by Dutch pirates, and near starvation on a desert island. Lobo finally reached Lisbon in December 1636.

Hoping to gain help for the beleaguered missions, Lobo had an audience in Lisbon with Princess Margarita, who sent him to Madrid to confer with Philip IV, ruler of Spain and Portugal. From there he traveled to Rome and remained in Italy the rest of the year.

On his return to Portugal, Lobo worked on the *Itinerário* from March 1639 to March 1640, when he embarked again for India.[7] For the next seventeen years he served the mission in a variety of administrative posts at Goa and at Bassein, but he was often involved in disputes with the civil authority and was the target of numerous charges ranging from high living to rumor-mongering about the viceroy. He was arrested and jailed in May 1648 and, despite extended negotiations, remained a prisoner for three years. Even after his release and return to his duties, his problems continued, and he was under pressure until he finally left Goa in 1657 for his last voyage home.

Lobo reached Lisbon in time to provide Balthasar Telles with vital information for the conclusion of his *Historia Geral de*

---

7. It was during this period, 1639–1640, Gonçalves da Costa argues (p. 97 ff.), that the *Itinerário* was written in the form that is now reposited in the Public Library at Braga (MS 813).

Ethiopia a Alta (1660), an abridgement of a manuscript history by Manuel de Almeida. The following year Lobo journeyed to Rome to report on the chaotic state of the embroiled Indian mission. Returning to Lisbon in 1660, he was appointed Vice-Prepositor of the Casa de San Roque, a post he held no more than two years because of friction with the Father Provincial. He remained, however, at San Roque where, in 1666, he received the British ambassador to Portugal, Sir Robert Southwell, who put him in touch with the Royal Society and its secretary, Henry Oldenburg. Lobo continued at San Roque until he died on 29 January 1678, renowned for his travels and his literary accounts.

Publication of the Lobo Material, 1660–1728

Although Lobo's works apparently were not published in Portuguese until the second half of the twentieth century,[8] various Lobo manuscripts have been the source over the years for abridgements, adaptations, and translations. Balthasar Telles, who had been in contact with Lobo some time after 1657, included in his *Historia* information gleaned from the returned traveller. In his prologue Telles indicates that he had seen the "Commentarios" of Father Lobo, and Lobo himself added a page attesting to the accuracy of Telles's account.[9]

Lobo's reputation was further strengthened by his association with Robert Southwell and the Royal Society. At Southwell's urging, Lobo produced short essays on five topics: the river Nile, the unicorn, the title Prester John, the reason for the name Red Sea, and the palm tree. Translated into English for the Society by Sir Peter Wyche, these were published in 1669, without the author's name being mentioned,[1] as *A Short Relation of the River Nile, Of its sourse and Current; Of its Overflowing the Campagnia of*

---

8. C. F. Beckingham describes the Lobo texts in "The 'Itinerario' of Jerónimo Lobo," *Journal of Semitic Studies*, x (1965), 262–64, and in "Jerónimo Lobo: His Travels and His Book," *Bulletin of the John Rylands University Library of Manchester*, 64 (1981), 10–26.

9. *Historia Geral de Ethiopia*, p. 3. Beckingham notes ("Jerónimo Lobo: His Travels and His Book," p. 13) that Lobo had presented an inscribed copy of the *Historia* to the Royal Society. The *Historia* was translated into English by John Stevens, appearing in London in 1710 as *The Travels of the Jesuits in Ethiopia*.

1. In "Jerónimo Lobo: His Travels and His Book," C. F. Beckingham discusses his detective work in establishing the book as Lobo's (pp. 12–14).

Aegypt, till it runs into the Mediterranean: And of other Curiosities: Written by an Eye-witnesse, who lived many years in the chief Kingdoms of the Abyssine Empire. This title provides some idea of the appeal of the work, and the multitude of translations of Wyche suggests its popularity. In the next few years translations of this version of Lobo appeared in French, German, Italian, and Dutch.[2]

The appearance of so many different translations of the manuscripts Lobo had entrusted to the Royal Society and the inclusion of his name on the title pages of many of them secured his reputation as an early authority on Abyssinia. The French translation of Wyche made him known to the French cleric Joachim Le Grand, who came across, and translated, a version of the *Itinerário*, the most extensive of the manuscripts, and he may have been known to Samuel Johnson even before Johnson had read Le Grand's translation at Oxford.

The manuscript used by Le Grand is not known, although nearly all of the Lobo manuscripts have now been found. For a long time the *Itinerário* was presumed to have been destroyed in the Lisbon earthquake of 1755. However, in 1947 that lengthy work of 174 manuscript folios (347 pages), covering the period from 1621 to 1638, was discovered by Father Manuel Gonçalves da Costa in the Biblioteca Pública of Braga in northern Portugal. The *Itinerário*, along with shorter manuscripts also unpublished, was edited in Portuguese by Father da Costa in collaboration with Professor C. F. Beckingham and Professor Donald M. Lockhart.[3]

The manuscript of the *Itinerário* indicates that for a time Lobo worked systematically making corrections. Around 1668, how-

2. A German edition was published at Nürnberg in 1670 entitled *P. Hieronymi eines Jesuiten in Portugal Neue Beschreibung und Bericht von der wahren Beschaffenheit*; Melchisedec Thévenot translated Wyche as *Relation de l'empire des Abyssins, des sources du Nil, de la licorne, &c. par le R. P. Ieronymo Lobo* (1673), and it was later added to printings of Thévenot's *Relations de divers voyages curieux* (1666–72). The Italian version of Wyche appeared in 1693 at Florence, translated by Lorenzo Magalotti: *Relazioni Varie sul Nilo cavate da una traduzione inglese dall' originale portoghese fatto da Girolamo Lobo gesuita*. And in 1707 Pieter vander Aa produced a Dutch edition with the title *Gedenk Waardige Aanteekeningen Van den Eerwaarden Vader Hieronymus Lobo, Aangaange het Rijk der Abyssinen de Oorsprongen des Nigls, den Eenhoorn, Pellikaan, Paradijs-vogel en de verscheyde soorten der Dadel-boomen, door eygen ondervinding in sijn Reys ondersogt en opgeteekent.*

3. The Hakluyt Society has published an English translation of *The Itinerário of geronimo Lobo* (London, 1984) by Donald M. Lockhart, edited by M. G. da Costa, with introduction and notes by C. F. Beckingham.

ever, he probably began work on the shorter version later used by Le Grand for his French translation and subsequently lost.[4] Almost all of the passages in Le Grand's first 136 pages can be compared to appropriate sections in the *Itinerário*, which is almost twice as long. The final section of the *Itinerário* (pp. 512–659), containing the long and eventful voyage back to Portugal, does not appear in Le Grand's book.

The French Translator

We move a step closer to Samuel Johnson's translation when we consider the man whose French text Johnson used. Joachim Le Grand was born at St. Lô in Normandy on 6 February 1653. After his earliest schooling he went to Caen to read philosophy.[5] In 1671 he entered the Oratorian School,[6] where he concentrated on literature and history.

During the years before publication of his translation of Lobo in 1728 Le Grand was employed, at various times, as secretary to the duc d'Estrées, the ambassador to Portugal; as a government historian-propagandist in the service of Jean-Baptiste Colbert, Marquis de Torcy, the influential secretary of state for foreign affairs; and, briefly, as royal censor. In Portugal he gathered information on the history of the Portuguese colonies and looked through various manuscripts, including the account of Lobo's travels. However, he did not immediately turn to translating this find; other interests and duties intervened. He demonstrated his command of Portuguese by translating the *Histoire de l'isle de Ceylan* (1701) from the Portuguese of Captain João de Ribeyro. Just as he would later augment his edition of Lobo, he

---

4. See Gonçalves da Costa's introduction, *Itinerário*, pp. 113–15.

5. Information about Joachim Le Grand is drawn from accounts in Jean Pierre Niceron, *Mémoires pour servir à l'histoire des hommes illustres dans la république des lettres*, XXVI (1734), 123–50; *Nouvelle biographie générale* (1859); and Joseph Klaits, *Printed Propaganda Under Louis XIV: Absolute Monarchy and Public Opinion* (1976), which utilizes manuscript materials in the Bibliothèque Nationale and the Archives Nationales to document Le Grand's career as propagandist; and my own examination of Le Grand's manuscript of the *Relation historique d'Abissinie* in the BN.

6. The French Oratory was established in 1611 and based on the Oratory founded by St. Philip Neri. Oratorians were secular, not regular priests, without vows of obedience; nevertheless, they strove to return to the simplicity of early Christianity with daily prayers, devotions, and sermons.

added to Ribeyro several chapters drawn from manuscripts shown him by Portuguese acquaintances.

The manuscript of the *Relation historique d'Abissinie* (BN, Ms. fr., 9094–95) reveals a careful writer and reviser. The first ninety-three folios, containing Lobo's account, are heavily re-written and interlined. Passages are rearranged and revised to reduce their length and tighten the style. A fair copy of this section, in another hand, contains a few changes by Le Grand. He also appears to have transcribed source materials for the dissertations, some of which (e.g., the first) he reworked exten-sively. In the manuscript the unnumbered "Dissertation sur la côte orientale d'Afrique" follows the fifteen numbered ones; in the published work, this appears between the third and fourth dissertations.

Le Grand's book was ready for publication by 29 March 1727. The following information appears on the title page of the 1728 quarto edition published in Paris:

> Relation Historique d'Abissinie, du R[évérend] P[ère] Jérome Lobo de la Compagnie de Jésus. Traduite du Portu-gais, continuée & augmentée de plusieurs Dissertations, Lettres, & Mémoires. Par M. Le Grand, Prieur de Neuville-les-Dames & de Prevessin. A Paris, Chez la Veuve d'Antoine–Urbain Coustelier, & Jacques Guérin Libraires, Quay des Augustins. 1728.

Three different title pages to this edition exist, although the typesettings throughout the text are the same. One title page is identical to the one cited above except for the substitution of "Voyage" for "Relation" and the incorrect retention of the feminine endings of "traduite," "continuée," and "augmen-tée."[7] A third state of the title page exists with "Voyage" as the opening word and with a different imprint: "A Paris & A La Haye, Chez P. Gosse & J. Neaulme. 1728." The running title is the same for all three versions: "Relation Historique d'Abissinie."

In addition to the quarto, a two-volume duodecimo edition was published at Amsterdam later in the same year. The errata

---

7. A clear discussion of these grammatical errors can be found in Donald M. Lock-hart, "Father Jeronymo Lobo's Writings Concerning Ethiopia" (Diss., Harvard Univ., 1958), p. 65. SJ probably translated from a copy with the *Voyage historique* ... title page, presumably a better seller.

noted at the end of the quarto version have been corrected and the feminine endings of the title changed to agree with the newly inserted masculine word, "Voyage."[8]

Only a few years after the publication of Lobo, Le Grand died of apoplexy on 1 May 1733 at the home of old friends in Paris. He was buried without ceremony, according to his request, at the Cemetery of St. Joseph in the parish of St. Eustache. One account of Le Grand concludes with the eulogy by an acquaintance who describes him as a man of great honour, truth, and religion, skilled in public law, erudite, and sagacious.

The *Voyage* in Context: 1735

Le Grand's French translation of 1728 and Johnson's English translation of 1735 should be seen against the background of the literature of travel, an extremely important genre in Great Britain and on the continent during the seventeenth and eighteenth centuries.[9] Collections by Ramusio in Italy (1550–59) and Hakluyt in England (1589) had appeared in print before Samuel Purchas published the first important collection of the seventeenth century, *Purchas His Pilgrimes* in 1625. Melchisedec Thévenot's *Relations de divers voyages curieux*, which contained a version of Lobo based on Telles' account, was published in Paris in 1674. Hardly a year went by without the publication of numerous individual accounts of journeys or—almost as frequently—of multi-volumed collections of voyages and travels whose title pages, like that of Johnson's *Voyage*, display highlights designed to awaken curiosity and stir the desire for vicarious adventure.[1] "The peculiar pleasure and improvement that

8. The precedence of the *Relation* title is indicated not only by the uniform running title and the grammatical implications of the feminine endings but also by the wording of the seal of approval dated 29 March 1727 for "un Manuscrit qui a pour Titre: *Relation historique de l'histoire de l'Abissinie . . .*" and by the citation of that title in the "Privilège du Roi" also appended to the book.

9. Generic distinctions are effectively applied by Charles L. Batten, Jr. in *Pleasurable Instruction: Form and Convention in Eighteenth-Century Travel Literature* (1978).

1. See Edward Godfrey Cox, *A Reference Guide to the Literature of Travel*, 3 vols., Univ. of Washington Publications in Language and Literature (IX, 1935; X, 1938; XII, 1949); G. R. Crone and R. A. Skelton, "English Collections of Voyages and Travels, 1625–1846," in *Richard Hakluyt and His Successors*, ed. Edward Lynan (1946); and Thomas M. Curley, *Samuel Johnson and the Age of Travel* (1976).

books of voyages and travels afford," one preface explained, "are sufficient reasons why they are as much, if not more read than any one branch of polite literature." [2]

Johnson himself, in addition to translating Lobo's *Voyage*, later contributed reviews of travel books to the *Gentleman's Magazine* and to the *Literary Magazine*, wrote a preface for John Newbery's collection, *The World Displayed*, discussed works of travels in a number of places, especially *Idler* 97, and, of course, incorporated oriental materials in *Irene*, *Rasselas*, and the various eastern tales of the *Rambler* and *Idler*. The list of books in his library relating to travel (geographies, histories, descriptions of antiquities as well as voyages)[3] and the comments he made throughout his life indicate that he read widely in this genre.

Like many of his contemporaries Johnson expected from such books information about the world beyond London, facts about men and manners. His injunctions to would-be travellers to keep detailed journals and to measure what could be measured, as well as his own responsible actions many years later on the tour of Scotland, suggest what he was looking for in his reading. Books of travel were but a substitute for travelling itself: "It is true," he wrote in the *Journey to the Western Islands of Scotland*,

> that of far the greater part of things, we must content ourselves with such knowledge as description may exhibit, or analogy supply; but it is true likewise, that these ideas are always incomplete, and that at least, till we have compared them with realities, we do not know them to be just. As we see more, we become possessed of more certainties, and consequently gain more principles of reasoning, and found a wider basis of analogy.[4]

Even in the last decade of his life he was writing to Warren Hastings in India urging him to "examine nicely the traditions and histories of the East, ... survey the remains of its ancient

2. John Harris, ed., *Navigantium atque itinerantium bibliotheca*, 2d ed. (1744).

3. Donald Greene, *Samuel Johnson's Library: An Annotated Guide*, English Literary Series, No. 1 (1975), p. 21, groups seventeen authors under "Geography, Topography, Travel." For the Abyssinian backgrounds of *Rasselas*, see Lockhart's "'The Fourth Son of the Mighty Emperor': The Ethiopian Background of Johnson's *Rasselas*," *PMLA*, LXXVIII (1963), 516–28.

4. *A Journey to the Western Islands of Scotland*, ed. Mary Lascelles (Vol. IX, Yale Edition of the Works of Samuel Johnson, 1971), p. 40.

edifices, and trace the vestiges of its ruined cities; [so] that at his return we shall know the arts and opinions of a race of men from whom very little has been hitherto derived." Johnson wants to know about "the natural productions animate and inanimate" because "our books are filled, I fear, with conjectures about things which an Indian peasant knows by his senses."[5]

The expectations expressed in Johnson's letter to Hastings are implied in the preface of the *Voyage to Abyssinia*, composed some forty years earlier. Johnson praises Lobo for not amusing his reader with "romantick absurdities or incredible fictions," for describing "things as he saw them," for consulting "his senses not his imagination." Unlike other books of travels, here are "no basilisks that destroy with their eyes." Lobo's crocodiles "devour their prey without tears, and his cataracts fall from the rock without deafening the neighbouring inhabitants."[6] He describes "no regions cursed with irremediable barrenness, or bless'd with spontaneous fecundity, no perpetual gloom or unceasing sunshine; nor are the nations here described either devoid of all sense of humanity, or consummate in all private and social virtues."[7] In short, one finds in Lobo "what will always be discover'd by a diligent and impartial enquirer, that wherever human nature is to be found, there is a mixture of vice and virtue, a contest of passion and reason, and that the Creator doth not appear partial in his distributions, but has balanced in most countries their particular inconveniences by particular favours."

Such praise for the accuracy and the impartiality of Father Lobo indicates that Johnson was able to distinguish between the Jesuit as missionary and the Jesuit as traveller. Indeed, only seven years after the publication of the *Voyage to Abyssinia*

---

5. *Letters* 353 (30 Mar. 1774).

6. As Donald J. Greene, *The Politics of Samuel Johnson* (1960), p. 303, points out, "these are not merely rhetoric, but references to actual passages in Lobo." Cf. pp. 22, 84, and 86 in this edition.

7. P. 3, below. Unlike SJ, James Bruce (*Travels to Discover the Source of the Nile*, 1790) was extremely critical of Lobo on a number of points, mostly having to do with geography; see especially IV. 324–32 and V. 105–106 (2d ed., 1804). In 1775, SJ, who had met Bruce at an earlier date, did not think him "a distinct relater," nor did he "perceive any superiority of understanding" (*Life*, II. 333–34). Some of the "errors" Bruce scornfully catalogued can be traced to Le Grand's translation of the Portuguese or to inaccurate footnotes appended to SJ's translation, probably by the Birmingham publisher. See, for example, pp. 9, 11, and 12 in this edition.

Johnson made explicit what is implicit in his praise of Lobo. In 1742 he published in the *Gentleman's Magazine* an "Essay on the Description of China," a translation of Du Halde's work recently printed by Edward Cave. Although most of the essay epitomizes Guthrie's translation, the opening paragraphs reveal Johnson's approbation of the Jesuits as nearly ideal travellers:

> For the Fathers of the mission, are obliged by the nature of their undertaking, to make the language of the nation in which they reside the[ir] first study, to cultivate a familiarity with the natives, to conform to their customs, observe their inclinations, and omit nothing that may produce influence, intimacy, or esteem.
>
> How well the Fathers, whose lot it was to be employed in the conversion of the Chinese practised all the arts of address, appears from the authority which they gained, and the employments in which they were engaged by the emperors, and which necessarily enabled them to examine every thing with their own eyes, and exempted them from the necessity of trusting to uncertain informations.[8]

Virtually all Johnson's recorded comments about the appropriate way to travel and to write about travelling stress the value of the eyewitness and the importance of first-hand knowledge. If, in addition to these advantages of the Jesuit travellers, an individual priest combines the virtues of truthfulness and objectivity, he "has a right to demand, that they should believe him, who cannot contradict him."[9] In Johnson's view, Father Lobo had this right.

The Religious Issues: Seventeenth and Eighteenth Centuries

Although travel books sold well, books on religious topics had an even wider appeal.[1] Publishers were continually bringing out sermons, church histories, hymnals, biographies of saints and

8. *Gentleman's Magazine*, XII (1742), 320–21. Arthur Sherbo, "Samuel Johnson's 'Essay' on Du Halde's *Description of China*," *Papers on English Language and Literature*, II (1966), 375, sees "the first fourteen paragraphs of the 'Essay' with their remarks on writers of travel literature and their praise of the learning and industry of the missionaries" as constituting "a largely independent essay" by Johnson, one which is clearly in agreement with his comments about Lobo in his Preface to the *Voyage*.
9. Preface, p. 3.
1. Curley, *Samuel Johnson and the Age of Travel*, p. 53.

churchmen, as well as discourses on religious themes. As a matter of fact, Johnson's Birmingham publisher, Thomas Warren, who had joined with Hector in urging Johnson to undertake the translation of Lobo, published a number of sermons, dialogues, and lectures on religious matters both before and after Johnson's book. The Birmingham Library has a half dozen or more religious books published by Warren between 1725 and 1738.

It seems clear that Warren had a clientele for such books. But a volume on the Jesuit missions to Abyssinia, along with a number of dissertations exploring the conflicts that divided the Abyssinian Church from the Roman Catholic Church, might well appeal to an even wider audience.

The isolation of Abyssinia and its development of an indigenous and idiosyncratic Christianity help to explain why it became a vicarious battleground for Protestant and Catholic polemicists in the seventeenth and eighteenth centuries. Their skirmishing resulted in a number of published attacks throughout the period. In 1681 the publication of Hiob Ludolf's *Historia Aethiopica* served to increase the tempo of the controversy. Scholarly though his approach was,[2] Ludolf's Lutheran interpretation of Abyssinian Church practices aroused antagonists throughout Catholic Europe. Whereas the Jesuits had asserted that the Abyssinian Church, with its rites of purification, circumcision, and others borrowed from the Jews, was immersed in heresy, Ludolf, drawing much first-hand information from the Abba Gregory, an Abyssinian, saw nothing heretical in such practices. On the contrary, he believed that the Abyssinian Church, untainted by Rome, could provide further justification for the Protestant Reformation. Moreover, the Jesuit insistence on the sinful condition of that church offered Protestants one more example of the wrongheadedness of the Church of Rome. These were the battle lines.

The contrast is sharply focused in *A Voyage to Abyssinia*. Jerónimo Lobo, the Portuguese Jesuit missionary, predictably criticizes the heretical Abyssinians; Hiob Ludolf, the Lutheran

---

2. He had already published a *Lexicon Aethiopico-Latinum* (1661) and a *Grammatica Aethiopica* (1661). Item 587 in the *Sale Catalogue* of SJ's library is "Ludolph's History of Ethiopia"; this is probably the English translation, dated 1682 (*Library*, p. 79).

Ethiopic scholar, is frequently brought into the dissertations in order that he may be refuted by Joachim Le Grand, the French Oratorian translator and propagandist; and Samuel Johnson, the Anglican translator (or epitomizer), has the final word on Lobo, Ludolf, and Le Grand. Given what we know about Le Grand's practices in his historical propaganda—the careful choice of authorities, the "great display of scholarly apparatus," and the general tone of erudition in the service of a specific point of view[3]—we should be suspicious of how he handles the evidence. Indeed, early in his eighth dissertation Le Grand remarks that Ludolf found nothing to blame among the Abyssinians except what they had in common with the Roman Catholic Church. Johnson in his Preface not surprisingly favors Ludolf: "The Portuguese, to make their mission seem more necessary, endeavour'd to place in the strongest light the differences between the Abyssinian and Roman church, but the great Ludolfus laying hold on the advantage, reduced these later writers to prove their conformity" (p. 5).

Johnson's opposition to ex cathedra authority and to dogmatism seems to affect his attitudes toward Roman Catholicism and the Jesuits and occasionally to dictate the language of his translation. Midway through his Preface, his phrasing becomes sharp and bitter:

> Let us suppose an inhabitant of some remote and superiour region, yet unskill'd in the ways of men, having read and considered the precepts of the Gospel, and the example of our Saviour, to come down in search of the *True Church*: if he would not enquire after it among the cruel, the insolent, and the oppressive; among those who are continually grasping at dominion over souls as well as bodies; among those who are employed in procuring to themselves impunity for the most enormous villanies, and studying methods of destroying their fellow-creatures, not for their crimes but their errors; if he would not expect to meet benevolence engaged in massacres, or to find mercy in a court of inquisition, he would not look for the *True Church* in the Church of Rome (pp. 4–5).

The powerful cumulative effect of the rhetoric leaves little doubt of the writer's point of view.

3. Joseph Klaits, *Printed Propaganda Under Louis XIV*, pp. 257–60.

In his Preface Johnson provides his readers with a counterbalance to the Catholic viewpoint by suggesting that if the reader "will not be satisfied with a popish account of a popish mission," he might turn to Michael Geddes's *The Church-History of Ethiopia*, "in which he will find the actions and sufferings of the missionaries placed in a different light" (p. 4). But Geddes, trying to unite the anti-papal forces, takes an extremely narrow view, and in his Dedication praises the Church of Abyssinia: "A church that was never at any time under the papal yoke, and which when its princes, instead of being nursing fathers, struggled hard of late years to have brought its neck under it; never rested until it had both broke that insupportable yoke asunder, and secured it self from ever having the like attempts made again upon its liberty." [4] Referring his reader to an author like Geddes does not, of course, imply that Johnson endorsed Geddes's vehement anti-papal opinions. He points out that Le Grand, too, "with all his zeal for the Roman Church," saw the missionaries in the same light as Geddes did and even "dared . . . in the midst of France to declare his disapprobation of the Patriarch Oviedo's sanguinary zeal" (p. 4). Johnson's approach in the Preface and in the translation itself is similar to the one he took a few years later in "The Life of Father Paul Sarpi."

The Political Context

In *The Politics of Samuel Johnson* Donald J. Greene comments on the international situation at the time Johnson was choosing his text and dictating his epitome to Edmund Hector:

> Johnson would have been aware . . . that friendship with [Cardinal] Fleury's France was the keystone of Walpole's structure of foreign relations, and that the Portuguese alliance, created by the Methuen treaty of 1703, was one of the showpieces of Whig diplomacy. It may be only a coincidence to find Johnson, at this early date, turning into English a book that is on the whole derogatory of Jesuit and Portuguese colonial activity; but in light of the vigorous

---

4. Michael Geddes, *Church-History of Ethiopia* (1696), A2r. In 1686, after having been chaplain to the English factory in Lisbon for eight years, Geddes was called before the Inquisition, threatened, "and strictly forbidden . . . to minister any more to his congregation" (Ibid., pp. xiv–xv).

opinions he was to express a few years later on the subjects of both Walpole and colonialism, it is an interesting one.[5]

Le Grand's role as chief propaganda writer in the last years of Louis XIV adds further nuances and makes the "coincidence" an even more interesting one. In the epitome itself the Portuguese do not fare well at the hands of the English "translator," but such treatment need not be imputed to any narrow political motives on Johnson's part. Greene's conclusion is probably correct: Johnson had "a strong suspicion that projects of colonialization and proselytization often cloak motives of aggrandizement and commercial gain."[6]

Regardless of any hypothetical opposition by Johnson to a British alliance with the Portuguese, his treatment of them in the *Voyage* reveals that he saw them as representatives of the "civilized" world. Believing that mankind was everywhere the same, and actuated by powerful theological and ethical convictions, Johnson could not condone the long exploitation of the Africans by the Portuguese. Johnson's views on this subject appear not to have changed much over the years. In 1759 his Introduction to John Newbery's collection, *The World Displayed*, provides an unequivocal point of view about an unprovoked Portuguese assault on the natives:

> On what occasion, or for what purpose cannons and muskets were discharged among a people harmless and secure, by strangers who without any right visited their coast; it is not thought necessary to inform us. The Portuguese could fear nothing from them, and had therefore no adequate provocation; nor is there any reason to believe but that they murdered the negroes in wanton merriment, perhaps only to try how many a volley would destroy, or what would be the consternation of those that should escape. We are openly told, that they had the less scruple concerning their treatment of the savage people, because they scarcely considered them as distinct from beasts; and indeed the practice of all the European nations, and among others of the English barbarians that cultivate the southern islands of America proves, that this opinion, however absurd and foolish, however wicked and injurious, still continues to

5. P. 71.
6. P. 72.

prevail. Interests and pride harden the heart, and it is in
vain to dispute against avarice and power.[7]

At times in the epitomizing of the *Voyage* Johnson colors
unfavorably the picture of the Portuguese by omitting details
that help to explain their actions. For instance, when the Jesuits
and the Portuguese soldiers have trouble with a recalcitrant
Moor, the master of the camels, Johnson's readers are simply
informed that the Moor was "knock'd down by one of our
soldiers" (p. 34). The account of his prior attack on a
Portuguese soldier is not translated. Moreover, in describing the
aftermath of this incident Johnson again leaves out some important elements:

Le vieillard fut contraint de rendre les cordes, mais il voulut nous quitter & fit décharger ses chameaux. Un Portugais & deux Mores des plus considérables trouvèrent moyen de l'apaiser, & depuis ce temps il parut un peu plus traitable. [p. 55]	he then restor'd the cords, and was more tractable ever after. [p. 34]

The English version provides no motive for the actions of the
Moor, and by omitting both the efforts at peacemaking and the
reason for striking the camel driver, Johnson heightens an impression of Portuguese cruelty and disdain. Similar deletions of
pertinent details suggest an anti-Portuguese bias occasionally at
work in Johnson's epitome.

The Techniques: "Not a translation but an epitome"

The eighteenth century gave birth to many theories of translation, some of which appeared contradictory.[8] The original
ideas should be faithfully reproduced—but not word for word.
The translator should strive for mimesis—but should provide a
sense of ease and originality. Most theoretical approaches, how-

---

7. Hazen, *Samuel Johnson's Prefaces & Dedications*, p. 227.
8. T. R. Steiner, *English Translation Theory, 1650–1800*, Approaches to Translation
Studies, No. 2 (Assen: The Netherlands, 1975). The first sixty pages of Steiner's useful
book bring together all of the pertinent theories.

ever, seem more applicable to literary originals like Homer or
Horace than to the kind of book Johnson was translating.
Johnson himself closes his account of translations in *Idlers* 68 and
69 with praise for the freer translations of recent years:

> Thus was translation made more easy to the writer, and
> more delightful to the reader; and there is no wonder if ease
> and pleasure have found their advocates. The paraphrastic
> liberties have been almost universally admitted, and
> Sherbourn, whose learning was eminent and who had no
> need of any excuse to pass slightly over obscurities, is the
> only writer who in later times has attempted to justify or
> revive the ancient severity.
>
> There is undoubtedly a mean to be observed. Dryden
> saw very early that closeness best preserved an author's
> sense, and that freedom best exhibited his spirit; he there-
> fore will deserve the highest praise who can give a represen-
> tation at once faithful and pleasing, who can convey the
> same thoughts with the same graces, and who when he
> translates changes nothing but the language.[9]

To the task of translating Le Grand's volume Johnson
brought an apparently self-taught competence in French, a
facility with words and rhetoric, a mind already stored with
facts and literature, a temperament that made him often speak
out in opposition, and an unwillingness to adhere slavishly to his
French text. "Such great liberties have been taken," he tells us
in his Preface, that at least the first part "is by no means a
translation but an epitome." Although it is tempting to conjecture at what point Johnson began dictating to Hector on the
basis of the closeness or looseness of translation or the amount of
epitomizing, there is no place at which a shift is clear. The
dissertations seem to contain fewer epitomes, but they are, of
course, a different genre from the earlier travel narrative.

A collation of the French and English versions of *A Voyage to
Abyssinia* reveals Johnson translating fairly closely in places,
epitomizing in others, omitting some sections, expanding others,
softening or adding asperity to the tone, rearranging elements
for greater clarity, balancing phrases for smoother syntax, inserting transitions for easier reading, and even inserting editorial comments to point a moral. These conclusions about the

---

9. Final paragraphs of *Idler* 69.

work on Lobo reinforce the judgments of John Lawrence Abbott about all of Johnson's French translations: in a given work, "what emerges is less a translation and more a recreation of the foreign text."[1]

Because the modern languages were not considered proper subjects for study in eighteenth-century schools and universities, Johnson, like many of his contemporaries, would have been forced to learn French on his own, perhaps working his way through a number of books with a dictionary beside him.[2] Nevertheless, even though his study of French was probably unsystematic, the general fluency of his translation suggests that he was at home with the language. Most of his errors in translating the *Voyage* occur with simple words—especially numerical terms—and probably indicate carelessness rather than unfamiliarity:

> "trois hommes"—"four of their company"
> "trois"—"two"
> "dix"—"six"
> "cent soixante & douze"—"an hundred and sixty-two"
> "trente jusqu'à cinquante"—"forty or fifty"
> "cinq ou six cens figues"—"five or six figs"
> "sixième siècle"—"sixteenth century"
> "Provinces Occidentales"—"Eastern Provinces"
> "vers le couchant"—"eastward"
> "coudes"—"hands"

Some of these occur more than once (e.g., "dix" as "six"). Occasionally the error is serious: his rendering of "quatre vingt" as "twenty four" leads to a misrepresentation of the purification rites of the Abyssinian Church. Such mistakes suggest that Johnson learned his French from books that seldom employed numerical terms: at any rate, he apparently felt that his knowledge of French was adequate enough to supply an equivalent for such terms without consulting a dictionary.

1. "No 'Dialect of France': Samuel Johnson's Translations from the French," *Univ. of Toronto Quarterly*, XXXVI (1967), 130.

2. Of the many French dictionaries published before Johnson's work on Lobo both Abel Boyer's *Royal Dictionary* (1699) and Pierre Richelet's *Dictionnaire François* (1710) are listed in the *Sale Catalogue* of Johnson's library in 1785, although they are not in the list of books he had at Oxford. The *Royal Dictionary* has two parts—French-English and English-French—while the *Dictionnaire François* is simply a dictionary of the French language.

One special characteristic of Johnson's translations, pointed out by Professor Abbott, is Johnson's odd handling of the French idiom "venir de" plus an infinitive. Johnson, as Abbott carefully notes in numerous citations, "chooses to render the meaning of this idiom in a variety of ways" but never with the usual sense of "'to have *just* done' something."[3]

Collation of the English edition with its French source quickly bears out Johnson's own remark that "great liberties have been taken." Virtually every page reveals him altering his text— cutting, expanding, rearranging, or commenting.[4] He omits sentences and paragraphs and even larger units such as the account of Lobo's first aborted voyage. He deletes names, dates, locations, and other details; he paraphrases longer passages; some epitomes turn lengthy first-person narratives and letters into compendious third-person accounts. But Johnson also expands material in Le Grand. Sometimes his enlargement grows out of ideas or phrases in parts already deleted; at other times his expansions clarify or emphasize, praise or blame. To cite only one example, we may consider how Johnson expands the brief passage on Grotius in Le Grand:

Grotius, qui a bien connu combien les impies tireraient d'avantage de ce raisonnement, l'a combattu de toute sa force, & a fait voir ... [p. 275]

Grotius, that name so justly celebrated, was sufficiently apprised how much this way of reasoning turn'd to the advantage of infidelity, and therefore opposed it with all the power of his learning, and was so successful in this laudable attempt, that he has made plain ... [p. 237][5]

3. John Lawrence Abbott, "Dr. Johnson's Translations from the French" (Diss., Michigan State Univ., 1963), p. 23. Boyer's *Royal Dictionary* renders the idiom as "to have just ...," and Abbott cites a few examples from the *Voyage*: "je viens de rapporter" / "I have been speaking of"; "qu'il venoit d'apprendre" / "that he had lately been informed"; "les auteurs que nous venons de citer" / "the authors already cited" (pp. 53–54).

4. A full discussion of the changes and their effects may be found in my article on "Johnson's Translation of Lobo," *PMLA*, LXXX (1965), 51–61.

5. In these parallel quotations page references for the French text are to Le Grand's *Relation*, and the page numbers for the English text refer to this edition of Johnson's *Voyage*.

While alterations like this expand upon an idea already present and augment the praise implied in the original, others clearly change the tone of the source. Compare the French and English versions of Lobo's reflections on the foolish savants who wrote of the Nile before the Portuguese discoveries:

<table>
<tr>
<td>

On ne peut aujourd'hui ne pas voir combien sont vains & ridicules les discours de ces philosophes, qui par une sotte vanité se sont imaginés que la nature se réglait & se gouvernait selon leurs caprices, & ont voulu assujettir tant de prodigieux effets que nous voyons tous les jours à la subtilté de leur imagination & de leurs raisonnements. [pp. 111–12]

</td>
<td>

I cannot help suspending my narration to reflect a little on the ridiculous speculations of those swelling philosophers, whose arrogance would prescribe laws to Nature, and subject those astonishing effects which we behold daily, to their idle reasonings, and chimerical rules. Presumptuous imagination! [p. 88]

</td>
</tr>
</table>

Certainly Lobo's criticism of "la subtilté de leur imagination & de leurs raisonnements" directs Johnson to a disapproving comment. But it does not account for the contempt which creeps into his phrasing: "idle reasonings, and chimerical rules." Nor does it explain that final crushing "Presumptuous imagination!" The cumulative effect of "ridiculous speculations," "swelling philosophers," "arrogance," and the rest serves to create an English version much more scornful than the French.

Other changes are more obviously stylistic. Sometimes Johnson adds phrases to connect paragraphs and ideas. Sometimes he prepares a reader for what is to come; at other times he bridges omitted material. Beyond the syntactical changes that might occur in any translation, Johnson in the *Voyage* will frequently provide balanced terms. Abbott suggests that "a doubling of a modifier (as 'une imitation fine,' in Johnson's rendition 'a remote and delicate imitation'), appears so frequently that it becomes a kind of signature and might be of value in identifying doubtful authorship." [6] Occasionally the process is complex. For example, Johnson employs new adjectives or additional terms to make the parallelism more effective at a

6. Abbott, "No 'Dialect of France': Samuel Johnson's Translations from the French," p. 130.

point in the journey when Lobo and his companions enter a mountain gorge:

Il semble que Dieu ait fait ce lieu exprès pour le soulagement des pauvres voyageurs, qui après avoir beaucoup souffert de la soif & de la chaleur, viennent se reposer entre ces montagnes. Ils y trouvent de l'eau, des arbres toujours verts, un frais agréable qu'entretient un vent qui ne manque jamais de s'élever à certaines heures du jour. [p. 56]

Heaven seems to have made this place on purpose for the repose of weary travelers, who here exchange the tortures of parching thirst, burning sands, and a sultry climate, for the pleasures of shady trees, the refreshment of a clear stream, and the luxury of a cooling breeze. [p. 35]

Here the elements have not only been carefully arranged; some of them have been created expressly to provide parallels which the original lacked. The skillful insertion of the verb "exchange" enables Johnson to set up his parallels. Consequently, he can exchange "tortures" for "pleasures," "refreshment," and "luxury," none of which appears in the original. Although Lobo's travellers suffered only from "soif & de la chaleur," they find "l'eau, des arbres ... un frais." Apparently believing that two disadvantages ought not to be traded for three advantages, Johnson manufactures a third evil, the "burning sands." Furthermore, he provides appropriate adjectives for the unadorned nouns he found in his source: thus, "soif" becomes "parching thirst," "chaleur" becomes "sultry climate" and, one may assume, produces those "burning sands." The adjectives in Lobo's second sentence are altered by Johnson: "l'eau" becomes "a clear stream," "arbres toujours verts" are transformed into "shady trees," and "un frais agréable," least altered, is rendered "a cooling breeze."

Obviously the intricate balance achieved by inventing and arranging details results from Johnson's careful planning, a process that must have been going on *while* Hector was writing down the previous phrases. In all of the foregoing it should be evident that the creative reshaping found throughout *A Voyage to Abyssinia* results in a recognizable "Johnsonian" style that links the writer of the text with the writer of the preface.

The various techniques at work throughout the book change significantly the picture of the Patriarch and the Jesuits afforded by the French source. Johnson's animus towards the Jesuits, apparent in the Preface, is also visible in the translation.[7] In virtually every place where Lobo speaks favorably of Patriarch Mendes, Johnson limits the praise or omits the passage. For instance, consider the difference between Johnson's epitome of the account of the Patriarch in exile and Lobo's fuller version:

jamais ce vertueux prélat ne perdit de vue sa chère Eglise d'Abissinie: toujours même attention, toujours même empressement pour soulager les catholiques qu'il avait laissés en ces pays-là; tant de voyages entrepris sans aucun fruit ne le rebutèrent pas. [p. 152]

that prelate whose thoughts were always intent upon his Church of Aethiopia ... [p. 131]

Eliminating the sympathetic phrasing, especially of "toujours même empressement pour soulager les Catholiques," changes the tone of the passage. Le Grand's French suggests the Patriarch's concern for the people as well as for the church; Johnson's English indicates only a possessive interest in "his" Church. And this is not an isolated instance.[8]

Moreover, Johnson frequently omits accounts of Jesuit or Roman Catholic ceremonies; for example, he deletes a detailed description of the Passion-Week activities. Whenever Lobo attributes miracles to God or interprets the will of God, Johnson

7. Professor Abbott has reached similar conclusions about the anti-Catholic bias that emerges in SJ's "Life of Father Paul Sarpi" (*Gentleman's Magazine* for November 1738), a translation based on Pierre-François Le Courayer's "Vie Abrégée de Fra-Paolo." Noting that SJ ignores some favorable points about Sarpi, Abbott observes that "Instead Johnson picked the most damning utterance Sarpi made about Rome and placed it in a crucial position in his article, toward the end, which leaves the reader with an impression of Sarpi which is not the one he gets from Le Courayer's text. Only in comparing the French and English texts, however, is it possible to see that to a certain extent the Sarpi of Johnson's version is a reflection of his own attitudes and prejudices and not always a faithful mirroring of the French" ("Dr. Johnson and the Making of 'The Life of Father Paul Sarpi,'" *Bulletin of the John Rylands Library*, XLVIII [1966], 267).

8. See, e.g., pp. 126 n. 8, 127 n. 4, 133 n. 5.

almost invariably weakens the impression of Lobo's personal knowledge of God's actions or intentions. What would appear to be a conscious bias even leads him to excise a particularly apt allusion from Lobo's account of the inhospitable village that resisted conversion (Le Grand, pp. 82–83; Johnson, pp. 57–58). Johnson translates almost literally the whole of Lobo's commentary up to the point when, the first lady of the community proving too difficult, the Jesuits decide to move on. But Johnson deletes the key line: "Nous fîmes ce qu'ordonne Jésus Christ; nous secouâmes la poussière de nos souliers." The single omitted element, the pertinent reference to Christ's advice to the apostles (Matthew x. 14), must disturb anyone who would argue that Johnson is omitting only that which is neither useful nor entertaining. Probably Johnson was struck by the literary justness of the remark, coming as it did from a missionary, but could not brook the religious implication of a direct descent from those first apostles to these. Such a line of reasoning seems more logical than assuming that Johnson thoughtlessly deleted one of the most appropriate images in the book.

One of Johnson's most common devices weakens the Jesuit case against the Abyssinians by substituting milder terms for words like "hérétique" and "schismatique." The English text seldom calls the Abyssinians heretics and schismatics even when the French plainly implies such a rendering. The frequency of these alterations indicates a determined effort to avoid the harsher terminology, to point out that "heretic" only meant one opposed to the Church of Rome. The evidence appears throughout *A Voyage to Abyssinia*.

Perhaps the most striking contrast occurs following the description of an edict requiring the people to renounce their errors and rejoin

l'eglise catholique, apostolique & romaine, ... & dans un combat qui se donna entre les hérétiques & les troupes du Sultan Segued ... [p. 114]	the Roman Church; ... and in a battle fought between these people that adhered to the religion of their ancestors, and the troops of Sultan Segued ... [p. 91]

What a remarkable shift in tone! Johnson deftly attracts the reader's sympathies for "les hérétiques" by transforming them into "these people that adhered to the religion of their ancestors." Point of view makes all the difference. Wherever Johnson renders epithets like "hérétiques" and "schismatiques" as "those opposed to the Church of Rome," he undercuts the Jesuit case against the Abyssinians.

A reader of the present edition of *A Voyage to Abyssinia* will find that the young translator was temperamentally incapable of producing a sustained literal translation; that he had strong opinions about both the subject matter and tone of his source; and that by striving for a clearer, more unified, more logical English text he eliminated many of Le Grand's details—proper names, footnotes, and the like.

Some additional conclusions may be drawn about the young Johnson. Disapproving of the Portuguese intruders, he seems never willing to grant them the benefit of the doubt—as we have seen—even in their encounters with wily camel drivers plotting betrayal (p. 36). His handling of Portuguese actions and motives in the *Voyage* therefore reveals a fairly consistent manipulation. Furthermore, his subtle omission of the missionaries' motives results in a noticeable weakening of Jesuit claims for a special knowledge of God's wishes and in a definite blunting of their criticism of the heretical Abyssinians. What we witness here is not merely Johnson's opposition to the implied religious superiority of the Jesuits, but also his deep-seated antagonism to the miraculous and intuitive in religion. The general tenor of his epitome, his attempt to discover the truth behind apparent fictions, and his unwillingness to credit God with performing miracles solely for the benefit of the Society of Jesus, all point to a fundamental rationality independent of religion. But again and again Johnson rejects mere rationality and questions whatever does not rest on a foundation of fact, preferably of direct observation. Johnson's rationality and empiricism lie at the heart of his systematic, unsympathetic retouching of Lobo and the Jesuits.

Johnson's antagonism to Portuguese high-handedness in general also seems occasionally to have affected his treatment of the Jesuit fathers. Although Johnson does not attack their Roman Catholic doctrine, he does disparage them because of their attempts to control the Abyssinians. His frequent detractions of Mendes, for example, may be traced to his dislike of the Patriarch's insensitive and often belligerent treatment of the population. Moreover, by playing down the Roman Catholic and Jesuit claims of belonging to the *true* "Apostolic" church and of professing the only correct interpretation of God's word, Johnson sharply limits the authority the Jesuits can muster to support their campaign against the Abyssinians. On the other hand, the Abyssinians are presented not as heretics or schismatics but rather as a people who are separated from or opposed to the Church of Rome, who wish not to be seduced from the true church, and who desire to hold fast to the faith of their ancestors. In their struggle to retain their old religion and customs against the inroads of the Jesuits, the Abyssinians clearly have Johnson's support.

Critical Annotation

Ordinarily an edition of a translation would not provide annotations for all divergences from the source. Any translator will necessarily clarify elements in his text, will adopt expressions for his own audience, will perhaps impose his style on the materials he translates, and will undoubtedly commit occasional errors. In this instance, however, I assume readers will want to know all they can about Johnson at work, even Johnson at the hack work that such translation required. For this reason, in addition to explanatory notes to provide necessary information about places, persons, or practices mentioned in the text, another sort of explanatory note accompanies the text. Where Johnson's rendering differs substantively from his source, the present edition indicates the degree of freedom and occasionally provides the French original (in modernized form) for the reader to compare. Page references in such notes are to the one-volume Paris edition of 1728 and will allow an interested reader to examine even more thoroughly the minute variations of Johnson's translation.

Through this extensive series of comparisons with the French original the present edition offers a unique opportunity to observe Johnson the translator. It risks, of course, overloading the text with footnotes that some readers might prefer to avoid. On the other hand, it does not attempt to take the place of those editions of Lobo's *Itinerário* published in Portuguese by the Livraria Civilização and in English by the Hakluyt Society.

In the Introduction and the notes, modern spellings of place names are employed and are taken from *The Times Atlas of the World*.

The Text

With the exceptions mentioned below, the text preserves the spelling and punctuation of the 1735 edition, the only one published during Johnson's lifetime. Since there is no reason to believe that Johnson saw the text after Hector took it to Warren's printer (or, indeed, that he even looked at Hector's manuscript version), there is certainly no authority for any other text. Occasionally, however, the 1789 text makes a substantive emendation that coincides with my own—e.g., changing the obviously incorrect phrasing of the Preface from "benevolence, engage in massacres" to "benevolence engaged in massacres." Such emendations are incorporated into the text and noted as a matter of some textual interest, but there is no evidence that Johnson left any instructions for correcting the 1735 text, or that he even commented upon it. It is possible that he helped provide the list of errata printed at the end of his Preface, but those corrections would as a matter of course be included in all future editions; they are here incorporated into the text and noted.[9]

Where the 1735 edition presents an incorrect version of a proper noun in the French text—e.g., *Falegur* for the correct *Fategur*—it is here corrected and noted to reflect Johnson's intention to follow his source. In a few instances, such as *Gasates/Gafates*, the Portuguese original as well as the French text is cited to justify an alteration in Johnson's text. Certain proper nouns appear in more than one form (e.g., Payz/Pays, Tellez/Telles, dos Santos/Dos-Santos, Gardafui/Guardafui) but should not cause any difficulties; alternative spellings are included in the Index. Modern spellings of place names, when different from Johnson's, may also be found in the Index. A few spellings acceptable in 1735 (e.g., *distitute* for *destitute*, *hippotamus* for *hippopotamus*) have been modernized and noted, but with these few exceptions, the often inconsistent spelling of the copy-text has been retained.

Italics in the 1735 edition are preserved only for emphasis, for book titles, for particular Abyssinian terms, and for quotations

---

9. The Errata read "In several places for Mazna r. Mazua." Since the name appears frequently in the 1735 text, always spelled "Mazna," it has been corrected throughout the present volume without notes.

from the Latin; italics used for all other quotations are here printed in roman type surrounded by double quotation marks. Extended quotations in English, usually indicated in the copy-text by inverted commas in the margin, are here indented. Obvious errors such as turned, omitted, or repeated letters or words are silently corrected. Capitalization, possessives, and typography (e.g., the occasional use of small capitals for emphasis) have been modernized in accordance with editorial practices observed in other volumes of this edition of Johnson's *Works*.

One characteristic of the 1735 edition is its frequent use of commas to separate independent clauses. In the few instances where such punctuation might confuse a modern reader, it is altered and the copy-text version is given in a note.

In the textual notes the following sigla are used to identify the various editions of the *Voyage*:

Itinerário	Lobo's account in Portuguese
Relation	Le Grand's translation
1735	Johnson's translation
1789	Gleig's edition

A VOYAGE TO ABYSSINIA

[The dedication of the 1735 edition]

To
John Warren, Esq;
of Trewern,
in the County of Pembroke.[1]

Sir,

The publication of the following sheets affording me an opportunity of testifying my gratitude, I could not forbear inscribing them to you; addresses of this kind being never less liable to censure than when offer'd like this, as acknowledgment of favours.

A generous and elevated mind is distinguish'd by nothing more certainly than an eminent degree of curiosity, nor is that curiosity ever more agreeably or usefully employ'd, than in examining the laws and customs of foreign nations. I hope, therefore, the present I now presume to make will not be thought improper, which, however, it is not my business, as a dedicator, to commend, nor, as a bookseller, to depreciate.

Such as it is, I entreat your acceptance of it, as a token of the highest respect and sincerest affection of,

Sir,
Your most obliged,
humble servant,
The Editor.

---

1. According to A. L. Reade, John Warren "was the representative of an old county family in South Wales. His place, Trewern, was in the parish of Nevern, in Pembrokeshire, of which county he, now a man of about sixty-two, had been High Sheriff in 1712" (*Johnsonian Gleanings*, v. 107). Reade speculates that Thomas Warren, "The Editor," and John Warren may have been related. Boswell "discern[s] [SJ's] hand" in the second paragraph of the Dedication (*Life*, 1. 89).

THE PREFACE

The following relation is so curious and entertaining, and the dissertations that accompany it so judicious and instructive, that the translator is confident his attempt stands in need of no apology, whatever censures may fall on the performance.

The Portuguese traveller, contrary to the general vein of his countrymen, has amused his reader with no romantick absurdities or incredible fictions;[a][2] whatever he relates, whether true or not, is at least probable, and he who tells nothing exceeding the bounds of probability, has a right to demand, that they should believe him, who cannot contradict him.

He appears by his modest and unaffected narration to have described things as he saw them, to have copied nature from the life, and to have consulted his senses not his imagination; he meets with no basilisks that destroy with their eyes, his crocodiles devour their prey without tears, and his cataracts fall from the rock without deafening the neighbouring inhabitants.[3]

The reader will here find no regions cursed with irremediable barrenness, or bless'd with spontaneous fecundity, no perpetual gloom or unceasing sunshine; nor are the nations here described either devoid of all sense of humanity, or consummate in all private and social virtues, here are no Hottentots without religion, polity, or articulate language, no Chinese perfectly polite, and compleatly skill'd in all sciences: he will discover, what will always be discover'd by a diligent and impartial enquirer, that wherever human nature is to be found, there is a

a. fictions, *1735*

---

2. Lobo himself makes a similar comment (p. 87).

3. Although he does not meet basilisks with deadly glances, Lobo is unwilling to discount the possibility that they exist (p. 22). Among incredible fictions, however, he cites crocodile tears (p. 86) and deafening cataracts (p. 84), the latter an allusion to Cicero's account of Scipio's dream: Africanus told Scipio that "the people who live near what are called the cataracts of the Nile, where the river sweeps down from high mountains, have lost the power of hearing because of the roar of waters ..." (*On the Commonwealth*, trans. George Holland Sabine and Stanley Barney Smith [1929], p. 263). I am grateful to Richard L. Eversole for drawing my attention to this passage.

3

mixture of vice and virtue, a contest of passion and reason, and
that the Creator doth not appear partial in his distributions, but
has balanced in most countries their particular inconveniences
by particular favours.

In his account of the mission, where his veracity is most to
be suspected, he neither exaggerates overmuch the merits of the
Jesuits, if we consider the partial regard paid by the Portugese
to their countrymen, by the Jesuits to their society, and by the
Papists to their church, nor aggravates the vices of the Abyssins;
but if the reader will not be satisfied with a popish account of
a popish mission, he may have recourse to the history of the
Church of Abyssinia, written by Dr. Geddes,[4] in which he will
find the actions and sufferings of the missionaries placed in a
different light, though the same in which Mr. Le Grand, with all
his zeal for the Roman Church, appears to have seen them.

This learned dissertator, however valuable for his industry
and erudition, is yet more to be esteem'd for having dared so
freely in the midst of France to declare his disapprobation of the
Patriarch Oviedo's sanguinary zeal, who was continually im-
portuning the Portuguese to beat up their drums for missionaries, who might preach the Gospel with swords in their
hands, and propagate by desolation and slaughter the true
worship of the God of Peace.

It is not easy to forbear reflecting with how little reason these
men profess themselves the followers of Jesus, who left this great
characteristick to his disciples, that they should be known "by
loving one another,"[5] by universal and unbounded charity and
benevolence.

Let us suppose an inhabitant of some remote and superiour
region, yet unskill'd in the ways of men, having read and considered the precepts of the Gospel, and the example of our
Saviour, to come down in search of the *True Church*: if he would
not enquire after it among the cruel, the insolent, and the
oppressive; among those who are continually grasping at do-
minion over souls as well as bodies; among those who are
employed·in procuring to themselves impunity for the most
enormous villanies, and studying methods of destroying their
fellow-creatures, not for their crimes but their errors; if he would

4. For Michael Geddes, see Introduc-   5. John xv. 17.
tion, p. xlv n. 4.

not expect to meet benevolence engaged[b] in massacres, or to find
mercy in a court of inquisition, he would not look for the *True
Church* in the Church of Rome.

Mr. Le Grand has given in one dissertation an example of
great moderation, in deviating from the temper of his religion,[6]
but in the others has left proofs, that learning and honesty are
often too weak to oppose prejudice. He has made no scruple of
preferring the testimony of Father du Bernat,[7] to the writings of
all the Portuguese Jesuits, to whom he allows great zeal, but
little learning, without giving any other reason than that his
favourite was a Frenchman. This is writing only to Frenchmen
and to Papists: a Protestant would be desirous to know why he
must imagine that Father du Bernat had a cooler head or more
knowledge; and why one man whose account is singular, is not
more likely to be mistaken than many agreeing in the same
account.

If the Portuguese were byass'd by any particular views, another byass equally powerful may have deflected the Frenchman
from the truth, for they evidently write with contrary designs;
the Portuguese, to make their mission seem more necessary,
endeavour'd to place in the strongest light the differences between the Abyssinian and Roman Church, but the great Ludolfus[8] laying hold on the advantage, reduced these later writers to
prove their conformity.

Upon the whole, the controversy seems of no great importance to those who believe the Holy Scriptures sufficient to teach
the way of salvation, but of whatever moment it may be
thought, there are not proofs sufficient to decide it.

His discourses on indifferent subjects, will divert as well as
instruct, and if either in these or in the relation of Father
Lobo, any argument shall appear unconvincing, or description
obscure, they are defects incident to all mankind, which, however, are not too rashly to be imputed to the authors, being,

---

b. Benevolence engaged *1789*] Benevolence, engage *1735*

---

6. Probably the ninth dissertation, especially pp. 60–61 and 65, in which Le
Grand criticizes the patriarchs.

7. Father du Bernat, a French Jesuit, is
quoted at length by Le Grand in the thirteenth dissertation and more briefly
elsewhere.

8. See the discussion of Hiob Ludolf in
the Introduction, pp. xliii–xliv.

sometimes, perhaps more justly chargeable on the translator.

In this translation (if it may be so call'd) great liberties have been taken, which, whether justifiable or not, shall be fairly confess'd, and let the judicious part of mankind pardon or condemn them.

In the first part the greatest freedom has been used, in reducing the narration into a narrow compass, so that it is by no means a translation but an epitome, in which whether every thing either useful or entertaining be comprised, the compiler is least qualified to determine.

In the account of Abyssinia, and the continuation, the authors have been follow'd with more exactness, and as few passages appeared either insignificant or tedious, few have been either shortened or omitted.[9]

The dissertations are the only part in which an exact translation has been attempted, and even in those, abstracts are sometimes given instead of literal quotations, particularly in the first; and sometimes other parts have been contracted.

Several memorials and letters, which are printed at the end of the dissertations to secure the credit of the foregoing narrative, are entirely left out.[1]

'Tis hoped, that, after this confession, whoever shall compare this attempt with the original, if he shall find no proofs of fraud or partiality, will candidly overlook any failure of judgment.

---

9. Although there are not as many contractions and omissions as in the first part, there are more than a "few."

1. These letters and memorials extend from page 359 to page 514 in the French text.

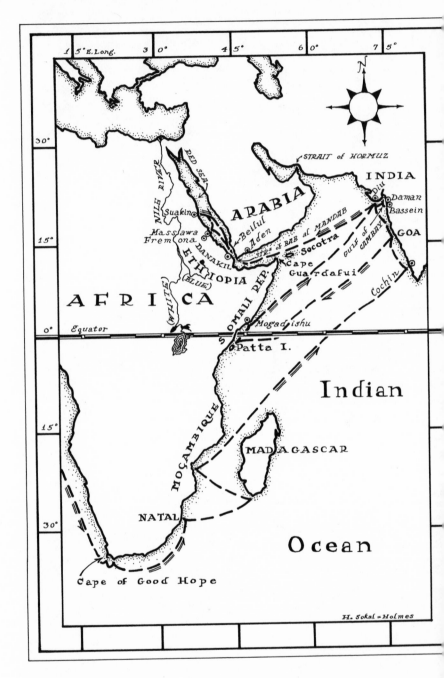

Map of Lobo's travels, 1622–1634, compiled and drawn by Hannah Sokal-Holmes.

A Voyage to Abyssinia

CHAPTER I

The author arrives after some difficulties at Goa. Is chosen for the mission of Aethiopia. The fate of those Jesuits who went by Zeila. The author arrives at the coast of Melinda.[1]

I embark'd in March 1622, in the same fleet with the Count Vidigueira, on whom the king had confer'd the viceroy-ship of the Indies, then vacant by the resignation of Alfonso Noronha,[2] whose unsuccessful voyage in the foregoing year had been the occasion of the loss of Ormus,* which being by the miscarriage of that fleet deprived of the succours necessary for its defence, was taken by the Persians and English.[3] The beginning of this voyage was very prosperous: we were neither annoy'd with the diseases of the climate, nor distress'd with bad weather, till we doubled the Cape of Good Hope, which was about the end of May. Here began our misfortunes; these coasts are remarkable for the many shipwrecks the Portuguese have suffer'd. The sea is for the most part rough, and the winds tempestuous, we had here our rigging somewhat damag'd by a storm of lightning which when we had repaired, we sailed forward to Mosam-

---

*Ormus. An island of great wealth and commodiousness in the Persian Gulf, since retaken by the Portuguese in 1729.[4]

---

1. Only the English text presents these brief chapter headings.

2. Having omitted Lobo's account of his ordination and subsequent aborted voyage toward the Indies, SJ compresses the more detailed opening of Lobo's second voyage, ignoring a list of ships and their commanders.

3. SJ has drawn these remarks about the loss of Ormus from the deleted story of the first voyage.

4. The note on Ormus (modern Hormoz) does not appear in the French text; it combines information taken from a geographical dictionary with the almost current news about the Portuguese victory.

bique,† where we were to stay some time.[5] When we came near
that coast, and began to rejoice at the prospect of ease and
refreshment, we were, on the sudden, alarmed with the sight of a
squadron of ships, of what nation we could not at first distinguish, but soon discovered that they were three English and
three Dutch, and were preparing to attack us. I shall not trouble
the reader with the particulars of this fight, in which though the
English commander ran himself a ground, we lost three of our
ships, and with great difficulty escap'd with the rest into the port
of Mosambique.[6]

This place was able to afford us little consolation in our uneasy
circumstances; the arrival of our company almost caused a scarcity of provisions: the heat in the day is intolerable, and the dews
in the night so unwholesome, that it is almost certain death to go
out with one's head uncover'd. Nothing can be a stronger proof
of the malignant quality of the air, than that the rust will immediately corrode both the iron and brass, if they are not carefully
covered with straw. We stay'd however in this place from the
latter end of July to the beginning of September, when having
provided our selves with other vessels, we set out for Cochim,*
and landed there after a very hazardous and difficult passage,
made so partly by the currents and storms which separated us
from each other, and partly by continual apprehensions of the
English and Dutch, who were cruising for us in the Indian seas.[8]
Here the Viceroy and his company were received with so much

---

†Mosambique, a city of Zanquebar on the coast of Africk in an island near the
continent, at the mouth of a river of the same name, which there falls into the Aethiopick
Sea.[7]

*A city of Asia in the East-Indies in the promontory of Malabar, a bishoprick under
the Archbishop of Goa, built by the Portuguese in 1503.

---

5. "we were neither ... some time"
epitomizes a page and a half of French
(pp. 5-6).

6. "When we came near ... port of
Mosambique" replaces an extensive account of this running battle (pp. 7-10).

7. This note and the ones that follow
are peculiar to the English text and may be
found almost *verbatim* in Laurence Echard,
The Gazetteer's: or Newsman's Interpreter, the

1692 edition of which is listed in SJ's
collection of books at Oxford. Numerous
editions (with a few changes) appeared
before 1735. This practice of inserting
footnotes ends after eleven notes and
sixteen pages of SJ's 1735 edition.

8. "we set out for Cochim ... Indian
seas" epitomizes a two-page description of
the difficult voyage (pp. 11-13).

ceremony, as was rather troublesome than pleasing to us who were fatigued with the labours of the passage;[9] and having staid here some time, that the gentlemen who attended the Viceroy to Goa,† might fit out their vessels, we set sail, and after having been detain'd some time at sea, by calms and contrary winds, and somewhat harrassed by the English and Dutch who were now encreased to eleven ships of war, arrived to Goa, on Saturday the 16th of December, and the Viceroy made his entry with great magnificence.

I lived here above a year, and compleated my studies in divinity; in which time some letters were received from the fathers in Aethiopia with an account, that Sultan Segued Emperor of Abyssinia was converted to the Church of Rome,[1] that many of his subjects had followed his example, and that there was a great want of missionaries to improve these prosperous beginnings. Every body was very desirous of seconding the zeal of our fathers and of sending them the assistance they requested; to which we were the more encouraged, because the Emperor's letters inform'd our provincial that we might easily enter his dominions by the way of Dancala,* but unhappily, the secretary wrote *Zeila*† for Dancala, which cost two of our fathers their lives.

We were, however, notwithstanding the assurances given us

---

†Goa, a city of Asia in the kingdom of Decan, in the peninsula on this side the Indus in a small island towards the mouth of the river Mandova, on the shores of the promontory of Cunean, on the west shore of the Cape of Malabar.

* Dancala, a city of Africk in the upper Aethiopia, upon the river Nile in the tract of Nubia, of which it is the capital.[2]

†Zeila, a city in the kingdom of Adel in Africk, at the mouth of the Red-Sea, upon the out-let of a river of the same name over-against Adel.

---

9. "Here the Viceroy ... passage" replaces a detailed account (pp. 13–14) of the reception; the remainder of the sentence is also an epitome.

1. The Sultan had "embrassé la religion catholique, apostolique & romaine" (p. 14), a formula SJ invariably omits. *Ramblers* 204 and 205 show SJ's later use of Sultan Segued.

2. The references to *Dancala* in the text and in this footnote, taken like the earlier ones from Echard's *Gazetteer*, should be to *Dancali*, an area on the coast of the Red Sea. Noting that ships from India would not be entering Abyssinia through an inland port, James Bruce observes that "Dr. Johnson, or his publisher, involves his reader in another strange perplexity" (2nd ed., IV. 326). Bruce's editor, however, points out that it is *Dancali* in Le Grand, p. 15.

by the Emperor sufficiently apprised of the danger, which we were exposed to in this expedition, whether we went by sea, or land. By sea, we foresaw the hazard we run of falling into the hands of the Turks, amongst whom we should lose, if not our lives, at least our liberty, and be for ever prevented from reaching the court of Aethiopia. Upon this consideration, our superiors divided the eight Jesuits chosen for this mission into two companies. Four they sent by sea, and four by land; I was of the latter number. The four first were the more fortunate, who though they were detain'd some time by the Turkish bassa, were dismissed at the request of the Emperor who sent him a *zeura* or wild-ass, a creature of large size, and admirable beauty.[3]

As for us who were to go by Zeila, we had still greater difficulties to struggle with: we were entirely strangers to the ways we were to take, to the manners, and even to the names of the nations through which we were to pass. Our chief desire was to discover some new road by which we might avoid having any thing to do with the Turks. Among great numbers whom we consulted on this occasion, we were informed by some that we might go through Melinda.* These men painted that hideous wilderness in charming colours, told us that we should find a country water'd with navigable rivers, and inhabited by a people that would either inform us of the way, or accompany us in it These reports charm'd us, because they flatter'd our desires; but our superiors finding nothing in all this talk that could be depended on, were in suspense, what directions to give us, till my companion and I upon this reflection, that since all the ways were equally new to us, we had nothing to do, but to resign our selves to the providence of God, ask'd and obtain'd the permission of our superiors to attempt the road through Melinda. So of we who went by land, two took the way of Zeila, and my companion and I, that of Melinda.

Those who were appointed for Zeila embark'd in a vessel that

---

* Melinda, the state of this country is now much changed, it is a kingdom of Africk upon the coast of Zanquebar, divided by the equator, with a city of the same name, subject to the Portuguese, who have (though the king is a Mahometan) churches for the exercise of their religion.

---

3. The French is less restrained: "Cet animal est fort grand & d'une beauté mer- veilleuse, & les plus beaux ne se trouvent que dans l'Abissinie" (p. 15).

was going to Caxume,* where they were well received by the
king, and accommodated with a ship, to carry them to Zeila,
they were there treated by the *check* with the same civility which
they had met with at Caxume. But the king being informed of
their arrival, order'd them to be convey'd to his court at Auxa,
to which place they were scarce come, before they were thrown
by the king's command into a dark and dismal dungeon, where
there is hardly any sort of cruelty that was not exercis'd upon
them. The Emperor of Abyssinia endeavour'd by large offers to
obtain their liberty, but his kind offices had no other effect than
to heighten the rage of the King of Zeila. This prince besides his
ill-will to Sultan Segued; which was kept up by some malecontents among the Abyssin nobility, who provok'd at the conversion of their master, were plotting a revolt, entertain'd an
inveterate hatred against the Portuguese for the death of his
grandfather, who had been kill'd many years before, which he
swore the blood of the Jesuits should repay. So after they had
languish'd for some time in prison, their heads were struck off. A
fate which had been likewise our own, had not God reserved us
for longer labours!

Having provided every thing necessary for our journey, such
as Arabian habits, and red caps, callicoes, and other trifles[5] to
make presents of to the inhabitants, and taking leave of our
friends,[6] as men going to a speedy death, for we were not
insensible of the dangers we were likely to encounter, amongst
horrid desarts, impassable mountains, and barbarous nations;[7]

---

* Caxume, a city of Africk, and the capital of the kingdom of Tigremahon in
Abyssinia, subject to the king of Abyssinia.[4]

---

4. Le Grand (p. 16) and the *Itinerário*
(p. 219) print "Caxem," correctly identified by Gonçalves da Costa as Qishn, a
city on the coast of Yemen. For a discussion of James Bruce's sneering response to
the mangled geography, see C. F.
Beckingham, "Jerónimo Lobo: His
Travels and His Book," *Bulletin of the John
Rylands Library* 64 (1981), 18–20, and
Joel J. Gold, "The Voyages of Jerónimo
Lobo, Joachim Le Grand, and Samuel
Johnson," *Prose Studies* (1982), pp. 34–35.
5. These items are part of a longer list

of apparel including "turban, robe, che-
mises ... écharpes ... souliers pointus"
and of small "bagatelles" like "quelques
toiles peintes" (p. 17).
6. Lobo and his companion resigned
themselves "entièrement à la volonté de
Dieu" (p. 17).
7. "barbarous nations" provides the
needed balance; it replaces a number of
obstacles: uncrossed forests, the avarice,
cruelty, and treachery of nations unfa-
miliar with white men. The concluding
remark is also deleted: "toutes choses très

we left Goa, on the 26th day of January in the year 1624, in a
Portuguese galliot that was order'd to set us ashore at Paté,*
where we landed without any disaster in eleven days together
with a young Abyssin, whom we made use of as our interpreter.[8]
While we stay'd here, we were given to understand that those
who had been pleased at Goa to give us directions in relation to
our journey, had done nothing but tell us lies. That the people
were savage, that they had indeed begun[a] to treat with the
Portuguese, but it was only from fear, that otherwise they were a
barbarous nation, who finding themselves too much crouded in
their own country, had extended themselves to the sea shore,
that they ravaged the country, and laid every thing waste,
where they came, that they were man-eaters,[9] and were on that
account dreadful in all those parts. My companion and I being
undeceiv'd by this terrible relation, thought it would be the
highest imprudence to expose ourselves both together to a death
almost certain and unprofitable, and agreed that I should go
with our Abyssin and a Portuguese to observe the country. That
if I should prove so happy as to escape being kill'd by the
inhabitants, and to discover a way, I should either return, or
send back the Abyssin or Portuguese. Having fix'd upon this, I
hired a little bark to Jubo, a place about forty leagues distant
from Paté, on board which I put some provisions, together with
my sacerdotal vestments, and all that was necessary for saying
mass; in this vessel we reached the coast, which we found in-

---

* Paté an isle and town on the coast of Zanquebar in Africk.

a. begun *1789*] began *1735*

---

capables de nous faire abandonner notre
entreprise, si Dieu pour l'amour duquel
nous nous exposions à tant de périls, ne
nous avoit soutenus & fortifiés par sa grâce
toute puissante" (p. 17).

8. Omitted are an account of the journey, a description of the island of Patta off
the coast of Kenya, and their reception
there by an Augustan friar (pp. 17–19).

9. SJ accurately renders Le Grand:
"s'étaient étendus jusqu'à la mer, pil-
lant & ravageant tout, & mangeant les
hommes" (p. 19). James Bruce, however,
ridicules Lobo for locating cannibals

where none existed. The problems had
been created by Le Grand's misunderstanding Lobo's metaphorical account of
the fierce Gallas, sallying out of their
country, conquering new lands, "e vierão
destruindo e comendo quanto encon-
travão até chegarem ao mar ... " (*Itin.*,
p. 225). They did not *eat* everyone they
met; they destroyed (devoured) everything in their path to the sea. For a fuller
discussion of this example, see my article
on "The Voyages of Jerónimo Lobo, Joachim Le Grand, and Samuel Johnson,"
Prose Studies (1982), pp. 35–36.

habited by several nations, each nation is subject to its own king, these petty monarchies are so numerous, that I counted at least ten, in less than four leagues.[10]

CHAPTER II

The author lands: the difficulty of his journey. An account of the Galles, and of the author's reception at the king's tent; their manner of swearing, and of letting blood. The author returns to the Indies, and finds the Patriarch of Aethiopia.

On this coast we landed, with an intention of travelling on foot to Jubo, a journey of much greater length, and difficulty than we imagined. We durst not go far from our bark, and therefore were obliged to a toilsome march along the windings of the shore, sometimes clambering up rocks, and sometimes wading through the sands, so that we were every moment in the utmost danger of falling from the one, or sinking in the other. Our lodging was either in the rocks or on the sands, and even that incommoded by continual apprehensions of being devoured by lyons and tygers.[1] Amidst all these calamities, our provisions failed us; we had little hopes of a supply, for we found neither villages, houses, nor any trace of a human creature, and had miserably perish'd by thirst and hunger, had we not met with some fishermen's boats, who exchanged their fish for tobacco.

Through all these fatigues we at length came to Jubo a kingdom of considerable extent, scituated almost under the Line and tributary to the Portuguese who carry on a trade here for ivory and other commodities. This region so abounds with elephants, that though the teeth of the male only are valuable, they load several ships with ivory every year.[2] All this coast is

---

10. Lobo describes a meeting with the king of the Abagnes, who came rowing up as naked as the rest of his people save for a hat upon his head. A bit of bread and a little fish satisfied his majesty (pp. 19–20).

1. And, Lobo notes, "nous ne pouvions ... attendre du secours que du Ciel" (p. 20).

2. SJ deletes a description of amber, cocoanuts, and the best slaves, the Maracates. Valuing chastity in their women, the Maracates sew up the genitals of female infants, the stitching to be undone only by the woman's future husband. Although "cette coûtume soit un peu barbare, on ne peut s'empêcher d'estimer le soin qu'ils ont de conserver parmi eux une vertu si rare par tout ailleurs" (p. 21).

much infested with ravenous beasts, monkeys and serpents, of which last here are some seven feet in length, and thicker than an ordinary man;[a] in the head of this serpent is found a stone about the bigness of an egg, resembling bezoar, and of great efficacy, as it is said, against all kinds of poison. I staid here some time to inform my self, whether I might, by persuing this road, reach Abyssinia, and could get no other intelligence, but that two thousand Galles (the same people who inhabited Melinda)[3] had encamped about three leagues from Jubo, that they had been induced to fix in that place by the plenty of provisions they found there. These Galles lay every thing, where they come, in ruin, putting all to the sword without distinction of age or sex, which barbarities, though their numbers are not great, have spread the terror of them over all the country. They chuse a king, whom they call *lubo*, every eighth year, they carry their wives with them, and expose their children without any tenderness in the woods, it being prohibited on pain of death, to take any care of those which are born in the camp. This is their way of living when they are in arms, but afterwards when they settle at home, they breed up their children. They feed upon raw cow's-flesh; when they kill a cow, they keep the blood to rub their bodies with, and wear the guts about their necks for ornaments, which they afterwards give to their wives.

Several of these Galles came to see me, and as it seem'd, they had never beheld a white man before, they gaz'd on me with amazement; so strong was their curiosity, that they even pull'd off my shoes and stockings, that they might be satisfied whether all my body was of the same colour with my face.[4] I could remark, that after they had observed me some time, they discovered some aversion from a white. However seeing me pull out my handkerchief, they ask'd me for it with a great deal of eagerness, I cut it into several pieces that I might satisfy them all, and distributed it amongst them; they bound them about their heads, but gave me to understand that they should have liked them better if they had been red: after this we were seldom

a. man, *1735*

3. This parenthetical identification does not appear in the French.

4. Cf. the Houyhnhnms' curiosity about Gulliver in the fourth voyage (Chap. 3).

without their company, which gave occasion to an accident, which tho' it seem'd to threaten some danger at first, turn'd afterward to our advantage.[5]

As these people were continually teazing us, our Portuguese one day threaten'd in jest to kill one of them. The black ran in the utmost dread to seek his comrades, and we were in one moment, almost covered with Galles, we thought it the most proper course to decline the first impulse of their fury, and retired into our house. Our retreat inspired them with courage, they redoubled their cries, and posted themselves on an eminence near at hand that overlooked us, there they insulted us by brandishing their lances and daggers. We were fortunately not above a stone's cast from the sea, and could therefore have retreated to our bark, had we found our selves reduced to extremities, this made us not very solicitous about their menaces. But finding that they continued to hover about our habitation, and being wearied with their clamours, we thought it might be a good expedient to fright them away by firing four muskets towards them, in such a manner, that they might hear the bullets hiss about two feet over their heads. This had the effect we wish'd, the noise and fire of our arms struck them with so much terror, that they fell upon the ground, and durst not for some time so much as lift up their heads. They forgot immediately their natural temper;[b] their ferocity and haughtiness were softened into mildness and submission;[6] they ask'd pardon for their insolence, and we were ever after good friends.

After our reconciliation we visited each other frequently, and had some conversation about the journey I had undertaken, and the desire I had of finding a new passage into Aethiopia. It was necessary on this account to consult their *lubo* or king; I found him in a straw-hut something larger than those of his subjects, surrounded by his courtiers who had each a stick in his hand, which is longer or shorter, according to the quality of the person admitted into the king's presence. The ceremony made use of at

b. temper, *1735*

---

5. "which gave ... advantage" appears only in the English text as a foreshadowing of what is to come.

6. "their ferocity ... submission" imposes a parallelism on the original: "ils devinrent plus doux que des agneaux ..." (p. 23).

the reception of a stranger is somewhat unusual; as soon[c] as he
enters, all the courtiers strike him with their cudgels till he goes
back to the door, the amity then subsisting between us, did not
secure me from this uncouth reception, which they told me,
upon my demanding the reason of it, was to shew those whom
they treated with, that they were the bravest people in the
world, and that all other nations ought to bow down before
them.[7] I could not help reflecting on this occasion, how impru-
dently I had trusted my life in the hands of men unacquainted
with compassion or civility, but recollecting at the same time
that the intent of my journey was such as might give me hopes of
the Divine protection, I banish'd all thoughts but those of
finding a way into Aethiopia.[8] In this streight it occur'd to me,
that these people, however barbarous, have some oath which
they keep with an inviolable strictness, the best precaution
therefore that I could use would be to bind them by this oath to
be true to their engagements. The manner of their swearing is
this; they set a sheep in the midst of them, and rub it over with
butter;[d] the heads of families who are the chief in the nation, lay
their hands upon the head of the sheep, and swear to observe
their promise. This oath (which they never violate) they explain
thus, the sheep is the mother of them who swear, the butter
betokens the love between the mother and the children, and an
oath taken on a mother's head is sacred. Upon the security of
this oath, I made them acquainted with my intention, an intention, they told me it was impossible to put in execution. From
the moment I left them, they said, they could give me no
assurance of either life or liberty, that they were perfectly
inform'd both of the roads and inhabitants, that there were no
fewer than nine nations between us and Abyssinia,[9] who were
always embroil'd amongst themselves, or at war with the
Abyssins, and enjoy'd no security even in their own territories.

c. as soon] assoon *1735*   d. butter, *1735*

7. Omitted here is the comment that
the Gallas had a very high opinion of the
Portuguese, whom they termed "les dieux
de la mer" (pp. 23–24).

8. "but recollecting . . . Aethiopia" fails
to reflect the tone of the original: Lobo
remarks that he undertook the journey

solely for the greater glory of God. "Je
mettais toute ma confiance en notre Seigneur, qui m'avait jusqu'alors délivré de
tant de périls, que je pouvais dire qu'il
m'avait tiré des portes de la mort" (p. 24).

9. The French provides a half-page
catalogue of the various tribes (p. 25).

We were now convinced that our enterprize was impracticable, and that to hazard our selves amidst so many insurmountable difficulties would be to tempt Providence; despairing therefore that I should ever come this way to Abyssinia, I resolved to return back with my intelligence to my companion; whom I had left at Paté.[1]

I cannot however leave this country, without giving an account of their manner of blood-letting, which I was led to the knowledge of[2] by a violent fever, which threaten'd to put an end to my life and travels together. The distress I was in, may easily be imagined, being entirely destitute of every thing necessary. I had resolved to let my self blood, though I was altogether a stranger to the manner of doing it, and had no lancet. But my companions hearing of a surgeon of reputation in the place, went and brought him. I saw with the utmost surprise an old Moor enter my chamber, with a kind of small dagger all over rusty, and a mallet in his hand, and three cups of horn about half a foot long. I started, and ask'd what he wanted? he told me to bleed me, and, when I had given him leave, uncovering my side, apply'd one of his horn cups which he stop'd with chew'd paper, and by that means made it stick fast;[e] in the same manner he fix'd on the other two, and fell to sharpening his instrument, assuring me that he would give me no pain. He then took off his cups and gave in each place a stroke with his poniard, which was followed by a stream of blood. He apply'd his cups several times, and every time struck his lancet into the same place;[f] having drawn away a large quantity of blood, he heal'd the orifices with three lumps of tallow. I know not whether to attribute my cure to bleeding, or my fear, but I had from that time no return of my fever.

When I came to Paté in hopes of meeting with my associate, I found that he was gone to Mombaza in hopes of receiving information, he was sooner undeceiv'd than I, and we met at the place where we parted,[3] in a few days, and soon afterwards left Paté to return to the Indies, and in nine and twenty days arrived

e. fast, *1735*   f. place, *1735*

---

1. The French reads "Ampasa" (a city on Patta Island). Having omitted earlier a description of the island, SJ here logically refrains from mentioning one of the cities.

2. These useful introductory clauses appear only in the English translation.

3. Having reached Pasa on Patta Island "le Dimanche de la Passion," Lobo participated in the services, but SJ omits his account: "nous étions quatre pretres

at the famous fortress of Diou.* We were told at this place, that Alfonso Mendes Patriarch of Aethiopia was arrived at Goa from Lisbon. He wrote to us, to desire that we would wait for him at Diou, in order to embark there for the Red Sea, but being informed by us that no opportunities of going thither were to be expected at Diou, it was at length determined that we should meet at Bazaim, it was no easy matter for me to find means of going to Bazaim. However, after a very uneasy voyage, in which we were often in danger of being dash'd against the rocks, or thrown upon the sands by the rapidity of the current, and suffer'd the utmost distress for want of water;[4] I landed at Daman,† a place about twenty leagues distant from Bazaim. Here I hired a *câtre* and four boys to carry me to Bazaim; these *câtres* are a kind of traveling couches, in which you may either lie or sit, which the boys, whose business is the same with that of chairmen in our country, support upon their shoulders by two poles, and carry a passenger at the rate of eighteen or twenty miles a day. Here we at length found the Patriarch with three more priests, like us, designed for the mission of Aethiopia. We went back to Daman, and from thence to Diou, where we arrived in a short time.[5]

CHAPTER III

The author embarks with the Patriarch, narrowly escapes shipwreck near the isle of Socotora: enters the Arabian Gulf, and the Red-Sea. Some account of the coast of the Red-Sea.

The Patriarch having met with many obstacles and disap-

---

* Diou an island and town at the mouth of the river Indus.
† Daman, a port upon the coast of the Gulf of Cambaya.

---

pour faire l'office de la semaine sainte dans la petite eglise d'Ampasa, avec soixante & dix chrétiens, ce qui ne s'était peut-être jamais vu auparavant, ni ne s'est vu depuis. L'office se fit de cette manière avec beaucoup de solemnité; ce peuple en parut extraordinairement touché, & il n'y eut pas un chrétien qui ne fit une confession générale, & qui ne donnât plusieurs

marques d'une véritable & sincère penitence. Nous passâmes la semaine sainte & l'octave de Pâques dans des exercices continuels de dévotion" (pp. 26–27).

4. "However ... water" epitomizes a long and detailed recounting of the voyage (pp. 27–29).

5. The French translation provides a brief specific description of the journey.

pointments in his return to Abyssinia, grew impatient of being so long absent from his church. Lopo Gomez d'Abreu[a][1] had made him an offer at Bazaim of fitting out three ships at his own expence, provided a commission could be procured him to cruise in the Red-Sea. This proposal was accepted by the Patriarch, and a commission granted by the Viceroy. While we were at Diou waiting for these vessels, we receiv'd advice from Aethiopia, that the Emperor unwilling to expose the Patriarch to any hazards, thought Dagher, a port in the mouth of the Red-Sea, belonging to a prince dependant on the Abyssins, a place of the greatest security to land at, having already written to that prince to give him safe passage thro' his dominions. We met here with new delays; the fleet that was to transport us did not appear, the Patriarch lost all patience, and his zeal so much affected the commander at Diou, that he undertook to equip a vessel for us, and push'd the work forward with the utmost diligence. At length the long expected ships enter'd the port, we were overjoy'd, we were transported, and prepar'd to go on board. Many persons at Diou seeing the vessels so well fitted out, desired leave to go this voyage along with us, imagining they had an excellent opportunity of acquiring both wealth and honour. We committed however one great error in the setting out; for having equip'd our ships for privateering, and taken no merchandise on board, we could not touch at any of the ports of the Red-Sea.[2] The Patriarch impatient to be gone, took leave in the most tender manner of the governour and his other friends, recommended our voyage to the Blessed Virgin, and in the field, before we went on shipboard, made a short exhortation, so moving and pathetick, that it touch'd the hearts of all who heard it.[3] In the evening we went on board, and early the next morning, being the 3d. of April, 1625 we set sail.[4]

After some days we discovered about noon the island Soco-

---

a. d'Abreu *Errata*] d'Abrea *1735*

---

1. He was, according to Gonçalves da Costa, a "fidalgo [nobleman] de Ponte de Lima" (*Itinerário*, p. 29).

2. This sentence appears much earlier in the paragraph in Le Grand (p. 30).

3. "recommended our voyage ... heard it" compresses Lobo's account of the ceremonies, the litanies, the Patriarch's blessings and exhortations, his embraces and words of edification for all (p. 31).

4. The year appears only in the English translation.

tora,* where we propos'd to touch. The sky was bright, and the
wind fair, nor had we the least apprehension of the danger into
which we were falling, but with the utmost carelessness and
jollity held on our course. At night, when our sailors, especially
the Moors were in a profound sleep, (for the Mahometans,
believing every thing forewritten in the decrees of God, and not
alterable by any human means, resign themselves entirely to
Providence)[5] our vessel ran aground upon a sand-bank at the
entrance of the harbour. We got her off with the utmost difficulty, and nothing but a miracle could have preserv'd us.[6]
We ran along afterwards by the side of the island, but were
entertain'd with no other prospect, than of a mountainous
country, and of rocks that jutted out over the sea, and seem'd
ready to fall into it.[7] In the afternoon putting into the most
convenient ports of the island, we came to anchor; very much to
the amazement and terror of the inhabitants, who were not us'd
to see any Portuguese ships upon their coasts, and were therefore
under a great consternation at finding them even in their ports.
Some ran for security to the mountains, others took up arms to
oppose our landing, but were soon reconciled to us, and brought
us fowls, fish, and sheep, in exchange for India callicoes, on
which they set a great value. We left this island, early the next
morning, and soon came in sight of Cape Gardafui, so celebrated heretofore under the name of the Cape of Spices, either
because great quantities were then found there, or from its
neighbourhood to Arabia the Happy, even at this day famous
for its fragrant products. 'Tis properly at this cape (the most
eastern part of Africa) that the Gulf of Arabia begins, which at
Babelmandel loses[b] its name, and is called the Red-Sea. Here,
though the weather was calm, we found the sea so rough, that we
were tossed, as in a high wind, for two nights;[c] whether this

---

* Socotora, an island near the mouth of the Streights of Babel-mandel.

b. looses *1735*   c. nights, *1735*

---

5. Lobo's moral is dropped: the sailors
are often lost "faute de prendre les précau-
tions nécessaires pour se sauver" (p. 31).

6. Here the "miracle" is simply a figure
of speech; Lobo, however, is more specific:
"de sorte que nous ne doutâmes point que

les prières de nos Pères, & le S. Sacrifice de
la messe ... n'eussent opéré ce miracle"
(p. 32).

7. A quarter-page description of the
island follows in the French (p. 32).

violent agitation of the water proceeded from the narrowness of the strait, or from the fury of the late storm, I know not;[d] whatever was the cause, we suffer'd all the hardships of a tempest. We continued our course towards the Red-Sea, meeting with nothing in our passage but a *gelve*, or kind of boat made of thin boards sewed together, with no other sail than a mat. We gave her chase, in hopes of being informed by the crew, whether there were any Arabian vessels at the mouth of the strait. But the Moors, who all entertain dismal apprehensions of the Franks,[8] ply'd their oars and sail with the utmost diligence, and as soon as they reach'd land, quitted their boat, and scour'd to the mountains. We saw them make signals from thence, and imagining they would come to a parley, sent out our boat with two sailors and an Abyssin, putting the ships off from the shore, to set them free from any suspicion of danger in coming down. All this was to no purpose, they could not be drawn from the mountain, and our men had orders not to go on shore, so they were obliged to return without information. Soon after we discovered the isle of Babelmandel, which gives name to the strait so call'd, and parts the sea that surrounds it into two channels;[e] that on the side of Arabia, is not above a quarter of a league in breadth, and through this pass almost all the vessels that trade to, or from the Red-Sea. The other on the side of Aethiopia, though much larger, is more dangerous by reason of the shallows, which make it necessary for a ship though of no great burthen, to pass very near the island where the channel is deeper and less embarrass'd. This passage is never made use of but by those who would avoid meeting with the Turks who are station'd on the coast of Arabia, 'twas for this reason that we chose it. We pass'd it in the night, and entered that sea so renowned on many accounts in history both sacred and profane.[9]

In our description of this famous sea, an account of which may justly be expected in this place, it is most convenient to begin

d. not, *1735*   e. channels, *1735*

---

8. Any western European.

9. This brief sentence is all that remains of Lobo's account of their thanksgivings: "nous chantâmes les litanies de la Sainte Vierge, & nous récitâmes d'autres prières, pour rendre grâces à Dieu de nous avoir donné jusqu'à lors un si heureux voyage, & pour lui demander de nous tenir toujours sous sa protection" (p. 35).

with the coast of Arabia, on which part at twelve leagues from the mouth stands the city of Moca, a place of considerable trade. Forty leagues farther is the isle of Camaram, whose inhabitants are annoy'd with little serpents, which they call basilisks, which, though very poisonous, and deadly, do not, as the ancients have told us, kill with their eyes, or, if they have so fatal a power, 'tis not at least in this place. Sailing ninety leagues farther,[1] you see the noted port of Jodda, where the pilgrims that go to Mecca and Medina, unlade those rich presents which the zeal of different princes is every day accumulating at the tomb of Mahomet. The commerce of this place, and the number of merchants that resort thither from all parts of the world are above description, and so richly laden are the ships that come hither, that when the Indians would express a thing of inestimable price, they say, "It is of greater value than a ship of Jodda." An hundred and eighteen leagues from thence lies Toro, and near it the ruins of an ancient monastry. This is the place, if the report of the inhabitants deserves any credit, where the Israelites miraculously pass'd through the Red-Sea on dry-land; and there is some reason for imagining the tradition not ill-grounded. For the sea is here only three leagues in breadth, all the ground about Toro is barren for want of water, which is only to be found, at a considerable distance, in one fountain, which flows out of the neighbouring mountains, at the foot of which, there are still twelve palm-trees. Near Toro are several wells which, as the Arabs tell us, were dug, by the order of Moses, to quiet the clamours of the thirsty Israelites. Suez lies in the bottom of the gulf, three leagues from Toro, once a place of note, now reduced, under the Turks, to an inconsiderable village, where the miserable inhabitants are forc'd to fetch water at three leagues distance. The ancient kings of Egypt convey'd the waters of the Nile to this place by an artificial canal, now so choak'd with sand, that there are scarce any marks remaining of so noble and beneficial a work.[2]

The first place to be met with in travelling along the coast of Africa is Rondelo, situate over-against Toro, and celebrated for

---

1. SJ seems to have added incorrectly; according to Lobo, the distance from Kamarān to Jiddah is sixty leagues plus forty-two leagues plus thirty leagues (p. 36).

2. SJ's adjectives "noble" and "beneficial" imply a judgment not present in the French: "comblé & plein de sable, & à peine il en reste quelques vestiges" (p. 37).

the same miraculous passage. Forty-five leagues from thence, is Cocir. Here ends that long chain of mountains that reaches from this place even to the entrance of the Red-Sea. In this prodigious ridge, which extends three hundred leagues, sometimes approaching near the sea, and sometimes running far up into the land, there is only one opening, through which all that merchandise, is convey'd, which is embark'd at Rifa, and from thence distributed through all the East: these mountains, as they are uncultivated, are in some parts shaded with large forests, and in others dry and bare: as they are exceedingly high, all the seasons may be here found together;[f] when the storms of winter beat on one side, on the other is often a serene sky and a bright sun-shine. The Nile runs here so near the shore, that it might without much difficulty be turned through this opening of the mountains into the Red-Sea, a design which many of the emperors have thought of putting in execution, and thereby making a communication between the Red-Sea, and the Mediterranean, but have been discouraged either by the greatness of the expence, or the fear of laying great part of Egypt under water, for some of that country lies lower than the sea.

Distant from Rondelo an hundred and thirty leagues is the isle of Suaquem, where the bassa of that country chuses his residence for the convenience of receiving the tribute with greater exactness, there being a large trade carried on here with the Abyssins.[3] The Turks of Suaquem, have gardens on the firm land not above a musket-shot from the island, which supply them with many excellent herbs and fruits,[4] of which I doubt whether there be not a greater quantity on this little spot, than on the whole coast of Africa besides, from Melinda to Suez. For if we except the dates which grow between Suez and Suaquem, the ground does not yield the least product; all the necessaries of life, even water is wanting.[5] Nothing can support itself in this region of barrenness, but ostriches, which devour stones, or any thing they meet with; they lay a great number of eggs, part of

f. together, *1735*

---

3. A two-thirds-page description of the Red Sea port of Suakin and the kingdom of Balou follows in the French (p. 38).

4. The French lists specific fruits and herbs: "des limons, des ananas, des cédrats, des canes de sucre, des melons d'eau

..." and so on (p. 38).

5. The French translation applies to this region the description in Psalm 62: "d'une terre déserte, impraticable, & où tout manque jusqu'à l'eau" (p. 39).

which they break to feed their young with. These fowls, of which I have seen many, are very tame, and when they are persued, stretch out their wings, and run with amazing swiftness: as they have cloven-feet, they sometimes strike up the stones when they run, which gave occasion to the notion that they throw stones at the hunters, a relation equally to be credited with those of their eating fire and digesting iron.[6] Those feathers which are so much valued, grow under their wings, the shell of their eggs powder'd is an excellent remedy for sore-eyes.

The burning wind spoken of in the sacred writings, I take to be that which the natives term *arur*, and the Arabs *uri*, which blowing in the spring brings with it so excessive an heat, that the whole country seems a burning oven; so that there is no travelling here in this dreadful season, nor is this the only danger to which the unhappy passenger is expos'd in these uncomfortable regions. There blows in the months June, July, and August, another wind, which raises mountains of sand and carries them thro' the air, all that can be done in this case is when a cloud of sand rises, to mark where it is likely to fall, and to retire as far off as possible, but 'tis very usual for men to be taken unexpectedly, and smothered in the dust. One day I found the body of a Christian,[g] whom I knew, upon the sand, he had doubtless been choak'd by these winds; I recommended his soul to the Divine Mercy and buried him. He seem'd to have been some time dead, yet the body had no ill smell. These winds are most destructive in Arabia the desert.[7]

CHAPTER IV

The author's conjecture on the name of the Red-Sea. An account of the coco-tree. He lands at Baylur.

To return to the description of the coast;[1] sixty leagues from

g. Christian; *1735*

---

6. SJ omits the comment that the ostriches are so swift that no horse can overtake them (p. 39).

7. This single sentence epitomizes a de-

tailed paragraph about the winds and the risks Lobo ran in traveling (p. 40).

1. This phrase avoids the awkwardness of the French: "Il est temps après cette

Suaquem is an island call'd Mazua, only considerable for its ports, which make the Turks reside upon it,[2] though they are forc'd to keep three barks continually employ'd in fetching water, which is not to be found nearer than at the distance of twelve miles. Forty leagues[3] from hence is Dalacha an island, where many pearls are found, but of small value. The next place is Baylur forty leagues from Dalacha, and twelve from Babelmandel.

There are few things upon which a greater variety of conjectures has been offer'd, than upon the reasons that induced the ancients, to distinguish this gulf, which separates Asia from Africk, by the name of the Red-Sea, an apellation that has almost universally obtain'd in all languages. Some affirm that the torrents, which fall after great rains from the mountains, wash down such a quantity of red-sand as gives a tincture to the water; others tell us, that the sun-beams being reverberated from the red rocks, give the sea on which they strike, the appearance of that colour. Neither of these accounts are satisfactory,[4] the coasts are so scorch'd by the heat that they are rather black than red: nor is the colour of this sea much altered by the winds or rains.[5] The notion generally received is, that the coral found in such quantities at the bottom of the sea, might communicate this colour to the water: an account merely chimerical.[6] Coral is not to be found in all parts of this gulf, and red coral in very few. Nor does this water in fact differ from that of other seas. The Patriarch and I have frequently amus'd our selves with making observations, and could never discover any redness, but in the shallows where a kind of weed grew which they call *gouesmon*, which redness disappear'd as soon[a] as we pluck'd up the plant.[7]

a. as soon] assoon *1735*

---

disgression, qui n'est peut-être que trop longue, de reprendre les suites de ma relation" (p. 40).

2. Replacing a description of the island, this clause has no counterpart in the French.

3. An error: "vingt lieues" (p. 40).

4. "Neither ... satisfactory" does not appear in the French. Lobo also considers and discounts a theory that wind-blown sand discolours the water (p. 41).

5. Still another opinion is deleted here: that the sea is made red by floating whale eggs (p. 41).

6. "an account ... chimerical" has no exact parallel in the French text, although it may be inferred from Lobo's observations, some of which SJ deletes.

7. "The Patriarch ... plant" epitomizes a much longer account (pp. 41–42) interrupted by a paragraph describing trees along the shore.

It is observable that St. Jerome confining himself to the Hebrew,
calls this sea, Jamsuf, *jam* in that language signifies sea, and *suf*
is the name of a plant in Aethiopia, from which the Abyssins
extract a beautiful crimson;[b] whether this be the same with the
gouesmon,[c] I know not, but am of opinion that the herb gives to
this sea both the colour and the name.

The vessels most us'd in the Red-Sea, tho' ships of all sizes
may be met with there, are *gelves*; of which some mention hath
been made already, these are the more convenient, because they
will not split, if thrown upon banks, or against rocks. These *gelves*
have given occasion to the report that out of the coco-tree alone,
a ship may be built, fitted out with mast, sails, and cordage, and
victual'd with bread, water, wine, sugar, vinegar, and oil. All
this indeed cannot be done out of one tree, but may out of several
of the same kind. They saw the trunk into planks, and sew them
together with thread which they spin out of the bark, and which
they twist for the cables; the leaves stitch'd together make the
sails. This boat thus equip'd may be furnish'd with all the
necessaries from the same tree. There is not a month in which the
coco does not produce a bunch of nuts, from twenty to fifty. At
first sprouts out a kind of seed or *capsula* of a shape not unlike
the scabbard of a scymetar, which they cut, and place a vessel
under, to receive the liquor that drops from it, this drink is call'd
soro, and is clear, pleasant, and nourishing. If it be boil'd, it
grows hard, and makes a kind of sugar much valued in the
Indies; distill this liquor and you have a strongwater, of which is
made excellent vinegar. All these different products are afforded
before the nut is formed, and while it is green it contains a
delicious cooling water; with these nuts they store their *gelves*,
and it is the only provision of water which is made in this
country. The second bark which contains the water, is so tender
that they eat it. When this fruit arrives to perfect maturity, they
either pound the kernel into meal, and make cakes of it, or draw
an oil from it of a fine scent and taste, and of great use in
medicine; so that what is reported of the different products of
this wonderful tree, is neither false nor incredible.[8]

b. crimson, *1735*   c. gouesmon *Errata*] gonesmon *1735*

8. "so that ... incredible" replaces a quarter-page list of the varied uses of the tree
(p. 44).

'Tis time we should come now to the relation of our voyage. Having happily past the straits at the entrance of the Red-Sea, we persued our course, keeping as near the shore as we could, without any farther apprehensions of the Turks. We were however under some concern that we were intirely ignorant, in what part of the coast to find Baylur, a port, where we proposed landing, and so little known, that our pilots, who had made many voyages in this sea, could give us no account of it. We were in hopes of information from the fishermen, but found that as soon as we came near they fled from us in the greatest consternation; no signals of peace or friendship could prevail on them to stay, they either durst not trust, or did not understand us. We ply'd along the coast in this uncertainty two days, till on the first of March having doubled a point of land, which came out a great way into the sea, we found ourselves in the middle of a fair large bay, which many reasons induced us to think was Baylur; that we might be farther assur'd we sent our Abyssin on shore, who returning next morning confirm'd our opinion. It would not be easy to determine whether our arrival gave us greater joy, or the inhabitants greater apprehensions, for we could discern a continual tumult in the land, and took notice that the crews of some barks that lay in the harbour, were unlading with all possible diligence, to prevent the cargo from falling into our hands, very much indeed to the dissatisfaction of many of our soldiers, who having engaged in this expedition with no other view than of filling their pockets, were, before the return of our Abyssin, for treating them like enemies, and taking them as a lawful prize. We were willing to be assured of a good reception in this port, the Patriarch therefore sent me to treat with them. I dress'd my self like a merchant,[9] and in that habit receiv'd the four captains of *gelves* which the *chec* sent to compliment me, and order'd to stay as hostages, whom I sent back, that I might gain upon their affections by the confidence I placed in their sincerity,[1] this had so good an effect, that the *chec*, who was trans-

---

9. SJ deletes the reason for the disguise: Lobo feared that in a country in which no one had ever seen a Jesuit, his garb might seem "un peu bizarre" (p. 45).

1. "that I might ... sincerity" imputes to Lobo crafty motives not actually stated in the French. The hostages admired the Portuguese and were pleased with their reception aboard ship. Kissing Lobo, they informed him that the sheik, convinced the Portuguese had come as friends, had sent them as reassurance and would come himself as soon as he could be certain of his own safety. Lobo's reply is natural: "Je

ported with the account the officers gave, of the civilities they had been treated with, came in an hour to visit me, bringing with him a Portuguese, whom I had sent ashore as a security for his return.[2] He inform'd me, that the king his master was encamp'd not far off, and that a *chec* who was then in the company was just arrived from thence, and had seen the Emperor of Aethiopia's letters in our favour; I was then convinced that we might land without scruple, and to give the Patriarch notice of it, order'd a volley of our muskets to be fired, which was answer'd by the cannon of the two ships, that lay at a distance for fear of giving the Moors any cause of suspicion by their approach. The *chec* and his attendants, though I had given them notice that we were going to let off our guns in honour of the king their master, could not forbear trembling at the fire and noise. They left us soon after, and next morning we landed our baggage, consisting chiefly of the Patriarch's library, some ornaments for the church, some images, and some pieces of callicoe, which were of the same use as money. Most of the soldiers and sailors were desirous of going with us, some from real principles of piety, and a desire of sharing the labours and merits of the mission, others upon motives very different, the hopes of raising a fortune. To have taken all who offered themselves would have been an injury to the owners of the ships, by rendering them unable to continue their voyage, we therefore accepted only of a few.

CHAPTER V

An account of Dancali. The conduct of *Chec* Furt. The author wounded, they arrive at the court of the King of Dancali; a description of his pavilion, and the reception they met with.

Our goods were no sooner landed, than we were surrounded

---

leur répondis que je ne doutais nullement de l'amitié du chec, qu'ils pouvaient l'assurer de celle des portugais, que je ne voulais point d'autres sûretés de sa parole, que sa parole même qu'il m'avait donnée; qu'ils pouvaient s'en retourner, & que

l'officier portugais, que j'envoyais avec eux, demeurerait en ôtage" (p. 46).

2. An omission: Lobo formed a reception line aboard ship and presented gifts to the sheik and his most important aides (p. 46).

with a crowd of officers, all gaping for presents, we were forced to
gratify their avarice by opening our bales, and distributing
among them some pieces of calicoe. What we gave to the *chec*
might be worth about a pistole, and the rest in proportion.
The kingdom of Dancali, to which this belongs, is barren,
and thinly peopled, the King is tributary to the Emperor of
Abyssinia, and very faithful to his sovereign. The Emperor had
not only written to him, but had sent a Moor and a Portuguese
as his embassadors to secure us a kind reception, these in their
way to this prince had come through the countries of Chumo-
Salamay and Senaa, the utmost confines of Abyssinia, and had
carried thither the Emperor's orders concerning our passage.

On Ascension-Day we left Baylur, having procured some
camels and asses to carry our baggage. The first day's march was
not above a league, and the others not much longer. Our guides
perform'd their office very ill, being influenced, as we imagined,
by the *Chec* Furt, an officer, whom, though unwillingly, we were
forced to take with us. This man who might have brought us to
the King in three days, led us out of the way through horrid
desarts destitute[a] of water, or where what we found was so foul,
nauseous, and offensive, that it excited a loathing and aversion
which nothing but extreme necessity would have over-come.[1]

Having travel'd some days, we were met by the King's
brother, to whom, by the advice of *Chec* Furt, whose intent in
following us, was to squeeze all he could from us, we presented
some pieces of Chinese workmanship, such as cases of boxes, a
standish,[2] and some earthen-ware, together with several pieces
of painted calicoe, which were so much more agreeable, that he
desired some other pieces instead of our Chinese curiosities, we
willingly made the exchange. Yet some time afterwards he ask'd
again for those Chinese goods which he had returned us, nor was
it in our power to refuse them. I was here in danger of losing my
life by a compliment which the Portuguese paid the prince of a
discharge of twelve muskets; one being unskillfully charged too

a. distitute *1735*

---

1. Cf. the less abstract description of   2. "A case for pen and ink" (*Dictionary*).
the water: "si sale & si puante, qu'il fallait   It is an apt translation for "une écritoire"
fermer les yeux & se boucher le nez pour   (p. 49).
en boire" (p. 48).

high, flew out of the soldier's hand, and falling against my leg
wounded it very much; we had no surgeon with us, so that all I
could do, was to bind it hard with some cloath. I was obliged by
this accident to make use of the *Chec* Furt's horse, which was the
greatest service we receiv'd from him in all our journey.

When we came[b] within two leagues and an half of the King's
court, he sent some messengers with his compliments, and five
mules for the chief of our company, our road lay through a
wood, where we found the ground cover'd over with young
locusts, a plague intolerably afflictive in a country so barren of it
self. We arriv'd at length at the bank of a small river, near which
the King usually keeps his residence, and found his palace at the
foot of a little mountain. It consisted of about six tents and
twenty cabins, erected amongst some thorns and wild trees,
which afforded a shelter from the heat of the weather. He
receiv'd us the first time in a cabin about a musket shot distant
from the rest, furnish'd out with a throne in the middle built of
clay and stones, and covered with tapistry and two velvet cush-
ions. Over-against him stood his horse with his saddle and
other furniture hanging by him, for in this country, the master
and his horse make use of the same apartment, nor doth the
King in this respect affect more grandeur than his subjects.
When we entred, we seated ourselves on the ground with our
legs cross'd, in imitation of the rest, whom we found in the
same posture. After we had waited some time, the King came in,
attended by his domesticks and his officers. He held a small lance
in his hand, and was dress'd in a silk robe, with a turbant on his
head, to which were fastned some rings, of very neat workmanship, which fell down upon his forehead.[3] All kept silence for
some time, and the King told us by his interpreter: that we were
welcome to his dominions, that he had been inform'd we were to
come, by the Emperor his father, and that he condoled the
hardships we had undergone at sea. He desired us not to be
under any concern at finding our selves in a country so distant
from our own, for those dominions, were ours, and he and the
Emperor his father, would give us all the proofs we could desire
of the sincerest affection. We returned him thanks for this prom-

b. came *1789*] come *1735*

---

3. There was more to the ceremony: Lobo and his party stood, were seated again,
were raised up, and were allowed to kiss the king's hand (p. 50).

ise of his favour, and after a short conversation went away. Immediately we were teazed by those who brought us the mules, and demanded to be paid the hire of them; and had advice given us at the same time, that we should get a present ready for the King. The *Chec*-Furt who was extremely ready to undertake any commission of this kind, would needs direct us in the affair, and told us, that our gifts ought to be of greater value, because we had neglected making any such offer at our first audience, contrary to the custom of that country. By these pretences he obliged us to make a present to the value of about twenty pounds,[4] with which he seem'd to be pleased, and told us we had nothing to do, but prepare to make our entry.[5]

CHAPTER VI

The King refuses their present. The author's boldness. The present is afterwards accepted. The people are forbidden to sell them provisions. The author
remonstrates against the usage. The King redresses it.

But such was either the hatred or avarice of this man, that instead of doing us the good offices he pretended, he advis'd the King to refuse our present, that he might draw from us something more valuable. When I attended the King in order to deliver the presents, after I had excused the smallness of them, as being, though unworthy his acceptance, the largest, that our profession of poverty, and distance from our country allow'd us to make, he examined them one by one with a dissatisfy'd look, and told me that, however he might be pleased with our good intentions, he thought our present such as could not be offer'd to a king without affronting him. And made me a sign with his hand to withdraw, and take back what I had brought. I obey'd, telling him, that perhaps he might send for it again, without having so much. The *Chec* Furt, who had been the occasion of all this, coming to us afterwards, blamed us exceedingly for having offered so little, and being told by us, that the present was pick'd out by himself, that we had nothing better to give, and that what

---

4. The English equivalent of "quatre cents livres" (p. 51).
5. This sentence epitomizes a more de-

tailed account of Furt's maneuvering and the Jesuits' gifts (p. 51).

we had left, would scarce defray the expences of our journey, he press'd us at least to add something, but could prevail no farther than to persuade us to repeat our former offer, which the King was now pleased to accept, tho' with no kinder countenance than before.[1]

Here we spent our time and our provisions, without being able to procure any more. The country indeed affords goats and honey, but no body would sell us any, the King as I was secretly inform'd, having strictly prohibited it, with a view of forcing all we had from us. The Patriarch sent me to expostulate the matter with the King, which I did in very warm terms, telling him, that we were assured by the Emperor of a reception in this country far different from what we met with, which assurances he had confirm'd by his promise, and the civilities we were entertain'd with at our first arrival; but that instead of friends who would compassionate our miseries, and supply our necessities, we found ourselves in the midst of mortal enemies that wanted to destroy us.[2]

The King who affected to appear ignorant[3] of the whole affair, demanded an account of the injuries I complain'd of, and told me that if any of his subjects should dare to attempt our lives, it should cost him his own. We are not, reply'd I, in danger of being stab'd or poison'd, but are doom'd to a more lingering and painful death by that prohibition which obliges your subjects to deny us the necessaries of life; if it be your highness's pleasure that we die here, we entreat that we may at least be dispatch'd quickly, and not condemned to longer torments.[4] The King, startled at this discourse, deny'd that he had given any such

---

1. Lobo and his party also presented gifts to the king's mother, brothers, and musicians (p. 52).

2. "but that ... destroy us" may lose some of the emotional impact of Lobo's direct discourse: "'Nous croyions avoir trouvé ici des amis qui pouvaient nous tenir lieu de ceux que nous avions quittés en venant dans un pays si eloigné du nôtre. Mais que nous nous sommes trompés! La liberté dont nous jouissons est une cruelle contrainte; nous sommes au milieu de nos plus cruels ennemis, qui en veulent à notre vie, & nous ne pouvons avoir re-

cours qu'à Dieu, qui écoutera nos plaintes, & punira les injustices & les violences que l'on nous fait'" (p. 52).

3. SJ infers this affectation from the king's response: "'qu'il ne savait ce que je lui voulais dire; qu'il ne croyait pas qu'il y eut un homme dans ses etats qui osât nous offenser'" (pp. 52–53).

4. SJ softens a vivid account of Lobo's boldness: suggesting that his majesty "'nous coupe la gorge tout d'un coup,'" Lobo advanced toward the king, "lui présentant la gorge" (p. 53).

orders, and was very importunate to know the author of our intelligence, but finding me determin'd not to discover him, he sent me away with a promise, that for the future we should be furnished with every thing we wanted, and indeed, that same day we bought three goats for about a crown, and some honey, and found ourselves better treated than before.

CHAPTER VII

They obtain leave with some difficulty, to depart from Dancali. The difficulties of their march. A broil with the Moors. They arrive at the plain of salt.

This usage, with some differences we had with a Moor,[1] made us very desirous of leaving this country, but we were still put off with one pretence or other, whenever we ask'd leave to depart;[a] tir'd with these delays, I apply'd my self to his favourite minister, with a promise of a large present if he could obtain us an audience of leave; he came to us at night to agree upon the reward, and soon accomplish'd all we desired, both getting us a permission to go out of the kingdom, and procuring us camels to carry our baggage, and that of the Abyssinian embassadors who were ordered to accompany us.

We set out from the kingdom of Dancali, on the fifteenth[2] of June, having taken our leave of the King who after many excuses for every thing that had happen'd, dismiss'd us with a present of a cow, and some provisions, desiring us to tell the Emperor of Aethiopia his father, that we had met with kind treatment in his territories, a request which we did not at that time think it convenient to deny.

Whatever we had suffer'd hitherto, was nothing to the difficulties we were now entering upon, and which God had decreed us to undergo for the sake of Jesus Christ. Our way now lay through a region scarce passable, and full of serpents, which were continually creeping between our legs, we might have

a. depart, *1735*

---

1. "with some ... Moor" epitomizes one third of a page recounting these differences (p. 53).
2. An error: "cinquième" (p. 54).

avoided them in the day, but being obliged, that we might avoid the excessive heats, to take long marches in the night, we were every moment treading upon them; nothing but a signal interposition of Providence could have preserved us from being bitten by them, or perishing either by weariness or thirst, for sometimes we were a long time without water, and had nothing to support our strength in this fatigue, but a little honey, and a small piece of cow's flesh dry'd in the sun. Thus we travel'd on for many days, scarce allowing our selves any rest, till we came to a channel or hollow worn in the mountains by the winter torrents, here we found some coolness, and good water, a blessing we enjoy'd for three days; down this channel all the winter runs a great river, which is dried up in the heats, or to speak more properly, hides it self under ground, we walk'd along its side sometimes seven or eight leagues without seeing any water, and then we found it rising out of the ground, at which places, we never fail'd to drink as much as we could, and fill our bottles.

In our march, there fell out an unlucky accident, which however did not prove of the bad consequence it might have done.[3] The master of our camels was an old Mahometan, who had conceived an opinion, that it was an act of merit to do us all the mischief he could; and in pursuance of his notion, made it his chief employment, to steal every thing, he could lay hold on; his piety even transported him so far, that one morning he stole and hid the cords of our tents. The Patriarch who saw him at the work, charg'd him with it, and upon his denial, shew'd him the end of the cord hanging from under the saddle of one of his camels. Upon this we went to seize them, but were opposed by him and the rest of the drivers, who set themselves in a posture of opposition with their daggers; our soldiers had recourse to their muskets, and four of them putting the mouths of their pieces to the heads of some of the most obstinate and turbulent, struck them with such a terrour, that all the clamour was still'd in an instant: none receiv'd any hurt but the Moor who had been the occasion of the tumult. He was knock'd down by one of our soldiers, who had cut his throat, but that the fathers prevented it, he then restor'd the cords, and was more tractable ever after.[4] In all my dealings with the Moors, I have always discover'd in

---

3. SJ creates this sentence to set the scene. The French paragraph begins simply: "Nous avions pour conducteur de nos chameaux ..." (p. 55).

4. "He was knock'd ... ever after" makes the Portuguese appear more brutal

them an ill-natur'd cowardise,[5] which makes them insupport-
ably insolent, if you shew them the least respect, and easily
reduced to reasonable terms, when you treat them with a high
hand.

After a march of some days, we came to an opening between
the mountains, the only passage out of Dancali into Abyssinia.
Heaven seems to have made this place on purpose for the repose
of weary travelers, who here exchange the tortures of parching
thirst, burning sands, and a sultry climate, for the pleasures of
shady trees, the refreshment of a clear stream, and the luxury of
a cooling breeze.[6] We arrived at this happy place about noon,
and the next day at evening left those fanning winds, and woods
flourishing with unfading verdure,[7] for the dismal barrenness of
the vast uninhabitable plains, from which Abyssinia is supply'd
with salt. These plains are surrounded with high mountains,
continually covered with thick clouds which the sun draws from
the lakes that are here, from which the water runs down into the
plain, and is there congealed into salt. Nothing can be more
curious, than to see the channels and aquaducts that nature has
formed in this hard rock, so exact and of such admirable contriv-
ance, that they seem to be the work of men. To this place
caravans of Abyssinia are continually resorting, to carry salt into
all parts of the empire, which they set a great value upon, and
which in their country is of the same use as money.[8] The super-
stitious Abyssins imagine, that the cavities of the mountains are
inhabited by evil spirits which appear in different shapes, calling

---

than does the French translation. SJ fails
to report that the Moor had attacked a
Portuguese soldier. Although the old man
returned the cords, "il voulut nous quitter
& fit décharger ses chameaux. Un portugais & deux mores des plus considér-
ables trouvèrent moyen de l'apaiser, &
depuis ce temps il parut un peu plus
traitable" (p. 55).

5. This phrase is not suggested in the
French: "un si mauvais naturel" (p. 55).

6. "Heaven ... breeze" represents a
careful revision of the French to provide
parallelism. Cf. "Il semble que Dieu ait
fait ce lieu exprès pour le soulagement des
pauvres voyageurs, qui après avoir beaucoup souffert de la soif & de la chaleur,

viennent se reposer entre ces montagnes.
Ils y trouvent de l'eau, des arbres toujours
verts, un frais agréable qu'entretient un
vent qui ne manque jamais de s'élever à
certaines heures du jour" (p. 56).

7. "left...verdure" does not appear in
the French. The alliteration, following the
carefully wrought passage above, suggests
that SJ was paying close attention to composition (p. 56).

8. Here Lobo repeats the comment
made in the third paragraph of this chapter: excessive heat limits travel to night-
time. SJ finds a more appropriate place for
the remark at the beginning of the next
paragraph.

those that pass, by their names as in a familiar acquaintance, who, if they go to them, are never seen afterwards. This relation was confirm'd by the Moorish officer who came with us, who, as he said, had lost a servant in that manner, the man certainly fell into the hands of the Galles, who lurk in those dark retreats, cut the throats of the merchants, and carry off their effects.

The heat making it impossible to travel through this plain in the day-time, we set out in the evening, and in the night lost our way, it is very dangerous to go through this place, for there are no marks of the right road but some heaps of salt, which we could not see. Our camel-drivers getting together to consult on this occasion, we suspected they had some ill design in hand, and got ready our weapons, they perceived our apprehensions, and set us at ease by letting us know the reason of their consultation.[9] Travelling hard all night, we found our selves next morning past the plain;[1] but the road we were in, was not more commodious, the points of the rocks pierc'd our feet; to encrease our perplexities we were alarmed with the approach of an arm'd troop, which our fear immediately suggested to be the Galles, who chiefly beset these passes of the mountains, we put our selves on the defensive, and expected them, whom upon a more exact examination, we found to be only a caravan of merchants come as usual to fetch salt.[2]

CHAPTER VIII

They lose their way, are in continual apprehensions of the Galles. They come to Duan, and settle in Abyssinia.

About nine the next morning we came to the end of this

---

9. One of the Portuguese had overheard "quelques paroles qui lui faisaient croire que ces gens machinaient quelque trahison" (p. 57). SJ's omission of this report leads us to infer that the Portuguese are unduly suspicious. Similarly, the camel drivers appear blameless. In the French translation the Moors are prudent scoundrels rather than misunderstood faithful guides: "Les chameliers con-

nurent à notre contenance que nous nous défiions d'eux, & que nous pourrions bien les prévenir" (p. 57).

1. This clause epitomizes five lines on the journey (p. 57).

2. Lobo notes that the merchants also took the Portuguese to be Gallas and that some of the Portuguese had resolved, if attacked, to kill the captain and the drivers (p. 57).

toilsome and rugged path, where the way divided into two, yet both led to a well, the only one that was found in our journey. A Moor with three others took the shortest,[1] without directing us to follow him, so we marched forwards we knew not whither, through woods and over rocks, without sleep or any other refreshment: at noon the next day we discovered that we were near the field of salt. Our affliction and distress is not to be express'd, we were all fainting with heat and weariness, and two of the Patriarch's servants, were upon the point of dying for want of water. None of us had any but a Moor, who could not be prevailed upon to part with it, at less than the weight in gold, we got some from him at last, and endeavour'd to revive the two servants, while part of us went to look for a guide that might put us in the right way. The Moors who had arrived at the well, rightly guessing that we were lost, sent one of their company to look[2] us, whom we heard shouting in the woods, but durst make no answer, for fear of the Galles. At length he found us, and conducted us to the rest,[3] we instantly forgot our past calamities, and had no other care than to recover the Patriarch's attendants. We did not give them a full draught at first, but poured in the water by drops, to moisten their mouths and throats, which were extreamly swell'd;[a] by this caution they were soon well. We then fell to eating and drinking, and though we had nothing but our ordinary repast of honey and dry'd flesh, thought we never had regal'd more pleasantly in our lives.

We durst not stay long in this place, for fear of the Galles who lay their ambushes more particularly near this well, by which all caravans must necessarily pass. Our apprehensions were very much encreased by our suspicion of the camel-drivers, who, as we imagined, had advertis'd the Galles of our arrival. The

a. swell'd, *1735*

---

1. "A Moor ... shortest" compresses and alters the ideas in the French translation: "Un more de notre compagnie fit prendre le chemin qui était le moins battu, nous assurant qu'il était le meilleur & le plus court; & véritablement c'est le chemin ordinaire des gens de pied: mais il y avait encore un autre sentier qui abrégeait beaucoup, & il s'en alla lui quatrième par là ..." (p. 58).

2. "to seek; to search for" (*Dictionary*).

3. SJ's translation does not reflect the suspicions of the Portuguese travelers: Lobo's party sent two men to accompany this guide, one to stay with him and the other to remain in the background with a musket (p. 58).

fatigue we had already suffer'd, did not prevent our continuing our march all night, at last we entred a plain, where our drivers told us, we might expect to be attack'd by the Galles; nor was it long before our own eyes convinc'd us, that we were in great danger, for we saw as we went along, the dead bodies of a caravan who had been lately massacred, a sight which froze our blood, and fill'd us with pity and with horror. The same fate was not far from overtaking us, for a troop of Galles, who were detach'd in search of us, miss'd us but an hour or two. We spent the next night in the mountains, but when we should have set out in the morning, were oblig'd to a fierce dispute with the old Moor, who had not yet lost his inclination to destroy us; he would have had us taken a road, which was full of those people we were so much afraid of;[b] at length finding he could not prevail with us, that we charg'd the goods upon him as belonging to the Emperor, to whom he should be answerable for the loss of them, he consented, in a sullen way, to go with us.[4]

The desire of getting out of the reach of the Galles, made us press forward with great expedition, and indeed, fear having entirely engross'd our minds, we were perhaps less sensible of all our labours and difficulties, so violent an apprehension of one danger, made us look on many others with unconcern; our pains at last found some intermission at the foot of the mountains of Duan[5] the frontier of Abyssinia which separates it from the country of the Moors, through which we had travel'd.

Here we imagined we might repose securely, a felicity we had long been strangers to, here we began to rejoice at the conclusion of our labours;[6] the place was cool, and pleasant, the water excellent, and the birds melodious; some of our company went into the wood to divert themselves with hearing the birds, and frightening the monkies, creatures so cunning, that they would not stir if a man came unarmed, but would run immediately

b. of, *1735*

---

4. "at length ... with us" epitomizes a more detailed account (pp. 59–60).

5. This paragraph freely summarizes (in half the space) Lobo's more specific relation of the dangers and hardships they

encountered (p. 60).

6. "Here we imagined ... labours" has no parallel in the French; SJ is bridging a gap produced by his omitting two thirds of a page (pp. 60–61).

when they saw a gun.[7] At this place our camel-drivers left us, to go to the feast of St. Michael, which the Aethiopians celebrate the sixteenth of June. We persuaded them however to leave us their camels and four of their company[8] to take care of them. We had not waited many days, before some messengers came to us, with an account, that Father Baradas with the Emperor's nephew, and many other persons of distinction waited for us at some distance; we loaded our camels, and following the course of the river, came in seven hours to the place, we were directed to halt at. Father Manuel Baradas and all the company, who had waited for us a considerable time, on the top of the mountain, came down when they saw our tents, and congratulated our arrival. It is not easy to express the benevolence and tenderness with which they embraced us, and the concern they shew'd at seeing us worn away with hunger, labour, and weariness, our cloaths tatter'd, and our feet bloody.[9]

We left this place of interview the next day, and on the 21st of June, arrived at Fremone the residence of the missionaries,[1] where we were welcom'd by great numbers of Catholicks, both Portuguese and Abyssins, who spar'd no endeavours to make us forget all we had suffer'd in so hazardous a journey, undertaken, with no other intention, than to conduct them in the way of salvation.[2]

---

7. Actually, the monkeys are not *quite* so cunning: "Tant que ces animaux ne virent point d'armes, ils ne s'enfuirent point; mais lorsqu'après plusieurs feintes, on prit tout de bon des fusils, ils disparurent en un instant" (p. 61).

8. An error: "trois hommes" (p. 61).

9. Lobo describes the camel drivers' fear of reprisal, "mais dès que nous fûmes avec nos frères, avec gens de même religion, nous oubliâmes tous nos maux, & toutes les injures que nous avions reçues" (p. 62).

1. The English does not reflect the tone of the French: "notre résidence, sanctifié par les sueurs & par la mort bienheureuse du P. André Oviedo qui a fini sa vie dans les travaux des missions, & par celles de plusieurs autres de nos pères, qui y sont enterrés" (p. 62).

2. SJ deletes an ingenuous concluding paragraph which offers to provide as briefly as possible a description of Abyssinia—its size, peoples, customs, government, and religion (p. 62).

A Description of Abyssinia[1]

CHAPTER I

The history of Abyssinia. An account of the Queen of Sheba, and of Queen Candace. The conversion of the Abyssins.

The original of the Abyssins like that of all other nations, is obscure, and uncertain. The tradition generally received, derives them from Cham the son of Noah, and they pretend, however improbably, that from his time till now, the legal succession of their kings, hath never been interrupted, and that the supreme power hath always continued in the same family. An authentick genealogy, traced up so high, could not but be extremely curious; and with good reason might the emperors of Abyssinia boast themselves the most illustrious and ancient family in the world. But there are no real grounds for imagining that Providence has vouchsafed them so distinguishing a protection,[2] and from the wars with which this empire hath been shaken in these latter ages, we may justly believe, that like all others it has suffer'd its revolutions, and that the history of the Abyssins is corrupted with fables. This empire is known by the name of the Kingdom of Prester-John. For the Portuguese having heard such wonderful relations of an ancient and famous Christian state call'd by that name, in the Indies, imagined it could be none but this of Aethiopia. Many things concurred to make them of this opinion: there was no Christian kingdom or state in the Indies, of which all was true which they heard of this land of Prester-John: And there was none in the other parts of the world who was a Christian separated from the Catholick Church, but what was known, except this kingdom of Aethiopia. It has therefore pass'd for the kingdom of Prester-John, since the

---

1. Unlike the chapter divisions, which appear only in the English translation, this division does occur in the French.

2. "But ... protection" is SJ's opinion, for which no parallel exists in the French.

time that it was discover'd by the Portuguese in the reign of
King John the Second. The country is properly call'd Abyssinia, and the people term
themselves Abyssins. Their histories count[a] an hundred and
sixty two reigns,[3] from Cham to Faciladas or Basilides; among
which some women are remarkably celebrated. One of the most
renowned is the Queen of Sheba, mention'd in Scripture, whom
the natives call Nicaula or Macheda, and in their translation of
the Gospel, *Nagista Azeb*, which in their language is Queen of the
South. They still shew the ruins of a city which appears to have
been once of note, as the place where she kept her court, and a
village which from its being the place of her birth, they call the
land of Saba: The kings of Aethiopia draw their boasted pedigree from Minilech the son of this queen and Solomon. The
other queen, for whom they retain a great veneration, is
Candace, whom they call Judith, and indeed if what they relate
of her, could be proved, there never was, amongst the most
illustrious and beneficent sovereigns, any to whom their country
was more indebted, for 'tis said, that she being converted by
Inda her eunuch whom St. Philip baptis'd, prevail'd with her
subjects, to quit the worship of idols, and profess the faith of
Jesus Christ. This opinion appears to me without any better
foundation, than another of the conversion of the Abyssins to the
Jewish rites, by the Queen of Sheba at her return from the court
of Solomon. They however, who patronise these traditions, give
us very specious accounts of the zeal and piety of the Abyssins
at their first conversion. Many, they say, abandon'd all the
pleasures and vanities of life for solitude, and religious austerities; others devoted themselves to God in an ecclesiastical life,
they who could not do these, set apart their revenues for building churches, endowing chapels, and founding monastries; and
spent their wealth in costly ornaments for the churches, and
vessels for the altars. 'Tis true, that this people has a natural
disposition to goodness, they are very liberal of their alms, they
much frequent their churches, and are very studious to adorn
them, they practise fasting and other mortifications, and notwithstanding their separation from the Roman Church, and the

a. count *Errata*] count up *1735*

_____

3. An error: "cent soixante & douze rois" (p. 64).

corruptions which have crept into their faith, yet retain in a great measure the devout fervour of the primitive Christians. There never were greater hopes of uniting this people to the Church of Rome, which their adherence to the Eutichian heresy[4] has made very difficult, than in the time of Sultan Segued, who called us into his dominions in the year 1625, from whence we were expell'd in 1634. As I have lived a long time in this country, and born a share in all that has passed, I will present the reader with a short account of what I have observed, and of the revolution which forced us to abandon Aethiopia, and destroyed all our hopes of reuniting this kingdom with the Roman Church.

The empire of Abyssinia hath been one of the largest which history gives us an account of, it extended formerly from the Red-Sea to the kingdom of Congo, and from Egypt to the Indian Sea. It is not long since it contain'd forty provinces; but it is now not much bigger than all Spain, and consists but of five kingdoms, and six provinces, of which, part is entirely subject to the Emperor, and part only pays him some tribute, or acknowledgement of dependance, either voluntarily or by compulsion. Some of these are of very large extent: The kingdoms of Tigre, Bagameder and Goiama, are as big as Portugal, or bigger; Amhara, and Damote, are something less. The provinces are inhabited by Moors, pagans, Jews, and Christians,[5] the last is the reigning and establish'd religion. This diversity of people and religion is the reason, that the kingdom in different parts is under different forms of government, and that their laws and customs are extremely various.

The inhabitants of the kingdom of Amhara, are the most civilized and polite, and next to them the natives of Tigre, or the true Abyssins. The rest, except the Damotes, the Gafates,[b] and the Agaus which approach somewhat nearer to civility, are

b. Gafates *Relation, Itinerário*] Gasates *1735*

---

4. Eutyches, a monk of Constantinople, argued in 446–447 against the doctrine of two perfect natures, divine and human, in Jesus Christ. According to Eutyches, before the incarnation there had been two natures, but afterwards the two natures blended, and only the divine remained. Although Eutyches was denounced for heresy, his monophysitism spread in the Alexandrian church. See the tenth dissertation, "On the errors of the Abyssins relating to the incarnation."

5. "chrétiens schismatiques" (p. 66). Le Grand is carefully translating Lobo's very specific phrase: "christão xismasticos" (*Itinerário*, p. 351).

Mountains of Tigre, from *Voyages and Travels, 1802–1806*, London, 1811, volume 4, by George Annesley, Viscount Valentia (later 2nd Earl of Mountnorris). Physical features had probably not changed significantly since Lobo's time. Reproduced by permission of the Yale University Library.

entirely rude and barbarous. Among these nations, the Galles, who first alarm'd the world in 1542, have remarkably distinguished themselves, by the ravages they have committed, and the terrour they have raised[6] in this part of Africa. They neither sow their lands, nor improve them by any kind of culture, but living upon milk and flesh, encamp like the Arabs, without any settled habitation.[7] They practise no rites of worship, though they believe that in the regions above, there dwells a being that governs the world: whether by this being they mean the sun or the sky is not known, or indeed whether they have not some conception of the God that created them. This deity they call in their language *Oac*.[c] In other matters they are yet more ignorant, and have some customs so contrary even to the laws of nature, as might almost afford reason to doubt, whether they are endued with reason.[8] The Christianity professed by the Abyssins is so corrupted with superstitions, errors, and heresies, and so mingled with ceremonies borrow'd from the Jews, that little besides the name of Christianity is to be found here, and the thorns may be said to have choaked the grain. This proceeds in a great measure from the diversity of religions which are tolerated there, either by negligence or from motives of policy; and the same cause hath produc'd such various revolutions, revolts, and civil wars within these latter ages. For those different sects do not easily admit of an union with each other, or a quiet subjection to the same monarch. The Abyssins cannot properly be said to have either cities or houses, they live either in tents, or in cottages made of straw and clay, for they very rarely build with stone. Their villages or towns consist of these huts, yet even of such villages they have but few, because, the grandees, the viceroys, and the Emperor himself are always in the camp, that they may be prepared upon the most sudden summons, to go

c. Oac *Relation (Errata), Itinerário*] Oul *1735*

---

6. "have remarkably ... raised" stems from more detailed phrasing: "mettant tout à feu & à sang, détruisant tous les lieux où ils passaient, & massacrant sans distinction d'âge n'y de sexe tous ceux qu'ils rencontraient" (p. 66).
7. Lobo notes that they elect a king every eight years (p. 66).
8. SJ omits a prediction by Patriarch

João Bermudes that in punishment for the country's stubbornness and treachery "l'Abissinie serait ravagée par une multitude de fourmis noires." Also deleted is the statement that the emperor was punished and the empire sharply reduced because of attacks "par les gentils, & par les mores ou Turcs" (pp. 66–67).

where the exigence of affairs demands their presence. And this precaution is no more than necessary for a prince every year engaged either in foreign wars, or intestine commotions.[9]

These towns have each a Governor, whom they call[d] *Gadare*, over whom is the *Educ*, or Lieutenant, and both are accountable to an officer call'd the *Afamacon*, or Mouth of the King, because he receives the revenues, which he pays into the hands of the *Relatina-Fala*, or Grand-Master of the Houshold; sometimes the Emperor creates a *Ratz*, or Viceroy, general over all the empire, who is superior to all his other officers.

Aethiopia produces very near the same kinds of provisions as Portugal, though by the extreme laziness of the inhabitants, in a much less quantity. However, there are some roots, herbs, and fruits, which grow there much better than in other places.[1] What the ancients imagined of the torrid zone being uninhabitable, is so far from being true, that this climate is very temperate, the heats indeed are excessive in Congo and Monomotapa, but in Abyssinia they enjoy a perpetual spring, more delicious and charming than that in our country. The blacks here are not ugly like those of the kingdoms I have spoken of, but have better features, and are not without wit and delicacy, their apprehension is quick, and their judgment sound. The heat of the sun, however it may contribute to their colour, is not the only reason of it, there is some peculiarity in the temper and constitution of their bodies, since the same men transported into cooler climates, produce children very near as black as themselves.

They have here two harvests in the year, which is a sufficient recompense for the small produce of each,* one harvest they have in the winter, which lasts through the months of July, August, and September, the other in the spring;[2] their trees are

---

*Une récolte se fait dans l'hiver, qui dure pendant les mois de Juillet, Aoust, et Septembre, et l'autre dans le printems.

d. whom they call *1789* (qu'ils nomment *Relation*)] whom they *1735*

---

9. This sentence embellishes the original idea: "Car il n'y a point d'année qu'il n'y ait quelque guerre, soit étrangère, soit domestique" (p. 67).

1. In the French text (p. 68) a paragraph on harvests interrupts the discussion at this point; SJ inserts it as his next paragraph.

2. For some reason the French sentence is translated *and* dropped to a footnote.

always green, and it is the fault of the inhabitants, that they produce so little fruit, the soil being well adapted to all sorts, especially those that come from the Indies. They have in the greatest plenty raisins, peaches, sour pomgranates, and sugar-canes, and some figs. Most of these are ripe about Lent, which the Abyssins keep with great strictness.[3]

After the vegetable products of this country, it seems not improper to mention the animals which are found in it,[4] of which here are as great numbers, of as many different species, as in any country in the world: it is infested with lyons, of many kinds, among which are many of that which is call'd the lyon royal. I cannot help giving the reader on this occasion, a relation of a fact which I was an eye-witness of. A lyon having taken his haunt, near the place where I lived, kill'd all the oxen and cows, and did a great deal of other mischief, of which I heard new complaints every day. A servant of mine having taken a resolution to free the country from this destroyer, went out one day with two lances, and after he had been some time in quest of him, found him with his mouth all smear'd with the blood of a cow he had just devour'd,[5] the man rush'd upon him, and thrust his lance into his throat with such violence that it came out between his shoulders, the beast with one dreadful roar, fell down into a pit, and lay struggling, till my servant dispatch'd him. I measured the body of this lyon, and found him, twelve feet between the head and the tail.[6]

CHAPTER II

The animals of Abyssinia, the elephant, unicorn, their horses and cows, with a particular account of the *moroc*.

There are so great numbers of elephants in Abyssinia, that in

---

3. In the French translation the point is that most of the fruits *die* during Lent, "que les Abissins jeûnent avec une extrême rigueur" (p. 68).

4. "After ... in it" provides a transition required because SJ has altered the original organization. Cf. Le Grand, p. 68.

5. The French translation presents a less gluttonous lion: he had eaten only part of the cow (p. 69).

6. SJ omits a second anecdote about a brave Abyssinian peasant who dispatched a lion with a dagger (p. 69).

one evening we met three hundred of them in three troops; as
they filled up the whole way, we were in great perplexity a long
time what measures to take;[a] at length, having implor'd the
protection of that Providence, that super-intends the whole
creation,[1] we went forwards through the midst of them, without
any injury. Once we met four young elephants, and an old one
that play'd with them, lifting them up with her trunk;[b] they
grew enraged on the sudden, and ran upon us; we had no way of
securing ourselves but by flight, which however would have
been fruitless, had not our persuers been stop'd by a deep ditch.
The elephants of Aethiopia are of so stupendous a size, that
when I was mounted on a large mule, I could not reach with my
hand within two spans of the top of their backs.[c] In Abyssinia is
likewise found the rhinoceros, a mortal enemy to the elephant.
In the province of Agaus, has been seen the unicorn, that beast
so much talk'd of, and so little known; the prodigious swiftness
with which this creature runs from one wood into another, has
given me no opportunity of examining it particularly, yet I have
had so near a sight of it as to be able to give some description of
it.[2] The shape is the same with that of a beautiful horse, exact
and nicely proportion'd, of a bay colour, with a black tail, which
in some provinces is long, in others very short; some have long
manes hanging to the ground. They are so timerous, that they
never feed but surrounded with other beasts that defend them.
Deer and other defenceless animals often herd about the elephant, which contenting himself with roots and leaves, preserves
those beasts that place themselves, as it were, under his protection, from the rage and fierceness of others that would devour
them.

The horses of Abyssinia are excellent, their mules, oxen, and
cows are without number, and in these principally consists the
wealth of this country. They have a very particular custom,

a. take, *1735*   b. trunk, *1735*   c. their backs *Errata*] his back *1735*

1. SJ here augments the French, which
reads simply: "après nous être recomman-
dés à Dieu" (p. 69).

2. This first-person account produces
an effect very different from that of the
French: "Comme cet animal passe vîte
d'un bois à un autre, on n'a pas eu le

temps de l'examiner; on l'a néanmoins
assez bien considéré pour pouvoir le dé-
crire" (p. 70). The *Itinerário* (pp. 360–61)
offers no support for SJ's reading. Here
and in the next note may be seen the
occasional peculiarity that results when
SJ translates "on" as "I."

which obliges every man that hath a thousand cows, to save every year one day's milk, of all his herd, and make a bath with it for his relations, entertaining them afterwards with a splendid feast. This they do so many days each year as they have thousands of cattle, so that to express how rich any man is, they tell you he bathes so many times. The tribute paid out of their herds to the king, which is not the most inconsiderable of his revenues, is one cow in ten every three years. The beeves are of several kinds; one sort they have without horns, which are of no other use than to carry burthens, and serve instead of mules. Another twice as big as ours which they breed to kill, fatting them with the milk of three or four cows. Their horns are so large the inhabitants use them for pitchers, and each will hold about five gallons. One of these oxen fat and ready to be kill'd, may be bought at most for two crowns. I have purchased five sheep, or five goats with nine kids for a piece of callicoe worth about a crown.

The Abyssins have many sort of fowls both wild and tame, some of the former we are yet unacquainted with: there is one of wonderful beauty, which I have seen in no other place except Peru,[3] it has instead of a comb, a short horn upon its head, which is thick, and round, and open at the top. The *feitan favez* or devil's-horse looks at a distance[4] like a man dress'd in feathers, it walks with abundance of majesty, till it finds itself persued, and then takes wing, and flies away. But amongst all their birds, there is none more remarkable than the *moroc*,[5] or honey-bird, which is furnished by nature with a peculiar instinct or faculty of discovering honey. They have here multitudes of bees of various kinds, some are tame like ours and form their combs in hives: of the wild-ones, some place their honey in hollow-trees, others hide it in holes in the ground, which they cover so carefully, that though they are commonly in the highway they are seldom found, unless by the *moroc*'s help, which, when he has discover'd any honey, repairs immediately to the road side, and when he

---

3. Lobo reached Brazil (not Peru) in his return from India. The inconsistency results from SJ's idiosyncratic translation of "un très beau que l'on ne trouve nulle part ailleurs qu'au Pérou" (p. 71).

4. SJ has added the qualification "at a distance."

5. Having omitted descriptions of cardinals, nightingales, partridges, turtle-doves, and pigeons, SJ provides this transitional clause.

sees a traveller, sings, and claps his wings, making many motions
to invite him to follow him, and when he perceives him coming,
flies before him from tree to tree, till he comes to the place where
the bees have stored their treasure,[6] and then begins to sing
melodiously. The Abyssin takes the honey, without failing to
leave part of it for the bird, to reward him for his information.[7]
This kind of honey I have often tasted, and do not find that it
differs from the other sorts in any thing but colour, it is somewhat blacker.[8] The great quantity of honey that is gathered, and
a prodigious number of cows that is kept here, have often made
me call Abyssinia a land of honey and butter.

CHAPTER III

The manner of eating in Abyssinia, their dress, their hospitality, and traffick.

The great lords, and even the Emperor himself, maintain
their tables with no great expence; the vessels they make use of
are black earthen-ware, which, the older it is, they set a greater
value on. Their way of dressing their meat, an European, till he
hath been long accustomed to it, can hardly be persuaded to
like, every thing they eat smells strong and swims with butter.
They make no use of either linnen or plates. The persons of rank
never touch what they eat, but have their meat cut by their
pages, and put into their mouths.[1] When they feast a friend, they
kill an ox, and set immediately a quarter of him raw upon the
table, (for their most elegant treat is raw beef newly kill'd) with
pepper and salt, the gall of the ox serves them for oil and vinegar;
some, to heighten the delicacy of the entertainment, add a kind
of sauce, which they call *manta*, made of what they take out of the
guts of the ox; this they set on the fire, with butter, salt, pepper,

---

6. "where ... treasure" replaces the
more matter-of-fact "au lieu où est le
miel" (p. 71).

7. The Abyssinian "ne manque jamais
d'en laisser une partie à cet oiseau"
(p. 72). It is SJ who notes that the bird was
being paid specifically for informing.

8. The French translation presents this
sentence earlier in the description of the

bees. It is followed by a reflection that the
honey must have been what sustained St.
John (p. 71).

1. It was considered the height of re-
finement to chew large mouthfuls of food
as noisily as possible: "n'y ayant que des
gueux, disent-ils, qui ne mangent que
d'un côté, & que des voleurs qui mangent
sans faire de bruit" (p. 72).

and onion. Raw beef, thus relish'd is their nicest dish, and is eaten by them with the same appetite and pleasure, as we eat the best partridges. They have often done me the favour of helping me to some of this sauce, and I had no way to decline eating it, besides telling them it was too good for a *missionary.*

The common drink of the Abyssins, is beer and mead, which they drink to excess, when they visit one another; nor can there be a greater offence against good manners, than to let the guests go away sober: their liquor is always presented by a servant who drinks first himself, and then gives the cup to the company, in the order of their quality.[2]

The meaner sort of people here dress themselves very plain, they only wear drawers, and a thick garment of cotton, that covers the rest of their bodies; the people of quality especially those that frequent the court run into the contrary extreme, and ruin themselves with costly habits. They wear all sorts of silks, and particularly the fine velvets of Turkey.

They love bright and glaring colours, and dress themselves much in the Turkish manner, except that their cloaths are wider, and their drawers cover their legs. Their robes are always full of gold and silver embroidery. They are most exact about their hair which is long and twisted, and their care of it is such, that they go bare-headed whilst they are young for fear of spoiling it, but afterwards wear red caps, and sometimes tur-bants after the Turkish fashion.

The ladies' dress is yet more magnificent and expensive, their robes are as large as those of the religious, of the order of St. Bernard, they have various ways of dressing their heads, and spare no expence in ear-rings, necklaces, or any thing that may contribute to set them off to advantage. They are not much reserv'd or confind, and have so much liberty in visiting one another, that their husbands often suffer by it: but for this evil there is no remedy, especially when a man marries a princess, or one of the royal family. Besides their cloaths, the Abyssins have no moveables or furniture of much value, nor[a] doth their manner of living admit of them.

a. or *1735.*

---

2. SJ omits Lobo's critical comment: the Abyssinians would have wine were it not so troublesome to make and preserve; but "ils aiment mieux s'en passer, que de se donner tant de peine" (p. 73).

One custom of this country deserves to be remarked:[3] when a stranger comes to a village, or to the camp, the people are obliged to entertain him and his company according to his rank; as soon as he enters an house, (for they have no inns in this nation) the master informs his neighbours that he hath a guest;[b] immediately, they bring in bread, and all kinds of provisions; and there is great care taken to provide enough, because if the guest complains, the town is oblig'd to pay double the value of what they ought to have furnish'd. This practise is so well establish'd, that a stranger goes into a house of one he never saw, with the same familiarity, and assurance of welcome, as into that of an intimate friend, or near relation, a custom very convenient, but which gives encouragement to great numbers of vagabonds throughout the kingdom.

There is no money in Abyssinia, except in the eastern provinces,[4] where they have iron coin. But in the chief provinces all commerce is managed by exchange; their chief trade consists in provisions, cows, sheep, goats, fowls, pepper, and gold, which is weigh'd out to the purchaser, and principally in salt which is properly the money of this country.[5]

When the Abyssins are engaged in a lawsuit, the two parties make choice of a judge, and plead their own cause before him, and if they cannot agree in their choice, the governor of the place appoints them one, from whom there lies an appeal to the Viceroy, and to the Emperor himself. All causes are determined on the spot, no writings are produced; the judge sits down on the ground in the midst of the high-road, where all that please, may be present. The two persons concerned stand before him, with their friends about them, who serve as their attornies. The plaintiff speaks first, the defendant answers him, each is permitted to rejoin three or four times, then silence is commanded, and the judge takes the opinions of those that are about him; if the evidence be deem'd sufficient, he pronounces sentence, which in

---

b. guest, *1735*

---

3. "One ... remarked" is an added transition.

4. A mistranslation of "provinces occidentales" (p. 74).

5. SJ deletes a third of a page in which

Lobo describes the use of salt for money, the rate of exchange, and the peculiar custom of friends who, upon meeting, lick each other's bits of salt (p. 74).

some cases is decisive and without appeal. He then takes the criminal into custody till he hath made satisfaction; but if it be a crime punishable with death, he is delivered over to the prosecutor, who may put him to death at his own discretion.

They have here a particular way of punishing adultery: a woman convicted of that crime is condemned to forfeit all her fortune, is turn'd out of her husband's house, in a mean dress, and is forbid ever to enter it again, she has only a needle given her to get her living with. Sometimes her head is shaved except one lock of hair which is left her, and even that depends on the will of her husband, who has it likewise in his choice, whether he will receive her again, or not;[c] if he resolves never to admit her, they are both at liberty to marry whom they will. There is another custom amongst them yet more extraordinary,[6] which is, that the wife is punished whenever the husband proves false to the marriage-contract, this punishment indeed extends no farther than a pecuniary mulct, and what seems more equitable,[7] the husband is obliged to pay a sum of money to his wife. When the husband prosecutes his wife's gallant, if he can produce any proofs of a criminal conversation, he recovers, for damages, forty cows, forty horses, and forty suits of cloaths, and the same number of other things; if the gallant be unable to pay him, he is committed to prison, and continues there during the husband's pleasure, who, if he sets him at liberty before the whole fine be paid, obliges him to take an oath, that he is going to procure the rest, that he may be able to make full satisfaction. Then the criminal orders meat and drink to be brought out, they eat and drink together, he asks a formal pardon, which is not granted at first;[d] however the husband forgives first one part of the debt, and then another, till at length the whole is remitted.

A husband that doth not like his wife may easily find means to make the marriage void, and, what is worse, may dismiss the second wife with less difficulty, than he took her, and return to the first: so that marriages in this country are only for a term of years, and last no longer than both parties are pleased with each other, which is one instance, how far distant these people are

c. not, *1735* d. first, *1735*

---

6. "There ... extraordinary" provides a useful transition not in the French.

7. "what ... equitable" has no parallel in the French translation.

from the purity of the primitive believers which they pretend to
have preserved with so great strictness. The marriages are in
short no more than bargains, made with this proviso, that when
any discontent shall arise on either side, they may separate, and
marry whom they please, each taking back what they brought
with them.

CHAPTER IV

An account of the religion of the Abyssins.

Yet though there is a great difference between our manners,
customs, civil government, and those of the Abyssins, there is yet
a much greater in points of faith; for so many errors have been
introduced, and ingrafted into their religion, by their ignorance,
their separation from the Catholick Church, and their intercourse with Jews, pagans, and Mahometans, that their present
religion, is nothing but a kind of confused miscellany of Jewish
and Mahometan superstitions, with which they have corrupted
those remnants of Christianity which they still retain.

. They have however preserved the belief of our principal
mysteries, they celebrate with a great deal of piety, the Passion
of our Lord, they reverence the cross, they pay a great devotion
to the Blessed Virgin, the angels, and the saints. They observe
the festivals, and pay a strict regard to the Sunday.[1] Every
month they commemorate the Assumption of the Virgin Mary,
and are of opinion, that no Christians beside themselves, have a
true sense of the greatness of the Mother of God, or pay her the
honours that are due to her. There are some tribes amongst
them, (for they are distinguish'd like the Jews by their tribes)
among whom the crime of swearing by the name of the Virgin, is
punished with forfeiture of goods, and even with loss of life: they
are equally scrupulous of swearing by St. George. Every week
they keep a feast to the honour of the apostles and angels; they
come to mass with great devotion, and love to hear the word of

---

1. Considering the Abyssinians' reverence for Saturday, the French "le
dimanche" should probably be translated
as Sabbath or Lord's Day. Lobo's original
term, however, is "os domingos," Sundays
(*Itinerário*, p. 374).

God. They receive the sacrament often, but do not always prepare themselves by confession. Their charity to the poor may be said to exceed the proper bounds, that prudence ought to set to it,[2] for it contributes to encourage great numbers of beggars, which are a great annoyance to the whole kingdom, and as I have often said, afford more exercise to a Christian's patience, than his charity: for their insolence is such, that they will refuse what is offer'd them, if it be not so much as they think proper to ask.

Though the Abyssins have not many images, they have great numbers of pictures, and perhaps pay them somewhat too high a degree of worship. The severity of their fasts is equal to that of the primitive church: in Lent they never eat till after sun-set. Their fasts are the more severe, because milk and butter are forbidden them, and no reason or necessity whatsoever can procure them a permission to eat meat, and their country, affording no fish, they live only on roots and pulse. On fast-days they never drink, but at their meat, and the priests never communicate till evening, for fear of profaning them. They don't think themselves obliged to fast till they have children either married, or fit to be married, which yet doth not secure them very long from these mortifications, because their youths marry at the age of ten years, and their girls younger.

There is no nation where excommunication carries greater terrours than among the Abyssins, which puts it in the power of the priests, to abuse this religious temper of the people, as well as the authority they receive from it, by excommunicating them, as they often do, for the least trifle in which their interest is concern'd.

No country in the world is so full of churches, monastries, and ecclesiasticks, as Abyssinia; it is not possible to sing in one church or monastry without being heard by another, and perhaps by several. They sing the psalms of David, of which as well as the other parts of the Holy Scriptures, they have a very exact translation in their own language, in which, though accounted canonical, the books of the Maccabees are omitted.[3] The instruments of musick made use of in their rites of worship, are little

---

2. The notion of prudence does not come from Lobo, who remarks only that their charity is carried to excess (p. 77).

3. According to two sentences which SJ omits, each monastery had two churches, one for men, one for women (p. 78).

drums, which they hang about their necks, and beat with both
their hands; these are carried even by their chief men, and by the
gravest of their ecclesiasticks. They have sticks likewise with
which they strike the ground, accompanying the blow with a
motion of their whole bodies. They begin their consort[4] by
stamping their feet on the ground, and playing gently on their
instruments, but when they have heated themselves by degrees,
they leave off drumming and fall to leaping, dancing, and
clapping their hands, at the same time straining their voices to
their utmost pitch, till at length they have no regard either to the
tune, or the pauses, and seem rather a riotous, than a religious
assembly. For this manner of worship they cite the psalm of
David. "O clap your hands all ye nations." [5] Thus they misapply
the sacred writings, to defend practises, yet more corrupt than
those I have been speaking of.

They are possess'd with a strange notion, that they are the
only true Christians in the world; as for us, they shun'd us as
hereticks, and were under the greatest surprize at hearing us
mention the Virgin Mary with the respect which is due to her,
and told us, that we could not be entirely barbarians, since we
were acquainted with the Mother of God. It plainly appears
that prepossessions so strong, which receive more strength from
the ignorance of the people, have very little tendency to.dispose
them to a re-union with the Catholick Church.[6]

They have some opinions peculiar to themselves about pur-
gatory, the creation of souls, and some of our mysteries.[7] They
repeat baptism every year, they retain the practise of circumcision, they observe the Sabbath, they abstain from all those sorts
of flesh which are forbidden by the law.[8] Brothers espouse the
wives of their brothers, and, to conclude, they observe a great
number of Jewish ceremonies.

Though they know the words which Jesus Christ appointed to
be used in the administration of baptism, they have without
scruple substituted others in their place, which makes the validity of their baptism, and the reality of their Christianity very

4. "A number of instruments playing together; a symphony. This is probably a mistake for *concert*" (*Dictionary*).
5. The French translation provides only the Latin title: *Omnes gentes plaudite manibus, jubilate Deo, &c.*

6. The concluding phrase is omitted: "ni à renoncer à leurs erreurs" (p. 78).
7. Lobo cites also their opinions on the Holy Ghost and the Son of God (p. 78).
8. And, the French adds, "les femmes sont obligées de se purifier" (p. 78).

doubtful. They have a few names of saints the same with those in the Roman martyrology, but they often insert others, as *Zama la Cota*, the Life of Truth, *Ongulavi*[a] the Evangelist, *Asca Georgi* the Mouth of Saint George.[9]

To bring back this people into the enclosure of the Catholick Church, from which they had been separated so many ages, was the sole view and intention, with which we undertook so long and toilsome a journey, cross'd so many seas, and pass'd so many desarts, with the utmost hazard of our lives: I am certain that we travelled more than seven thousand leagues before we arrived at our residence at Fremona.[b][1]

We came to this place anciently call'd Maigoga,[c] on the twenty-first of June, as I have said before, and were obliged to continue there till November, because the winter begins here in May, and its greatest rigour is from the middle of June, to the middle of September. The rains that are almost continually falling in this season make it impossible to go far from home, for the rivers overflow their banks, and therefore in a place like this, where there are neither bridges nor boats, are, if they are not fordable, utterly impassable. Some indeed have cross'd them by means of a cord fasten'd on both sides of the water, others tie two beams[2] together, and placing themselves upon them, guide them as well as they can, but this experiment is so dangerous, that it hath cost many of these bold adventurers their lives. This is not all the danger,[3] for there is yet more to be apprehended from the unwholesomeness of the air, and the vapours which arise from the scorch'd earth at the fall of the first showers, than

a. Ongulavi *Relation*] Onguelavi *Itinerário*; Ongulari *1735*   b. Fremona *Errata*]
Maigoga *1735*   c. Maigoga *Errata*] Fremona *1735*

---

9. "Asca ... Saint George" is an error. Omitting seven names, SJ appears to have fused two lines in the French text, which reads:

Alfa Christos, bouche de Christ ...
Asca Georgis, os de S. Georges ... (p. 79).

1. A long discussion (pp. 79–80) of the naming of Fremona (near Aksum) and its function as a refuge for Patriarch André Oviedo and his company is omitted. Famous "par l'exil, par les souffrances, par la mort & par la sépulture du Père

André Oviedo & de ses compagnons," it was a fitting location for the Jesuit residence.

2. "two beams" appears to be a guess at "deux outres," which Boyer's *Royal Dictionary* (1699) defines as bottles made of goatskin or leather. The *Itinerário* is more specific: "dous valentes odres das pelles de duas vaquas e cheos de vento" (p. 384); i.e., two large wineskins from the skins of two cows and filled with air.

3. An added clause.

from the torrents and rivers. Even they who shelter themselves
in houses, find great difficulty to avoid the diseases, that proceed
from the noxious qualities of these vapours. From the beginning
of June to that of September, it rains more or less every day. The
morning is generally fair and bright, but about two hours after
noon the sky is clouded, and immediately succeeds a violent
storm, with thunder and lightning flashing in the most dreadful
manner. While this lasts which is commonly three or four hours,
none go out of doors. The ploughman upon the first appearance
of it unyokes his oxen, and betakes himself with them into
covert. Travellers provide for their security in the neighbouring
villages, or set up their tents, every body flies to some shelter, as
well to avoid the unwholesomeness as the violence of the rain.
The thunder is astonishing, and the lightning often destroys
great numbers, a thing I can speak of from my own experience,
for it once flash'd so near me, that I felt an uneasiness on that
side for a long time after;[d] at the same time it kill'd three young
children, and having run round my room went out, and kill'd a
man and woman three hundred paces off.[4] When the storm is
over, the sun shines out as before, and one would not imagine it
had rain'd, but that the ground appears deluged. Thus passes
the Abyssinian winter, a dreadful season, in which the whole
kingdom languishes with numberless diseases, an affliction,
which however grievous, is yet equal'd, by the clouds of grashoppers,[5] which fly in such numbers from the desart, that the
sun is hid and the sky darken'd; whenever this plague appears,
nothing is seen through the whole region, but the most ghastly
consternation, or heard but the most piercing lamentations, for
wherever they fall, that unhappy place is laid wast and ruin'd,
they leave not one blade of grass, nor any hopes of a harvest.[6]
    God, who often makes calamities subservient to his will,

d. after, *1735*

---

4. SJ omits Lobo's conclusion: "Dieu
par sa bonté infinie, me preserva de cet
accident qui coûta la vie à cinq personnes"
(p. 81).
    5. "an affliction ... grashoppers" pro-
vides a transition not found in the French
(p. 81).
    6. "whenever this plague ... harvest"

is SJ's imaginative rendering of the following: "Lorsque ce fléau arrive, tout le
monde tombe dans une consternation
épouvantable, & crie miséricorde. En effet
ces insectes couvrent tout un pays, mangent l'herbe jusqu'à la racine, & ne lais-
sent aucune espérance de récolte" (p. 81).

permitted this very affliction, to be the cause of the conversion of many of the natives, who might have otherwise died in their errors; for part of the country being ruin'd by the grashoppers that year in which we arrived at Abyssinia, many, who were forced to leave their habitations, and seek the necessaries of life in other places, came to that part of the land where some of our missionaries were preaching, and laid hold on that mercy which God seem'd to have appointed for others.

As we could not go to court before November, we resolved, that we might not be idle, to preach and instruct the people in the country; in pursuance of this resolution, I was sent to a mountain, two days' journey distant from Maigoga. The lord or governor of the place was a Catholick, and had desired missionaries, but his wife had conceived an implacable aversion both from us and the Roman Church, and almost all the inhabitants of that mountain were infected with the same prejudices as she. They had been persuaded, that the hosts which we consecrated and gave to the communicants, were mix'd with juices strain'd from the flesh of a camel, a dog, a hare, and a swine, all creatures, which the Abyssins look upon with abhorrence, believing them unclean, and forbidden to them, as they were to the Jews. We had no way of undeceiving them, and they fled from us whenever we approach'd. We carried with us our tent, our chalices and ornaments, and all that was necessary for saying mass. The lord of the village, who like other persons of quality throughout Aethiopia, lived on the top of a mountain, received us with very great civility. All that depended upon him, had built their huts round about him, so that this place compared with the other towns of Abyssinia seems considerable: as soon as we arrived he sent us his compliments, with a present of a cow, which among them, is a token of high respect. We had no way of returning this favour, but by killing the cow, and sending a quarter smoking, with the gall, which amongst them is esteemed the most delicate part. I imagined for some time, that the gall of animals was less bitter in this country than elsewhere, but upon tasting it, I found it more; and yet have frequently seen our servants drink large glasses of it, with the same pleasure that we drink the most delicious wines.

We chose to begin our mission with the lady of the village, and hoped that her prejudice and obstinacy, however great, would in time yield to the advice and example of her husband, and that

her conversion would have a great influence on the whole
village, but having lost several days without being able to
prevail upon her to hear us on any one point, we left the place,[7]
and went to another mountain, higher and better peopled:
when we came to the village on the top of it where the lord lived,
we were surprised with the cries and lamentations of men that
seem'd to suffer, or apprehend some dreadful calamity; and were
told, upon enquiring the cause, that the inhabitants had been
persuaded that we were the devil's missionaries, who came to
seduce them from the true religion,[8] that foreseeing some of
their neighbours would be ruin'd by the temptation, they were
lamenting the misfortune which was coming upon them. When
we began to apply our selves to the work of the mission, we could
not by any means persuade any but the lord and the priest to
receive us into their houses; the rest were rough and untractable
to that degree, that, after having converted six, we despaired of
making any farther progress, and thought it best to remove to
other towns where we might be better received.[9]

We found however a more unpleasing treatment at the next
place, and had certainly ended our lives there, had we not been
protected by the governor, and the priest, who, though not
reconciled to the Roman Church, yet shew'd us the utmost
civility;[1] the governor inform'd us of a design against our lives,
and advis'd us not to go out after sunset, and gave us guards to
protect us from the insults of the populace.

We made no long stay in a place where they stop'd their ears
against the voice of God,[2] but returned to the foot of that
mountain which we had left some days before; we were sur-

---

7. SJ's very close translation omits only
one idea, an apt Biblical echo: "nous fîmes
ce qu'ordonne Jésus Christ; nous secouâmes la poussière de nos souliers ..."
(p. 83). See the Introduction (p. liv) for a
fuller discussion of this passage.

8. "who came ... religion" implies a
point of view not apparent in the French:
"qui venions pour les tenter & les faire
changer de religion" (p. 83).

9. "towns ... received" suggests a self-
interest not apparent in the French: "aller
à d'autres villages qui nous appellaient"

(p. 83).

1. "certainly ended ... civility" alters
the terminology: "je crois que nous aurions
fini notre martyre" there were it not for
these two men who were "schismatiques"
(p. 83).

2. "We made ... God" abbreviates the
French with its emphasis on obedience to
God's will: "Nous ne demeurâmes pas longtemps dans un lieu où Dieu ne vouloit pas
sitôt faire entendre sa voix; nous allâmes
porter les lumières de l'évangile à d'autres
qui en étaient plus dignes" (p. 83).

rounded, as soon as we began to preach, with a multitude of auditors, who came either in expectation of being instructed, or from a desire of gratifying their curiosity, and God[3] bestowed such a blessing upon our apostolical labours, that the whole village was converted in a short time. We then remov'd to another at the middle of the mountain, situated in a kind of natural *parterre*, or garden: the soil was fruitful, and the trees that shaded it from the scorching heat of the sun, gave it an agreeable and refreshing coolness. We had here the convenience of improving the ardour and piety of our new converts, and at the same time, of leading more into the way of the true religion.[4] And indeed our success exceeded the utmost of our hopes, we had in a short time great numbers whom we thought capable of being admitted to the sacraments of baptism and the mass.

We erected our tent, and placed our altar under some great trees, for the benefit of the shade; and every day before sunrising, my companion and I began to catechise and instruct these new Catholicks; and used our utmost endeavours to make them abjure their errors. When we were weary with speaking, we placed in ranks those who were sufficiently instructed,[5] and passing through them with great vessels of water, baptized them according to the form prescribed by the Church. As their number was very great, we cried aloud, those of this rank are named Peter, those of that rank Anthony. And did the same amongst the women, whom we separated from the men. We then confessed them, and admitted them to the Communion. After mass we applyed our selves again to catechise, to instruct, and receive the renunciation of their errors, scarce allowing our selves time to make a scanty meal, which we never did more than once a day.

After some time had been spent here, we removed to another town not far distant; and continued the same practise. Here I was accosted one day by an inhabitant of that place, where we had found the people so prejudiced against us, who desired to be

---

3. "God" replaces "le Père des Missions" (p. 84).

4. "leading ... religion" avoids some of the religious overtones of the French: "préparer les voies du Seigneur pour ceux qu'il voulait faire entrer dans le droit chemin" (p. 84).

5. "those ... instructed" is less specific than the French translation: "ceux que nous croyions en état de recevoir le baptême." Omitted too is Lobo's comment that "nous leur faisions faire quelques actes de foi & de contrition" (p. 84).

admitted to confession. I could not forbear asking him some questions, about those lamentations, which we heard upon our entring into that place. He confess'd with the utmost frankness and ingenuity, that the priests and religious, had given dreadful accounts both of us, and of the religion we preached, that the unhappy people was taught by them, that the curse of God attended us wheresoever we went, that we were always followed by the grashoppers, that pest of Abyssinia, which carried famine and destruction over all the country: that he seeing no grashoppers following us, when we pass'd by their village, began to doubt of the reality of what the priests had so confidently asserted, and was now convinced that the representation they made of us, was calumny and imposture. This discourse gave us double pleasure, both as it proved that God had confuted the accusations of our enemies, and defended us against their malice without any efforts of our own, and that the people who had shun'd us with the strongest detestation, were yet lovers of truth, and came to us on their own accord.[6]

Nothing could be more grosly absurd than the reproaches which the Abyssinian ecclesiasticks aspers'd us and our religion with. They had taken advantage of the calamity that happen'd the year of our arrival; and the Abyssins, with all their wit, did not consider that they had often been distress'd by the grashoppers, before there came any Jesuits into the country; and indeed before there were any in the world.[7]

Whilst I was in these mountains, I went on Sundays and Saints days sometimes to one church, and sometimes to another; one day I went out with a resolution not to go to a certain church, where I imagined there was no occasion for me, but before I had gone far, I found my self press'd by a secret impulse, to return back, to that same church. I obey'd the influence, and discovered it to proceed from the mercy of God to three young children who were destitute[e] of all succour, and at the point of

e. distitute *1735*

---

6. The evangelical flavour of the French is missing. These people loved "la vérité" and came to us with "grandes dispositions à devenir bientôt de vrais & zelés catholiques" (p. 85).

7. In an omitted section (about one third of a page) Lobo conjectures that

God allowed the plague of grasshoppers in order to save souls: whole villages came seeking food and, aided by the Jesuits' charity, were willing to listen to their message. Many were baptized; a few were stubborn (pp. 85–86).

death: I found two very quickly in this miserable state,[8] the mother had retired to some distance that she might not see them die, and when she saw me stop, came and told me that they had been obliged by want to leave the town they lived in, and were at length reduced to this dismal[9] condition, that she had been baptized, but that the children had not. After I had baptized and relieved them, I continued my walk, reflecting with wonder on the mercy of God,[1] and about evening discovered another infant, whose mother, evidently a Catholick, cried out to me to save her child, or at least, that if I could not preserve this uncertain and perishable life, I should give it another certain and permanent.[2] I sent my servant to fetch water with the utmost expedition, for there was none near, and happily baptized the child before it expired.

Soon after this,[3] I returned to Fremona, and had great hopes of accompanying the Patriarch to the court; but, when we were almost setting out, receiv'd the command of the Superior of the mission to stay at Fremona, with a charge of the house there, and of all the Catholicks that were dispersed over the kingdom of Tigre, an employment very ill proportion'd to my abilities. The House of Fremona has always been much regarded, even by those emperors who persecuted us; Sultan Segued annex'd nine large manors to it for ever, which did not make us much more wealthy, because of the expensive hospitality which the great conflux of strangers obliged us to. The lands in Abyssinia yield but small revenues, unless the owners themselves set the value upon them, which we could not do.

The manner of letting farms in Abyssinia differs much from that of other countries: the farmer, when the harvest is almost

---

8. "in this ... state" is an added comment.

9. An inserted adjective.

1. According to the French, Lobo was reflecting "aux grâces que Dieu fait à ceux qu'il a prédestinés de toute éternité" (p. 86).

2. "if I ... permanent" is constructed from the original plea of the mother "que si je ne pouvais pas lui conserver la vie qu'il pouvait perdre, je lui en donnasse une autre qu'il ne perdrait jamais" (p. 87).

3. This transition bridges a deletion of

half a page describing Lobo's fruitless attempt to convert the headstrong wife who had blocked the Jesuits earlier, and his reluctant compliance with the request of his superiors that he change his name because the Abyssinians disliked "Lobo" (p. 87). Although Lobo does not inform us what name he chose, Gaspar Pais, a contemporary, refers in January 1626 to Jerónimo Lobo, now known as "Brandão" (quoted from *Braga, doc.* XXIII, f. 13 in *Itinerário*, p. 398, n. 2). The name comes from his mother's family: she was D. Maria Brandão de Vasconcelos.

ripe, invites the *chumo* or steward, who is appointed to make an estimate of the value of each year's product, to his house, entertains him in the most agreeable manner he can; makes him a present, and then takes him out to see his corn. If the *chumo* is pleased with the treat and present, he will give him a declaration, or writing to witness that his ground which afforded five or six sacks of corn, did not yield so many bushels, and even of this it is the custom to abate something; so that our revenue did not encrease in proportion to our lands; and we found ourselves often obliged to buy corn, which, indeed is not dear, for in fruitful years, forty or fifty[4] measures weighing each about twenty-two pounds may be purchased for a crown.

Besides the particular charge I had of the House of Fremona, I was appointed the Patriarch's grand vicar, through the whole kingdom of Tigre. I thought that to discharge this office as I ought, it was incumbent on me to provide necessaries as well for the bodies as the souls of the converted Catholicks. This labour was much encreased by the famine which the grashoppers had brought that year upon the country.[5] Our house was perpetually surrounded by some of those unhappy people, whom want had compell'd to abandon their habitations, and whose pale cheeks and meagre bodies were undeniable proofs of their misery and distress.[6] All the relief I could possibly afford them, could not prevent the death of such numbers, that their bodies filled the highways; and to encrease our affliction, the wolves having devoured the carcasses, and finding no other food fell upon the living; their natural fierceness being so encreased by hunger,[7] that they drag'd the children out of the very houses. I saw myself a troop of wolves tear a child of six[8] years old in pieces before I, or any one else could come to its assistance.

While I was entirely taken up with the duties of my ministry, the Viceroy of Tigre receiv'd the commands of the Emperor, to search for the bones of Don Christopher de Gama: on this occasion it may not be thought impertinent to give some ac-

---

4. An error: "trente jusqu'à cinquante" (p. 88).

5. The French mentions "la plaie," but only SJ reminds us of its cause, the grasshoppers.

6. "whose pale ... distress" lends pathos

to the original idea: "dont les visages exténués marquaient assez la nécessité où ils étaient" (p. 88).

7. "their natural ... hunger" has no parallel in the French (p. 88).

8. An error: "dix" (p. 88).

count of the life and death of this brave and holy Portuguese, who, after having been successful in many battles fell at last into the hands of the Moors, and compleated that illustrious life by a glorious martyrdom.

CHAPTER V

The adventures of the Portuguese, and the actions of Don Christopher de Gama in Aethiopia.

About the beginning of the sixteenth century, arose a Moor near the Cape of Gardafui,[1] who, by the assistance of the forces sent him from Moca by the Arabs and Turks, conquered almost all Abyssinia, and founded the kingdom of Adel. He was call'd Mahomet Gragnè or the Lame.[2] When he had ravaged Aethiopia fourteen years, and was master of the greatest part of it, the Emperor David sent to implore succour of the King of Portugal, with a promise, that when those dominions were recovered which had been taken from him, he would entirely submit himself to the Pope, and resign the third part of his territories to the Portuguese. After many delays occasion'd by the great distance between Portugal and Abyssinia, and some unsuccessful attempts, King John the Third, having made Don Stephen de Gama son of the celebrated Don Vasco de Gama, Viceroy of the Indies, gave him orders to enter the Red-Sea in pursuit of the Turkish gallies, and to fall upon them where-ever he found them, even in the port of Suez. The Viceroy in obedience to the King's commands, equip'd a powerful fleet, went on board himself, and cruis'd about the coast without being able to discover the Turkish vessels. Enrag'd to find, that with this great preparation he should be able to effect nothing,[a] he landed at Mazua four hundred Portuguese under the command of Don Christopher de Gama, his brother, he was soon joined by some

a. nothing; *1735*

---

1. The Cape of Guardafui juts out into the Gulf of Aden and the Indian Ocean.
2. The French "le gaucher" (p. 89) should be translated as "the left-handed."

Cf. SJ's translation (p. 256) and the Portuguese term, "esquerdo" (left) in the *Itinerário* (p. 403).

Abyssins, who had not yet forgot their allegiance to their sovereign,[3] and in his march up the country, was met by the Empress Helena, who receiv'd him as her deliverer. At first nothing was able to stand before the valour of the Portuguese, the Moors were driven from one mountain to another, and were dislodged even from those places, which it seem'd almost impossible to approach, even unmolested by the opposition of an enemy.

These successes seem'd to promise a more happy event, than that which follow'd them. It was now winter, a season in which, as the reader hath been already inform'd,[4] it is almost impossible to travel in Aethiopia. The Portuguese unadvisedly engaged themselves in an enterprise, to march thro' the whole country, in order to join the Emperor who was then in the most remote part of his dominions. Mahomet, who was in possession of the mountains, being inform'd by his spies, that the Portuguese were but four hundred, encamped in the plain of Balut, and sent a message to the general, that he knew the Abyssins had imposed on the King of Portugal, which, being acquainted with their treachery, he was not surprised at, and that in compassion of the commander's youth,[5] he would give him and his men, if they would return, free passage, and furnish them with necessaries; that he might consult upon the matter, and depend upon his word, reminding him, however, that it was not safe to refuse his offer.

The general presented the ambassador with a rich robe, and returned this gallant answer; "That he, and his fellow soldiers were come with an intention to drive Mahomet out of these countries, which he had wrongfully usurped; that his present design was, instead of returning back the way he came, as Mahomet advised, to open himself a passage through the country of his enemies; that Mahomet, should rather think of determining whether he would fight or yield up his ill-gotten territories, than of prescribing measures to him: that he put his

3. "who had ... sovereign" expands "qui étaient demeurés fidèles" (p. 89).

4. "as the reader ... inform'd" appears only in the English translation.

5. SJ deletes a key phrase. According to Lobo, Grañ took pity on the youth of

da Gama and of his "moines; c'est ainsi qu'il appelait, par mépris, nos portugais" (p. 90). The Portuguese reaction to the sneering phrase was an important factor in their determination to resist.

whole confidence[b] in the omnipotence of God, and the justice of his cause, and that to shew how just a sense he had of Mahomet's kindness, he took the liberty of presenting him with a looking-glass, and a pair of pincers."

This answer and the present so provok'd Mahomet, who was at dinner when he receiv'd it, that he rose from table immediately to march against the Portuguese, imagining he should meet with no resistance, and indeed any man, however brave, would have been of the same opinion; for his forces consisted of fifteen thousand foot, beside a numerous body of cavalry, and the Portuguese commander had but three hundred and fifty men, having lost eight in attacking some passes, and left forty at Mazua, to maintain an open intercourse with the Viceroy of the Indies. This little troop of our countrymen were upon the declivity of a hill near a wood; above them stood the Abyssins, who resolved to remain quiet spectators of the battle, and to declare themselves on that side which should be favour'd with victory.

Mahomet began the attack with only ten horsemen, against whom as many Portuguese were detach'd, who fir'd with so much exactness, that nine of the Moors fell, and the tenth with great difficulty made his escape. This omen of good fortune gave the soldiers great encouragement; the action grew hot, and they came at length to a general battle, but the Moors, dismay'd by the advantages our men had obtain'd at first, were half defeated before the fight. The great fire of our muskets and artillery broke them immediately. Mahomet preserv'd his own life not without difficulty; but did not lose his capacity with the battle:[6] he had still a great number of troops remaining, which he rallied, and entrench'd himself at Membret, a place naturally strong, with an intention to pass the winter there, and wait for succours.

The Portuguese, who were more desirous of glory than wealth, did not encumber themselves with plunder, but with the utmost expedition pursued their enemies, in hopes of cutting them entirely off. This expectation was too sanguine;[7] they found them encamped in a place naturally almost inaccessible,

b. confidence *1789* (confiance *Relation*)] confi- *1735*

6. "did not ... battle" produces a neat parallelism based on "il ne perdit pas le jugement dans sa défaite" (p. 91).

7. This opening clause is SJ's addition.

and so well fortified, that it would be no less than extreme
rashness to attack them. They therefore entrench'd themselves
on a hill over-against the enemies' camp,[8] and, though victorious, were under great disadvantages. They see new troops
arrive every day at the enemies' camp, and their small number
grew less continually, their friends at Mazua could not join
them, they know not how to procure provisions, and could put
no confidence in the Abyssins; yet recollecting the great things
atchieved by their countrymen, and depending on the Divine
protection, they made no doubt of surmounting all difficulties.

Mahomet on his part was not idle,[9] he solicited the assistance
of the Mahometan princes, pressed them with all the motives of
religion, and obtain'd a reinforcement of two thousand mus-
queteers from the Arabs, and a train of artillery from the Turks.
Animated with these succours, he march'd out of his trenches to
enter those of the Portuguese, who received him with the utmost
bravery, destroy'd prodigious numbers of his men, and made
many sallies with great vigour, but losing every day some of their
small troops, and most of their officers being kill'd, it was easy to
surround, and force them.

Their general had already one arm broken, and his knee
shatter'd with a musket-shot, which made him unable to repair
to all those places where his presence was necessary to animate
his soldiers. Valour was at length forced to submit to superiority
of numbers, the enemy entred the camp, and put all to the
sword.[1] The general with ten more escaped the slaughter, and by
means of their horses retreated to a wood, where they were soon
discover'd by a detachment sent in search of them, and brought
to Mahomet, who was overjoy'd to see his most formidable
enemy in his power, and order'd him to take care of his uncle
and nephew, who were wounded, telling him, that he should
answer for their lives; and, upon their death, tax'd him with
hastening it. The brave Portuguese made no excuses, but told
him, he came thither to destroy Mahometans, and not to save
them.[2] Mahomet enraged at this language, order'd a stone to be

---

8. SJ deletes half a page describing
Grañ's retreat and a dialogue with his
uncle about the debacle (pp. 91–92).

9. An added transitional clause.

1. "put all . . . sword" is an extension of

"ne firent quartier à personne" (p. 92).

2. SJ creates this pithy rejoinder by revising the French phrasing: da Gama said,
"qu'il n'était pas venu des Indes pour
sauver la vie à des mores" (p. 93).

ut on his head, and exposed this great man to the insults and reproaches of the whole army: after this they inflicted various kinds of tortures on him,[3] which he endured with incredible resolution, and without uttering the least complaint, praising the mercy of God who had ordain'd him to suffer in such a cause.

Mahomet, at last satisfied with cruelty, made an offer of sending him to the Viceroy of the Indies, if he would turn Musulman;[4] the hero took fire at this proposal, and answer'd with the highest indignation, that nothing should make him forsake his heavenly master to follow an impostor, and continued in the severest terms to vilify their false prophet, till Mahomet struck off his head.

Nor did the resentment of Mahomet end here, he divided his body into quarters, and sent them to different places. The Catholicks gathered the remains of this glorious martyr[5] and inter'd them. Every Moor that pass'd by, threw a stone upon his grave, and rais'd in time such an heap, as I found it difficult to remove, when I went in search of those precious reliques.

What I have here related of the death of Don Christopher de Gama, I was told by an old man, who was an eye-witness of it: and there is a tradition in the country, that in the place where his head fell, a fountain sprung up of wonderful virtue, which cur'd many diseases otherwise past remedy.

CHAPTER VI

Mahomet continues the war and is kill'd. The stratagem of Peter Leon.

Mahomet, that he might make the best use of his victory, ranged over a great part of Abyssinia, in search of the Emperor Claudius, who was then in the kingdom of Dambia. All places submitted to the Mahometan, whose insolence encreased every

---

3. All the gruesome details are omitted: da Gama was stripped, led through the camp, splattered with mud, beaten, and cursed; his beard was plucked bristle by bristle, and his flesh was torn by those same pincers which he had sent to Grañ (p. 93).

4. Actually da Gama was offered a choice: either to become a Moslem or to reveal the position of the remaining Portuguese.

5. "This glorious martyr" has no parallel in the French (p. 93).

68 A VOYAGE TO ABYSSINIA

day with his power, and nothing after the defeat of the Portu
guese was supposed able to put a stop to the progress of his arms.

The soldiers of Portugal, having lost their chief, resorted to
the Emperor, who, though young, promised great things, and
told them[1] that since their own general was dead, they would
accept of none but himself. He received them with great kindness, and hearing of Don Christopher de Gama's misfortune
could not forbear honouring with some tears the memory of a
man who had come so far to his succour, and lost his life in his
cause.

The Portuguese, resolved at any rate to revenge the fate of
their general, desired the Emperor to assign them the post
opposite to Mahomet, which was willingly granted them. That
king flush'd with his victories and imagining to fight was undoubtedly to conquer,[2] sought all occasions of giving the
Abyssins battle. The Portuguese, who desired nothing more
than to reestablish their reputation by revenging the affront put
upon them by the late defeat,[3] advised the Emperor to lay hold
on the first opportunity of fighting. Both parties joined battle
with equal fury; the Portuguese directed all their force against
that part where Mahomet was posted. Peter Leon who had been
servant to the general, singled the king out among the croud,
and shot him into the head with his musket. Mahomet, finding
himself wounded, would have retired out of the battle, and was
followed by Peter Leon, till he fell down dead; the Portuguese
alighting from his horse, cut off one of his ears. The Moors being
now without a leader, continued the fight but a little time, and
at length fled different ways in the utmost disorder; the Abyssins
pursued them, and made a prodigious slaughter; one of them
seeing the king's body on the ground, cut off his head, and
presented it to the Emperor; the sight of it fill'd the whole camp
with acclamations, every one applauded the valour and good
fortune of the Abyssin, and no reward was thought great enough
for so important a service. Peter Leon, having stood by some
time, asked, whether the king had but one ear? "If he had two,"

---

1. An error: "ils lui déclarèrent" (p. 94).

2. "imagining ... conquer" is SJ's revision of "était persuadé qu'une bataille
suffirait pour le rendre maître de toute
l'Abissinie; & se croyant sûr de la gagner

..." (p. 94).

3. SJ omits a second, more important
reason for the Portuguese zeal: the need to
avenge the deaths of their captain and
their comrades (p. 94).

says he, "it seems likely that the man who kill'd him cut off one, and keeps it as a proof of his exploit."[4] The Abyssin stood confus'd, and the Portuguese produced the ear out of his pocket; every one commended the stratagem, and the Emperor commanded the Abyssin to restore the presents he had receiv'd, and delivered them with many more to Peter Leon.[5]

I imagined the reader would not be displeased to be informed who this man was, whose precious remains were search'd for by a viceroy of Tigre, at the command of the Emperor himself. The commission was directed to me, nor did I ever receive one that was more welcome on many accounts; I had contracted an intimate friendship with the Count de Vidigueira viceroy of the Indies, and had been desired by him, when I took my leave of him, upon going to Melinda, to inform my self where his relation was buried, and to send him some of his reliques.

The Viceroy, son-in-law to the Emperor,[6] with whom I was joined in the commission, gave me many distinguishing proofs of his affection to me, and of his zeal for the Catholick religion. It was a journey of fifteen days, thro' a part of the country possessed by the Galles, which made it necessary to take troops with us for our security; yet, notwithstanding this precaution, the hazard of the expedition appeared so great, that our friends bad us farewell with tears, and look'd upon us as destin'd to unavoidable destruction. The Viceroy had given orders to some troops to join us on the road, so that our little army grew stronger, as we advanced. There is no making long marches in this country; an army here is a great city well peopled, and under exact government; they take their wives and children with them, and the camp hath its streets, its market-places, its churches, courts of justice, judges, and civil officers.

Before they set forward, they advertise the governors of provinces through which they are to pass, that they may take care to furnish what is necessary for the subsistance of the troops. These governors give notice to the adjacent places, that the army is to march that way on such a day, and that they are assess'd such a

---

4. "as ... exploit" appears only in the English translation.

5. The final comment is deleted: his reputation became so great that to praise a man one had only to say, "qu'il était un autre Pierre Leon" (p. 95).

6. SJ silently corrects the French, which here erroneously refers to the viceroy as "beau-frère de l'empereur" (p. 95); that the error is Le Grand's is made clear by the *Itinerário*, which has "genrro" (p. 416), or son-in-law.

quantity of bread, beer, and cows. The peasants are very exact in supplying their quota, being oblig'd to pay double the value in case of failure, and very often when they have produced their full share, they are told, that they have been deficient, and condemned to buy their peace with a large fine.[7]

When the providore has received these contributions, he divides them according to the number of persons, and the want they are in; the proportion they observe in this distribution is twenty pots of beer, ten of mead, and one cow to an hundred loaves. The chief officers and persons of note carry their own provisions with them, which I did too, though I afterwards found the precaution unnecessary, for I had often two or three cows more than I wanted, which I bestowed on those whose allowance fell short.

The Abyssins are not only obliged to maintain the troops in their march, but to repair the roads, to clear them, especially in the forests, of brambles and thorns, and by all means possible to facilitate the passage of the army. They are by long custom, extremely ready at encamping; as soon as they come to a place they think convenient to halt at, the officer that commands the van-guard, marks out with his pike the place for the king's or viceroy's tent; every one knows his rank and how much ground he shall take up; so the camp is form'd in an instant.

CHAPTER VII

They discover the reliques. Their apprehension of the Galles. The author converts a criminal, and procures his pardon.

We took with us an old Moor, so enfeebled with age, that they were forced to carry him: he had seen, as I have said, the sufferings and death of Don Christopher de Gama: and a Christian, who had often heard all those passages related to his father, and knew the place where the uncle and nephew of Mahomet were buried, and where they inter'd one quarter of the Portuguese martyr. We often examined these two men, and

---

7. This long sentence has been placed here by SJ; in the French translation it   occurs after the first sentence of the next paragraph. Cf. *Relation*, p. 96.

always apart; they agreed in every circumstance of their relations, and confirm'd us in our belief of them, by leading us to
the place, where we took up the uncle and nephew of Mahomet,
as they had described. With no small labour we removed the
heap of stones which the Moors according to their custom, had
thrown upon the body, and discover'd the treasure we came in
search of.[1] Not many paces off, was the fountain where they had
thrown his head with a dead dog, to raise a greater aversion in
the Moors. I gathered the teeth and the lower jaw. No words can
express the extasies I was transported with, at seeing the reliques
of so great a man, and reflecting that it had pleased God to make
me the instrument of their preservation, so that one day, if our
holy Father the Pope shall be so pleased, they may receive the
veneration of the faithful. All burst into tears at the sight: we
indulg'd a melancholly pleasure in reflecting what that great
man had achiev'd for the deliverance of Abyssinia, from the
yoke and tyranny of the Moors; the voyages he had undertaken,
the battles he had fought, the victories he had won, and the
cruel and tragical death he had suffered. Our first moments were
so entirely taken up with these reflexions, that we were incapable of considering the danger we were in of being immediately surrounded by the Galles: but as soon as we awaked to
that thought, we contrived to retreat as fast as we could; our
expedition, however, was not so great, but we saw them on the
top of a mountain ready to pour down upon us. The Viceroy
attended us closely with his little army, but had been probably
not much more secure than we, his force consisting only of foot,
and the Galles entirely of horse, a service at which they are very
expert. Our apprehensions, at last prov'd to be needless, for the
troops we saw were of a nation at that time, in alliance with the
Abyssins.[2]

Not careing, after this alarm, to stay longer here, we set out on
our march back, and in our return, passed through a village
where two men who had murther'd a domestick of the Viceroy,
lay under an arrest; as they had been taken in the fact, the law of
the country allow'd that they might have been executed the
same hour, but the Viceroy having order'd that their death

---

1. "treasure ... search of" paraphrases
"ces précieuses reliques" (p. 97).
2. SJ has reduced a more detailed ac-

count (a fifth of a page) to this sentence
(pp. 98–99).

should be defer'd till his return, delivered them to the relations of the dead, to be disposed of as they should think proper. They made great rejoicings all the night, on account of having it in their power to revenge their relation, and the unhappy criminals had the mortification of standing by, to behold this jollity, and the preparations made for their execution.

The Abyssins, have three different ways of putting a criminal to death; one way is to bury him to the neck, to lay a heap of brambles upon his head, and to cover the whole with a great stone. Another is to beat him to death with cudgels. A third, and the most usual, is to stab him with their lances. The nearest relation gives the first thrust, and is followed by all the rest according to their degrees of kindred, and they to whom it does not happen to strike while the offender is alive, dip the points of their lances in his blood, to shew that they partake in the revenge. It frequently happens, that the relations of the criminal, are for taking the like vengeance for his death, and sometimes pursue this resolution so far, that all those who had any share in the prosecution lose their lives.

I being inform'd that these two men were to die, wrote to the Viceroy, for his permission to exhort them, before they entred into eternity, to unite themselves to the Church. My request being granted, I apply'd myself to the men, and found one of them so obstinate that he would not even afford me an hearing, and died in his error. The other I found more flexible, and wrought upon him so far,[3] that he came to my tent to be instructed: after my care of his eternal welfare had met with such success, I could not forbear attempting something for his temporal,[4] and by my endeavours, matters were so accommodated, that the relations were willing to grant his life on condition he paid a certain number of cows, or the value. Their first demand was of a thousand, he offered them five, they at last were satisfied with twelve, provided they were paid upon the spot. The Abyssins are extremely charitable, and the women on such occasions, will give even their necklaces, and pendants, so that, with what I gave my self, I collected in the camp, enough to pay the fine, and all parties were content.

---

3. "wrought ... so far" has no parallel in the French translation (p. 99).

4. "after my care ... temporal" is SJ's contribution.

CHAPTER VIII

The Viceroy is offended by his wife. He complains to the Emperor but without redress. He meditates a revolt, raises an army, and makes an attempt to seize upon the author.

We continued our march, and the Viceroy having been advertised that some troops had appeared in an hostile manner on the frontiers, went against them; I parted from him, and arrived at Fremona, where the Portuguese expected me with great impatience. I reposited the bones of Don Christopher de Gama in a decent place, and sent them the May following to the Viceroy of the Indies, together with his arms which had been presented me by a gentleman of Abyssinia, and a picture of the Virgin Mary, which that gallant Portuguese always carried about him.

The Viceroy during all the time he was engaged in this expedition, heard very provoking accounts of the bad conduct of his wife, and complain'd of it to the Emperor, intreating him either to punish his daughter himself, or to permit him to deliver her over to justice, that, if she was falsely accused, she might have an opportunity of putting her own honour, and her husband's out of dispute. The Emperor took little notice of his son-in-law's remonstrances, and, the truth is, the Viceroy was somewhat more nice in that matter, than the people of rank in his country generally are. There are laws, 'tis true, against adultery, but they seem to have been made only for the meaner people, and the women of quality, especially the *Ouzoros* or Ladies of the Blood-Royal, are so much above them, that their husbands have not even the liberty of complaining; and certainly to support injuries of this kind without complaining, requires a degree of patience, which few men can boast of.[1] The Viceroy's virtue was not proof against this temptation, he fell into a deep melancholly, and resolved to be revenged on his father-in-law. He knew the present temper of the people, that those of the greatest interest and power were by no means pleased with the changes of religion, and only waited for a fair

---

1. "to support ... boast of" is a reworking of: "il faut être bien chrétien pour souffrir de tels affronts, & les supporter sans murmurer" (p. 99).

opportunity to revolt; and that these discontents were ever
where heighten'd by the monks and clergy. Encouraged by
these reflections,[2] he was always talking of the just reasons h
had to complain of the Emperor, and gave them sufficient roon
to understand, that if they would appear in his party, he woulc
declare himself for the ancient religion, and put himself at the
head of those who should take arms in the defence of it. The chie
and almost the only thing that hindred him from raising ;
formidable rebellion,[3] was the mutual distrust they entertain'c
of one another, each fearing that as soon as the Emperor shoul
publish an Act of Grace, or general amnesty, the greatest par
would lay down their arms, and embrace it; and this suspicior
was imagined more reasonable of the Viceroy than of any other
Notwithstanding this difficulty, the priests who interested them
selves much in this revolt, ran with the utmost earnestness from
church to church, levelling their sermons against the Empero
and the Catholick religion: and that they might have the bette
success in putting a stop to all ecclesiastical innovations, the
came to a resolution of putting all the missionaries to the sword;
and that the Viceroy might have no room to hope for a pardon
they obliged him to give the first wound to him that should fal
into his hands.

As I was the nearest, and by consequence the most exposed
an order was immediately issued out for apprehending me, i
being thought a good expedient to seize me, and force me to
build a citadel, into which they might retreat, if they shoulc
happen to meet with a defeat. The Viceroy wrote to me, to
desire that I would come to him, he having, as he said, an affai
of the highest importance to communicate.

The frequent assemblies which the Viceroy held, had already
been much talk'd of; and I had received advice, that he wa
ready for a revolt, and that my death was to be the first signal o
an open war. Knowing that the Viceroy had made many com
plaints of the treatment he receiv'd from his father-in-law,
made no doubt that he had some ill design in hand; and ye
could scarce persuade my self that after all the tokens of friend

---

2. An added transition.
3. "raising...rebellion" has no counterpart in the French (p. 100).
4. "and that they ... sword" expands

and explains the point in the French: "I
résolurent pour mieux engager l'affaire
de massacrer tous les missionnaires'
(p. 100).

ship I had receiv'd from him, he would enter into any measures for destroying me. While I was yet in suspence, I dispatch'd a faithful servant to the Viceroy with my excuse for disobeying him; and gave the messenger strict orders to observe all that passed, and bring me an exact account. This affair was of too great moment not to engage my utmost endeavours to arrive at the most certain knowledge of it, and to advertise the court of the danger. I wrote therefore to one of our fathers who was then near the Emperor, the best intelligence I could obtain of all that had passed, of the reports that were spread through all this part of the empire, and of the disposition which I discover'd in the people to a general defection; telling him, however, that I could not yet believe that the Viceroy, who had honour'd me with his friendship, and of whom I never had any thought, but how to oblige him, could now have so far chang'd his sentiments, as to take away my life.

The letters which I receiv'd by my servant and the assurances he gave that I need fear nothing, for that I was never mention'd by the Viceroy without great marks of esteem, so far confirm'd me in my error, that I went from Fremona with a resolution to see him. I did not reflect that a man who could fail in his duty to his king, his father-in-law, and his benefactor, might without scruple do the same to a stranger, tho' distinguish'd as his friend; and thus sanguine and unsuspecting[5] continued my journey, still receiving intimation from all parts to take care of my self: at length when I was within a few days' journeys of the Viceroy, I receiv'd a billet in more plain and express terms than any thing I had been told yet, charging me with extreme imprudence in putting my self into the hands of those men who had undoubtedly sworn to cut me off.

I began upon this to distrust the sincerity of the Viceroy's professions, and resolved, upon the receit of another letter from the Viceroy, to return directly: in this letter having excused himself, for not waiting for my arrival, he desired me in terms very strong and pressing to come forward, and stay for him at his own house, assuring me, that he had given such orders for my entertainment, as should prevent my being tired with living here. I imagined at first that he had left some servants to provide for my reception, but being advertis'd at the same time,

---

5. The two adjectives are introduced by SJ.

that there was no longer any doubt of the certainty of his revolt
that the Galles were engaged to come to his assistance, and tha
he was gone to sign a treaty with them; I was no longer in
suspence what measures to take, but returned to Fremona.

Here I found a letter from the Emperor, which prohibited me
to go out, and the orders which he had sent through all these
parts, directing them to arrest me wherever I was found, and to
hinder me from proceeding on my journey. These orders came
too late to contribute to my preservation, and this prince'
goodness had been in vain, if God, whose protection I have often
had experience of in my travels, had not been my conductor[6] in
this emergency.

The Viceroy hearing that I was returned to my residence, did
not discover any concern, or chagrin as at a disappointment, for
such was his privacy and dissimulation, that the most penetrat
ing could never form any conjecture that could be depended on
about his designs, till every thing was ready for the execution o
them. My servant, a man of wit, was surprised as well as every
body else, and I can ascribe to nothing but a miracle,[7] my escape
from so many snares as he laid to entrap me.

There happen'd during this perplexity of my affairs an ac
cident of small consequence in itself, which yet I think deserve
to be mention'd, as it shews the credulity and ignorance of the
Abyssins. I receiv'd a visit from a religious, who passed, though
he was blind, for the most learned person in all that country, he
had the whole Scriptures in his memory, but seem'd to have
been at more pains to retain, than understand them; as he talk'd
much, he often took occasion to quote them, and did it almost
always improperly: having invited him to sup and pass the nigh
with me, I set before him some excellent mead, which he liked so
well, as to drink somewhat beyond the bounds of exact temper
ance:[8] next day, to make some return for this entertainment, he
took upon him to divert me with some of those stories which the
monks amuse simple people with, and told me of a devil tha
haunted a fountain, and us'd to make it his employment to
plague the monks that came thither to fetch water, and con

---

6. "mon conducteur & mon sauveur"
(p. 101).

7. "un miracle de la Providence de
Dieu sur moi" (p. 102).

8. "as to drink ... temperance" is
more decorous rendering of the French
"il en but largement & même trop; il n
s'en plaignit pas" (p. 102).

inued his malice, till he was converted by the founder of their
order, who found him no very stubborn proselyte till they came
to the point of circumcision; the devil was unhappily prepossessed with a strong aversion from being circumcised,[9] which
however, by much persuasion he at last agreed to, and afterwards taking a religious habit, died ten years after with great
signs of sanctity. He added another history, of a famous
Abyssinian monk, who kill'd a devil two hundred feet high, and
only four feet thick, that ravaged all the country; the peasants
had a great desire to throw the dead carcase from the top of a
rock, but could not with all their force remove it from the place,
but the monk drew it after him with all imaginable ease, and
push'd it down. This story was follow'd by another, of a young
devil that became a religious of the famous monastry of Aba-
Garima.[a] The good father would have favour'd me with more
relations of the same kind, if I had been in the humour to have
heard them, but, interrupting him, I told him that all these
relations confirm'd, what we had found by experience, that the
monks of Abyssinia, were no improper company for the devil.[1]

CHAPTER IX

The Viceroy is defeated and hanged. The author narrowly escapes being
poison'd.

I did not stay long at Fremona, but left that town, and the
province of Tigre, and soon found that I was very happy in that
resolution, for scarce had I left the place, before the Viceroy
came in person to put me to death, who, not finding me, as he
expected, resolved to turn all his vengeance against the Father
Gaspard Paes a venerable man, who was grown grey in the

a. Aba-Garima *Relation*; Abagarima *Itinerário*] Aba-Gatima *1735*

9. The phrasing—"no very stubborn proselyte" and "unhappily prepossessed with a strong aversion"—augments the French: "qu'il n'avait eu de difficulté que sur le point de la circoncision" (p. 102).

1. By revising the sentence SJ sharpens the retort: Lobo's response was that these stories confirmed the fact "qu'il y avait bien des diables en Abissinie cachés sous des habits de religieux, & que pour être moines, ils n'en étaient pas moins méchants" (p. 102).

missions of Aethiopia, and five other missionaries, newly arrived
from the Indies: his design was to kill them all at one time
without suffering any to escape; he therefore sent for them all,
but one happily being sick, another staid to attend him; to this
they owed their lives, for the Viceroy finding but four of them,
sent them back, telling them, he would see them all together.
The fathers, having been already told of his revolt, and of the
pretences he made use of to give it credit, made no question of his
intent to massacre them,[1] and contrived their escape so, that
they got safely out of his power.

The Viceroy disappointed in this scheme, vented all his rage
upon Father James, whom the Patriarch had given him, as his
confessor;[2] the good man was carried, bound hand and foot, into
the middle of the camp, the Viceroy gave the first stab in the
throat, and all the rest struck him with their lances, and dipped
their weapons in his blood, promising each other that they
would never accept of any act of oblivion, or terms of peace, by
which the Catholick religion was not abolish'd throughout the
empire, and all those who professed it either banished or put to
death. They then order'd all the beads, images, crosses and
reliques which the Catholicks made use of to be thrown into the
fire.

The anger of God was now ready to fall upon his head for
these daring and complicated crimes;[3] the Emperor had already
confiscated all his goods, and given the government of the
kingdom of Tigre to Keba Christos a good Catholick, who was
sent with a numerous army to take possession of it. As both
armies were in search of each other, it was not long before they
came to a battle. The revolted Viceroy[4] Tecla Georgis placed all
his confidence in the Galles his auxiliaries. Keba Christos, who
had march'd with incredible expedition to hinder the enemy
from making any entrenchments, would willingly have refreshed

1. SJ deletes the remainder of the sentence: "& en faire les premières victimes de son apostasie & de sa rébellion" (p. 103).

2. The laudatory description of Father James is deleted: "un des plus excellents maîtres de la vie spirituelle, qui fût dans toute l'Abissinie" (p. 103). Gonçalves da Costa, quoting Beccari, gives "6 de Novembro de 1628" as the date of Jacobo Alexandre's death (Itinerário, pp. 432–33, n. 3).

3. "for these ... crimes" replaces the phrase, "de ce malheureux apostat" (p. 103).

4. This opening phrase appears only in the English translation.

his men a few days before the battle, but finding the foe vigilant, thought it not proper to stay till he was attack'd, and therefore resolved to make the first onset; then presenting himself before his army without arms and with his head uncover'd, assured them that such was his confidence in God's protection of those that engaged in so just a cause, that though he were in that condition and alone, he would attack his enemies.

The battle began immediately, and of all the troops of Tecla Georgis only the Galles made any resistance, the rest abandon'd him without striking a blow. The unhappy commander seeing all his squadrons broken,[5] and three hundred of the Galles with twelve ecclesiasticks kill'd on the spot, hid himself in a cave, where he was found three days afterwards, with his favourite and a monk. When they took him they cut off the heads of his two companions in the field, and carried him to the Emperor, the procedure against him was not long, and he was condemn'd to be burnt alive. Then imagining that, if he embraced the Catholick faith, the intercession of the missionaries, with the entreaties of his wife and children might procure him a pardon,[6] he desired a Jesuit to hear his confession, and abjured his errors. The Emperor was inflexible both to the entreaties of his daughter, and the tears of his grand-children, and all that could be obtained of him, was that the sentence should be mollified, and changed into a condemnation to be hanged. Tecla Georgis renounced his abjuration, and at his death persisted in his errors. Adero his sister who had born the greatest share in his revolt, was hanged on the same tree fifteen days after.

I arrived not long after[7] at the Emperor's court, and had the honour of kissing his hands, but staid not long in a place, where no missionary ought to linger, unless obliged by the most pressing necessity; but being order'd by my superiors into the kingdom of Damote; I set out on my journey, and on the road was in great danger of losing my life by my curiosity[8] of tasting an herb which I found near a brook, and which, though I had often heard of it, I did not know. It bears a great resemblance to our

5. "The unhappy ... broken" does not occur in the French (p. 104).
6. "Then imagining ... pardon" is a more formal rendering of: "Il crut que s'il se convertissait, les missionnaires, sa femme, ses enfants parlans pour lui, il pourrait avoir sa grâce" (p. 104).
7. An error: "peu de jours avant ce tragique événement" (p. 104).
8. Cf. "ma gourmandise" (p. 104).

radishes, the leaf and colour were beautiful, and the taste not
unpleasant; it came into my mind when I began to chew it, that
perhaps it might be that venomous herb, against which no
antidote hath yet been found, but persuading my self afterwards
that my fears were merely chimerical, I continued to chew it, till
a man accidentally meeting me, and seeing me with a handful of
it cry'd out to me, that I was poison'd, I had happily not
swallow'd any of it, and throwing out what I had in my mouth, I
return'd God thanks for this instance of his protection.[9]

I cross'd the Nile the first time in my journey to the kingdom
of Damote, my passage brought into my mind all that I had read
either in ancient or modern writers, of this celebrated river; I
recollected the great expences at which some emperors had
endeavour'd to gratify their curiosity of knowing the sources of
this mighty stream, which nothing but their little acquaintance
with the Abyssins made so difficult to be found. I passed the river
within two days' journeys of its head, near a wide plain which is
entirely laid under water when it begins to overflow the banks.
Its channel is even here so wide, that a ball shot from a musket
can scarce reach the farther bank. Here is neither boat nor
bridge, and the river is so full of hippopotames,[a] or river-horses,
and crocodiles, that it is impossible to swim over without danger
of being devoured. The only way of passing it, is upon flotes
which they guide as well as they can, with long poles. Nor is even
this way without danger, for these destructive animals overturn
the flotes, and tear the passengers in pieces. The river-horse,
which lives only on grass and branches of trees, is satisfied with
killing the men, but the crocodile being more voracious feeds
upon the carcasses.

But since I am arrived at the banks of this renown'd river,
which I have pass'd and repass'd so many times, and since all
that I have read of the nature of its waters, and the causes of its
overflowing, is full of fables, the reader may not be displeased to
find here an account of what I saw my self, or was told by the
inhabitants.

a. hippopotames *Errata*] hippotames *1735*

9. Lobo was even more grateful than
SJ's translation suggests: "je remerciai
Dieu de toutes les grâces qu'il me faisait
en toute occasion" (p. 105).

CHAPTER X

A description of the Nile.[1]

The Nile, which the natives call *Abavi*, that is, the Father of Waters, rises first in Sacala a province of the kingdom of Goiama, which is one of the most fruitful and agreeable of all the Abyssinian dominions. This province is inhabited by a nation of the Agaus, who call themselves Christians, but[a] by daily inter-marriages they have allied themselves to the pagan Agaus, and adopted all their customs and ceremonies. These two nations are very numerous, fierce, and unconquerable, inhabiting a country full of mountains, which are covered with woods, and hollow'd by nature into vast caverns, many of which are capable of containing several numerous families, and hundreds of cows;[2] to these recesses the Agaus betake themselves when they are driven out of the plain, where it is almost impossible to find them, and certain ruin to pursue them.[3] This people encreases extremely, every man being allowed so many wives as he hath hundreds of cows, and it is seldom that the hundreds are re-quired to be compleat.

In the eastern part of this kingdom on the declivity of a mountain, whose descent is so easy that it seems a beautiful plain, is that source of the Nile, which has been sought after at so much expence of labour, and about which such variety of con-jectures hath been form'd[4] without success. This spring, or rather these two springs, are two holes each about two feet diameter, a stone's cast distant from each other, the one is but about five feet and an half in depth;[b] at least we could not get

a. who ... but *1789*] which but only call themselves Christians, for *1735*; "for which but, r[ead] who call, but" *Errata*   b. depth, *1735*

---

1. This heading does appear in the French (p. 105).

2. "several numerous ... cows" is less specific than the French, which refers to "deux ou trois familles nombreuses, avec plus de trois ou quatre cents vaches" (p. 106).

3. "where it ... pursue them" alters the meaning: "Il est très difficile de découvrir ces caches, & presque impossible d'en chasser les Agaus, quand on les a décou-verts" (p. 106).

4. "about which ... form'd" is SJ's addition.

our plummet farther, perhaps because it was stopped by roots, for the whole place is full of trees; of the other which is somewhat less, with a line of ten feet we could find no bottom, and were assured by the inhabitants, that none ever had been found. 'Tis believed here, that these springs are the vents of a great subterraneous lake, and they have this circumstance to favour their opinion;[5] that the ground is always moist, and so soft, that the water boils up under foot as one walks upon it; this is more visible after rains, for then the ground yields and sinks so much, that I believe it is chiefly supported by the roots of trees, that are interwoven one with another: such is the ground round about these fountains. At a little distance to the south, is a village named Guix, through which the way lies to the top of the mountain, from whence the traveller discovers a vast extent of land, which appears like a deep valley, though the mountain rises so imperceptibly, that those who go up or down it, are scarce sensible of any declivity.

On the top of this mountain is a little hill which the idolatrous Agaus have in great veneration, their priest calls them together at this place once a year, and having sacrificed a cow, throws the head into one of the springs of the Nile; after which ceremony, every one sacrifices a cow or more, according to their different degrees of wealth or devotion. The bones of these cows have already form'd two mountains of considerable height, which afford a sufficient proof that these nations have always paid their adorations to this famous river. They eat these sacrifices with great devotion, as flesh consecrated to their deity. Then the priest anoints himself with the grease and tallow of the cows, and sits down on an heap of straw, on the top and in the middle of a pile which is prepared, they set fire to it, and the whole heap is consumed without any injury to the priest, who while the fire continues, harangues the standers-by, and confirms them in their present ignorance and superstition. When the pile is burnt, and the discourse at an end, every one makes a large present to the priest, which is the grand design of this religious mockery.

To return to the course of the Nile, its waters, after the first rise,[6] run to the eastward for about a musket-shot, then turning

---

5. "and they...opinion" is a transition not found in the French.

6. "To return ... rise" replaces a sen-

tence in the French about a tributary of the Nile (p. 107).

to the north, continue hidden in the grass and weeds for about a quarter of a league, and discover themselves for the first time among some rocks, a sight not to be enjoy'd without some pleasure, by those who have read the fabulous accounts of this stream delivered by the ancients, and the vain conjectures and reasonings which have been form'd upon its original, the nature of its water, its cataracts, and its inundations, all which we are now entirely acquainted with, and eye-witnesses of.[7]

Many interpreters of the Holy Scriptures pretend that Gihon mention'd in Genesis,[8] is no other than the Nile, which encompasseth all Aethiopia; but as the Gihon had its source from the terrestrial paradise, and we know that the Nile rises in the country of the Agaus, it will be found I believe no small difficulty[9] to conceive how the same river could arise from two sources so distant from each other, or how a river from so low a source should spring up and appear in a place perhaps the highest in the world; for if we consider, that Arabia and Palestine are in their situation almost level with Egypt, that Egypt is as low if compared with the kingdom of Dambia, as the deepest valley in regard of the highest mountain, that the province of Sacala is yet more elevated than Dambia, that the waters of the Nile must either pass under the Red-Sea, or take a great compass about, we shall find it hard to conceive such an attractive power in the earth, as may be able to make the waters rise through the obstruction of so much sand, from places so low, to the most lofty region of Aethiopia.

But leaving these difficulties, let us go on to describe the course of the Nile. It rowls away from its source with so inconsiderable a current, that it appears unlikely to escape being dried up by the hot season, but soon receiving an encrease from the Gemma, the Keltu, the Bransu and other less rivers, it is of such a breadth in the plain of Boad, which is not above three days' journeys from its source, that a ball shot from a musket will scarce fly from one bank to the other. Here it begins to run northwards, deflecting,

---

7. "all which ... eye-witnesses of" avoids the awkwardness of the French translation: "toutes choses que présentement nous connaissons, que nous touchons, pour ainsi dire, du doigt & que nous voyons à l'oeil" (p. 107).

8. Genesis ii. 13: "And the name of the second river is Gihon: the same is it that compasseth the whole land of Ethiopia."

9. "it will ... difficulty" expands "il faut voir ..." (p. 107).

however, a little towards the east, for the space of nine or ten
leagues and then enters the so much talk'd of Lake of Dambia,
call'd by the natives *Barhar Sena* the resemblance of the sea, or
Bahar Dambia the Sea of Dambia. It crosses this lake only at one
end, with so violent a rapidity that the waters of the Nile may be
distinguish'd through all the passage, which is six leagues. Here
begins the greatness of the Nile. Fifteen miles[1] farther, in the
land of Alata, it rushes precipitately from the top of a high rock,
and forms one of the most beautiful waterfalls in the world,[2] I
pass'd under it without being wet, and resting myself there for
the sake of the coolness, was charm'd with a thousand delightful
rainbows which the sun-beams painted on the water in all their
shining and lively colours. The fall of this mighty stream from so
great an height, makes a noise that may be heard to a considerable distance; but I could not observe that the neighbouring inhabitants were at all deaf, I conversed with several, and
was as easily heard by them, as I heard them. The mist that rises
from this fall of water, may be seen much farther, than the noise
can be heard. After this cataract, the Nile again collects its
scatter'd stream among the rocks,[3] which seem to be disjoined in
this place only to afford it a passage. They are so near each other,
that in my time a bridge of beams, on which the whole imperial
army passed, was laid over them.[4] Sultan Segued hath since
built here a bridge of one arch in the same place, for which
purpose he procured masons from India. This bridge, which is
the first the Abyssins have seen on the Nile, very much facilitates
a communication between the provinces, and encourages commerce among the inhabitants of his empire.

Here the river alters its course, and passes through many
various kingdoms; on the east it leaves Begmeder, or the Land of
Sheep, so call'd from great numbers that are bred there, *beg*, in
that language signifying sheep, and *meder* a country. It then
waters the kingdoms of Amhara, Olaca, Choaa, and Damote,
which lie on the left side, and the kingdom of Goiama which it

---

1. An appropriate rendering of "cinq
lieues" (p. 108), yet only a line earlier SJ
has translated "six lieues" as "six leagues."

2. SJ omits both Lobo's comment that
this is the first cataract and Le Grand's
marginal note that Mendes calls it the
second (p. 108).

3. "the Nile again ... rocks" is fash-
ioned from: "le Nil se resserre tellement
entre des rochers" (p. 108).

4. SJ deletes the remark that there are
even some men bold enough, agile enough,
and strong enough to leap from one rock
to another (p. 109).

bounds on the right, forming by its windings a kind of peninsula. Then entering Bezamo a province of the kingdom of Damot, and Gamarcausa part of Goiama, it returns within a short day's journey of its spring, though to persue it through all its mazes, and accompany it round the kingdom of Goiama, is a journey of twenty nine days. So far, and a few days' journeys farther, this river confines itself to Abyssinia, and then passes into the bordering countries of Fazulo and Ombarca.

These vast regions we have little knowledge of: they are inhabited by nations entirely different from the Abyssins, their hair is like that of the other blacks short and curl'd. In the year 1615 Rassela Christos lieutenant general to Sultan Segued, enter'd those kingdoms[c] with his army in an hostile manner, but being able to get no intelligence of the condition of the people, and astonished at their unbounded extent, he return'd without daring to attempt any thing.

As the empire of the Abyssins terminates at these desarts, and as I have followed the course of the Nile no farther, I here leave it to range over barbarous kingdoms, and convey wealth and plenty into Egypt, which owes to the annual inundations of this river, its envyed fertility. I know not any thing of the rest of its passage, but that it receives great encreases from many other rivers, that it has several cataracts like the first already described, and that few fish are to be found in it, which scarcity doubtless is to be attributed to the river-horses, and crocodiles, which destroy the weaker inhabitants of these waters,[5] and something may be allow'd to the cataracts, it being difficult for fish to fall so far without being kill'd.

Although some who have travelled in Asia and Africa have given the world their descriptions of crocodiles and hippopotamus[d] or river-horse; yet as the Nile has at least as great numbers of each as any river in the world, I cannot but think my account of it would be imperfect, without some particular mention of these animals.

The crocodile is very ugly, having no proportion between his length and thickness; he hath short feet, a wide mouth, with two rows of sharp teeth, standing wide from each other, a brown skin

c. kingdom *1735*   d. hippotamus *1735*

5. "which ... waters" is an expansion of "qui le dépeuplent" (p. 110).

so fortified with scales even to his nose, that a musket-ball cannot penetrate it. His sight is extremely quick and at a great distance. In the water he is daring and fierce,[6] and will seize on any that are so unfortunate as is to be found by him bathing;[7] who if they escape with life, are almost sure to leave some limb in his mouth. Neither I, nor any with whom I have convers'd about the crocodile, have ever seen him weep, and therefore I take the liberty of ranking[8] all that hath been told us of his tears, amongst the fables which are only proper to amuse children.

The hippopotamus[e] or river-horse grazes upon the land, and brouses on the shrubs, yet is no less dangerous than the crocodile. He is the size of an ox,[9] of a brown colour without any hair, his tail is short, his neck long, and his head of an enormous bigness; his eyes are small, his mouth wide, with teeth half a foot long; he hath two tusks like those of a wild boar, but larger; his legs are short, and his feet part into four toes. It is easy to observe from this description that he hath no resemblance of an horse, and indeed nothing could give occasion to the name, but some likeness in his ears, and his neighing and snorting like an horse when he is provoked, or raises his head out of water. His hide is so hard that a musket fired close to him can only make a slight impression, and the best temper'd lances push'd forcibly against him are either blunted or shivered, unless the assailant has the skill to make his thrust at certain parts which are more tender. There is great danger in meeting him, and the best way is, upon such an accident, to step aside, and let him pass by. The flesh of this animal doth not differ from that of a cow, except that it is blacker and harder to digest.

The ignorance, which we have hitherto been in, of the original of the Nile, hath given many authors an opportunity of presenting us very gravely with their various systems, and conjectures about the nature of its waters, and the reason of its overflows.

It is easy to observe how many empty hypotheses and idle

e. hippotamus *1735*

6. The two adjectives replace a single one: "hardi" (p. 110).

7. "and will ... bathing" extends Lobo's brief comment: "il attaque ceux qui se baignent" (p. 110).

8. "I take ... ranking" grows out of "je mets" (p. 110).

9. Lobo says the crocodile is "gros comme deux boeufs" (p. 110).

reasonings, the phaenomenons of this river have put mankind to the expence of.[1] Yet there are people so biggotted to antiquity, as not to pay any regard to the relation of travellers who have been upon the spot, and by the evidence of their eyes can confute all that the ancients have written. It was difficult, it was even impossible to arrive at the source of the Nile, by tracing its channel from the mouth; and all who ever attempted it, having been stop'd by the cataracts, and imagining none that follow'd them could pass farther, have taken the liberty of entertaining us with their own fictions.[2]

It is to be remembred likewise, that neither the Greeks nor Romans, from whom we have received all our information, ever carried their arms into this part of the world, or ever heard of multitudes of nations that dwell upon the banks of this vast river; that the countries where the Nile rises, and those through which it runs, have no inhabitants but what are savage and uncivilized; that before they could arrive at its head, they must surmount the insuperable obstacles of impassable forests, inaccessible cliffs, and desarts crouded with beasts of prey, fierce by nature, and raging for want of sustenance.[3] Yet if they who endeavoured with so much ardour, to discover the spring of this river, had landed at Mazua on the coast of the Red-Sea, and march'd a little more to the south than the south-west, they might perhaps have gratified their curiosity at less expence, and in about twenty days might have[f] enjoyed the desired sight of the sources of the Nile.

But this discovery was reserved for the invincible bravery of our noble countrymen,[4] who not discouraged by the dangers of a navigation in seas never explor'd before, have subdued kingdoms and empires, where the Greek and Roman greatness, where the names of Caesar and Alexander were never heard of:

f. might have] might *1735*

1. "the phaenomenons ... expence of" has no counterpart in the French translation.
2. "have taken ... fictions" embellishes the French: "ils ont inventé milles fables" (p. 111). SJ echoes this line in his Preface.
3. "they must surmount ... sustenance" is a creative rendering of the following

passage: "il faut traverser des montagnes affreuses, des forêts impénétrables, des déserts pleins de bêtes féroces, qui à peine y trouvent de quoi vivre" (p. 111).
4. "invincible ... countrymen" improves on Lobo's reference to "nos braves & vaillants Portugais" (p. 111).

who first steer'd an European ship into the Red-Sea through the
Gulf of Arabia, and the Indian Ocean, who have demolish'd the
airy fabricks of renoun'd hypotheses, and detected those fables
which the ancients rather chose to invent of the sources of the
Nile, than to confess their ignorance.[5] I cannot help suspending
my narration to reflect a little[6] on the ridiculous speculations of
those swelling[7] philosophers, whose arrogance would prescribe
laws to nature, and subject those astonishing effects which we
behold daily, to their idle reasonings, and chimerical rules.
Presumptuous imagination![8] that has given being to such numbers of books, and patrons to so many various opinions about the
overflows of the Nile. Some of these theorists have been pleas'd
to declare it as their favourite notion,[9] that this inundation is
caused by high winds which stop the current, and so force the
water to rise above its banks, and spread over all Egypt. Others
pretend a subterraneous communication between the ocean and
the Nile, and that the sea being violently agitated swells the
river. Many have imagined themselves bless'd with the discovery when they have told us, that this mighty flood proceeds
from the melting of snow on the mountains of Aethiopia, without reflecting that this opinion is contrary to the receiv'd notion
of all the ancients, who believed that the heat was so excessive
between the tropicks, that no inhabitant could live there. So
much snow, and so great heat are never met with in the same
region. And indeed I never saw snow in Abyssinia, except on
Mount Semen in the kingdom of Tigre, very remote from the
Nile, and on Narea[g] which is indeed not far distant, but where
there never falls snow sufficient to wet the foot of the mountain,
when it is melted.[1]
    To the immense labours and fatigues of the Portuguese man-
kind is indebted for the knowledge of the real cause of these

g. Narea *Relation* (*Errata*)] Namera *1735*

---

5. "who have demolish'd ... ignorance"
has its beginnings in: "qui ont fait voir
que l'antiquité n'a inventé tant de fables
touchant la source du Nil, que pour cacher
son ignorance" (p. 111).
    6. "I cannot ... little" has no parallel
in the French.
    7. An inserted adjective.

8. The final ejaculation is another of
SJ's additions to the French (p. 112).
    9. "Some ... notion" is a slightly ironic
expansion of "Les uns ont voulu ... "
(p. 112).
    1. "when ... melted" appears only in
the English translation.

inundations so great and so regular. Their observations inform us, that Abyssinia where the Nile rises, and waters vast tracts of land, is full of mountains, and in its natural situation much higher than Egypt; that all the winter, from June to September, no day is without rain; that the Nile receives in its course all the rivers, brooks and torrents which fall from those mountains; these necessarily swell it above the banks, and fill the plains of Egypt with the inundation. This comes regularly about the month of July, or three weeks after the beginning of a rainy season in Aethiopia. The different degrees of this flood are such certain indications of the fruitfulness or sterility of the ensuing year, that it is publickly proclaim'd in Cairo, how much the water hath gain'd each night. This is all I have to inform the reader of concerning the Nile, which the Aegyptians adored as the deity in whose choice it was to bless them with abundance, or deprive them of the necessaries of life.

CHAPTER XI

The author discovers a passage over the Nile. Is sent into the province of Ligonous, which he gives a description of. His success in his mission. The stratagem of the monks to encourage the soldiers. The author narrowly escapes being burned.

When I was to cross this river at Boad, I durst not venture myself on the flotes, I have already spoken of, but went up higher in hopes of finding a more commodious passage. I had with me three or four men that were reduced to the same difficulty with myself. In one part seeing people on the other side, and remarking that the water was shallow, and that the rocks and trees which grew very thick there, contributed to facilitate the attempt, I leap'd from one rock to another, till I reach'd the opposite bank, to the great amazement of the natives themselves, who never had tried that way, my four companions follow'd me with the same success, and it hath been call'd since the passage of Father Jerome.

That province of the kingdom of Damot, which I was assign'd to by my superior is call'd Ligonous, and is perhaps one of the most beautiful and agreeable places in the world; the air is healthful and temperate, and all the mountains, which are not very high, shaded with cedars. They sow and reap here in every season, the ground is always producing, and the fruits ripen throughout the year: so great, so charming[1] is the variety, that the whole region seems a garden, laid out and cultivated, only to please. I doubt whether even the imagination of a painter has yet conceiv'd a landskip as beautiful as I have seen. The forests have nothing uncouth or savage, and seem only planted for shade and coolness. Among a prodigious number of trees which fill them, there is one kind which I have seen in no other place, and to which we have none that bears any resemblance. This tree which the natives call *enseté* is wonderfully useful, its leaves, which are so large as to cover a man, make hangings for rooms, and serve the inhabitants instead of linnen for their tables, and carpets.[2] They grind the branches and the thick parts of the leaves, and when they are mingled with milk find them a delicious food, the trunk and the roots are even more nourishing than the leaves or branches, and the meaner people, when they go a journey make no provision of any other victuals. The word *enseté* signifies the tree against hunger, or the poor's tree, though the most wealthy often eat of it. If it be cut down within half a foot of the ground, and several incisions made in the stump, each will put out a new sprout, which, if transplanted, will take root, and grow to a tree. The Abyssins report, that this tree when it is cut down, groans like a man, and on this account, call cutting down an *enseté* killing it. On the top grows a bunch of five or six figs, of a taste not very agreeable,[3] which they set in the ground to produce more trees.

I staid two months in the province of Ligonous, and during that time procured a church to be built of hewn stone, roofed and wainscotted with cedar, which is the most considerable in the whole country. My continual employment was the duties of the mission, which I was always practising in some part of the province, not indeed with any extraordinary success at first, for I

---

1. An added adjective.

2. This sentence rearranges some details and omits others: "Ses feuilles sont si grandes, que deux suffisent pour couvrir un homme devant & derrière. Cet arbre qu'on nomme *enseté* est d'une utilité merveilleuse; comme les feuilles sont fort

longues & fort larges, on en tapisse des chambres, on s'en sert au lieu de tapis de pied, de nappes, & de serviettes" (p. 113).

3. Epitomizing a longer passage, SJ errs in the number of figs: "cinq ou six cents figues" (p. 114).

found the people inflexibly obstinate in their opinions, even to so great a degree, that when I first publish'd the Emperor's edict requiring all his subjects to renounce their errors, and unite themselves to the Roman Church;[4] there were some monks, who, to the number of sixty, chose rather to die by throwing themselves headlong from a precipice, than obey their sovereign's commands: and in a battle fought between these people that adhered to the religion of their ancestors,[5] and the troops of Sultan Segued, six hundred religious placing themselves in the head of their men, march'd towards the Catholick army[6] with the stones of the altars upon their heads, assuring their credulous followers, that the Emperor's troops would immediately at the sight of those stones fall into disorder and turn their backs. But, as they were some of the first that fell, their death had a great influence upon the people, to undeceive them, and make them return to the truth. Many were converted after the battle, and when they had embraced the Catholick faith, adhered to that with the same constancy and firmness with which they had before persisted in their errors.

The Emperor had sent a viceroy into this province whose firm attachment to the Roman Church, as well as great abilities in military affairs, made him a person very capable of executing the orders of the Emperor, and of suppressing any insurrection that might be rais'd, to prevent those alterations in religion which they were design'd to promote: a farther view in the choice of so warlike a deputy, was, that a stop might be put to the inroads of the Galles,[7] who had kill'd one viceroy, and in a little time after kill'd this.

It was our custom to meet together every year about Christmas, not only that we might comfort and entertain each other, but likewise that we might relate the progress and success of our missions, and concert all measures that might farther the con-

4. "l'eglise catholique, apostolique & romaine" (p. 114).

5. "people … ancestors" is hardly a literal translation of "les hérétiques" (p. 114).

6. "towards … army" is SJ's clarifying insertion.

7. The entire paragraph to this point is an embellished version of the sentence: "L'empereur avait envoyé pour vice-roi dans ce royaume un catholique très zélé & très bon officier, afin de tenir ces peuples en bride, pendant qu'il voulait leur faire embrasser la religion catholique, & de pouvoir en même temps arrêter les courses des Galles …" (p. 115).

version of the inhabitants.[8] This year our place of meeting was
the Emperor's camp, where the Patriarch and Superior of the
missions were. I left the place of my abode, and took in my way
four fathers, that resided at the distance of two day's journeys, so
that the company, without reckoning our attendants was five.
There happen'd nothing remarkable to us till the last night of
our journey, when taking up our lodging, at a place belonging to
the Empress, a declared enemy to all Catholicks, and in particular, to the missionaries, we met with a kind reception in
appearance, and were lodged in a large stone house cover'd with
wood and straw, which had stood uninhabited so long, that
great numbers of red ants had taken possession of it; these, as
soon as we were laid down, attack'd us on all sides, and tor-
mented us so incessantly, that we were obliged to call up our
domesticks. Having burnt a prodigious number of these troublesome animals, we try'd to compose our selves again, but had
scarce closed our eyes, before we were awaked by the fire that
had seiz'd our lodging: our servants, who were, fortunately, not
all gone to bed, perceiv'd the fire as soon as it began, and
inform'd me who lay nearest the door. I immediately alarm'd all
the rest, and nothing was thought of, but how to save ourselves,
and the little goods we had, when to our great astonishment, we
found one of the doors barricaded in such a manner, that we
could not open it; nothing now could have prevented our perishing in the flames, had not those who kindled them omitted to
fasten that door near which I was lodged. We were no longer in
doubt, that the inhabitants of the town had laid a train, and set
fire to a neighbouring house, in order to consume us; their
measures were so well laid, that the house was in ashes in an
instant, and three of our beds were burnt which the violence of
the flame would not allow us to carry away. We spent the rest of
the night in the most dismal apprehensions, and found next
morning that we had justly charg'd the inhabitants with the
design of destroying us, for the place was entirely abandon'd,
and those that were conscious of the crime, had fled from the
punishment. We continued our journey, and came to Gorgora,
where we found the fathers met, and the Emperor with them.

---

8. Cf. "la conversion de ces hérétiques" (p. 115).

CHAPTER XII

The author is sent into Tigre, is in danger of being poison'd by the breath of a serpent; is stung by a serpent. Is almost kill'd by eating *anchoy*. The people conspire against the missionaries, and distress them.

My superiors intended to send me into the farthest parts of the empire, but the Emperor over-ruled that design, and remanded me to Tigre where I had resided before; I passed in my journey by Ganete Ilhos, a palace newly built, and made agreeable by beautiful gardens,[1] and had the honour of paying my respects to the Emperor who had retired thither, and receiving from him a large present for the finishing of an hospital, which had been begun in the kingdom of Tigre. After having return'd him thanks, I continued my way, and in crossing a desart two day's journeys over, was in great danger of my life, for, as I lay on the ground, I perceiv'd myself seiz'd with a pain which forc'd me to rise, and saw about four yards from me one of those serpents that dart their poison at a distance. Although I rose before he came very near me, I yet felt the effects of his poisonous breath, and, if I had lain a little longer, had certainly died; I had recourse to bezoar[2] a sovereign remedy against these poisons which I always carried about me. These serpents are not long, but have a body short and thick, and their bellies speckled with brown, black, and yellow, they have a wide mouth, with which they draw in a great quantity of air, and having retain'd it some time, eject it with such force, that they kill at four yards distance,[3] I only

---

1. "a palace ... gardens" epitomizes "L'empereur s'y était retiré depuis quelque temps, il se plaisait beaucoup en ce lieu-là, il y avait fait planter quelques jardins & bâtir un palais" (p. 116). Cf. *Itinerário*, which adds: "Ganete Ilhos, que quer dizer Paraizo de Ilhos" or "Island Paradise" (p. 464). Gonçalves da Costa notes that the name was "Gannete Jesus." This pleasure palace with gardens built by Sultan Segued is a likely source for *Ramblers* 204 and 205. Almeida refers to it as well. Contemporary maps place it on the north shore of Lake Tana in Ethiopia.

2. "A medicinal stone, formerly in high esteem as an antidote, and brought from the East Indies, where it is said to be found in the dung of an animal of the goat kind, called *pazan*; the stone being formed in its belly, and growing to the size of an acorn, and sometimes to that of a pigeon's egg. The peculiar manner of its formation, is now supposed to be fabulous" (*Dictionary*).

3. James Bruce singles out this passage for comment: "Now, as this is warranted, by one of such authority as Dr. Johnson, to be neither imagination nor falsehood, we must think it a new system of natural phi-

escaped by being somewhat farther from him. This danger
however was not much to be regarded in comparison of another
which my negligence brought me into. As I was picking up a
skin that lay upon the ground, I was stung by a serpent, that left
his sting in my finger, I at least pick'd an extraneous substance
about the bigness of an hair out of the wound which I imagined
was the sting. This slight wound I took little notice of, till my
arm grew inflamed all over; in a short time the poyson infected
my blood, and I felt the most terrible convulsions, which were
interpreted as certain signs that my death was near, and in-
evitable. I receiv'd now no benefit from bezoar, the horn of the
unicorn, or any of the usual antidotes,[4] but found my self obliged
to make use of an extraordinary remedy which I submitted to
with extreme reluctance; this submission and obedience brought
the blessing of Heaven upon me. Nevertheless I continued indis-
posed a long time, and had many symptoms which made me fear
that all the danger was not yet over: I then took cloves of garlick,
though with a great aversion both from the taste and smell; I was
in this condition a whole month, always in pain, and taking
medicines the most nauseous in the world,[5] at length youth[6] and
an happy constitution surmounted the malignity, and I recovered my former health.

I continued two years at my residence in Tigre, entirely taken
up with the duties of the mission, preaching, confessing, baptising, and enjoyed a longer quiet and repose than I had ever done
since I left Portugal. During this time one of our fathers, being
always sick, and of a constitution which the air of Abyssinia was
very hurtful to, obtain'd a permission from our superiors to
return to the Indies; I was willing to accompany him through
part of his way, and went with him over a desart, at no great

---

losophy, and consider it as such; and, in
the first place, I would wish to know from
the author, who seems perfectly informed,
what species of serpent it is that he has
quoted, as darting their poison at a distance" (2d ed., IV. 330). Despite Bruce's
mocking treatment of the incident—and
he goes on for a full paragraph—such
spitting cobras are not uncommon in
Africa.

4. In a footnote, Gonçalves da Costa

points out that bezoar and the horn of the
unicorn were highly esteemed as antidotes
(*Itinerário*, p. 466, n. 1).

5. "the most ... world" goes beyond
the French: "souffrant toujours, ayant de
très grands dégoûts" (p. 117).

6. The French word, "l'âge" (p. 117),
would not have been defined as "youth";
and for Lobo at 33, "youth" seems in-
appropriate.

distance from my residence, where I found many trees loaded
with a kind of fruit call'd by the natives *anchoy*, about the bigness
of an apricot, and very yellow, which is much eaten without any
ill effect. I therefore made no scruple of gathering and eating it,
without knowing that the inhabitants always peel'd it, the rind
being a violent purgative: so that eating the fruit and skin
together I fell into such a disorder as almost brought me to my
end.[7] The ordinary dose is six of these rinds, and I had devour'd
twenty.

I removed from thence to Debaroa, fifty four miles[8] nearer the
sea, and crossed in my way the desart[9] of the province of Saraoe,
the country is fruitful, pleasant, and populous; there are greater
numbers of Moors in these parts than in any other province of
Abyssinia, and the Abyssins of this country are not much better
than the Moors.

I was at Debaroa when the prosecution was first set on foot
against the Catholicks;[a] Sultan Segued who had been so great a
favourer of us, was grown old, and his spirit and authority
decreased with his strength. His son who was arrived at man-
hood, being weary of waiting so long for the crown he was to
inherit, took occasion to blame his father's conduct, and found
some reason for censuring all his actions; he even proceeded so
far,[1] as to give orders sometimes contrary to the Emperor's. He
had embraced the Catholick religion, rather through complaisance than conviction, or inclination; and many of the Abyssins,
who had done the same, waited only for an opportunity of
making publick profession of the ancient erroneous opinions,
and of re-uniting themselves to the Church of Alexandria. So
artfully can this people dissemble their sentiments, that we had
not been able hitherto to distinguish our real from our pretended favourers, but as soon as this prince began to give evident
tokens of his hatred, even in the life-time of the Emperor, we saw

a. Catholicks, *1735*

---

7. This generalized "disorder" replaces Lobo's more specific but less decorous "un vomissement & un dévoyement
qui me mirent à deux doigts de la mort"
(p. 117).

8. Figuring a league at three miles
(*Dictionary*), SJ has rendered "dix-huit

lieues" (p. 117) as 54 miles.

9. Given the description of the country,
"wilderness" might be a more appropriate translation of "désert" (p. 117) than
SJ's "desart."

1. "even ... far" is SJ's insertion.

all the courtiers and governors who had treated us with such a shew of friendship declare against us, and persecute us as disturbers of the publick tranquillity, who had come into Aethiopia with no other intention, than to abolish the ancient laws and customs of the country, to sow divisions between father and son, and preach up a revolution.

After having born all sorts of affronts and ill treatments, we retired to our house at Fremona, in the midst of our countrymen, who had been settling round about us a long time; imagining we should be more secure there, and that at least during the life of the Emperor, they would not come to extremities, or proceed to open force. I laid some stress upon the kindness, which the Viceroy of Tigre had shown to us, and in particular to me; but was soon convinced that those hopes had no real foundation, for he was one of the most violent of our persecutors. He seized upon all our lands, and advancing with his troops to Fremona, blocked up the town. The army had not been station'd there long, before they committed all sorts of disorders, so that one day a Portuguese, provoked beyond his temper, at the insolence of some of them, went out with his four sons and wounding several of them, forced the rest back to their camp.

We thought we had good reason to apprehend an attack, their troops were increasing, our town was surrounded, and on the point of being forced; our Portuguese therefore, thought, that without staying till the last extremities, they might lawfully repel one violence by another, and sallying out to the number of fifty, wounded about threescore of the Abyssins, and had put them to the sword, but that they fear'd it might bring too great an odium upon our cause. The Portuguese were some of them wounded, but, happily, none died on either side.

Though the times were by no means favourable to us, every one blamed the conduct of the Viceroy, and those who did not commend our action, made the necessity we were reduc'd to of self-defence an excuse for it. The Viceroy's principal design was to get my person into his possession, imagining that if I was once in his power, all the Portuguese would pay him a blind obedience. Having been unsuccessful in his attempt by open force, he made use of the arts of negociation, but with an event not more to his satisfaction. This viceroy being recall'd, a son-in-law of the Emperor's succeeded, who treated us even worse than his predecessor had done.

When he entered upon his command, he loaded us with kindnesses, giving us so many assurances of his protection, that while the Emperor liv'd, we thought him one of our friends; but no sooner was our protector dead, than this man[2] pull'd off his mask, and quitting all shame, let us see that neither the fear of God nor any other consideration was capable of restraining him, when we were to be distress'd. The persecution then becoming general, there was no longer any place of security for us in Abyssinia; where we were look'd upon by all as the authors of all the civil commotions, and many councils were held to determine in what manner they should dispose of us. Several were of opinion, that the best way would be to kill us all at once, and affirmed that no other means were left of re-establishing order and tranquillity in the kingdom.

Others more prudent were not for putting us to death with so little consideration, but advis'd that we should be banished to one of the isles of the Lake of Dambia, an affliction more severe than death itself. These alledged in vindication of their opinions, that, it was reasonable to expect, if they put us to death,[3] that the Viceroy of the Indies would come with fire and sword, to demand satisfaction. This argument made so great an impression upon some of them, that they thought no better measures could be taken, than to send us back again to the Indies: this proposal however, was not without its difficulties, for they suspected, that when we should arrive at the Portuguese territories, we would levy an army, return back[4] to Abyssinia, and under pretence of establishing the Catholick religion, revenge all the injuries we had suffered.

While they were thus deliberating upon our fate, we were imploring the succour of the Almighty with fervent and humble supplications, intreating Him in the midst of our sighs and tears, that He would not suffer His own cause to miscarry, and that however it might please Him to dispose of our lives, which, we pray'd, He would assist us to lay down with patience and resignation worthy of the faith for which we were persecuted, He would not permit our enemies to triumph over the truth.[5]

---

2. Cf. "cet hypocrite" (p. 119).

3. "These alledged ... death" is an expansion of: "Ces derniers laissaient entendre que, comme nous étions Portugais ..." (p. 119).

4. The French translation suggests that they would return with troops; it does not

mention "levying" (p. 120).

5. "and that however ... truth" paraphrases and epitomizes direct discourse: "'Vous pouvez, Seigneur, lui disions-nous dans l'excès de notre douleur, vous pouvez disposer de nos vies. Donnez nous seulement la force & le courage néces-

Thus we pass'd our days and nights in prayers, in affliction, and tears,[6] continually crouded with widows and orphans, that subsisted upon our charity, and came to us for bread, when we had not any for ourselves.

While we were in this distress we received an account that the Viceroy of the Indies, had fitted out a powerful fleet against the King of Mombaza, who having thrown off the authority of the Portuguese, had kill'd the governor of the fortress, and had since committed many acts of cruelty. The same fleet as we were informed, after the King of Mombaza was reduced, was to burn and ruin Zeila, in revenge of the death of two Portuguese Jesuits, who were kill'd by the king in the year 1624.[b] As Zeila was not far from the frontiers of Abyssinia, they imagined, that they already saw the Portuguese invading their country.

The Viceroy of Tigre had enquired of me a few days before how many men one India ship carried, and being told that the complement of some was a thousand men, he compared that answer with the report then spread over all the country, that there were eighteen Portuguese vessels on the coast of Adel, and concluded that they were man'd by an army of eighteen thousand men; then considering what had been achiev'd by four hundred, under the command of Don Christopher de Gama, he thought Abyssinia already ravaged or subjected to the King of Portugal. Many declar'd themselves of his opinion, and the court took its measures with respect to us from these uncertain and ungrounded rumours. Some were so infatuated with their apprehensions that they undertook to describe the camp of the Portuguese, and affirm'd that they had heard the report of their cannons.

All this contributed to exasperate the inhabitants,[7] and

b. 1624 *Relation*] 1604 *1735*

saires, pour souffrir tous les torments les plus cruels, nous serons trop heureux de mourir pour votre S. nom; mais que deviendront ces pauvres âmes que vous avez rachetées par votre sang, ayez pitié d'elles, ayez pitié de nous, ne permettez pas que vos ennemis & les nôtres triomphent de la vérité, & portent la corruption dans le sanctuaire; mangeons, s'il le faut, le pain de douleur, & buvons l'eau d'amertume;

mais, Seigneur, accourez à notre aide, hâtez-vous de nous assister; il est temps'" (p. 120).

6. "in prayers ... tears" provides three terms where the French has only two: "dans les afflictions & dans les larmes" (p. 120).

7. Cf. the French translation: "Tout cela ne contribuait pas peu à augmenter la haine qu'on avait contre nous" (p. 121).

reduc'd us often to the point of being massacred. At length they came to a resolution of giving us up to the Turks, assuring them that we were masters of a vast treasure, in hope that after they had inflicted all kinds of tortures on us, to make us confess where we had hid our gold, or what we had done with it, they would at length kill us in rage for the disappointment.[8] Nor was this their only view, for they believed that the Turks would by killing us, kindle such an irreconcileable hatred between themselves and our nation, as would make it necessary for them to keep us out of the Red-Sea, of which they are intirely masters: so that their determination was as politick as cruel.[9] Some pretend that the Turks were engaged to put us to death as soon as we were in their power.

CHAPTER XIII

The author relieves the Patriarch and missionaries, and supports them. He escapes several snares laid for him by the Viceroy of Tigre. They put themselves under the protection of the Prince of Bar.

Having concluded this negociation, they drove us out of our houses and robbed us of every thing, that was worth carrying away, and not content with that,[1] inform'd some banditti, that were then in those parts, of the road we were to travel through, so that the Patriarch and some missionaries were attack'd in a desart by these rovers with their captain at their head, who pillag'd his library, his ornaments, and what little baggage the missionaries had left, and might have gone away without resistance or interruption, had they satisfied themselves with only robbing;[2] but when they began to fall upon the missionaries and their companions, our countrymen finding that their lives could only be preserved by their courage,[3] charged their enemies

---

8. "kill us ... disappointment" interprets the original comment: "nous faire mourir si nous persistions à dire que nous n'en avions pas" (p. 121).

9. "so that ... cruel" has little relation to its source in the French translation: "Tout ce dessein n'était pas mal conçu" (p. 121).

1. "and not ... that" is not in the French (p. 121).

2. "and might have ... robbing" expands "Tant qu'ils ne voulurent que piller, on les laissa faire" (p. 121).

3. "our countrymen ... courage" compresses the original phrasing: they "crurent qu'il était temps de se défendre, s'ils voulaient sauver leur vie" (p. 121).

with such vigour, that they kill'd their chief, and forced the rest to a precipitate flight. But these rovers being acquainted with the country, harrass'd the little caravan till it was past the borders.

Our fathers then imagined they had nothing more to fear, (but too soon) were convinced of their error, for they found the whole country turn'd against them, and met every where new enemies to contend with, and new dangers to surmount. Being not far distant from Fremona where I resided, they sent to me for succour; I was better inform'd of the distress they were in than themselves; having been told that a numerous body of Abyssins had posted themselves in a narrow pass, with an intent to surround and destroy them. Therefore without long deliberation, I assembled my friends, both Portuguese and Abyssins, to the number of fourscore, and went to their rescue, carrying with me provisions and refreshments, of which I knew they were in great need. These glorious confessors I met, as they were just entring the pass design'd for the place of their destruction, and doubly preserv'd them from famine and the sword. A grateful sense of their deliverance made them receive me as a guardian angel.[4] We went together to Fremona, and being in all a patriarch, a bishop, eighteen Jesuits, and four hundred Portuguese, whom I supply'd with necessaries, though the revenues of our house were lost, and though the country was dis-affected to us, in the worst season of the year. We were obliged for the relief of the poor, and our own subsistance, to sell our ornaments and chalices, which we first broke in pieces, that the people might not have the pleasure of ridiculing our mysteries, by prophaning the vessels made use of in the celebration of them; for they now would gladly treat with the highest indignities what they had a year before look'd upon with veneration.

Amidst all these perplexities, the Viceroy did not fail to visit us and make us great offers of service in expectation of a large present. We were in a situation in which it was very difficult to act properly;[5] we knew too well the ill intentions of the Viceroy,

4. "design'd for ... guardian angel" adds some flourishes to the French: Lobo met them as they were about to enter the pass, "de sorte que je leur rendis deux fois la vie, & en leur portant de quoi manger, & en les retirant du péril qui paraissait inévitable; aussi me reçurent-ils comme un ange tutélaire" (p. 122).

5. "a situation ... properly" produces some nuances not in the French: "une situation bien terrible" (p. 122).

but durst not complain, or give him any reason to imagine that we knew them. We longed to retreat out of his power, or at least to send one of our company to the Indies, with an account of the persecution we suffer'd, and could without his leave neither do one nor the other. When it was determined that one should be sent to the Indies, I was at first singled out for the journey, and it was intended that I should represent at Goa, at Rome, and at Madrid, the distresses[6] and necessities of the mission of Aethiopia. But the fathers reflecting afterwards, that I best understood the Abyssinian language, and was most acquainted with the customs of the country, altered their opinions, and continuing me in Aethiopia either to perish with them, or preserve them, deputed four other Jesuits, who in a short time set out on their way to the Indies.

About this time[7] I was sent for to the Viceroy's camp, to confess a criminal, who, though falsely, was believed a Catholick, to whom after a proper exhortation, I was going to pronounce the form of absolution, when those that waited to execute him, told him aloud, that if he expected to save his life by professing himself a Catholick,[8] he would find himself deceived, and that he had nothing to do but prepare himself for death. The unhappy criminal had no sooner heard this, than rising up he declared his resolution to die in the religion of his country, and being delivered up to his prosecutors, was immediately dispatch'd with their lances.

The chief reason of calling me, was not that I might hear this confession; the Viceroy had another design of seizing my person, expecting that either the Jesuits or Portuguese would buy my liberty with a large ransom, or that he might exchange me for his father, who was kept prisoner by a revolted prince. That prince would have been no loser by the exchange, for so much was I hated by the Abyssinian monks, that they would have thought no expence too great to have gotten me into their hands, that they might have glutted their revenge[9] by putting me to the most painful death they could have invented. Happily, I found means to retire out of this dangerous place, and was follow'd by

---

6. An added term.
7. SJ's transition.
8. "by professing ... Catholick" simplifies the French: "qu'en se confessant ou

pour s'être confessé ..." (p. 123).
9. SJ contributes this idea of glutting their revenge.

the Viceroy almost to Fremona, who being disappointed, desired me either to visit him at his camp, or appoint a place where
we might confer. I made many excuses, but at length agreed to
meet him at a place near Fremona, bringing each of us only
three companions. I did not doubt but he would bring more,
and so he did, but found that I was upon my guard, and that my
company encreased, in proportion to his. My friends were resolute Portuguese, who were determin'd to give him no quarter,
if he made any attempt upon my liberty: finding himself once
more countermin'd he return'd asham'd to his camp, where a
month after, being accused of a confederacy in the revolt of
that prince, who kept his father prisoner, he was arrested, and
carried in chains to the Emperor.

The time now approaching in which we were to be delivered
to the Turks, we had none but God to apply to for relief, all the
measures we could think of were equally dangerous; resolving
nevertheless to seek some retreat, where we might hide ourselves
either altogether or separately, we determined at last to put
ourselves under the protection of the Prince John Akay, who
had defended himself a long time in the province of Bar against
the power of Abyssinia.

After I had concluded a treaty with this prince, the Patriarch
and all the fathers put themselves into his hands, and being
receiv'd with all imaginable kindness and civility, were conducted with a guard to Adicota, a rock excessively steep, about
nine miles from his place of residence. The event was not agreeable to the happy beginning of our negociation; for we soon
began to find that our habitation was not likely to be very
pleasant. We were surrounded with Mahometans, or Christians
who were inveterate enemies to the Catholick faith,[1] and were
oblig'd to act with the utmost caution. Notwithstanding these
inconveniences,[2] we were pleased with the present tranquillity
we enjoy'd, and lived contentedly on lentils and a little corn
that we had, and I, after we had sold all our goods, resolved to
turn physician, and was soon able to support my self by my
practise.

---

1. "Christians ... faith" avoids the   2. This transitional phrase replaces
harsher "hérétiques" (p. 124).   "mais" (p. 124).

I was once consulted by a man troubled with an asthma, who presented me with two *alquieres*, that is, about twenty eight pound weight of corn,[3] and a sheep, the advice I gave him, after having turn'd over my books, was to drink goats' urine every morning, I know not whether he found any benefit by following my prescription, for I never saw him after.[4]

Being under a necessity of obeying our *acoba* or protector, we changed our place of abode as often as he desired it, though not with out great inconveniences from the excessive heat of the weather, and the faintness, which our strict observation of the fasts and austerities of Lent as it is kept in this country, had brought upon us. At length wearied with removing so often, and finding that the last place assigned for our abode was always the worst, we agreed that I should go to our sovereign, and complain.

I found him entirely taken up with the imagination of a prodigious treasure affirmed by the monks to be hidden under a mountain, he was told that his predecessors had been hindred from discovering it by the demon that guarded it, but that the demon was now at a great distance from his charge, and was grown blind and lame, that having lost his son, and being without any children, except a daughter that was ugly and unhealthy,[5] he was under great affliction, and entirely neglected the care of his treasure, that if he should come, they could call one of their ancient brothers to their assistance, who being a man of a most holy life would be able to prevent his making any resistance: to all these stories, the Prince listen'd with unthinking[6] credulity. The monks encouraged by this, fell to the business,[7] and brought a man above an hundred years old, whom, because he could not support himself on horseback, they had tyed on the beast, and covered him with black wool. He was follow'd by a black cow design'd for a sacrifice to the demon of

---

3. SJ has taken the parenthetical explanation from a marginal note in Le Grand's text: "Une alquière est une mesure de blé du poids d'environ dix-neuf livres" (p. 124). Two *alquières* would actually be around thirty-eight pounds.

4. SJ deletes Lobo's final wry comment: "mais nous trouvâmes son mouton excellent" (p. 124).

5. She was also, we are told, "bigle," or squint-eyed (p. 125).

6. SJ's added adjective.

7. "encouraged ... business" has no parallel in the French (p. 125).

the place, and by some monks that carried mead, beer, and parch'd corn, to compleat the offering.

No sooner were they arrived at the foot of the mountain, than every one began to work; bags were brought from all parts to convey away the millions which each imagined would be his share. The *xumo*[8] who superintended the work would not allow any to come near the labourers, but stood by, attended by the old monk, who almost sung himself to death. At length, having removed a vast quantity of earth and stones, they discover'd some holes made by rats or moles; at sight of which a shout of joy run through the whole troop, the cow was brought and sacrificed immediately, and some pieces of flesh were thrown into these holes: animated now with assurance of success, they lose no time,[9] every one redoubles his endeavours, and the heat though intolerable was less powerful than the hopes they had conceiv'd. At length, some not so patient as the rest, were weary and desisted. The work now grew more difficult, they found nothing but rock, yet continued to toil on, till the Prince, having lost all temper, began to enquire with some passion when he should have a sight of this treasure,[1] and after having been sometime amused with many promises by the monks, was told that he had[a] not faith enough to be favour'd with the discovery.

All this I saw myself, and could not forbear endeavouring to convince our protector, how much he was imposed upon; he was not long before he was satisfied, that he had been too credulous, for all those that had so industriously search'd after this imaginary wealth, within five hours, left the work in despair, and I continued almost alone with the Prince.

Imagining no time more proper to make the proposal I was sent with, than while his passion was still hot against the monks, I presented him with two ounces of gold, and two plates of silver, with some other things of small value, and was so successful that

a. had *Errata*] ad *1735*

---

8. *Xumo* or *shum*: a local chieftain. SJ also spells the word *chumo*.

9. "animated now ... time" appears only in the English translation.

1. "the heat though intolerable ... treasure" is a revision and expansion of

the French: "La chaleur était grande, quelques-uns moins patients que les autres s'ennuient & s'en vont; la peine & le travail redoublent, on ne trouve que de la pierre. Le xumo s'impatiente aussi, il demande quand ce trésor paraîtra" (p. 125).

he gratified me in all my requests,[2] and gave us leave to return to Adicota,[b] where we were so fortunate to find our huts yet uninjured and entire.

About this time the fathers who had staid behind at Fremona, arrived with the new viceroy, and an officer fierce in the defence of his own religion, who had particular orders to deliver all the Jesuits up to the Turks, except me, whom the Emperor was resolv'd to have in his own hands alive or dead. We had received some notice of this resolution from our friends at court, and were likewise informed, that the Emperor their master, had been persuaded that my design was to procure assistance from the Indies, and that I should certainly return at the head of an army. The Patriarch's advice upon this emergency, was, that I should retire into the woods, and by some other road join the nine Jesuits who were gone towards Mazua; I could think of no better expedient,[3] and therefore went away in the night between the 23d and 24th of April, with my comrade an old man very infirm and very timerous. We cross'd woods never cross'd, I believe, by any before; the darkness of the night and the thickness of the shade spread a kind of horror round us; our gloomy journey was still more incommoded by[4] the brambles and thorns which tore our hands; amidst all these difficulties I apply'd myself to the Almighty, praying Him to preserve us from those dangers which we endeavoured to avoid, and to deliver us from those to which our flight exposed us. Thus we travelled all night till eight next morning without taking either rest or food; then imagining ourselves secure, we made us some cakes of barley meal and water, which we thought a feast.

We had a dispute with our guides, who though they[c] had bargain'd to conduct us for an ounce of gold, yet when they saw us so intangled in the intricacies of the wood, that we could not possibly get out without their direction, demanded seven ounces of gold, a mule and a little tent which we had;[d] after a long

b. Adicota *Relation*] Adicora *1735*   c. though they *Errata*] they thought *1735*
d. had, *1735*

---

2. "was so successful ... requests" extends Lobo's "j'obtiendrois ce que je demandois" (p. 125).

3. "I could ... expedient" replaces

"J'obéis" (p. 126).

4. "our gloomy ... incommoded by" is SJ's invention.

dispute we were forced to come to their terms. We continued to travel all night, and to hide ourselves in the woods all day; and here it was that we met the three hundred elephants I spoke of before. We made long marches, travelling without any halt, from four in the afternoon to eight in the morning.

Arriving at a valley where travellers seldom escape being plundered, we were obliged to double our pace, and were so happy as to pass it without meeting any misfortune, except that we heard a bird sing on our left-hand; a certain presage among these people of some great calamity at hand. As there is no reasoning them out of superstition, I knew no way of encouraging them to go forward, but, what I had already made use of on the same occasion, assuring them that I heard one at the same time on the right. They were, happily, so credulous as to take my word,[5] and we went on till we came to a well, where we staid a while to refresh our selves. Setting out again in the evening, we pass'd so near a village where these robbers had retreated, that the dogs bark'd after us: next morning we joined the fathers who waited for us;[e] after we had rested ourselves some time in that mountain, we resolved to separate and go two and two, to see for a more convenient place where we might hide ourselves: we had not gone far before we were surrounded by a troop of robbers, with whom, by the interest of some of the natives who had join'd themselves to our caravan, we came to a composition, giving them part of our goods to permit us to carry away the rest, and after this troublesome adventure[6] arrived at a place something more commodious than that which we had quitted, where we met with bread, but of so pernicious a quality, that after having eat it we[f] were intoxicated to so great a degree, that one of my friends seeing me so disorder'd, congratulated my good fortune of having met with such good wine, and was surprised when I gave him an account of the whole affair. He then offered me some curdled milk very sour, with barley-meal, which we boil'd, and thought it the best entertainment we had met with a long time.

e. us, *1735*   f. we, *1735*

---

5. "They were ... word" alters the tone: "heureusement ils me crurent" (p. 127).

6. "after ... adventure" is an added transition.

CHAPTER XIV

They are betray'd into the hands of the Turks. Are detain'd a while at Mazua: are threatned by the Bassa of Suaquem: they agree for their ransom, and are part of them dismissed.

Sometime after we received news that we should prepare ourselves to serve the Turks, a message which fill'd us with surprise, it having never been known that one of these lords had ever abandoned any, whom he had taken under his protection; and it is on the contrary one of the highest points of honour amongst them, to risque[a] their fortunes and their lives in the defense of their dependants who have implor'd their protection. But neither law nor justice were of any advantage to us, and the customs of the country were doom'd to be broken when they would have contributed to our security.[1]

We were obliged to march in the extremity of the hot season, and had certainly perish'd by the fatigue, had we not entred the woods which shaded us from the scorching sun. The day before our arrival at the place, where we were to be delivered to the Turks, we met with five elephants that persued us, and if they could have come to us, would have prevented the miseries we afterwards endured, but God had decreed otherwise.[2]

On the morrow we came to the banks of a river, where we found fourscore Turks that waited for us arm'd with muskets. They let us rest a while, and then put us into the hands of our new masters, who setting us upon camels, conducted us to Mazua; their commander seeming to be touch'd with our misfortunes, treated us with much gentleness and humanity, he offered us coffee, which we drank, but with little relish. We came next day to Mazua in so wretched a condition, that we were not surprised at being hooted by the boys, but thought ourselves well used that they threw no stones at us.[3]

a. risque *Errata*] rescue *1735*

---

1. This sentence embellishes the French: "mais il n'y avait plus ni justice, ni lois, ni de bonnes coûtumes pour nous" (p. 127).

2. "would have prevented ... otherwise" bears little resemblance to its source: "mais notre heure n'était pas en-core venue, nous étions destinés à de plus longues souffrances" (p. 128).

3. The French translation describes briefly the fortifications, cannon, gardens, and watermelons of Massawa (p. 128).

As soon as we were brought hither, all we had was taken from us, and we were carried to the governor, who is placed there by the Bassa of Suaquem. Having been told by the Abyssins that we had carried all the gold out of Aethiopia, they search'd us with great exactness, but found nothing except two chalices, and some relicks of so little value, that we redeemed them for six sequins. As I had given them my chalice upon their first demand, they did not search me, but gave us to understand, that they expected to find something of greater value which either we must have hidden, or the Abyssins must have imposed on them. They left us the rest of the day at a gentleman's house who was our friend, from whence the next day they fetch'd us to transport us to the island, where they put us into a kind of prison, with a view of terrifying us into a confession of the place where we had hid our gold, in which, however, they found themselves deceived.

But I had another affair upon my hands which was near costing me dear. My servant had been taken from me, and left at Mazua, to be sold to the Arabs; being advertised by him of the danger he was in, I laid claim to him, without knowing the difficulties which this way of proceeding would bring upon me. The governor sent me word that my servant should be restored me upon the payment of sixty piastres,[4] and being answer'd by me that I had not a penny for my self, and therefore could not pay sixty piastres to redeem my servant, he inform'd me by a renegade Jew, who negociated the whole affair, that either I must produce the money, or receive an hundred blows of the *battoon*:[5] knowing that those orders are without appeal, and always punctually executed, I prepar'd my self to receive the correction I was threatned with, but, unexpectedly, found the people so charitable as to lend me the money. By several other threats of the same kind they drew from us about six hundred crowns.

On the 24th of June, we embarked in two gallies for Suaquem, where the Bassa resided; his brother who was his deputy at Mazua, made us promise before we went, that we would not mention the money he had squeezed from us. The season was not very proper for sailing, and our provisions were but short. In

---

4. "Piaster. An Italian coin, about five shillings sterling in value" (*Dictionary*).

5. "Batoon. A staff or club" (*Dictionary*).

a little time we began to feel the want of better stores, and thought ourselves happy in meeting with a *gelve*, which though small, was a much better sailer than our vessel in which I was sent to Suaquem, to procure camels and provisions. I was not much at my ease, alone[6] among six Mahometans, and could not help apprehending that some zealous pilgrim of Mecca might lay hold on this opportunity in the heat of his devotion, of sacrificing me to his prophet.

These apprehensions were without ground,[7] I contracted an acquaintance which was soon improved into a friendship with these people, they offered me part of their provisions, and I gave them some of mine. As we were in a place abounding with oysters, some of which were large and good to eat, others more smooth and shining in which pearls are found, they gave me some of those they gather'd. But whether it happen'd by trifling our time away in oyster-catching, or whether the wind was not favourable, we came to Suaquem later than the vessel I had left, in which were seven of my companions.

As they had first landed, they had suffered the first transports of the Bassa's passion, who was a violent tyrannical man, and would have kill'd his own brother for the least advantage, a temper which made him fly into the utmost rage at seeing us poor, tatter'd, and almost naked, he treated us with the most opprobrious language, and threatned to cut off our heads. We comforted ourselves in this condition, hoping that all our sufferings would end, in shedding our blood for the name of Jesus Christ. We knew that the Bassa had often made a publick declaration before our arrival, that he should die contented, if he could have the pleasure of killing us all with his own hand; this violent resolution was not lasting, his zeal gave way to his avarice, and he could not think of losing so large a sum, as he knew he might expect for our ransom: he therefore sent us word, that it was in our choice either to die, or to pay him thirty thousand crowns, and demanded to know our determination.[8]

We knew that his ardent thirst of our blood was now cold,[9]

---

6. "seul chrétien" (p. 129).
7. This transitional clause grows out of Lobo's comment: "J'en fus quitte pour la peur" (p. 129).
8. "and demanded ... determination"

has no counterpart in the French (p. 130).
9. Cf. "Nous connûmes bien que le bacha n'avait plus d'envie de nous faire mourir" (p. 130).

that time, and calm reflection, and the advice of his friends had all conspired to bring him to a milder temper, and therefore willingly began to treat with him; I told the messenger, being deputed by the rest to manage the affair, that he could not but observe the wretched condition we were in, that we had neither money nor revenues, that what little we had, was already taken from us; and that therefore all we could promise, was to set a collection on foot, not much doubting but that our brethren would afford us such assistance, as might enable us to make him an handsome present according to custom.

This answer was not at all agreeable to the Bassa, who return'd an answer that he would be satisfied with twenty thousand crowns, provided we paid them on the spot, or gave him good securities for the payment. To this we could only repeat what we had said before, he then proposed to abate five thousand of his last demand, assuring us that unless we came to some agreement, there was no torment so cruel but we should suffer it, and talk'd of nothing but impaling, and fleaing us alive, the terror of these threatnings was much encreased by his domesticks, who told us of many of his cruelties. This is certain, that some time before, he had used some poor pagan merchants in that manner, and had caused the executioner to begin to flea them. When some Bramin touch'd with compassion, generously contributed the sum demanded for their ransom. We had no reason to hope for so much kindness, and having nothing of our own, could promise no certain sum.

At length some of his favourites whom he most confided in, knowing his cruelty and our inability to pay what he demanded, and apprehending that if he should put us to the death he threatned, they should soon see the fleets of Portugal in the Red-Sea, laying their towns in ashes to revenge it,[1] endeavoured to soften his passion, and preserve our lives, offering to advance the sum we should agree for, without any other security than our words;[b] by this assistance after many interviews with the Bassa's agents, we agreed to pay four thousand three hundred crowns, which were accepted on condition that they should be paid down, and we should go on board within two hours: but chang-

b. words, *1735*

1. The French does not mention the burning of the towns (p. 131).

ing his resolution on a sudden, he sent us word by his treasurer that two[2] of the most considerable among us should stay behind for security, while the rest went to procure the money they had promised. They kept the Patriarch, and two more fathers, one of which was above fourscore years old, in whose place I chose to remain prisoner, and represented to the Bassa, that being worn out with age, he perhaps might die in his hands which would lose the part of the ransom, which was due on his account, that therefore it would be better to chuse a younger in his place, offering to stay my self with him, that the good old man might be set at liberty.

The Bassa agreed to another Jesuit, and it pleased Heaven that the lot fell upon Father Francis Marquez. I imagined that I might with the same ease get the Patriarch out of his hand, but no sooner had I began to speak, but the anger flash'd in his eyes, and his look was sufficient to make me stop and despair of success.[3] We parted immediately, leaving the Patriarch and two fathers in prison, whom we embraced with tears, and went to take up our lodging on board the vessel.

CHAPTER XV

Their treatment on board the vessel. Their reception at Diou. The author applies to the Viceroy for assistance, but without success; he is sent to solicite in Europe.

Our condition here was not much better than that of the illustrious captives, whom we left behind.[1] We were in an Arabian ship, with a crew of pilgrims of Mecca, with whom it was a point of religion to insult us. We were lodged upon the deck exposed to all the injuries of the weather, nor was there the meanest workman or sailor,[2] who did not either kick or strike us. When we went first on board, I perceived a humour in my finger, which I neglected at first, till it spread over my hand, and swell'd up my arm, afflicting me with the most horrid torture. There was neither surgeon nor medicines to be had, nor could I

2. A mistranslation: "trois" (p. 131).

3. This despair appears only in the English translation.

1. "whom ... behind" is SJ's added

clarification.

2. SJ employs these specific labels, "workman" and "sailor," in place of the impersonal "on" of the French (p. 131).

procure any thing to ease my pain, but a little oyl, with which I anointed my arm, and in time found some relief. The weather was very bad, and the wind almost always against us, and to encrease our perplexity,[3] the whole crew, though Moors, were in the greatest apprehension of meeting any of those vessels which the Turks maintain in the strait of Babel-mandel; the ground of their fear was, that the captain had neglected the last year, to touch at Moca, though he had promised, thus we were in danger of falling into a captivity perhaps more severe than that we had just escaped from. While we were wholly engaged with these apprehensions, we discover'd a Turkish ship and galley were come upon us; it was almost calm, at least there was not wind enough to give us any prospect of escaping, so that when the galley came up to us, we thought ourselves lost without remedy, and had probably fallen into their hands,[4] had not a breeze sprung up just in the instant of danger, which carried us down the channel between the main land and the isle of Babelmandel. I have already said that this passage is difficult and dangerous, which nevertheless we passed in the night, without knowing what course we held, and were transported at finding ourselves next morning out of the Red Sea, and half a league from Babelmandel. The currents are here so violent, that they carried us against our will to Cape Guardafui, where we sent our boats ashore for fresh water, which we began to be in great want of. The captain refused to give us any, when we desired some, and treated us with great insolence,[5] till coming near the land, I spoke to him in a tone more lofty and resolute than I had ever done, and gave him to understand, that when he touch'd at Diou he might have occasion for our interest. This had some effect upon him, and procured us a greater degree of civility than we had met with before.

At length after forty[6] days' sailing we landed at Diou, where we were met by the whole city, it being reported that the Patriarch was one of our number; for there was not a gentleman who was not impatient to have the pleasure of beholding that good man, now made famous by his labours and sufferings.[7] It is

---

3. to encrease ... perplexity" is SJ's addition.

4. This probability does not appear in the French (p. 132).

5. The French translation says nothing of insolence (p. 132).

6. Mistranslation: "cinquante-deux" (p. 132).

7. "That good man" replaces "ce saint homme," and "his labours" replaces "ses travaux apostoliques" (p. 132).

not in my power to represent the different passions they were affected with, at seeing us pale, meagre, without cloaths, in a word, almost naked, and almost dead with fatigue and ill usage.[8] They could not behold us in that miserable condition without reflecting on the hardships we had undergone, and our brethren then underwent in Suaquem and Abyssinia. Amidst their thanks to God for our deliverance they could not help lamenting the condition of the Patriarch and the other missionaries, who were in chains, or at least in the hands of profess'd enemies to our holy religion. All this did not hinder them from testifying in the most obliging manner, their joy for our deliverance, and paying such honours as surprised the Moors, and made them repent in a moment of the ill treatment they had shown us on board. One who had discovered somewhat more humanity than the rest, thought himself sufficiently honour'd when I took him by the hand, and presented him[a] to the chief officer of the custom-house who promised to do all the favours that were in his power.[9]

When we passed by in sight of the fort, they gave us three saluts with their cannon, an honour only paid to generals. The chief men of the city, who waited for us on the shore, accompanied us through a crowd of people, whom curiosity had drawn from all parts of our college. Though our place of residence at Diou, is one of the most beautiful in all the Indies, we staid there only a few days, and as soon as we had recovered our fatigues, went on board the ships that were appointed to convoy the northern fleet, I was in the admiral's: we arrived at Goa in some vessels bound for Camboia:[b] here we lost a good old Abyssin convert, a man much valued in his order, and who was actually prior of his convent when he left Abyssinia, chusing rather to forsake all for religion, than to leave the way of salvation which God had so mercifully favour'd him with the knowledge of.[1]

We continued our voyage, and almost without stopping sailed by Surate, and Damam, where the rector of the college came to

---

a. presented him Errata] presented 1735   b. Camboia Errata] Camberia 1735

---

8. "with fatigue ... usage" is SJ's addition.

9. The officer promised only "de lui rendre service" (p. 133).

1. "chusing rather ... knowledge of"

expands the comment and heightens the impression of the prior's piety. Cf. the French: "aimant mieux tout quitter que d'abandonner la voie que Dieu lui avait montrée" (p. 133).

see us, but so sea sick, that the interview was without any satisfaction on either side. Then landing at Bazaim we were received by our fathers with their accustomed charity, and nothing was thought of but how to put the unpleasing remembrance of our past labours out of our minds; finding here an order of the Father Provincial[c] to forbid those who returned from the missions, to go any farther, it was thought necessary to send an agent to Goa, with an account of the revolutions that had happened in Abyssinia, and of the imprisonment of the Patriarch. For this commission I was made choice of, and I know not by what hidden decree[d] of Providence, almost all affairs whatever the success of them was, were transacted by me. All the coasts were beset by Dutch cruisers, which made it difficult to sail without running the hazard of being taken; I went therefore by land from Bazaim to Tana, where we had another college, and from thence to our house of Chaul. Here I hired a narrow light vessel, and placing eighteen oars on a side, went close by the shore, from Chaul to Goa, almost eighty leagues. We were often in danger of being taken, and particularly when we touch'd at Dabal, where a cruiser block'd up one of the channels, through which ships usually sail, but our vessel requiring no great depth of water, and the sea running high, we went through the little channel, and fortunately escaped the cruiser. Though we were yet far from Goa, we expected to arrive there on the next morning, and row'd forward with all the diligence we could. The sea was calm and delightful, and our minds were at ease,[2] for we imagined our selves past danger; but soon found we had flatter'd ourselves too soon with security,[3] for we came within sight of several barks of Malabar, which had been hid behind a point of land which we were going to double. Here we had been inevitably taken, had not a man call'd to us from the shore,[4] and inform'd us, that among those fishing boats there, some cruisers would make us a prize. We

---

c. Provincial *Errata*] Provinad *1735*   d. decree *Errata*] degree *1735*

---

2. "and our minds ... ease" is SJ's addition.

3. "but soon found ... security" provides an element of suspense lacking in the French (p. 134).

4. According to the French, the man "fût venu à la nage," phrasing which suggests swimming rather than calling (p. 134).

rewarded our kind informer for the service he had done us, and lay by till night came, to shelter us from our enemies.[5] Then putting out our oars, we landed at Goa next morning about ten, and were received at our college. It being there a festival day, each had something extraordinary allow'd him, the choicest part of our entertainments was two pilchers,[6] which were admired because they came from Portugal.

The quiet I began to enjoy did not make me lose the remembrance of my brethren, whom I had left languishing among the rocks of Abyssinia, or groaning in the prisons of Suaquem,[7] whom since I could not set at liberty without the Viceroy's assistance, I went to implore it, and did not fail to make use of every motive which could have any influence.[8]

I described in the most pathetick manner I could, the miserable state to which the Catholick religion was reduced, in a country where it had lately flourished so much by the labours of the Portuguese; I gave him in the strongest terms, a representation of all that we had suffered since the death of Sultan Segued; how we had been driven out of Abyssinia; how many times they had attempted to take away our lives; in what manner we had been betrayed, and given up to the Turks; the menaces we had been terrified with; the insults we had endured; I laid before him the danger the Patriarch was in of being either impaled or flead alive; the cruelty, insolence, and avarice of the Bassa of Suaquem, and the persecution that the Catholicks suffered in Aethiopia. I exhorted, I implored him by every thing I thought might move him, to make some attempt for the preservation of those who had voluntarily sacrificed their lives for the sake of God. I made it appear with how much ease the Turks might be driven out of the Red-Sea, and the Portuguese enjoy all the trade of those countries. I inform'd him of the navigation of that sea, and the situation of its ports, told him which it would be necessary to make ourselves masters of first, that we might upon any unfortunate encounter retreat to them. I cannot deny that some degree of resentment might appear in

5. "to shelter ... enemies" is SJ's addition.
6. A herring-like fish.
7. "my brethren ... Suaquem" embellishes the French: "mes frères, dont les uns étaient cachés dans les rochers, les autres gémissaient dans les fers" (p. 135).
8. "I went to implore ... influence" greatly expands Lobo's remark: "j'allai le chercher aussitôt" (p. 135).

my discourse; for though revenge be prohibited to Christians, I should not have been displeased to have had the Bassa of Suaquem and his brother in my hands, that I might have reproached them with the ill treatment we had met with from them. This was the reason of my advising to make the first attack upon Mazua, to drive the Turks from thence, to build a citadel, and garrison it with Portuguese.

The Viceroy listned with great attention to all I had to say, gave me a long audience, and asked me many questions. He was well pleased with the design of sending a fleet into that sea, and to give a greater reputation to the enterprise proposed making his son commander in chief, but could by no means be brought to think of fixing garrisons, and building fortresses there, all he intended was to plunder all they could, and lay the towns in ashes.

I left no art of persuasion untry'd to convince him, that such a resolution would injure the interests of Christianity;[9] that to enter the Red-Sea only to ravage the coasts, would so enrage the Turks, that they would certainly massacre all the Christian captives, and for ever shut the passage into Abyssinia, and hinder all communication with that empire.[1] It was my opinion that the Portuguese should first establish themselves at Mazua, and that an hundred of them would be sufficient to keep the fort that should be built. He made an offer of only fifty, and proposed that we should collect those few Portuguese who were scatter'd over Abyssinia: these measures I could not approve.

At length when it appeared that the Viceroy had neither forces nor authority sufficient for this undertaking, it was agreed, that I should go immediately into Europe, and represent at Rome and Madrid, the miserable condition of the missions of Abyssinia. The Viceroy promised, that, if I could procure any assistance, he would command in person the fleet and forces raised for the expedition, assuring, that he thought he could not employ his life better than in a war so holy, and of so great an importance, to the propagation[2] of the Catholick faith.

---

9. "I left ... Christianity" expands Lobo's "Je tâchai de lui faire connaître que ce serait tout perdre ... " (pp. 135–36).

1. No reference to the interruption of communication occurs in the French (p. 136).

2. "Propagation" has no counterpart in the French (p. 136).

Encouraged by[3] this discourse of the Viceroy, I immediately prepared my self for a voyage to Lisbon, not doubting to obtain upon the least solicitation[4] every thing that was necessary to re-establish our mission. Never had any man a voyage so troublesome as mine, or interrupted with such variety of unhappy accidents:[5] I was shipwreck'd on the coast of Natal; I was taken by the Hollanders, and it is not easy to mention the danger which I was exposed to both by land and sea, before I arrived at Portugal.

---

3. SJ's added transition.
4. "upon . . . solicitation" is not in the French (p. 136).
5. "Never had . . . accidents" augments

Lobo's comment: "Mais jamais naviga- tion n'a été plus traversée que la mienne" (p. 136).

The Sequel of the Account of Abyssinia[1]

CHAPTER I

The calamities that befell the missionaries in Aethiopia. A counterfeit bishop is detected in Abyssinia; another, imagined a favourer of the Catholicks, is chosen.

Scarcely had Father Jerome Lobo left Suaquem, before a report was spread, that the Portuguese fleet had enter'd the Red-Sea, made a descent upon the coasts of Abyssinia, and were come with a design of conquering the empire. The terror caused by this report, very far from stopping the persecution, much contributed to exasperate it. The Portuguese, who had been settled a long time in this kingdom, were constrained to retire farther into the country, having leave only to take with them one missionary, and even that consolation they were soon depriv'd of; for the Father John Pereira, who had offered to run all hazards with them, was obliged to conceal himself for the preservation of his life, by an edict publish'd about the same time, which, after declaring that the Emperor thought himself not secure while there was a single missionary in his dominions, enjoin'd all his subjects to make strict search, and put to death, or deliver to justice all that they could find.

Caflamariam kept near his person the Fathers Apollinaro d'Almeida[a] Bishop of Nice,[2] and Hyacinto Francisco a Florentine, and informing them, after the edict was publish'd, that he could preserve them no longer, he conducted them to some rough unfrequented mountains, where indeed they lay hid

---

a. d'Almeida *Relation*] d'Almerda *1735*

---

1. Unlike the chapter divisions peculiar to the English translation, this division and heading does occur in Le Grand's text. "Chapter I" does not, nor does the précis that follows.

2. Nicée in the French (modern İznik, in Turkey). Although "Nice" is listed in Echard's *Gazetteer*, "Nicea" is listed with it and would be a less ambiguous translation for modern readers.

secure enough from their persecutors,[3] but were every moment in danger of being devoured by ravenous beasts, or perishing with hunger. The report that they were dead made them less sought after. Caflamariam upon reflection considering the danger of their present abode, conducted the Bishop of Nice to the place where Father Francis Rodriguez had chosen his retreat, and no small pleasure did these two confessors[4] feel at their meeting; that they might live together and assist each other was an inexpressible satisfaction. The Father Francisco changed his place of retirement, but not for the better; he was a whole year without seeing the light of the sun, not daring to go out for air, but in the night, and even that liberty cost him dear; so that having nothing to satisfy his avaricious host with any longer, he was forced to seek for protection in another place.

The same misfortune befel the Fathers Lewis Cardeira, and Bruno Bruni. They hid themselves in the house of Zerr Jannes, who after having shown them the highest respect and civility, till he had got all their ornaments and vessels into his hands, then threatned to sell them to the Turks, and could not be prevailed on to dismiss them, or diverted from his perfidious resolution, but by the payment of eleven ounces of gold for their ransom.

Bruno Bruni went to join the Fathers Gaspar Payz and John Pereira, who lay conceal'd at Assa, ten miles from Fremona, under the protection of Tecla Emanuel. This faithful friend and protector of the missionaries being soon recalled from his government, gave notice to the fathers, that his brother Melca Christos was named for his successor, advising them to be cautious of reposing any trust in him, he being nearly allied to some of the most hot and violent persecutors of the Catholick faith. These fathers had made use of this information, had they known whither to fly, or whom to trust; but having so often been abandoned and betrayed by those who had given them marks of the sincerest friendship, they were now unable to determine what course to take: they continued thus wavering and uncertain till it was told them that Melca Christos the new governor desired to see them; who immediately came in sight with a troop of guards, having laid another party in ambush; he told the fathers with an affected melancholly, that he had been lately

---

3. "from their persecutors" is SJ's addition.

4. "Confesseurs de la foi de Jésus Christ" (p. 138).

informed, that his brother was laid in chains by the king's command, for having protected them; and that he was sorry, to tell them, a necessary regard to his own security,[5] forced him to desire them to remove.

Scarcely had he spoke the last words, before his soldiers, to the number of an hundred and thirty, poured upon the missionaries, who[6] resolving to suffer every thing for the religion they had come to preach, exhorted their attendants to retire. The Father Gaspar Payz, who had neither strength nor inclination to defend himself, covering his face with his handkerchief, lean'd against a tree, and in that posture was run through with lances. The rest after a gallant defence being overborn and wearied by the numbers of their adversaries, ended their labours by a glorious death,[7] except Bruno Bruni, who being left as dead, was cured afterwards by a Cafre slave.[8]

During the time of this cruel persecution, the Jacobite Church of Abyssinia suffer'd one of the greatest reproaches that had ever happen'd to it. A man who was bringing some Nubia[b] horses into the province of Narea,[c] had the impudence, without being so much as shorn, to take upon himself the stile of Abuna of Abyssinia, and to exercise all the offices of a bishop. Being known by an Aegyptian, he was so enraged that he kill'd him: a crime like this could not be kept private, and the Emperor Basilides by his own authority deposed this Abuna, and banished him into the isle of Dek.[d]

He that came from Alexandria to supply his place, was not much better, for he arrived at Abyssinia accompanied by his wife and children, and lived in so scandalous a manner, that the Emperor sent him the same year with a strong guard to a rock almost unaccessible, and having confined him there, demanded another bishop from Alexandria. The Father Agatange de Vendome superior of the mission of Capuchins in Egypt, being informed of the miserable state of religion in Aethiopia, went to

b. Nubia *Errata*] Nabia *1735*   c. Narea *Relation*] Narca *1735*   d. Dek *Relation*] Bek *1735*

---

5. "a necessary ... security" has no parallel in the French translation (p. 138).
6. The pronoun replaces the phrase, "Ces saints confesseurs" (p. 139).
7. "The rest ... death" epitomizes a brief account of the battle, filled with the names of the priests (p. 139).
8. SJ deletes the concluding comment on Father Bruno Bruni: "Dieu le réservant sans doute à de plus grands travaux, & à un supplice en apparence plus ignominieux" (p. 139).

the Patriarch of Alexandria, imploring him to have pity upon the Christians of Abyssinia, and to send them a bishop of such conduct and moderation, as might by his prudence and charity appease the spirits of the people, too much heated by these commotions.[9] The Patriarch promised him all he desired, and proceeded so far, as to write to King Basilides, that the Christians of the Roman Church might be treated in his dominions with less rigour.[1] The Abbé Mark who was made Abuna or Metropolitan of Abyssinia, was one of Father Agatange's friends, they had conversed often, and the good Capuchin was persuaded, that he had favourable sentiments of the Roman Church, as it appears by a letter which he wrote on this occasion to the Patriarch Alphonso Mendez at Suaquem,[2] wherein he informs him, that this Abuna was fully persuaded of the truth of the doctrines of the Church of Rome, that, though he could not affirm him to be a Catholick, yet that he was well inclined towards them, that he held the same opinions concerning our Saviour, and the superiority of the sovereign Pontiff, and would treat those of the Roman Church as orthodox; and desires of the Patriarch that he would in regard of his affection for the Church, shew him all the kindness in his power, and recommend him to the admiral of the Portugal fleet.

The Patriarch did not find the new Abuna's opinions agreeable to this account of them, for he had imposed upon the Capuchin father,[3] and far from being either a Catholick or inclined to favour their opinions, he became, when he was invested with his authority, one of the most furious of their persecutors, as Father Agatange[e] had himself experience of.

e. Agatange *Errata*] Agantange *1735*

9. "by ... commotions" is SJ's addition.

1. SJ deletes the second part of the request: "& de s'abstenir de répandre de sang humain" (p. 140).

2. "Suaquem" is added for clarity. The remainder of this paragraph epitomizes a first-person letter that covers three quarters of a page. SJ omits seven lines which describe the German Lutheran, "un grand obstacle à la propagation de la foi" (p. 140), who accompanied the Abuna.

3. "The Patriarch ... Capuchin father" replaces a more specific passage in the French translation: "Le patriarche Alphonse Mendez était à Suaquem, où l'Abuna Marc & Pierre Heyling, ce jeune lutherien allemand, lui rendirent cette lettre. Il eut plusieurs entretiens avec eux, & jugea de ces deux hommes tout autrement que le Père Agatange. Il trouva que l'Abuna avait trompé ce bon capucin ..." (pp. 140–41).

CHAPTER II

The Patriarch and his companions suffer great miseries; are ransomed, and arrive at Diou. Their reception there; with the fate of the other missionaries in Abyssinia.

To return to the Patriarch and two Jesuits who were left at Suaquem:[1] never was captivity more severe than what they endured. The Bassa, a man whose cruelty was not to be appeased, or avarice satiated,[2] began his injustice by taking all they had from them, then demanded immense sums, making every day some new proposition more unreasonable than the last. The Patriarch at length wearied with incessant injuries and oppressions, made application to the French consul in Egypt, that he might give notice at Rome, of the condition they were in, nor were they without hopes, that he might procure letters in their favour from the Bassa of Cairo, on whom he of Suaquem is dependant.

The consul employed his interest, but without any advantage to the captives at Suaquem, whom the Bassa loaded with irons heavier than before, fastening them to the ground by the feet and neck, so that they could not move. The Count de Linares Viceroy of the Indies, having received information of the miseries these confessors underwent, gave directions to some merchants to treat about their ransom. The Bassa was offered four thousand crusades, but he insisted on six thousand for only the Patriarch, and there was no way of procuring his liberty, but by satisfying this unreasonable demand.[3]

The Patriarch much desired to take the Bishop of Nice away with him, and directed him to meet him with the utmost expedition, but whether the letter miscarried, or any thing else

---

1. This transition bridges an omission of half a page in which the Patriarch describes Peter Heyling (see n. 3, p. 121) more fully: his ingratiating manner, his learning, and the futility of his attempt to spread Lutheranism in Abyssinia. The Patriarch believed he would soon have converted Heyling had the Bassa not jailed the Jesuits (p. 141).

2. "The Bassa ... satiated" expands and balances the French: "Le bacha, homme d'une avarice insatiable" (p. 141).

3. "and there was ... demand" extends the original brief remark: "& il fallut les donner" (p. 142). The "crusade" was a Portuguese coin (*crusado*) bearing an emblem of a cross.

interven'd, the Bishop did not appear, and they went away without him. The ship which had waited for them from the 4th of April, set sail on the 24th of August, and arrived on the 23d, of the next month at Diou. The Governor went to receive the Patriarch at his landing, and offered to convey him to the city in his own chair, which, after having excused himself, he was obliged to accept of, for upon trying to walk, he found his legs so weak, and his head so disorder'd, that he was not able to move a step. He kept his bed several days, and continued six weeks at Diou, to recover from the fatigues of so long a voyage after so severe a confinement. He landed at Goa, on the 19th of December, and had a publick audience soon after of Don Pedro de Silva, who had succeeded the Count de Linares in the government of the Indies, at which he gave him an account of the labours of the missionaries, of the progress they made in the reign of Sultan Segued, and the calamities they had suffer'd since the accession of Basilides, of their exile, their captivity, and of the danger their brethren were in, who chose to continue their residence in Abyssinia. He represented the urgent necessity of assisting the rise, and cherishing the growth of the Catholick religion, but the methods he proposed[4] discover'd more of the spirit of the warriour than of the bishop or missionary. He declar'd it as his opinion that Mazua, and Arkiko ought to be seiz'd, a strong citadel to be built, and maintained by a numerous garrison; that one of the princes of Abyssinia ought to be got into Catholick hands by winning over or conquering the commander that kept him prisoner, that he ought to be set on the throne, and a civil war by that means be raised in Abyssinia.

Father Jerome Lobo spoke in much the same strain at Rome; which gave occasion to the Pope, the cardinals, and all who were concerned in these affairs, to suspect, that the missionaries had infected their preaching and all their conduct with a little of the martial spirit too natural to the Portuguese nation. The resistance made at Assa and Fremona, the many expedients put into practise to bring back Rassela Christos from his exile, the disobedience, or, to say more, the revolt of Zamariam, that zealous

---

4. "assisting ... proposed" balances ideas found in the French translation: "Il représenta le besoin que cette catholicité naissante avait d'être promptement secourue; mais les moyens qu'il proposa pour conserver & augmenter notre religion en ce pays-là ..." (p. 142).

Catholick, and eminent protector of the Jesuits, who joining himself to the enemies of the king at Mount-Lasta, died with his sword drawn against his sovereign, confirm'd them in their opinion, that the Catholicks and missionaries of Abyssinia, were not sheep that would be drag'd to the slaughter without murmuring.

The Fathers Bruno Bruni, and Lewis Cardeira retired with Zamariam to Mount Salam, whom 'tis said, they proposed to leave when he engaged in arms; however they wrote to the Bishop of Nice, and to the Fathers Hyacinto Francisco, and Francisco Rodriguez, to come to them, but were answer'd by the pious missionaries,[5] that they came hither to suffer and to labour, not to hide themselves, or lye useless, that their lives were in the hands of God, and that they were resolv'd to resign them entirely to the disposal of His providence. In which noble resolution they continued unshaken, and were not long before they obtained that crown which God hath prepared for those who leave all for Him, being seized in June 1638, and hanged immediately. The other two fathers, notwithstanding[a] the care they took to lye undiscovered, being at length found out, met the same fate with their glorious brethren. There now remained no more Jesuits in Abyssinia, and all the endeavours of the Patriarch to send some thither were without effect.

CHAPTER III

Other missionaries are sent into Abyssinia, their persecution and death. The Patriarch attempts to send more. The vigilance of the Emperor; who seizes his brother on suspicion, and puts him to death.

The Pope and cardinals being prejudiced against the conduct of the Jesuits, gave the charge of this mission to six French Capuchins, who under the direction of Father Agatange attempted the way into Abyssinia. Two of them arriving at Mazua were well received by the Bassa there, but no sooner enter'd into Abyssinia, than they were apprehended in the disguise of

a. notwithstanding, *1735*

5. "Pious missionaries" is SJ's addition.

Armenian merchants, and brought to Mark the Abuna, who discovering them to be Catholick priests, who came (as he said) to oppose and destroy the Church of Alexandria, so enraged the people against them,[1] that they were stoned on the spot. Such was his recompense of the civilities he receiv'd from Father Agatange, and such the effect of the friendship contracted between them.

Two more[2] were massacred at Magadoxo, and such had been the fate of the other two, had they not with great prudence continued at Mazua, under the protection of the Bassa, where their labours were so successful, that they brought back into the way of salvation several Abyssin merchants, who had been converted formerly by the Jesuits, but, for want of preachers and instructions, had relapsed into their former errors. The harvest in time grew too great for the labourers, and one of them worn out by those holy employments died in the beginning of the year 1642.

The other continuing to practise the duties of the mission, was assisted by two other fathers who came to share his labours. Their arrival gave the alarm to the Emperor Basilides who, having conceiv'd a firm opinion that all the Catholick princes were in league with the Portuguese, was in continual apprehensions of some design against his empire or life;[3] so that scarcely could a ship put in at Mazua or Suaquem, but he imagined it a fleet sent to invade his dominions. He therefore upon the first account of the arrival of some Europeans at Suaquem sends an ambassador to the Bassa with a large present,[4] entreating him either to drive them out of the country or put them to death.

This Bassa was not that generous man who had protected the Capuchins, but was as cruel and avaricious as his predecessor was human and dis-interested. No sooner had he received the embassador's present, than he order'd the fathers to be seiz'd, and calling for those two who came last thither,[5] commanded

---

1. "so enraged ... them" differs from the French phrasing: "Ce discours fut un arrêt de mort contre ces religieux" (p. 143).

2. Throughout this section names and details appear in the French translation (p. 144) which SJ replaces with more general terms: "one of them," "the other," "this last," and so forth.

3. "of some ... life" has no counterpart in the French (p. 144).

4. SJ deletes the specific details: "un présent de cent cinquante onces d'or, & de cinquante esclaves" (p. 144).

5. The French provides their names: "les pères Felix de S. Severin & Joseph Tortulani" (p. 144).

their heads to be struck off in his presence; as he had some acquaintance with him that had resided longer there, he paid him the compliment[a] of sending for his head.[6] After the death of this last, it was impossible to receive any account of the state of affairs in Abyssinia, though the Patriarch considering himself entrusted with the charge of the Church of Aethiopia, omitted no endeavours to send assistance to the new converts.[7] Those Jesuits who had already shar'd with him the labours of the mission, and had been forced with him out of Aethiopia, rather animated than discouraged by the death of their companions, offered to expose themselves to the same dangers by returning thither, and accused their own cowardice which had lost them the crown of martyrdom.

One of these pious fathers[8] hoping by the credit of the Banians at Diou, who carry on a great trade in the Red-Sea, to be well receiv'd at Mazua, engaged in this undertaking,[9] and arriving at Suaquem on the 16th of May, went to pay his compliments to the Bassa as factor of the ship; he was well receiv'd, but notwithstanding his disguise some time after discovered to be a Jesuit and a Portuguese; this was sufficient to alarm the whole country.[1] The crafty Bassa sent for Father Calaca and telling him of good-will he entertain'd towards the Jesuits and Portuguese, order'd him to return to the Indies with propositions for establishing a commerce with the Viceroy. The father was to no purpose apprised of his intention;[b] though he saw the snare, there was no avoiding it. He therefore went, and was no sooner out of the port than the Bassa seiz'd all his goods for his own use.

a. compliment *Errata*] like compliment *1735*   b. intention, *1735*

---

6. SJ's avoidance of names causes some awkwardness in this account of the beheading: "Comme il connaissait le père Antoine de Petra Sancta, il lui épargna la peine de le venir trouver, il se contenta qu'on lui apportât sa tête" (p. 144). Both translations offer their own attempts at humor.

7. "the new converts" is SJ's substitute for "tant de chrétiens orthodoxes, qu'il avait enfantés en Jésus Christ" (pp. 144–45).

8. This phrase is all that SJ retains of a four-line description of Father Damien Calaca and the esteem in which he was held (p. 145).

9. "engaged ... undertaking" replaces the comment that "là il pourrait attendre les occasions que la Providence lui offrirait de rentrer en Abissinie" (p. 145).

1. The French translation suggests that the Bassa himself might have spread the rumor in order to extort more from the king and the missionaries (p. 145).

As to the proposals of traffick, the Bassa was in no care about them, the condition of a Turkish officer is too uncertain to allow him to entertain prospects of future advantages, he seiz'd what was then within his reach, and was unconcern'd at any thing further.

Father Botelho afterwards being desirous to try his fortune, landed at Suaquem in a Turkish habit; immediately upon his arrival advice was sent to the Emperor of Abyssinia, that a Portuguese Jesuit was come to that port;[2] this intelligence raised all his passion, for being possess'd by an opinion that the Portuguese were in arms against him, supported by all the powers of Europe, he made the strongest application to the Bassa, that he would not suffer a single Portuguese to reside in the neighbourhood of his dominions,[3] and imagining that Claudius his young brother held a private correspondence with the Jesuits, he put him under an arrest.

This young prince's only crime was, that he was imagined to adhere to the Roman Church, because he frequently, as the licentious lives of the Abuna, and the rest of the clergy fell under his observation, would compare them with the constancy, piety and modesty of the Patriarch,[4] affirming that the King his brother had not in his empire a preacher equal to him; than this and the discharge of some of his domesticks for having abjured the Church of Rome there needed nothing more to make the prince criminal at a time when to profess the Catholick religion was treason.[5]

The King resolving to secure the person of his brother, having placed some officers and soldiers in his palace, sends for the prince under pretence of having some weighty affair to communicate, then leading him through several appartments, gives the sign to some men who were hid on purpose, to seize him. They fell upon him in an instant, and loading him with chains,

---

2. And, SJ omits, "pourrait être suivi de plusieurs autres" (p. 146).

3. The French translation indicates that this request, accompanied by luxurious gifts, was sent simultaneously to Massawa, to Al Mukhā, and to Yemen (p. 146).

4. Omitted is part of the prince's high praise of the Patriarch and the Jesuits: "Il disait qu'en les chassant on avait pris l'ivraie pour le bon grain, le cuivre pour l'or, dont on s'était défait mal à propos" (p. 146).

5. "treason" compresses the following idea: "c'était être traître au roi & à l'etat, & coupable de toutes sortes de crimes" (p. 146).

led him to a prison fortified on purpose to secure him. All his
children and dependants were arrested at the same time. The
manner of proceeding against him was very compendious,[6]
the army was assembled, and the prince brought out bound;
the King then, in an harangue to the multitude, accused his
brother, of having abandoned the religion of his ancestors,[7] of
designing to introduce the Portuguese into Abyssinia, and con-
spiring against his government and life.

When a man is accused by his king in person, before a
prejudiced croud, incapable of separating the truth from the
falshood, he is easily found guilty: no sooner had the King ceased
to speak, than the whole audience cry'd out for justice on a man
so infamous for apostacy and treason;[8] a sentence thus pronounced never fails to be speedily executed; the prince was
remanded back to prison, and the same night lost his head.

This execution prepared a way for many others, and all who
were suspected of favouring either the prince or the Roman
Church shared in his sentence, and had their goods confiscated,
and their persons confined; the persecution was carried on
without regard to dignity, age, or sex.[9] All these severities were
not able to set the Emperor's mind at quiet, for imagining that
he had rather excited than suppress'd the murmurs of his
people, and encreased the numbers, as well as aggravated the
malice of the malecontents,[1] he thought it necessary to secure
himself on his throne by leagues and alliances, and therefore
sends ambassadors to a Mahometan prince, with proposals of
tolerating the exercise of his religion, in Abyssinia, and a request that some of their learned men might be sent to instruct his
people.

This important commission was trusted jointly to a Christian and Mahometan, but the Mahometan, being more fully

---

6. "The manner ... compendious" is
SJ's inserted transition.

7. Abandoned it "pour embrasser celle
de Rome" (p. 147).

8. "a man ... treason" softens the original plea to be delivered from "ce traître,
de cet apostat, de cet ennemi du roi, de ce
parricide qui n'avait vécu que trop long
temps & qu'on se dépêchat de le faire
mourir" (p. 147).

9. This general account of the persecution epitomizes a more specific paragraph (p. 147).

1. "imagining ... malecontents" expands and balances the following: "Il crut
au contraire qu'ils avaient augmenté le
nombre des mécontents, & que pouvant
être attaqué au dedans & au dehors ..."
(p. 147).

instructed in the full extent of the Emperor's project, treated his colleague with a contempt which is never forgiven, and engrossed all the honours and presents which they were complimented with in the Mahometan country.[2] Resentment of such usage made the Christian turn his whole thoughts upon defeating the design,[3] and scarce were they arrived at the frontiers of Abyssinia, before he publickly declared the whole intent of the negociation.[4] The monks at this news were the first who took up arms, and the people by their persuasion and example made a general insurrection; nothing now was talked of but dethroning King Basilides, and setting up another prince more capable of standing up in defense of the religion of his country.

Never was Basilides more terrified;[c] the people, tumultuous and enraged,[5] could scarcely be prevailed upon to hear any defense; he denied all he had been charged with, and threw the whole upon the queen his mother, who still retain'd a great affection for the Mahometans from whom she descended. This plea was confuted by the many personal interviews he had been observ'd to have with the Mahometan doctor, who came back with the ambassador of the same religion. Finding that neither his crown nor his life could be preserved without bidding farewel to his new scheme,[6] he sent away the Mahometan with as little noise as he could, loaded with honours and with riches.

This account, however disputed by Mr. Ludolf, who denies that any such design was ever on foot, and attempts to prove by political arguments the inconsistency of it with the Emperour's interest,[7] affirming the Emperor never was so cruel as to put his brother to death, is supported by the testimony of the Father

---

2. The French translation describes more fully the bickering of the envoys and the imprisonment of the Christian (p. 148).

3. "Resentment ... design" provides a motive not mentioned in the French (p. 148).

4. The French sets forth the specific charges made by the Christian (p. 148).

5. The description of the people has no parallel in the French (p. 148).

6. "without bidding ... scheme" is SJ's insertion.

7. "This account ... interest" is a revision of the following sentence: "Comme le projet de Basilides ne put être exécuté à cause de la très grande opposition qu'il trouva de la part de ses sujets, Mr. Ludolf soutient que jamais Basilides n'a pu avoir cette pensée; il tâche de le prouver par plusieurs raisons de convenance" (p. 148).

Bernard Nogueire, who was then in Aethiopia, of Torquato
Pisani, who, as it is reasonable to believe, was at Mazua, and
of^d Alphonso Mendez who heard it from some Abyssins who
came into the Indies:[8] facts proved by so many testimonies
ought to be confuted by some more solid arguments, than vain
conjectures, and uncertain reasonings.

The persecution grew hotter every day, and there were left
but five Portuguese and four Abyssin priests to administer the
sacraments to those who still continued stedfast in the Catholick
religion; these, though they had hitherto escaped the fate of their
brethren, suffered all the inconveniences of nakedness and
hunger.[9]

CHAPTER IV

The Patriarch sends letters to Father Nogueira. The Emperor renews the
persecution. His ill success in his other affairs.

Alphonso Mendez not discouraged by the ill success of so
many adventurers, was continually studying new means for the
relief of the Abyssinian Catholicks; two of his domesticks were
fortunate enough to find the way into Aethiopia, one of whom I
take to be that Gregory made so famous by the history of Mr
Ludolf, and the time in which Gregory reports himself to have
made his voyage, strengthens my conjecture. After this, there
was no possibility of sending any messages to Abyssinia, or
receiving any accounts from thence.[1] The miserable state which
the Catholicks were apprehended to be in, was represented to
the bishops and Governor of the Indies, in a most pathetick
letter by Father Nogueira, who though worn out himself with
miseries, could not forbear attempting something for the service

d. of *1789*] of the *1735*

---

8. Mendes presents this account in
Book IV, Chap. 22 (Beccari, IX. 373–77).

9. Deleted are the names of these
Portuguese and Abyssinian clerics who
"étaient nus, mourants de faim, man-
quants de tout, & toujours sur le point

d'être égorgés, comme ils le furent presqu
tous" (p. 149).

1. Jesuits and others returning from
Suakin or Massawa were able to bring ou
only "des bruits confus de ce qui se passa
en ces pays-là" (p. 149).

of the converts of Abyssinia, and apply'd himself to the Banians. But those men, whose tenderness and compassion[2] would not suffer them to put the most contemptible animal to death, could hear the moving entreaties and sorrowful relation of the father without being affected.[3]

His letter[4] however could not be read by the Patriarch without the strongest emotions; that prelate whose thoughts were always intent upon his Church of Aethiopia,[5] after having fail'd in all his attempts to send Jesuits into that country, at length pitch'd upon one George an Abyssin, who had been many[6] years in the service of the fathers, imagining, that he being acquainted with the country, would be better enabled to elude the diligence of the guards who were posted at the avenues.

This man with a Banian his companion, after some delays occasion'd by a difference between the Governor of Moca, and the Bassa of Mazua, which had interrupted all commerce between those two ports, and consequently left them no means of travelling,[7] arrived at Mazua, and by presents having easily procured free passage through the Bassa's district, they continued their journey for two days, then stopping at Engana, sent

---

2. "whose ... compassion" does not appear in the French (p. 149).

3. "could hear ... affected" epitomizes a more detailed version: the Banians "virent couler les larmes de Nogueira sans être touchés, son visage abattu, son corps nu & exténué, le récit de ses misères & de celles de ses compagnons ne furent point capables d'exciter leur compassion, & il s'en retourna sans avoir le moindre soulagement" (pp. 149–50).

4. SJ deletes this two-page letter, the first half of which, Nogueira says, was dictated to him by Rassela Christos, " 'sanglotant & fondant en larmes' " (p. 151). Rassela Christos regrets his sins, bemoans the abandonment of his country by the Pope and the Catholic world, and hopes for deliverance from "cette hérésie & de cette captivité d'Égypte." Then Nogueira recounts the miseries, imprisonments, deaths, and apostasy in Abyssinia (pp. 150–52).

5. "that prelate ... of Aethiopia" is a rather spare rendering of the following: "jamais ce vertueux prélat ne perdit de vue sa chère Eglise d'Abissinie: toujours même attention, toujours même empressement pour soulager les catholiques qu'il avait laissés en ces pays-là; tant de voyages entrepris sans aucun fruit ne le rebutèrent pas" (p. 152).

6. "cinq" (p. 152).

7. The "difference" that disrupted trade is explained in the French translation: Christian slaves aboard one of the Bassa's galleys revolted, slew the officers, and became pirates. After robbing and killing without mercy they were captured and executed; the ship was returned to the Bassa, who was not quite appeased. Also omitted is the news of the Abuna Marc's ouster and the arrival of Michael, his successor. SJ's deletion amounts to two thirds of a page (pp. 152–53).

letters to Father Nogueira, who lay concealed in the country of the Agaus. It is not easy to describe his surprise at hearing that he was discovered, and enquired after. He could not be convinced that the messengers were any other than officers sent with a plausible pretence to ensnare and apprehend him; he read the letters over and over, and still continued incredulous: nor could he be brought to entertain any other opinion, though they gave him such tokens, as, had he been less disturb'd, he would have known could be sent by none but the Patriarch.[8] At length, by the advice of his friends[9] he was prevail'd with to go with the messengers, and came on the 24th of March to Engana, where with a strange mixture of joy and grief, they heard and told their own calamities and those of their brethren.[1]

About this time the Emperor being alarm'd by some groundless reports of the preparations of the Portuguese, a tale which never fail'd to fill him with terror, and exasperate him against the Catholicks, renew'd the persecution with great fury, and issued out a proclamation for apprehending Father Nogueira, and having by the information of some who had return'd to their former religion, detected many Portuguese Catholicks, put them all to death without mercy.[2]

This emperor was only artful and fortunate in his attempts against his Catholick subjects, for almost every other undertaking miscarried.[3] His general Bela Christos lost his army in the mountains of Lasta: the Galles having ravaged one of his provinces, retreated without being attack'd; his army revolted; and one of his kingdoms refused their tribute: the next year was even more unfortunate: his army under Bela Christos was almost entirely cut off.[4] And to compleat his misfortunes, the King of

---

8. "such tokens ... the Patriarch" avoids the specific details of the French: "on lui demandait les cantiques que Rassela-Christos avait composés en l'honneur de l'Eglise Romaine, une vie de la Vierge composée en Latin par le père Antoine Fernandés que le patriarche avait laissée chez Laurent Martinés son premier secretaire & interprète; circonstance qui ne pouvait guère être sue que par le patriarche" (p. 153).

9. "At length ... friends" treats more briefly Nogueira's doubt and final decision (pp. 153–54).

1. "where with ... brethren" epitomizes a third of a page taken up with specific news (p. 154).

2. This paragraph abridges more than a page of detailed description of the persecution (pp. 154–55).

3. "for almost every ... miscarried" simplifies the original idea: "quoique les rois les plus braves & les plus sages perdent des batailles, il est rare que tout leur réuississe mal, & en même temps" (p. 155).

4. Throughout this discussion of the emperor's problems SJ is epitomizing and omitting details (pp. 155–56).

Adel hearing of all these losses, seiz'd some rocks in his dominions, and from thence made inroads into his country. Mr. Ludolf notwithstanding all these unhappy accidents, affirms, that no emperor had ever a reign of more honour and tranquillity than Basilides after the expulsion of the Jesuits; but his conjectures are often only founded upon prejudice, and are not to be opposed to facts proved by such authentick testimonies as we can produce.

At this time the Patriarch Alphonso Mendez died, in the seventy seventh year of his age;[a] he had all the qualities of a good and useful missionary,[5] being bless'd with an extraordinary degree of patience, resolution, zeal, and learning;[6] yet his conduct seems liable to some censure, and it is not easy to excuse[7] the rigour with which he insisted on the abolition of some ancient customs, which the Abyssins had receiv'd with the truths of the Gospel, and which have never yet been condemned by the Church.[8]

After the death of this prelate we have very little knowledge of what happen'd in the interiour regions of Abyssinia, and have no other memoirs to make use of for continuing our relation, than what we have receiv'd from Cairo.[9]

a. age, *1735*

---

5. Cf. "toutes les qualités d'un saint & vertueux missionnaire" (p. 156).

6. The French adds "piété" (p. 156).

7. "yet ... to excuse" expands the French: "On ne laisse pas d'être quelquefois surprise ..." (p. 156).

8. SJ omits a third of a page criticizing Ludolf for excusing Judaic customs among the Abyssinians and for ignoring Wansleben's evidence (p. 157). Johann Michael Wansleben, a Lutheran and a student of Ludolf's, was sent by the Duke of Saxe to find Ethiopian liturgies which would, as Ludolf had suggested, prove favorable to Lutheranism. Reading the first manuscripts he purchased, Wansleben is said to have recognized his errors, converted to Catholicism, and become a Dominican. His second search for liturgies resulted in the discovery of more than five hundred manuscripts which were sub-

sequently deposited in the Bibliothèque du Roi. His *Conspectus Aethiopicarum* was published in Paris (1671). An English translation "Collected out of a Manuscript History Written in Latin by Jo. Michael Wansleben, a Learned Papist" (1679) has the revealing title: *A Brief Account of the Rebellions and Bloodshed Occasioned by the Anti-Christian Practices of the Jesuits and other Popish Emissaries in the Empire of Ethiopia.*

9. The French includes a paragraph on Wansleben and Charles Jacques Poncet as travellers to the interior (p. 157). As the following chapter explains, Poncet, a French physician, visited Ethiopia at the end of the seventeenth century. His *Voyage to Aethiopia* was published in English in 1709; the best edition, under the title, "A Narrative by Charles Jacques Poncet of his Journey from Cairo into Abyssinia and

CHAPTER V

Mr. Poncet goes into Aethiopia, comes back with a pretended embassador. Is well received at Paris and at Rome. An envoy arrives at Paris from the Patriarch of Alexandria.

Agi Ali factor to the King of Abyssinia, was afflicted with the same distemper with the king his master and the prince, and had applied himself in his enquiry for a physician to the Franciscan missionaries of Italy; which the consul of France hearing of, procured that Agi Ali should have recourse to him. After some conversation about the king's distemper, the consul told him of a physician among his attendants, who had more skill than any other in the world, and engaged the Abyssin to make use of him. This learned physician was James Charles Poncet, a surgeon of Franche-Comptè, who undertook and perform'd the cure. This success so encreased his reputation, that nothing now was talk'd of but the French physician.[1]

Every thing was got ready for the departure of Monsieur Poncet, and his journey into Abyssinia, the Father Brevedent, a Jesuit of Roan,[2] who was influenced by no motives but zeal and charity, was resolved to go as companion of this surgeon newly dignified with the title of physician, and without so much as waiting for the orders of his superiors, changing his dress, and his name, went away with Mr. Poncet.

Two companions of tempers more different were never known; the surgeon was a man of a roving mind, without the least sense of either honour or religion, and of parts below the middle rank of mankind, who knew nothing but lying, and imposed upon all that had any thing to do with him. The Jesuit was a man full of religious sentiments, of a placid and soft temper, and of great learning, and sacrificed himself with no other view than of promoting the glory of God. Agi Ali the

---

Back 1698–1700," appears in *The Red Sea and Adjacent Countries at the Close of the Seventeenth Century*, ed. by Sir William Foster for the Hakluyt Society, 2nd Series, No. 100 (1949), pp. 93–172.

  1. SJ omits almost a page describing the territorial conflict between "les

jésuites français & les pères récollets italiens, au sujet des missions de Nubie & d'Abissinie" (p. 158). "James Charles Poncet" should, of course, be Charles James Poncet.

  2. "Rouen" (p. 158).

principal man of the company was more subtle, and crafty than Mr. Poncet, and like him made no scruple of sacrificing his honesty to his interest.[3]

They set out with the caravan, which was obliged to stay a long time in Upper-Egypt, for fear of the Arabs;[4] the only letter that was ever receiv'd from Father Brevedent, was dated from Sanaar on the 15th of February 1699. In this letter he informs us that they left Cantara, on the banks of the Nile, the 2d of October, that they travelled for five days cross a desart which begins at that place, without finding any water, except within a day's journey of Helaone, a large village inhabited by Turks, and governed by a *chec*, whose jurisdiction extends to thirty smaller villages. That after having travelled in two days from Helaone to Chab, and in three from Chab to Selima, they entred an horrid desart, where no living animal, not even a fly was to be seen, and the ways were mark'd by the carcases of camels that had died in passing it. No other creature is capable of undergoing such fatigues, and he was told by an old man of the company, that the camels of those caravans that march westward from the banks of the Nile, are sometimes forty days without eating, for they cannot eat unless they drink, and they sometimes find no water in that time. After passing this desart they stop'd at Machou to refresh themselves after the labours of so fatiguing a march. Here the men and women wear no other cloaths than an apron, the women only dress their heads by braiding their hair. The men of quality distinguish themselves by hanging a sword at their left arm, and carrying a lance in their right. Their houses are nothing but huts of clay and the straw of *doras*, a grain of which they make sour bread, and a drink very intoxicating. This country breeds excellent horses and is governed by a *cheik*.

Not far distant is the isle of Argo, which hath its governor or *ahab*; here the physician gave remedies to the *cheik* and governor, and perform'd several cures. Here are many houses along the bank of the Nile. A day's journey from Machou or Moscho is the village of Harril. On the 13th of November, the caravan arrived at Dongola, the commander of which takes upon him the stile of king or *malek*, which is corruptly pronounced *mek*, though he is

---

3. "like him ... interest" improves on: "comme lui, fourbe & intéressé à l'excès" (p. 159).

4. An omitted paragraph describes an attempt to hinder Father Brevedent (p. 159).

set up and deposed at the pleasure of the king of Sanaar. During a long stay which they made at Dongola, the *Cheik* Gandil treated the physician and father several days at Corty[a] a place two days' journey from Dongola, and gave them provisions to pass the desart of Bihouda.[b] They left Dongola, the 19th of January, and on the 23d came to Derreira on the Nile, which they had left for some days, marching to the westward, to escape those troops that had revolted from the king of Sanaar. On the 26th they left Derreira, and on the 28th pass'd a branch of the Nile, and lodged that evening at Guelri, where they found the country better peopled than any they had pass'd thro, after they came from Egypt;[c] the villages are large and the roofs on account of the rains rais'd in form of a pyramid. On the 6th of February having cross'd the river again, they lodged at Herbagi, and having rested there two days, arrived on the 12th at Sanaar. Thus far Father Brevedent.[5]

These travellers were detain'd three whole months at Sanaar, so that the rains began before they came to Jesim, a place in the midway between Sanaar and the frontiers of Abyssinia. The Father Brevedent weaken'd by a distemper, and harrass'd beyond his strength by so toilsome a march, died at Braco, with that hope and consolation which accompanies the last hours of those who have lived in the fear, and died in the service of God.[6]

Nothing being heard either from Father Brevedent or Mr. Poncet, the Fathers Grenier and Paulet two Jesuits, being impatient to go into Aethiopia, set out on their journey thither without staying for proper informations. By the recommendation of the French consul, they were well receiv'd at Sanaar, and being introduced to the Abyssinian ambassador[7] who was then concluding a peace between the two kingdoms, left Sanaar in his

a. Corty *Relation*] Corry *1735*   b. Bihouda *Relation*] Bebouda *1735*   c. Egypt, *1735*

5. SJ deletes a few lines recounting how the murder of a young Abyssinian in the king's palace had disrupted trade between Sennar in the Sudan and Abyssinia (pp. 160–61).

6. Omitting references to Father Brevedent's three days of agony, his feelings of piety, and his continual prayers, SJ has revised the concluding clause: "envisageant la mort avec cette consolation qui accompagne ordinairement ceux qui ayant vécu dans la crainte de Dieu, meurent de la mort des justes" (p. 161).

7. Cf. "un envoyé du Prêtre-Jean" (p. 161).

train on the 26th of May. Had they staid at Cairo long enough to have seen Mr. Poncet's letters, which came sometime after their departure, they would perhaps have been less eager of entering into a kingdom, which it is so difficult to return out of. Mr. Poncet tells the French consul in his letter to him,[8] that in his opinion no missionary will ever be receiv'd in Aethiopia, such an inveterate hatred being conceiv'd there against the Franks, that upon the news of his arrival, the religious to the number of an hundred thousand rose in a tumultuous manner, and the like insurrection happened upon advice that an English ship was seen on their coast; he tells of great favours receiv'd from Negus,[9] and that Agi Ali for having robb'd him and his companion on the road, was closely confined, and that his house was sold for Mr. Poncet's use. This letter was written at Gedda on the 6th of December 1700. In the beginning of January Mr. Poncet set out on his return, and wrote from Suez, that he had seen the Abyssinian ambassador; he arrived at Cairo the 20th of June, and the ambassador on the next day.

Different opinions have been form'd of Murat Eben Magdeloun, for so the ambassador was named; some affirm that they have seen him before at Cairo, in a condition very different from the character he assumed, others say he was the son[1] of Murat, who was then the Emperor's prime minister, and of whom it may not be improper to give some account.[2]

This man settling in Abyssinia in the time of the Emperor Basilides, made several voyages on account of trade to Batavia, and went thither in 1678, where he had those conferences with Paul de Roo[d] which Mr. Ludolf hath publish'd under the name of the *Present State of Aethiopia*. He was receiv'd as Envoy of the Emperor, and persuaded the Dutch to fit out some vessels in prospect of an advantageous trade with the Abyssins, but these vessels returned back with the same lading which they took out. Murat coming again some time after took back with him an envoy from the Dutch[3] East-India Company, and when they

d. Paul de Roo *Relation*] Paul de Rod *1735*

---

8. The information in this clause is extracted from a marginal note (p. 161).
9. The Negus was a ruling prince.
1. The French word is "parent," or kinsman (p. 162).

2. "of whom ... account" substitutes for: "Il est nécessaire pour les raisons qu'on va voir de faire connaître le vieux Murat" (p. 162).
3. SJ has inserted the modifier.

came to Moca, promised to fetch him a passport, which was
necessary for his entering that empire, and demanded the presents which were designed for the Emperor, but being refused
them went away, and the Hollander, having waited a year to no
purpose, came back to Batavia.

Murat Eben Magdeloun was not so dexterous as old Murat;
he imposed on none, but those that were willing to be cheated,
and it was prudent advice which was given him to stay at Cairo,
and entrust Father Verseau superior of the missions of Syria,
the consul's chancellor, and Mr. Poncet, with the letters and
presents from the Emperor of Abyssinia to the King. These
three deputies came to Paris about the end of the year 1701, and
Mr. Poncet made his appearance in that city with a robe and a
bracelet presented him in Abyssinia.

Whilst this surgeon or physician was carried about from house
to house, where being in no danger of contradiction, he vented
his falshoods without scruple; Murat's credentials were examined by persons skill'd in the oriental tongues and acquainted
with the customs and history of the Abyssinians, who could not
find in it any proofs of its being a credential letter, but detected
many faults of the expression and orthography; the confession of
faith which the kings of Abyssinia always make in the beginning
of their letters was very imperfect, and especially they were
surprised to find at the end of the letter, "Given at Gondar, the
capital of Aethiopia." For the word *gondar* or *guender*, as Mr.
Ludolf writes it, signifies only a camp, and Axuma is the capital
of Abyssinia.

Notwithstanding these proofs of forgery, Murat was considered as an ambassador, presents were sent him for himself,
and his master, his charges at Cairo were defray'd by the King's
order, and it was resolved that this embassy should be return'd
by another, and a mission of Jesuits maintain'd in Aethiopia at
the King's expence.

This was what the fathers of the missions wish'd for, and
nothing was talk'd of but uniting to the Catholick Church,
infinite numbers so long separated from it;[4] in the midst of this
discourse arrived at Paris one Ibrahim d'Hanna of the religion

---

4. Cf. the French translation: "réunir à l'eglise catholique une infinité de schisma
tiques ..." (p. 164).

of the Maronites, sent by the Patriarch of Alexandria,[5] who on his landing at Marseilles, wrote by Father Fleuriau's means to the Secretary of the Navy, that the affair might be kept secret, for fear of awakening the jealousy of the Turks; this precaution was too late, the Turks having already published their *olla* or edict[6] to prohibit the Francs from passing into Abyssinia.

While Ibrahim d'Hanna was in France, Father Verseau and Mr. Poncet were pressing the affair at Rome with the most earnest solicitations, being introduced to an audience of the Pope by the Cardinal de Janson himself, and well receiv'd by his Holiness, who in an encomium on the Jesuits term'd them the pillars of the church.[7] But the reformed monks of St. Francis in Italy, having obtain'd two years before a grant of the mission of Aethiopia, in opposition to the claim of the Jesuits, spake with great contempt of the Patriarch of Alexandria, and made no scruple to affirm that the letters brought by Murat[8] and presented to his Holiness by Father Verseau, were counterfeit, and that they had the true ones. It was uncertain which of these bold competitors ought to be credited, Mr. Poncet's letters, however seem to carry evident marks of forgery, as will appear from the words in which the Emperor addresses the Pope.[9] "I am convinced," says he, "that the calamities with which my kingdoms and people have been afflicted, proceed from no other cause than our separation from the head of the Church. Send me two or three skillful missionaries to instruct me in the faith, and repair the loss of Father Brevedent." This good and pious missionary, who died before his arrival at Gondar, was never seen by the Emperor, or known in Abyssinia by any other name than that of Joseph, nor is he mention'd by any other name in the letters to the King of Sanaar.

---

5. Le Grand notes that an account written by this envoy will be found translated into French; it appears in the last third of the *Relation* (pp. 489–97), which SJ did not translate. The Maronite religion is a branch of Roman Catholicism which follows the Syrian of Antioch liturgy, celebrated in Syriac and Arabic.

6. SJ contributes the explanatory paraphrase.

7. And, on the contrary, according to

Le Grand, the Pope "blâma beaucoup la conduite des religieux réformés de Saint François d'Italie" (p. 164).

8. SJ omits the Franciscans' opinion that Murat was "un fourbe & un imposteur" (p. 164).

9. "It was uncertain ... Pope" expands and alters the French translation: "On ne savait qui croire des uns & des autres; mais peut-on penser que le roi d'Abissinie ait écrit au pape en ces termes" (pp. 164–65).

Ibrahim d'Hanna had his charges at Paris defrayed by the mission of Syria, and was treated as an embassador being admitted to many conferences with the Minister of the Navy; he had the honour of concerting the affair with the King, who agreed to all the Patriarch's proposals; and being presented with a gold medal, and furnished with money for his voyage, he left Paris at the end of October, and came to Rome in the beginning of the year 1703, where he had audience of the Pope and of Cardinal Barberino Prefect of the Congregation for Propagating the Faith.[1] Yet notwithstanding the protection and countenance of the Cardinal de Janson, his credit, and the reality of his commission were call'd in question. Nor would the court of Rome come to any determination,[2] till they had sent one Gabriel a Maronite, who was then at Rome, to Cairo, that he might examine the matter to the bottom.

The Patriarch of Alexandria[3] freely own'd that he had sent him, though he had before denied it to the consul of France; and being ask'd whether he had resolved to submit himself to the Pope, and acknowledge the authority of the Church of Rome, he gave the messenger a profession of his faith, sound and orthodox enough, but could never be prevailed on to sign it: this ambiguous behaviour sufficiently acquitted Ibrahim from any suspicion of fraud, but made the intentions of the Patriarch very much suspected.[4]

CHAPTER VI

The miscarriage of Mr. Poncet's second voyage. Mr. du Roule sets out on his journey to Abyssinia; is opposed and calumniated; he arrives at Sanaar, and is assasinated there by the King's command.

In the mean time Mr. Poncet arrived from Rome at Cairo, and made all the necessary dispositions for a second voyage into

---

1. "where he ... Faith" epitomizes a long letter describing in detail the envoy's reception, his interview with the Pope, and a final suggestion that the Pope is going to grant him a secret audience (pp. 165–67).

2. "Nor would ... determination" is based upon: "on résolut avant que de rien faire ... " (p. 167).

3. SJ adds "of Alexandria" for clarification.

4. According to the French, the patriarch's "catholicité" was "très suspecte" (p. 167).

Abyssinia, being accompanied by Murat the ambassador, who was now sent back loaded with presents and testimonials of his good conduct, with letters for the King his master and the prime minister.[1] This company left Cairo on the 6th of October, 1703, in order to go to Suez, where Father de Bernat a Jesuit waited for them, and embarked for Gedda on the 3d of December. They were soon so unhappy as to disagree amongst themselves, Mr. Poncet in a letter makes heavy complaints of Murat, whose disposition, he says, he did not know before this voyage to Gedda. He forgets that it was he who raised him to the dignity of an ambassador, that he was receiv'd upon his word, and being now somewhat dissatisfy'd with his behaviour, endeavours to represent him as a man of the vilest character, and a declared enemy to all Francs, who will, as far as he can, hinder their reception in Aethiopia, and to confirm his assertions, he appeals to Father Bernat. For his own part he declares himself ready to shed his blood for the honour of the King; yet in the midst of all these protestations instead of going forward into Abyssinia, he wanders into other countries, with the chest of medicines bought at the King's charge for this voyage; and abandoning the large possessions which had been given him in Aethiopia, and the wife which he had married there, he after having rambled from place to place,[2] died at Ispahan. Such was the fate of this worthless man who had been too much caressed and believed.

Murat fearing the punishment, which would certainly be inflicted on him at his return into Aethiopia, under pretence of going to Mazua, went to Mascate, and ended his life there. Father Bernat, much chagrin'd at finding himself in so bad company, and entirely disabled from continuing his journey, returned to Cairo in the beginning of April.[3]

All these miscarriages might have discouraged James[a] de Noir better known by the name of Du Roule, who was pitch'd upon to go as ambassador to the Emperor of Aethiopia. He was so far

---

a. James *Errata*] Janus *1735*

---

1. According to the French, they were accompanied by Elias, a Syrian, "précurseur du ministre du roi & son truchement" (p. 167).

2. The French is more specific: he went to Surat (on the west coast of India) from Yemen (p. 168).

3. SJ deletes another reference to Elias, the Syrian.

from being ignorant of what had pass'd, that he had born a
principal part in all these affairs,[4] yet was resolved after having
concerted measures with the Minister of the Navy to run the
hazard. No voyage was ever undertaken with omens less auspi-
cious, or concluded with success less happy.

He embark'd at Toulon on the 26th of December 1703, in
a ship commanded by the Chevalier de Fourbin, who was
appointed to convey thirty six merchant ships to several coasts of
the Mediterranean.[5] In the afternoon there rose so violent a
tempest that the fleet was all dispers'd, and so shatter'd that they
were incapable of pursuing their voyage till the 8th of February.
It is unnecessary to trouble the reader with all the tempests they
felt, all the dangers they were exposed to, and all the obstacles
they met with,[6] which were so many, that they were four months
in sailing from Toulon to Egypt.

Here the ambassador lost no time, but prepared every thing
with the utmost diligence for his journey into Abyssinia, but
some knowledge of his design having, notwithstanding all his
care to keep it secret, got abroad, many difficulties occur'd,
which were only to be surmounted by the power of money.[7]

The Sieur du Roule left Cairo on the 19th of July 1704, and
was followed to the boat by great numbers of people with tears in
their eyes.[8] 'Tis said that the merchants who had openly opposed this expedition at Cairo, still continued to use all their arts
to force him to return, and that the Italian Franciscans imagining that by his means a mission of Jesuits would be established in
Abyssinia, caballing with the merchants,[9] gave notice to the
Arabs of the departure of the Envoy, and engaged them to
threaten that they would rob the caravan, if he was admitted to
travel with it. The Envoy himself adds, that a report was spread

4. The French provides some details of
his involvement (p. 168).

5. "Mediterranean" replaces "Levant"
(p. 168).

6. "It is unnecessary ... met with" has
no equivalent in the French: it epitomizes
a dozen lines of specific details (pp. 168–
69).

7. The French mentions certain individuals who were won over with bribes
(p. 169).

8. SJ deletes the motive for their tears:

they were thinking of "les dangers presque
inévitables où il allait être exposé"
(p. 169).

9. "imagining that ... merchants" attributes to the Franciscans a motive not
found in the French and substitutes for the
term "se joignirent" the less neutral "caballing": the merchants "se joignirent aux
pères de la réforme de Saint François
d'Italie; que les uns & les autres ..."
(p. 169).

at Siout, that he was going to the King of Abyssinia to teach him to make powder and cast cannon, and to engage him in a war against the Turks. The reports, though void of all appearance of truth, were sufficient however to gain credit with this people, who besides their natural suspicion and jealousy, were pleas'd with every thing that gave them an opportunity of squeezing money from him.

The Sieur du Roule had been at great expence in presents to secure Belac the chief of the caravan in his interest, and had received from him many promises of service confirmed by the most solemn oaths, which however had been all broken had not a messenger arrived with fresh orders from the Bassa of Cairo to the commander of Siout, which being read to the chiefs of the caravan,[1] they swore never to separate from the Envoy, but to run all hazards with him.

The commander of Siout told the Envoy all the measures concerted between the French merchants and Italian Franciscans to disappoint his design, and Belac inform'd him that the Patriarch of the Cophtes had insinuated to the chief persons of the caravan, that the Francs who were travelling with them were not merchants, and that their intention was to cut the banks of the Nile, for which reason they ought to be cautious of admitting them into their company.

The caravan left Siout on the 12th of Sept. and after having passed the two desarts,[2] came on the 18th of October to Moscho, where the Envoy was inform'd, that the Italian Franciscans had left Sanaar, whether on their own accord or by compulsion he doth not say. This was the last letter receiv'd from the Sieur du Roule, what news was afterwards heard of him came by indirect ways, and a report was spread about the country that he was assassinated, a melancholly presage of what afterwards came to pass.

He arrived at Sanaar about the end of May 1705, where he was received with great marks of respect; the King sent two of his officers to meet him,[3] and lodged him in the house of his late

---

1. "had received ... caravan" reduces a third of a page of detailed description (pp. 169–70).

2. "after having ... desarts" is more succinct than the detailed quarter-page account in the French with its remarks on a greedy governor who had to be bribed (p. 170).

3. The French adds that a feast was arranged for the envoy and presents exchanged (p. 171).

prime minister, whom he had not long before put to death. The minister who succeeded him, seem'd inclined to enter into an intimate acquaintance with the French Envoy, coming often to see him, and entertaining him at his own house with great familiarity; he even gave him some hints that he had a mind to go with him into Abyssinia.

Hitherto every thing answer'd the Envoy's wishes, and 'tis said, that the cause of his fatal end, was, that he reposed too much confidence in the King and his first minister, and neglecting to secure the good-will of the other officers, exasperated them to his ruin. The accident which put it in their power to do him so great an injury, was this.[4] The King having obtain'd a victory over his rebels, there was a publick feast kept at Sanaar. The Envoy thinking he ought on this occasion to display all his magnificence, had set out some looking-glasses, which brought all the city to his house; the King's women who are rarely permitted to go out, could not forbear gratifying their curiosity with a view of these rarities, and above all were astonish'd at those glasses which multiply objects, and imagining this could not be the effect of natural causes, represented the Envoy and his retinue as magicians, who had ill designs against the King. The whole show added new incitements to the avarice of the officers, and perhaps of the King himself, so that, a few days after, he sent to demand of the Envoy three thousand piasters, and being refused, let the ambassador know by Macé his interpreter, that his refusal might bring him and his retinue into danger. The demand was repeated several times, and Mr. du Roule still continued obstinate. Not to protract the relation,[5] on the 25th of November the King sent three hundred men to seize the Envoy in his house with all his retinue, and carrying them into the market-place, first cut him in pieces,[6] and afterwards his attendants. The Envoy underwent his fate with great resolution, and exhorted his company to behave themselves in the same manner. Their bodies lay exposed for some time, and it was observed that neither bird nor beast of prey did them any injury.

4. This sentence replaces Le Grand's comment that "les irrita à un point que tous conspirèrent de le ruiner dans l'esprit du roi leur maître & de le perdre. Ils eurent assez de peine à en venir à bout" (p. 171).

5. "Not ... relation" grows from "Enfin" (p. 171).

6. "first cut ... pieces" adds a nasty flourish to: "il fut massacré le premier" (p. 171).

CHAPTER VII

Several revolutions happen'd in Abyssinia. The Emperor's letter relating to the death of Mr. du Roule. The endeavours of the French consul to revenge it.

One Elias a Syrian who was to have attended Mr. du Roule as his interpreter, had arrived at the dominions of Negus,[1] and having told that prince, according to his instructions, that the French profess'd the same religion with the Cophtes, had been well received, and upon this recommendation was permitted by the Emperor[2] to return to Mr. du Roule, and one of his officers was named to go with him in compliment to the Envoy, and was order'd to provide him all the carriages he had occasion for in his journey from Sanaar. This officer unhappily spent too much time either in getting ready his equipages, or other amusements, and came to Sanaar, three days after the murther of the Envoy.

The King of Sanaar and his council imagined they might excuse their crime by charging Mr. du Roule and his company with magick, but the Abyssin returned very little satisfied with this plea.

A great revolution happen'd at that time in Abyssinia, by a revolt of the people, who being headed by the Emperor's eldest son, dethroned the Emperor and put him to death. The cause of this general defection is not known, indeed if we could be convinced of the genuineness of the letter presented by the Recolet missionaries to the Pope, there would be no need of enquiring farther. It appears from Mr. Poncet's narrative how nice the nation and particularly the clergy are in every thing that bears the least relation to religion, and how much they detest the Europeans; their aversion even extends to every thing that is white.

It was not known at Cairo, when the account was received of the assassination of the Envoy, what was the fate of the deposed Emperor, some affirmed that he was kill'd, others maintain'd that he conceal'd himself in some corner of his kingdom, in expectation of a favourable opportunity to attack his son.

---

1. Having suppressed earlier references to Elias, SJ here introduces him with the phrase, "One Elias." His arrival "at the dominions of Negus" is once again an odd translation of "au pays du Negus" (p. 172).

2. "le Prêtre-Jean" (p. 172).

Elias the interpreter, who was on the road to meet the Envoy, having heard of this new revolution in Abyssinia, went back, and put the letters which he had receiv'd from Jasou[a] the late King, into the hands of Teklimanout who had newly taken possession of the throne. Teklimanout directed that they should be copied in his own name, and commanded Elias to take the road to Sanaar; Elias in pursuance of the King's order set out, and was come within three day's journeys of Sanaar, when he heard of the Envoy's unfortunate end, then thinking it not proper to proceed farther, returned to the Emperor, who was enraged at the relation of the massacre, and in his passion wrote the following letter.[3]

> To the Pacha, and the Lords Commanders of the Militia at Cairo, from the King of Abyssinia, the King Teklimanout, Son of the King of the Church of Abyssinia.

> From the august King, powerful arbiter of nations; the shadow of God upon earth, the guide of the kings who profess the religion of the Messiah, the most mighty of Christian kings, he who keeps peace between the Musulmans and Christians, protector[b] of the boundaries of Alexandria; observer of the precepts of the Gospel, inheriting from his father a mighty kingdom; issue of the lineage of David, and Solomon. May the blessing of Israel be upon our Prophet, and upon them; may their felicity be lasting, their power permanent, and their mighty forces always formidable. To the mighty Lord exalted by his power, venerable for his merits, distinguish'd by his strength and wealth among the Musulmans, the refuge of all that reverence him, whose prudence governs and guides the army of the noble empire, and commands upon its frontiers, the victorious Viceroy of Egypt, the confines of which shall always be defended and reverenced, so be it. And to all illustrious princes, judges, doctors, and other officers, who are constituted for the support of order and government, and in general to all potentates; may God preserve them in their high stations,

a. Jasou Relation] Jason 1735   b. protectors 1735

---

3. The literal translation of the letter (pp. 173–74) contrasts with SJ's general practice.

and in the dignity of salvation. It is known to you that our ancestors have never been at enmity with other kings, nor ever given them any molestation, or shown any token of malice. But on the contrary, afforded proofs of their friendship on all occasions, in generously assisting them, in relieving their necessities, whether in matters relating to the caravan and pilgrims of Mecca, in Arabia the Happy, in India, Persia, or other remote and unfrequented places, in succouring those who labour'd under pressing necessities. Nevertheless the King of France our brother, who professeth the same law, and the same faith, having been moved by such tokens of amity exhibited on our part, as ought to be practised, and having sent an ambassador to us, I am inform'd, that you have stop'd him at Sanaar and also Morad the Syrian, sent by us to the ambassadors, whom you have put under an arrest, and have by so doing violated the law of nations; since the ambassadors of kings ought to be at liberty, and to pass where they will, and to be treated with honour, and not hinder'd or molested: neither ought any dues or tribute to be exacted from them. It is in our power to return the injury, if we pleas'd to revenge the insult offer'd by you to our messenger. The Nile might be made the instrument of our vengeance, God having placed in our hands its fountain, its passage, and its encrease, and put it in our power to make it do good or harm.[4] At present we require and exhort you to cease from offering any injury to our ambassadors, and from disquieting us by stopping those who are on their way to us. You shall suffer them without hindrance to continue their journey, going and coming freely according to their own convenience, whether they be our subjects or those of France, and whatever you shall do to them, we shall esteem done to our selves.

Subscribed. To the Pacha, Princes, and Lords Commanders in the city of Grand Cairo, whom God favour with his mercies. This letter is written in Arabick without date.

The crime of Teklimanout in robbing his father of his crown and life, made him detested by all mankind, his reign was short

---

4. "and put it ... good or harm" goes a step beyond the French translation "& que nous pouvons en disposer pour faire le mal" (p. 174).

and unquiet, and ended at last in his being assassinated by his own troops as he was preparing to march against the King of Sanaar. Tetilis the brother of Ayasou[c] or Jasou[5] succeeded him, and after a reign of three years and some months was dethroned by Oustas his sister's son and his first minister. Oustas was soon deposed by David, the second son of Ayasou.[c] All these revolutions happening in a very short time prevented the Abyssins from punishing the murder of Mr. du Roule. The French[6] consul who had born the greatest part in the direction of this embassy, sought all opportunities of revenging the Envoy's death, and calling the French merchants at Cairo together, told them how he had been cut in pieces[7] in sight of the King of Sanaar, animating them to join with him in seeking some means of revenging so publick an injustice. They immediately came to an agreement to discharge all the Nubians that were in their service. A memorial was likewise given to the Bassa who was going to take upon him the command of Suaquem and Mazua, and that side of Aethiopia, entreating him to lend his assistance in the punishment of the King of Sanaar for a crime committed against the law of nations, and in the recovery of thirty thousand piasters, and four thousand sequins, which the Envoy had with him at the time when he was kill'd. The largeness of this sum is a sufficient proof at how vast an expence this mighty design of penetrating into Abyssinia, and of establishing a trade, and the Catholick religion in that country is to be carried on, a design which to all who have any knowledge of that empire and its inhabitants will appear chimerical and impracticable.[8]

c. Ayasou *Relation*] Ayason *1735*

---

5. SJ adds the alternative name Jason (here corrected to Jasou).

6. SJ inserts the nationality.

7. "had been . . . pieces" is not required

by the French: "avait été assassiné" (p. 174).

8. SJ adds this final adjective.

Dissertations Relating to the History of Abyssinia

A DISSERTATION UPON MR. LUDOLF'S
HISTORY OF ABYSSINIA

I know not any man in Europe who has apply'd himself to the study of the Abyssin language with so much assiduity as the late Mr. Ludolf, he hath labour'd in it near sixty years with very little assistance, and without being discouraged by any difficulties. If this language be not more known in Europe than it is, or is likely ever to be, 'tis not to be imputed to him, who has spared no pains to facilitate the study of it. He has given us a grammar and a dictionary, and has inserted in his history long passages written in that language, extracted out of manuscripts; yet all this hath not yet prevail'd with many to become his disciples. We have scarce any intercourse with the Abyssins, it is difficult to pass into their country, and still more difficult to pass out of it, and had not the Portuguese been at several times call'd into Abyssinia, we had known no more of it than we do of the more inland kingdoms of Africa, or of those southern countries into which no man hath yet entred. Besides there are very few writings in that language, either printed or manuscript;[a] the Abyssins excelling in no kind of literature, have publish'd scarce any books, and those which they have publish'd, cannot be procur'd; no man would employ his life in mastering a language of no use either in commerce or learning. The example of Mr. Ludolf himself far from giving any invitation to that study, is sufficient to divert any such design,[1] for after having made the knowledge of that tongue his principal employment, after having laid out all his time upon it, and read every thing that could be found written in it, he had[b] not been in a condition to write ten pages of the history of Abyssinia, had he not had recourse to that of Father Baltazar Tellez a Portuguese Jesuit.[2]

---

a. manuscript, *1735*   b. he had *Errata*] had *1735*

---

1. "Besides there are ... design" rearranges elements in the French translation (p. 178; misnumbering of the inner forme of this gathering results in the following pagination: 177, 182, 183, 180, 181, 178, 183. Citations will refer to the *actual* page rather than to the page as numbered in Le Grand.).

2. For Telles, see Introduction, p. xxxiv–xxxv.

Gregory that learned Abyssin, on whom he heaps so many commendations is certainly a very bad guide, and we cannot help saying, that either Mr. Ludolf and Gregory did not understand one another, or that Gregory was very ignorant in his own religion; for no Abyssin who had enjoy'd the least advantages of instruction ever embraced those sentiments or declared them: but whatever might be his qualities the Patriarch Alphonso Mendez, who hath taken so much care to transmit to posterity the names of those that adhered to him, hath not said a word of him. This omission is no proof that he had greater abilities, or an exacter knowledge of his religion than others, and his whole conduct, and all his answers to Mr. Ludolf are contradictions to the many praises bestow'd upon him. Where this Abyssin fails him, Mr. Ludolf produces another evidence whose authority is of equal weight. This is Murat the Armenian, who, when he was trading at Batavia, was examined, at Mr. Ludolf's request, about the present state of religion in Abyssinia. Murat whose thoughts were more upon his merchandise, than any thing else, was not very capable of making any satisfactory answer to their enquiries; nor can I easily persuade myself that he would have gratified them with an exact information though he had been able to do it; this was the man[3] who imposed upon the Hollanders with promises of a wealthy commerce on the coasts of the Red-Sea as hath been already related.[4]

But what need there was of the testimony of either Gregory or Murat is not easy to understand; nor can any just reason be assign'd, why he did not rather consult the liturgies which he had in his possession; why he neglected to publish them when he was press'd to it; why he wrote to Batavia rather than to Cairo, and enquired of the Dutch merchants rather than of the Patriarch of Alexandria. We should wonder at the conduct of that man who should write to Armenia, for information about the religion of the Moscovites, and should address himself to the Armenian traders rather than to the Patriarch of Moscow: there would be strong reasons for saying that if his search was after truth, he took very uncommon methods to discover it, yet in this manner has Mr. Ludolf acted, and has been guilty of the greatest absurdities in his account of the creed of the Abyssins.

---

3. "un vieux fourbe" (p. 178).   about the unsuccessful Dutch trading mis-
4. "as ... related" replaces a comment   sions to the Red Sea ports (p. 178).

Several learned men were dissatisfied with Mr. Ludolf's work, and amongst the rest Mr. Piques one of his correspondents wrote his opinion to him with so much freedom, that notwithstanding the friendship between them, it was the occasion of a difference.[5] Some of the letters that pass'd between them having been communicated to the author of these dissertations by Father Le Quien, the reader may not be displeased with an extract from them.

Mr. Ludolf observes[6] to Mr. Piques the necessity of a nice discernment to distinguish truth from falshood in the relations of the Abyssinian affairs, and remarks how little credit is to be given to the narratives of the missionaries, who prove their zeal for the Catholick religion by inventing false accounts, or by depending upon false information. Some from ignorance and unskilfulness, others from insincerity and disregard of truth;[7] and charges Wansleb of having been guilty of the latter in those accounts of Egypt which he hath published in Europe, loading both his writings, and his personal character with the severest censures.[8] He speaks of a collection of the subscriptions of the eastern bishops, testifying their belief of the doctrine of transubstantiation, kept in the Abby of St. German. On this he lays no great stress, and declares it as his opinion, that the eastern churches, if they hold a transubstantiation, believe only that the bread is changed into the body of Christ, according to his words literally taken. "This is my body which is given for you," and not into his person as consisting of soul and body, of the divine and the human nature, and consequently that since they do not imagine it transformed into the divine nature, they do not adore it as God. The soul and divine nature of our Saviour (they say) was not given for us, and therefore admitting the literal sense of the words, the bread is not transformed into that nature. He approves the notion of Mr. de Piques, that in order to arrive at the knowledge of the religion of any country, their catechisms

---

5. This sentence epitomizes a paragraph quoting Renaudot, who refers to a number of writers disagreeing with Ludolf. In addition to Piques, Thévenot and d'Herbelot are cited (p. 179).

6. After ignoring the first half page of this letter, SJ occasionally translates literally but more often epitomizes throughout

the long paragraph that follows. Cf. pp. 180–81 in Le Grand.

7. "others from ... truth" alters the French somewhat: "quelques-uns aussi par malice & méchanceté" (p. 180).

8. "loading both ... censures" is SJ's evaluative summary of the comments in the letter. Cf. pp. 180–81.

and liturgies ought to be consulted; and that it is^c not safe to depend upon depositions procured *prece vel pretio*, by entreaties or bribes,[9] or answers made to questions proposed by one party, without admitting those of the contrary opinion to use the same method of examination. He says that the ambassador who procured this heap of testimonies, by convening an assembly of bishops and priests who subscribed to these opinions, might have saved both his labour and his money, if he had only made extracts of their confessions, catechisms and liturgies, which would have sufficiently explain'd their true sentiments.[1] He concludes with a postscript that Mr. de Piques does him wrong in imagining he gives more credit to the Armenian than to Wansleb or Olearius.

Mr. de Piques in his answer to Mr. Ludolf,[2] observes that to inform one's self of the religion of a country, it is not sufficient to enquire of the first man that can be met with, that application ought to be made to those who profess it, and that even the answers of one of those can never be a sufficient foundation for a positive assertion unless corroborated by the authority of more.[3] That it is unfair to embarrass them with studied and sophistical interrogatories, and that the most probable way of discovering the truth, is to desire a plain narrative account of their opinions and practice, and to act as if we were desirous of being their converts. There is nothing in this conduct (says he) of artifice or insidiousness. He then taxes Mr. Ludolf with a neglect of this method, and with endeavouring by various questions, to insnare Gregory, and draw from him an answer conformable to his own inclinations; and remarks with an air of triumph, that the answers of Murat the Armenian are not agreeable to the character of ignorance given him by Mr. Ludolf. He relates a conversation with two gentlemen who having read Mr. Ludolf's book, make no difficulty of insinuating that he has been defective in impartiality and sincerity, and in a second letter after some

c. it is] is *1735*

9. SJ provides a translation not found in Le Grand (p. 182) for the Latin phrase.
1. Ludolf's letter concludes with a paragraph of miscellaneous information on books and other matters (p. 182).
2. SJ deletes the first two paragraphs of

Piques's letter (p. 183).
3. "that application ought...of more" expands the remark: "qu'il faut s'adresser à un homme de la profession, & même à plusieurs consécutivement" (p. 183).

compliments pursues his design of proving the same opinions to be held by the Aethiopian as by the Roman Church.[4]

These two letters were written with so much heat and zeal in defence of the Roman Church which he perceived attack'd, that Mr. Ludolf could not bear the freedom taken with his character, and his resentment rose so high, that their correspondence was intirely broken off.

These letters may furnish us with instances of some inconsistency in Mr. Ludolf's conduct, who has given the world[5] the answers of the Armenian Murat or Morad, as an authentick and satisfactory account of the present state of Abyssinia, particularly with respect to religion;[6] he is pleas'd to forget that the Armenian merchants who like Murat ramble over the world, seldom have any other religion than their traffick. But when in a private correspondence he is press'd to declare the truth, he confesses that the Armenian is a man so ignorant that, like Mahomet, he neither could write nor read, and adds in the conclusion of his letter; you do me wrong if you imagine I give more credit to the Armenian than to Wansleb or Olearius. How Mr. Ludolf will reconcile this character of his informer, with the regard which he has shewn to his information is not easy to discover; he has publish'd the answers of this illiterate Armenian, in thirty two folio pages, with the pompous title[7] of, *A New Account of the Present State of Abyssinia, lately brought from the Indies.* It was sure with some other intention than of swelling his volume, or of shewing that besides his knowledge of the Aethiopick language which was of little use to him in compiling his history, he had nothing that could recommend him to the esteem of the world.[8]

---

4. "He then taxes ... Roman Church" is one of the more succinct epitomes SJ offers, summarizing Piques's two letters (pp. 183–92).

5. "These letters ... world" is more general than the French: "Mais nous ne pouvons nous empêcher d'observer ici combien M. Ludolf varie dans ses sentiments, lui qui traite si mal Wansleb pour n'avoir pas pensé de même étant catholique & religieux, qu'il faisait étant protestant. M. Ludolf n'a point de honte de faire imprimer ... " (p. 192).

6. The questions and answers appear (pp. 25–31) in the *Appendix ad Historiam Aethiopicam Iobi Ludolfi Illiusque Commentarium, ex Nova Relatione, De hodierno Habessiniae Statu ...* (1693).

7. SJ has added the phrase, "with the pompous title," and has translated the Latin title into English (p. 193).

8. "he had nothing ... world" bears little resemblance to the French: "il ne savait guère de chose, & que son *nasus criticus,* n'était pas fort long" (p. 193).

His answer to the second question proposed to him is a sufficient proof either of his ignorance or his falshood.[9] Being ask'd, "Who was the present King of Abyssinia, what was his name, and who were his progenitours." He answers, "That Susneus who embraced the Roman religion, after having struggled with many bloody wars, and intestine commotions died in the year 1632, leaving his kingdom involved in calamities; but his son Basilides having thrown off the religion of Rome, and expell'd the fathers of the mission, reigned thirty two years undisturb'd, and by many victories re-establish'd the power of the Abyssins then almost expiring, and restor'd his kingdom to a flourishing condition."[1] Murat, 'tis evident was either himself unacquainted with the subject he talk'd of, or knowingly imposed upon the enquirers, when he told them of the quiet reign of Basilides. The persecution of the Jesuits began in 1632, they were expell'd in 1634, after which many missionaries and Catholicks were put to death. The many calamities that happen'd to the kingdom, are related in a letter of Father Bernard Nogueira, which affords abundant proof, that King Basilides was guilty of putting his brother to death, and of sending to the King of Yemen for Mahometan preachers to convert his people, so that Mr. Ludolf has no just reason to call in question facts so well attested;[2] but he sometimes supplies a deficiency in his memoirs out of his own imagination, and expects of his readers that they should be satisfied with weak reasons when he has no stronger to offer. While Mr. Ludolf had Gregory with him, he made him say what he pleas'd, and Gregory was his only favourite; he procured his picture to be engrav'd and wrote his encomium. "Now," says he, "we come to Gregory the Abyssin, to whom we are indebted for a great part of our Aethiopick history, and for a more exact knowledge of the Abyssinian tongue. He had in his youth applied himself to learning, and such was his proficiency, that he acquired great reputation among his countrymen, and was dignified with the title of Abba."[3]

---

9. This sentence has no counterpart in the French (p. 193).

1. SJ translates the question and answer from the Latin (p. 193).

2. "The many calamities ... attested"

compresses and rearranges material; SJ omits Le Grand's defence of Father Telles against Ludolf's attacks (pp. 193–94).

3. SJ translates this quotation from the Latin (p. 194).

Mr. Ludolf would have been perhaps much at a loss, if it had been demanded, what course of studies this celebrated Abyssin had pass'd through; and what became of his genius after he arrived at Germany; for however he may praise him, he sometimes makes him speak like a man whose genius was not very elevated, or learning very extensive, and has himself very much diminish'd his encomiums in the preface to the last edition of his dictionary. "As to Gregory my Abyssinian," says he, "whose authority I sometimes made use of in the preface to my former edition, he, though a man of some learning, was often doubtful about the signification of words which more rarely occur, and of very many was entirely ignorant, as he made no scruple to confess in his letters and conversation."[4] This is the doctor, whom Mr. Ludolf consults, and follows in his account of the religion of Abyssinia, this is the man whose authority he prefers to the liturgies that were in his hands and which he was importuned to make publick. No man, 'tis true, in Europe hath ever equal'd, or perhaps ever will equal Mr. Ludolf in the knowledge of the Ethiopick language; but that knowledge hath been of no great advantage to him in writing his history. As to any use it might have been of to the Church, Mr. Ludolf's insincerity hath deprived us of it. The Abyssins are Jacobites, but he hath represented them as Lutherans or Calvinists, and while he endeavours to excuse some abuses which have crept in amongst them, charges them with erroneous tenets which they do not hold. He hath transformed the Church of Abyssinia into an imaginary church which hath no existence but in his own imagination.[5]

John-Michael Wansleb, whom Mr. Ludolf treats with so much severity,[6] was a native of Erford, who having learn'd the Ethiopick language under Mr. Ludolf, was sent by the Duke of Saxony to pass, if possible, into Abyssinia, and collect all the liturgies he could meet with; Mr. Ludolf having insinuated to

4. SJ translates this quotation from the Latin (p. 195).

5. SJ omits a page in which Le Grand discusses Ludolf's defence of Peter Heyling, the Lutheran proselytizer, as a traveller among the Abyssinians; Le Grand praises Wansleben for having been in upper Egypt and criticizes Ludolf for merely conjecturing about the Ethiopian religion (pp. 195–96).

6. An inserted descriptive clause.

this prince that those liturgies would furnish some arguments in favour of Lutheranism. Wansleb could not go into Abyssinia, but met, however, with a great number of liturgies, part of which he purchased, and upon examining them was convinced of his errors, and, being converted, took the Dominican habit at Rome. Afterwards going into France, he was presented to Mr. Colbert,[7] by Mr. Bosquet Bishop of Montpellier, as a person of extraordinary skill in the Oriental tongues. That minister, whose chief enquiry was after men capable of executing those grand designs he had form'd of spreading his master's glory through the world, was in extasies at meeting this man, whom he sent very soon into the Levant, with a commission to purchase all the Oriental manuscripts he could find. Wansleb bought above five hundred manuscripts and sent them to the King's library, but could not pursue his orders of passing into Aethiopia. He return'd to France, in 1676, and died a few years after.

He had printed at London in 1661, the liturgy of Dioscorus Patriarch of Alexandria, and publish'd in 1671 before he embark'd in his second voyage, a project or list of the books he proposed to publish in the Aethiopick language, with an account in Italian of the present state of Egypt. And after his return he gave the world a journal of his voyage to Egypt in 1672 and 1673, and after that an history of the Church of Alexandria.[8]

Whoever reads these works will be surprized to find him spoken of by Mr. Ludolf with such an air of contempt; though Mr. Ludolf was his master in the Aethiopick language, there were many things in which he might have been his scholar.[9] After all Mr. Ludolf is not to be refused the praises he deserves, for having apply'd himself with so much diligence and labour to the study of a language, which before his time had been very little known in Europe.

7. Jean-Baptiste Colbert, Minister of Louis XIV and uncle of Colbert de Torcy, Le grand's employer.
8. Wansleben's *Histoire de l'eglise d'Alexandrie* was published in Paris (1677).
9. SJ omits a passage which criticizes Ludolf, suggests that his reputation has deceived people, and concludes: "Comme nous aurons occasion de parler dans les Dissertations suivantes des fautes particulières dans lesquelles il est tombé, nous nous contenterons de ce que nous en venons de dire" (p. 197).

DISSERTATION THE SECOND,
UPON AETHIOPIA, OR ABYSSINIA

The ancients have call'd all those countries that extend themselves beyond Egypt on each side of the Red-Sea indifferently India or Aethiopia. Strabo tells us that the country on the south coast was nam'd Aethiopia,[1] which appellation though these regions have since taken several names, they have long preserv'd. In Scripture all the black nations are call'd *Chus*, which word not only by the author of the Vulgar, but likewise by all the interpreters as well Greek as Latin, is universally render'd Aethiopia or Aethiopian. We read in the 12th chapter of Numbers, that Aaron and Miriam were extremely enraged at Moses for having married an Aethiopian woman. Now Sephora, the wife of Moses and Raguel her brother were Midianites, which puts it beyond all controversy, that the country now call'd Arabia, was heretofore call'd the Eastern Aethiopia, to distinguish it from the Aethiopia of Africk. The eastern people on the contrary call'd those kingdoms India which we call Ethiopia or Abyssinia. Both their historians, and the Greek and Latin writers say, that St. Frumentius who travel'd into Ethiopia, was sent by St. Athanasius to India, and that the Indians had desired bishops from Simon the Syrian, Patriarch of Alexandria: and the Persians to this day call an Ethiopian, Siah, Hindou, or Hindi. It is difficult to assign the exact limits of the Asiatick Ethiopia on the east side, we are only certain that it was separated from that of Africa by the Red-Sea. Thus Theodoret having ask'd who the people of Saba were, the answer is, they are a nation of Ethiopia.[2] " 'Tis said, that this nation inhabits the coast of the Indian-Sea; they are call'd Homerites, and are

---

1. Of the seventeen surviving books in Strabo's *Geography*, Book 16 treats the Ethiopian coasts and Arabia, and Book 17 is concerned with Egypt, Ethiopia, and northern Africa. Item 347 in *The Sale Catalogue of Samuel Johnson's Library* is "Strabonis geographia"; as Greene notes, "there were several 16th- to 18th-century editions" (*Library*, p. 107).

2. Theodoret, fifth-century B.C. Greek historian and Bishop of Cyrrhus in northern Syria, was a friend of Nestorius and consequently an opponent of Cyril, Patriarch of the Church of Alexandria. A translation of his work appeared in 1612 as *The Ecclesiasticall History of Theodoret Bishop of Cyrus*.

opposite to the Axumites with nothing but the sea between them; that admirable woman was their queen whose zeal hath been praised[a] by our Saviour Jesus Christ. Philostorgus places the Sabaeans among the nations of India.[3] The Sabaeans a people of India, so named from Saba the capital of their country, are the same with the Homerites." L. 3. C.4.[4]

These Sabaeans or Homerites were a powerful nation, and possessed a country of wide extent between the Persian and Arabian Gulph, and so numerous were their people that 'tis pretended, the Abyssins are a colony from them. In this almost all authors agree. Uranius in Stephanus, Byzantinus, Ptolomy, and Arrian, even place the Abyssins in Arabia.[5] 'Tis yet highly probable that this excursion was made long before these historians and geographers, and perhaps before the Sabaeans or Homerites were known, or distinguish'd by those names. Eusebius declares,[6] that the Abyssins removed out of Asia into Africk in the time that the Jews were in Egypt, that is about the 2345th year from the creation of the world, Syncellus[7] places this migration somewhat later, about the age of the Judges.

Diodorus of Sicily[8] however maintains that the Ethiopians

a. praised *1789* (loué *Relation*)] practised *1735*

3. Existing only in fragments, the church history of Philostorgius covers the period from 300 to 430 and is written from an Arian point of view. An edition of the *Ecclesiasticae Historiae* with dissertations by Jacques Godefroy (Gothofredus) appeared in 1642. See *Library*, p. 91.

4. SJ includes the bare reference to L. 3. C. 4. as he found it in Le Grand, who seems to have taken it from Ludolf's *Commentarius*. A version of the quoted material appears in Godefroy's dissertation on Book 3, Chap. 4 of Philostorgius's *Ecclesiasticae Historiae* (1642), p. 105.

5. Some time after A.D. 400 Stephanus of Byzantium wrote a massive geographical lexicon which "must have included many extracts from ancient authors, with notices of historical events and famous personages" (Sandys, I, 371). In the *History* Ludolf remarks: "Stephanus in his book concerning cities, upon the word

Abasseni, writes, Abasseni, a nation of Arabia, and relates out of the Arabicks of Uranius, that they bordered upon the Sabeans" (p. 8). Ptolemy of Alexandria, writing between A.D. 121 and 151, produced a *Geography* consisting of eight books and an atlas of maps; see *Library*, p. 94. Among the works of Arrian, a second-century governor of Cappadocia in Asia Minor, is the *Indike*, an account of India.

6. Eusebius (*c.* 260–*c.* 340), Bishop of Caesarea in ancient Palestine, probably best known for his *History of the Christian Church*. SJ owned a number of copies (*Library*, p. 57).

7. Probably George Syncellus (d. *c.* 810), who lived for a time in Palestine and wrote a chronicle of the world up to the reign of Diocletian.

8. Diodorus Siculus wrote a history of the world in 40 books up to the time of Caesar's Gallic War.

never knew any other country than that which they inhabit, and that they never had been corrupted by foreign customs; but the Abyssins are so different from the neighbouring nations, that no man will suppose they have the same original. The Abyssins are well shap'd, their features are commonly sufficiently regular, their eyes large and lively, their colour rather olive than black, and their hair long which they have a thousand ways of dressing. The women of distinction are there tolerably white. The other Ethiopians have noses big and wide, thick lips,[9] and hair curled like wool.

Auleddin Aboulfadhi surnamed Assiouthi, hath written two books on those people[1] which the Arabs comprehend under the general name of Soudans or blacks; one of these books is one continued encomium on the Ethiopians, whom he stiles flowers that grow round the thrones of the sultans, because those princes generally employ'd them near their persons, and in offices of the greatest trust. Whatever is the reason, there hath always been a great intercourse between the Abyssins and Sabaeans, or Homerites. The passage from one kingdom to the other is neither long nor difficult, and perhaps they have been formerly under the same master, and the Queen of the South ruled over all these countries. Theodoret, Procopius of Gaza, and Procopius of Caesarea[2] call them equally Aethiopians, distinguishing those of Asia by the addition of Homerites, and those of Africa by that of Axumites, from Axum, or Axuma, the capital in former times of Abyssinia.

The Aethiopia of Africa hath been of much greater extent than that of Asia; Homer tells us, that it reach'd from one sea to the other, and beheld both the rising and the setting sun.[3] It is now divided into three parts; the western Aethiopia containing the kingdoms of Congo, Angola and Benguela, the eastern Aethiopia of which Father John des Santos a Portuguese Dominican hath given us a large and curious history more than an

---

9. SJ omits one other attribute: "le teint très noir" (p. 200).

1. Assiouthi, or Abulfeda, a Syrian prince (d. 1331), wrote both a geography and a history. SJ owned a 1723 translation and abridgement of his life of Mohammed (*Library*, p. 25).

2. Procopius of Gaza, a rhetorician active between 491 and 527, is best known for his paraphrases of Homer; Procopius of Caesarea, a historian and public official in Constantinople, traveled in Asia and Africa before his death in 565.

3. *Odyssey*, I, 22 ff.

hundred years since;[4] this division extends from Sofala to Cape
Gardafui, and runs far up into the inland parts. The third is
upper Aethiopia, of which the reader hath here met with an
account, and which I am endeavouring to make more known.
Abyssinia heretofore extended itself from the seventh degree
to the seventeenth, and comprised thirty-six kingdoms and
provinces,[5] but its territories are much contracted since the
revolt of the Galles, which began about the year 1537. So that
the Emperor of Abyssinia now is only master of the kingdoms of
Tigre, Dambia, Bagameder, Goiam, Amhara, part of Choaa,
and Narea, with the provinces of Mazaga, Salent, Ogara,
Abargale, Seguade, Olcait, Semen, Salaoa, Holeca, and Doba.
The kingdom of Tigre is the most considerable part of
Abyssinia, its length from Mazua to the desart of Aldoba and
Mount-Semen is three hundred Italian miles,[6] its breadth from
the province of Bur to the same desart is near equal. Axum or
Axuma which the Portuguese who first visited this country
call'd by corruption Cachumo or Chassumo, hath been the
capital of this kingdom and of all Abyssinia, and hath in some
measure given its name to the whole country. As the Abyssins
were heretofore ignorant of the use of lime,[7] the buildings of this
city could not be very extraordinary; yet there may still be seen
the remains of a magnificent temple which have supported
themselves against the injuries of time. It is an hundred and ten
feet in length,[8] it had two wings on each side, and a double
porch, with an ascent of twelve steps; the Emperor, when he is
crown'd here, sits on a throne of stone in the inner-porch.
Behind this temple are several obelisks of different bigness, some

---

4. João dos Santos, *Ethiopia Oriental, e
Varia Historia de Cousas notaveis do Oriente*
(Evora, 1609).

5. SJ omits half a page of detailed geographical information drawn, according
to Le Grand's marginal note, from a
manuscript of Patriarch Afonso Mendes
(pp. 200–01).

6. Echard's *Gazetteer* (1724 ed.) indicates that an English mile of 5280
"London feet" is a little longer than an
Italian mile; 69 English miles "and somewhat more" equal "a degree of the earth's

surface, though a degree has generally
been reckoned but 60 miles" while "76
Italian miles are nearest a degree"
(A3v–A4r).

7. The 1735 text prints "the line" for
"lime," either a printing or aural error
which might have occurred during SJ's
dictation to Hector: the word in the
Relation is "la chaux" (p. 201), or lime,
used in making mortar.

8. Cf. "Il pouvait avoir deux cents vingt
palmes de longueur sur cent de largeur"
(p. 201).

of which have been thrown down by the Turks, others are yet standing; among the rubbish is a great square stone on which appear the remains of an inscription so effaced by time, that it is not legible, and nothing can be distinguish'd except some Greek and Latin letters and the word *basilius*.

Three leagues distant from Axum is Fremona, the first and principal seat of the Jesuits, formerly call'd Maegoga, from the murmur of a rivulet that runs near it, which the fathers changed to that of Fremona, in honour of Saint Fremona or Frumentius the apostle of the Abyssins. There is reason to believe that this place already illustrious by the death of the holy Father Andrew Oviedo, patriarch of Aethiopia, and other venerable missionaries, would have encreas'd in reputation, had it pleas'd God to have continued his blessing to the Aethiopian mission.

The Patriarch Alphonso Mendez pretends, that there are forty four governments in the kingdom of Tigre:[9] Mr. Ludolf reckons up but twenty seven, and seven maritime governments which being separated from the general viceroyship of the kingdom, have a peculiar deputy assigned them, with the title *Bahr Nagus*, or Intendant of the Sea.

The kingdom of Angote is almost entirely laid waste by the Galles, and only a small part of it is now subject to the Emperor. The kingdom of Bagameder lyes westward of Angote, and extends to the Nile, it is now only sixty leagues in length, and twenty in breadth, it was formerly much larger, but several provinces are now dismembred from it, as Abargale, Semen, Ogara, Segued, Olcait, and joined to the kingdom of Tigre. Amhara is situate southwards from Bagameder from which it is divided by the little river Baixillo, as it is on the east by the Nile from Goiam. It is divided into several little countries, and hath pass'd for the most valuable of all the Abyssinian kingdoms. In this kingdom is Guexon the famous rock on which the sons and brothers of the Emperor were confin'd till their accession to the throne. This custom establish'd about 1260, hath been abolish'd for two ages.[1]

The kingdoms of Holeca and Chaoa or Xaoa, are divided on

---

9. In Beccari, VIII. 26.

1. For a discussion of this passage and of other sources for the prison in *Rasselas* see Donald M. Lockhart, "'The Fourth Son of the Mighty Emperor': The Ethiopian Background of Johnson's *Rasselas*," *PMLA*, LXXVIII (1963), 516–28.

the east from Goiam by the Nile, on the west of Chaoa is Oifate,[b]
or Ifate, and on the south of these kingdoms are those of Fategar,
Ogge, Gaus, and Amut which is somewhat more remote and
borders upon Narea, the farthest province of Abyssinia to the
south-west, which was governed by its own princes, till it was
subdued by Sultan Segued, who made the kings hereditary
governors; nor have the emperors of Abyssinia any subjects
more faithful or obedient. 'Tis said that this country produces
abundance of gold. Those natives of Narea who have been
converted[2] are good Christians, but there are still great numbers of idolaters. Ogara is situated more to the north than
almost any of these kingdoms, and lies between Olcait, Segued,
Tigre, Bagameder, and Dambia, is of much greater length than
breadth, and hath nothing in it remarkable except the mountain of Lamalmon. In the time of the Patriarch Alphonso
Mendez, the kings of Abyssinia generally resided in the kingdom
of Dambia, which was a strong reason for the Jesuits establishing
themselves there; the houses and the churches which they built
have been no prejudice to the beauty of the country. Sultan
Segued gave to the Patriarch Enfras with its whole territory,
who chose to reside for the most part at Depsan about a league
from the Lake of Dambia, and equally distant from Dancas,
where Sultan Segued generally kept his court.[3]

The kingdom of Goiam which is made a peninsula by being
almost encompass'd by the Nile, hath been thought by the
Jesuits for that reason to be the Meroe of the ancients. Mr.
Ludolf on the contrary maintains that Goiam cannot be the isle
of Meroe, because nothing related of Meroe by Diodorus of
Sicily, Strabo, or Pliny, is applicable to that kingdom; Meroe
being much nearer Egypt.[4] The strongest reason he offers is that
if Meroe had been Goiam, and the ancients had known that
country, they must have consequently known the source of the
Nile. The greatest part of the authorities alleged by him rather

---

b. Chaoa is Oifate (Chaoa, est Oifate *Relation*)] Chaoais, Oifate *1735*

---

2. "Converted" replaces: "ont embrassé la foi de Jésus Christ" (p. 203).

3. SJ omits Le Grand's comment that a
discussion of the Lake of Dambée (Lake
Tana in northern Ethiopia) will be found

in the next dissertation (p. 203).

4. Despite the variety of ancient historians cited in this long paragraph, the
actual source is Ludolf's *Historia*, Book I,
Chap. 4 and the *Commentarius*, pp. 88–93.

shew his learning than prove his opinion. Solinus says,[5] that
Meroe is the first island form'd by the Nile, and that it is six
hundred miles distant from the sea.[c] If Father Jerome Lobo may
be credited, from the sea to the head of the Nile, is a journey of
twenty days length: from Mazua to the Agaus, are an hundred
and fifty Portuguese leagues, which are at least six hundred
Italian miles.[6] Mela as corrected by Salmasius[7] says very near
the same with Solinus. Pausanius[8] writes that the Greeks and
Aethiopians who had been beyond Syene and Meroe reported,
that the Nile entred a great lake, and after it had passed through
it, traversed the whole country of Aethiopia: all this is very
agreeable to the kingdom of Goiam. Vossius,[9] who is of opinion,
that Goiam is not Meroe, affirms that the river now call'd
Mareb is the Astaboras of the ancients, and that the capital of
Meroe, is a city, Baroo or Baroa, situated in the sixteenth degree
22 minutes, where the Bahrnagash generally resides, the neighbourhood of Syris[d] or Syene confirms this opinion; for the way
from Egypt to Meroe lay through Syene, which was somewhat
above two hundred French leagues[1] distant from it. But Vossius
is mistaken in affirming that the Mareb falls into the Tacaza, for
the Mareb loses itself in the sands. And I am more inclined to
believe that the Astusapes mention'd by Pliny, book the 5th, is
the Mareb.[2] If the Astaborus be as Pliny says, on the left of the

c. the sea] sea *1735*   d. Syris *Errata*] Syrio *1735*

---

5. The *Collectanea Rerum Memorabilium* (*c*. A.D. 200) of Solinus is a summary of world geography drawn almost entirely from Pliny and from Pomponius Mela, whose first-century geographical survey (*De Chorographia*) is regarded as a popular summary of known facts.

6. According to the discussion "Of Divers Measures" in Echard's *Gazetteer*, "The Spanish league is estimated at four Italian miles, and are reckoned seventeen and an half to a degree" (A4r).

7. Ludolf's *Commentarius* (p. 90) is the source for this version of Mela corrected by Salmasius (Claude de Saumaise), whose *Plinianae Exercitationes* (1629) is a "remarkable work ... in which more than 900 pages are devoted to the elucidation of

the portions of Pliny included in the geographical compendium of Solinus" (Sandys, II, 285). SJ owned copies of Salmasius: see *Library*, p. 100.

8. A traveller himself, Pausanias was familiar with both Egypt and Palestine.

9. Isaac Vossius, professor of history at Amsterdam, was the editor of Pomponius Mela; in the section of the *Commentarius* (p. 88) from which Le Grand takes this material Ludolf is discussing Chapter 16 of Vossius, *De Origine Nili & Fluminum*.

1. According to Echard's *Gazetteer*, "A French league is the 25th part of a degree, being near 2 English miles, and three quarters" (A3v).

2. Pliny, Book V, Chap. 9; *Commentarius*, p. 89.

Nile, 'tis probably the Melecca, and then the notion of the learned Father Hardouin,[e] who places Meroe between the Nile and the Melecca,[3] will have a greater appearance of truth than that of Vossius. But, after all, the ancients were so little acquainted with this part of Aethiopia, and the accounts they have left us of the isle of Meroe are so different and confused, that there is as much reason for affirming as for denying that it was Goiama.

Mr. Ludolf,[4] I know not for what reason has left out the nation of the Agaus in his account, who are mention'd by other writers, and of whom Father Jerome Lobo hath said so much.[5] This people inhabits about the fountains of the Nile,[6] and is[f] not to be confounded with another nation of almost the same name that dwells in the mountains of Lasta, and revolting from Sultan Segued, engaged him in a bloody war.

A man is not to expect in Aethiopia, either valuable pictures, or beautiful statues, or busts of admirable workmanship,[7] or grand buildings, there is not a city in the empire; their houses are nothing but cabins built of clay and straw, all the polite arts are utterly unknown here, and nothing is to be met with but nature savage and uncultivated.

Here are mountains of so stupendous an height that the Alps and Pireneans which seem to us to rise into the sky, are hillocks if compared with Guza, which yet is but the basis of Lamalmon; these two mountains are in the confines of Tigre and Dambia, and are to be pass'd over by those who travel from one kingdom into the other.

When the traveller has surmounted the fatigue of climbing Mount Guza,[8] he finds an agreeable plain, where he reposes

---

e. Hardoüin *Relation*] Hardurn *1735*   f. is *Errata*] are *1735*

3. Jean Hardouin, a Jesuit of Quimper, edited the Delphin Pliny.

4. Cf. "Mr. Ludolf, qui n'a trouvé aucune carte de l'Abissinie à son gré" (p. 204).

5. Ludolf is criticized for deviating from his source without setting forth his reasons: "Il semble qu'il aurait dû dire les raisons qui l'ont obligé à s'en écarter" (p. 204).

6. "This people ... Nile" has been moved from the end of the paragraph where it was followed by a sentence (omitted by SJ) concerning the religion of the Agaus: "Le christianisme qu'ils professent est mêlé de beaucoup d'idolâtrie, & ils ressemblent peu aux autres Abissins" (p. 205).

7. Cf. "excellents bustes" (p. 205).

8. "When ... Guza" expands the French: "Lorsqu'on est arrivé au haut du mont Guça ..." (p. 205).

himself before he attempts Lamalmon; from these mountains he enjoys a free prospect of the whole kingdom of Tigre, where Semen, and the other mountains which cross and divide it into so many places, appear little more than molehills.

The kingdom of Amhara is yet more mountainous, the Abyssins call those steep rocks Amba, there are many of them which appear to the sight like great cities; and one is scarcely convinced even upon a near view that one doth not see walls, towers and bastions. It was on the barren summit of Ambaguexa, that the princes of the blood-royal pass'd their melancholly life, being guarded by officers who treated them often with great rigour and severity.[9]

The Father Balthazar Tellez tells a story which deserves not to be forgotten on this occasion: one of these guards an exact and severe man observing one of the princes to be better dress'd than the rest, and take care of his cloaths, not only inform'd the Emperor, but tore the suit, and threatned the prince to procure him one he should be less pleased with. Some time after, that prince mounted the throne, and sending for the officer, presented him with a magnificent habit, and bad him return to his charge, with these memorable words.[1] "As you have served my father, I hope you will serve me, you have hitherto done your duty, I approve of you, continue to do it." Such examples are illustrious and rare, and Ethiopia may boast of more officers thus severe, than princes thus generous.[2] The highest of all these mountains according to the Patriarch Alphonso Mendez is Thabat-Mariam, which is vastly large and rises far above the clouds, its foot is watered by two rivers. Here are seven churches, of which that of the Invocation of St. John is extremely wealthy, it was formerly the burying place of the kings of Abyssinia, and there are still to be seen five tombs hung with tapistry wrought with the arms of Portugal, which are supposed to be those hangings which King Emanuel presented to the Emperor David.[3]

Among so many craggy mountains the air cannot be always

---

9. In *Rasselas*, SJ transforms this mountain prison into the Happy Valley.

1. SJ's added phrase.

2. "Ethiopia may ... generous" provides a greater balance than the French does: "on trouve plus de gardes durs & sévères que des princes tels que ce roi d'Ethiopie" (p. 206). The anecdote may be found in Telles, p. 47.

3. Mendes describes Thabat Mariam in exactly this manner (Beccari, VIII. 35).

alike, and perhaps there is no country in the world in which so
many different seasons may be found in so small a compass.
Along the coasts of the Red-Sea, and twelve leagues within the
country the winter begins in December and ends in February,
and the rains in that time are not much. Higher in the country,
July, August and September, are the three winter months.

The heats are not excessive in Abyssinia, notwithstanding its
situation between the line and the tropick, and if the land doth
not produce great abundance of every necessary of life, it is to be
attributed not to the sterility of the soil, but the laziness of the
natives.

The rivers bring down with their streams some grains of gold,
which gives room to suspect that the mountains are full of it, and
that there is no want in this country of either metals or other
minerals, but whether reasons of state as some imagine, or
carelessness be the cause, they have never yet discover'd any
mines. The little gold to be seen in Abyssinia, is brought from the
province of Narea, or received in their small traffick with the
other Ethiopians who have great plenty of that metal; the most
valuable mineral in Abyssinia is salt.

DISSERTATION THE THIRD, UPON THE NILE

The greatest men of antiquity have passionately wish'd to find
the head of the Nile, and have thought after all their conquests
that their glory was not compleat without this discovery. Cambyses lost in this search much time and great numbers of men.[1]
When Alexander consulted the oracle of Ammon, the first enquiry he made was after the sources of the Nile, and having
afterwards encamp'd at the head of the river Indus, which he
imagined to be that of the Nile, was overjoy'd at his success.
Ptolomy Philadelphus, one of his successors carried his arms
with this view into Ethiopia; where he took the city of Axuma, as
appears by the inscriptions preserv'd down to us by Cosmas
Indoplustes,[2] which he copied upon the spot in the time of the
Emperor Justin the First.

---

1. The story about Cambyses, son of
Cyrus the Great of Persia, like most of the
material in this paragraph, is found in
Commentarius (p. 121).

2. Cosmas Indicopleustes had visited
Aksum around A.D. 525 and describes the
area in *Christian Topography*, trans. and ed.
J. W. McCrindle (Hakluyt Soc., 1897).

Lucan puts it into the mouth of Caesar, that his highest ambition is to discover the head of Nilus, and the causes that act upon it, which have been a secret to so many generations; and that, could he be assured of enjoying the sight of its fountains, he would bid adieu to the civil war.[3]

> ———— *Nihil est quod noscere malim*
> *Quam fluvij causas per secula tanta latentis,*
> *Ignotumque caput; spes sit mihi certa videndi*
> *Niliacos fontes, bellum civile relinquam.*[4]

Nero had the same desire upon other motives, and sent out whole armies to make the discovery, the report brought back to him, took away all hopes of success.

The ancients having thus to no purpose sought after the head of this river and the causes of its inundations, have had recourse to fable, and have endeavoured to conceal their ignorance by inventing mysteries. The interpreters of the Holy Scriptures have not been themselves free from this error, who knowing no other Aethiopia than that of Africa, have imagined that Gihon mention'd in Genesis is the Nile, and not daring to contradict the Scripture which says that the Gihon rising in the terrestrial paradise waters the land of Chus or Aethiopia,[5] have conducted it under lands and seas and made it appear again in Aethiopia.

Great numbers of learned men have labour'd to clear these fables, and have invented many different hypotheses for this purpose. Mr. Huet, Bishop of Avranches, maintains in his treatise on the terrestrial paradise,[6] that the Gihon is an eastern

---

3. In this paragraph SJ rearranges and rephrases the French: "Lucain fait dire à Cesar qu'il aurait abandonné le dessein de faire la guerre à sa patrie, s'il avait crû être assez heureux pour voir le lieu où le Nil prenait sa source, qui était la chose qu'il désirait le plus" (p. 207).

4. [There's nought I more desire to know at all
Than Niles hid head, and strange original
So many years unknown: grant but to me
A certain hope the head of Nile to see,
Ile leave off civil war.]
—Thomas May translator, Lucan, *Pharsalia*, x. 189–92.

SJ owned copies of the 1728 edition and of the 1740 edition of Lucan's *Pharsalia* (*Library*, p. 78).

5. SJ inserts the parenthetical "or Aethiopia."

6. Pierre Daniel Huet, general editor of the Latin works in the Delphin Classics, wrote the *Traité de la situation du paradis terrestre* (Paris, 1691); an English translation followed quickly: *A Treatise of the Situation of Paradise* (London, 1694). The relevant discussion of the Gihon appears in Chap. 12.

branch of the Euphrates, which taking its rise from the country of Eden passes along that of Chus call'd even at this day Chusostam. He adds that Homer makes it descend from Jupiter, and that this is the reason that Plautus says of a river which he doth not name, that its fountain is in heaven, and springs up under the throne of Jupiter.

There is no reason to wonder that the poets have honour'd the Nile with a divine original, the Egyptians who are indebted to its inundations for the fertility of their soil, after having made the river a divinity thought themselves, as well as the Gymnosophists and Aethiopians, obliged to stand in defence of their ancient errors, how absurd soever,[7] and therefore built temples, rais'd altars, and appointed festivals to his honour, and paid their adorations to him under the name of Osiris.

The Jews and Mahometans however averse from idolatry, have yet attributed a peculiar blessedness and sanctity to its waters, and we find in the foregoing relation, that the Agaus who inhabit the country round about its sources, though instructed in the Christian religion, continue still to offer sacrifices to the river. In this manner does obstinacy and folly support those superstitions and idolatries which ignorance introduced.

The Nile hath passed under various names in different ages, and in different countries through which it runs, "not being call'd Nilus," says Pliny, B. 5. C. 9. "till it collects its disunited streams into one channel, and even then for some miles, keeping the name of Siris; it is call'd in general by Homer Aegyptus, and by others Triton."[8] Pliny doth not tell us whether the Nile first gave the name to Egypt, or receiv'd like many other rivers its name from the country it waters. Hesychius affirms, that the Nile being originally call'd Aegyptus, communicated its name to that kingdom;[9] Aegyptus however, was not the first name, it was known by, for it was first call'd Oceanus, then Aetus or Aquila, afterwards Aegyptus, and since, from its having born

---

7. "the Egyptians ... soever" preceded the rest of the material in Le Grand's paragraph; SJ here inserts it in the middle of what was a single sentence in the French (p. 208). The Gymnosophists were a sect of ascetic Hindu philosophers known to the Greeks through reports made by Alexander's companions.

8. SJ translates the quotation from the Latin (pp. 208–09).

9. Hesychius, a lexicographer of Alexandria, is quoted by Le Grand in French, Greek, and Latin (p. 209); SJ limits himself to a single version. SJ owned a first edition (1514) of Hesychius's dictionary (*Library*, p. 67).

those three names, Triton. At length it came to be known both to
the Greeks, and Romans by no other appellation than that of
Nilus. The Fathers Pays and Lobo inform us that the Abyssins
call this river Abavi, or the Father of Waters, and according to
Pliny, it takes the name of Siris in passing through Syene. The
Egyptians, who ascribed the wonderful fruitfulness of their
country to its waters, call'd it by the venerable names of the
Preserver, the God, the Sun, sometimes the Father.

Mr. Ludolf maintains that *abavi* does not signify father in the
Abyssinian language, observing at the same time,[1] that it would
be a very improper name, because the Nile receives part of its
waters from other rivers that discharge themselves into it, as the
Tacaza and the Mareb, but no river takes its rise from the Nile.[2]
He says farther, that in that dialect which the men of learning
make use of, it is nam'd Gejon, and thinks it might be so call'd
from the Gihon which Moses speaks of in his description of paradise.[3] Vatable in his exposition of the word *Cusch* or Ethiopia,[4]
says it is to be understood of eastern Ethiopia. The Nile or Gejon
does not encompass all Ethiopia, but only one part of it, the
kingdom of Goiama.

Cosmas the hermit whom we have quoted is the first that hath
inform'd us of the true way to the head of the Nile; who having
been in Ethiopia, hath made appear by the account which he
hath given, that he was acquainted with the country: yet Father
Peter Pays, a Portuguese Jesuit, was the first European, who had
a sight of the two springs which give rise to this celebrated[5]
stream, and therefore I imagine most will be pleased to meet
with his account of it, as preserved to us by Father Kircher,[a]
another famous Jesuit.[6]

a. Kircher *Relation*] Kercher *1735*

1. "observing ... time" is SJ's added
transition. The discussion in Ludolf's *New
History* may be found in Book I, Chap. 8.

2. "because ... from the Nile" expands
the French: "parce que tous les fleuves,
comme le Mareb, le Tacaze, se perdent
dans son sein & n'en sortent point"
(p. 209).

3. The Latin quotation from Genesis ii.
13, is deleted: "*Et nomen fluvii secundi Gehon;
ipse est qui circumit omnem terram Aethiopiae*"

(p. 209). [And the name of the second
river *is* Gihon: the same *is* it that compasseth the whole land of Ethiopia.]

4. Franciscus Vatablus published *Liber
Psalmorum Davidis* at Geneva (1556).

5. SJ adds the adjective.

6. *New History*, Book I, Chap. 8, quotes
Athanasius Kircher, a German Jesuit,
who presents Paez's account in *Oedipus
Aegyptiacus* (Rome, 1662), I. 57–59.

On the 21st of April, in the year 1618,[b] I accompanied, says
he, the Emperor, who was then at the head of his army in the
kingdom of Goiama, he was encamped in the province of Sacala, in the country of the Agaus, near a little mountain, that did
not seem of any considerable height, because it was surrounded
by others much higher. As I was looking round about me with
great attention, I discover'd two round springs one of which
might be about two feet diameter;[7] the sight fill'd me with a
pleasure which I know not how to express, when I considered
that it was what Cyrus, Cambyses, Alexander and Julius Caesar, had so ardently and so much in vain desired to behold. I did
not perceive any other spring towards the top of the mountain:
the second spring breaks out about a stone's cast westward from
the first. The natives affirm that the whole mountain is full of
water, and I am inclin'd to the same opinion, for the ground
shakes and the water boils up under foot round about these
springs. The water having a steep fall, runs with great rapidity
to the foot of the mountain, so that the fountains never flood the
ground. The inhabitants told me, that the year having been
extremely dry the mountain was observ'd to quake, and that
sometimes the trembling was so violent that it was dangerous to
walk upon it, which was confirmed by the Emperor. Below the
top of the mountain, a league from the spring, is the village of
Guix, which appears to the sight but a short cannon shot distant.
The mountain is of a difficult ascent except on the north side.

A league from the mountain springs another rivulet which
soon loses itself in the Nile; it is imagined to rise from the same
fountain and to run under ground for some space; it runs
eastward, and afterwards turning to the north receives another
brook, which, rising among the rocks is enlarged by two others
that spring toward the east, and the Nile being augmented by all
these petty streams soon swells into a considerable river, and
after continuing its course a day's journey, receives a large
encrease from the Gemma, a river no less than it self; it soon after
declines to the west, but turning again eastward, it enters a lake
which it crosses with great impetuosity, preserving its water
unmix'd. Having pass'd through that lake, it wanders thro' a

b. 1618 *Relation*] 1613 *1735*

---

7. Cf. "quatre palmes de diamètre" (p. 210).

long maze of windings to the south, and waters the plains of
Alaba. About five leagues from the lake it falls fourteen feet[8]
down a precipice with so much violence, that at a distance all
the water seems to be turn'd into mist and foam; a little after it is
so confin'd among the rocks, that it can scarcely be perceived,
for they approach so near to each other, that with the help of a
few beams and planks, the King and his whole army passed over
it.

This river after having left the kingdom of Bagameder on the
east, runs through Amhara, Olaca, Schaoa, and Damota, with
the countries of Bizamo and Gumancana, and almost surrounds
Goiama, returning within a day's journey of its original source,
and afterwards traversing the kingdoms of Fazalo and Ombarca, which Rassela[c] Christos conquered in 1613, naming them
Aysolam or Hadisalem, that is the New World, in allusion to
their vast extent, and to their being so little known before to the
Abyssins. The Nile afterwards bidding farewell[9] to Abyssinia,
after having passed through several kingdoms, falls at length
into Egypt, and discharges itself into the Mediterranean.

Father Payz, having nothing more concerning the course of
the Nile, and scarce saying any thing of it, after it hath left
Abyssinia, I choose to present the reader with the account which
Mr. Ludolf received from Gregory the Abyssin,[1] taking notice
only of that part of the letter which relates to its passage after it is
out of the Abyssinian dominions.

After it has run between Bizamo and Goiam, it enters the
country of the Shankelas, then turning to the right, leaves on the
left the west part of the land, and passes through Sanaar, having
already received the Tacaza which rises in the kingdom of Tigre,
and the Gangua which comes from Dambia. From Sanaar it
enters the country of Dangola, and flows into Nubia, afterwards
turning still more to the right, it comes into the country of
Abrim, where all the vessels stop, that pass up the stream from
Egypt, the rocks which interrupt so frequently the course of the
river, making it impossible to sail any higher.

c. Razzela *1735*

---

8. Cf. "quatorze brasses de haut" (p. 211).
(p. 211).
9. "afterwards bidding farewell" is SJ's
poetic equivalent of "quittant alors"

1. Gregory's account is found in *New History*, Book I, Chap. 8.

I cannot comprehend the distinction made here between Sanaar and Nubia, one being only the ancient, the other the modern name. We have already given an account of the Nile from Cairo to Dangola, out of the letter of Father Brevedent.[2]

The Nile afterwards says he,[3] enters Egypt, it bounds on the east the countries of Sanaar and Nubia. Those who come down out of Abyssinia and Sanaar into Egypt, keep always the Nile on the right hand, and when they have travelled through Nubia, cross upon camels, a desert fifteen days' journey over, where nothing but sand is to be found, then arriving at Rif, or Upper-Egypt, they quit their camels, and pass the remaining part of their way upon the water; some go by land on foot.

The Nile, continues the same Gregory, receives as it runs, all other rivers both great and small, except the Hanazo, which rises in the kingdom of Angote,[d] and Aoaxe, or Hawash which runs through the kingdoms of Dawara and Fategur.[e]

'Tis not unlikely that the Hanazo mention'd by Gregory is the same river that runs by Mount-Senaf, where the Patriarch Alphonso Mendez and his companions had their first pleasing interview with Father Emanuel Baradas.

The Patriarch has described this river as one of the most agreeable that the world can boast of, where the traveller is delighted with trees and aromatick herbs that flourish along its banks.[4]

The account which the Patriarch gives of the other rivers being at least as curious as any thing that Gregory tells us of the Nile, seems to deserve to be set down in a compendious manner.[5]

The Nile receives several rivers, the most remarkable of which are the Baxilo or Bachilo, which divides the kingdoms of Baga-

---

d. Angote *Relation*] Angolè *1735*   e. Fategur *Relation*] Falegur *1735*

---

2. In the French this paragraph appears as a longer, more detailed marginal note (pp. 211–12).

3. As a result of the preceding interpolated paragraph, this inserted clause is confusing: "he" refers not to Father Brevedent but to Gregory.

4. "that the world ... banks" adds some flourishes to the French: one of the most agreeable "qu'on puisse voir, à cause du grand nombre d'arbres & d'herbes odoriférantes dont elle est bordée" (p. 212). Mendes describes the river in greater detail (Beccari, VIII. 134).

5. The description in the next two paragraphs is taken from Mendes (Beccari, VIII. 33).

meder and Amhara; the Guecem[f] which bounds the same kingdom of Amhara and Oleca, the Maleck and Anguer[g] which
having joined their streams, water[h] the countries of Damot,
Narea, Bizamo, the Gafates, and the Gongas. The Tacaza call'd
by the ancients Astaboras hath three different sources near the
mountains, which separate the two kingdoms of Angote and
Bagameder, it runs towards the west through the desart of
Oldeba, then entring Dambar falls into a large bed of sands, and
afterwards having cross'd part of the kingdom of Decan discharges itself into the Nile. 'Tis said that besides crocodiles and
river-horses, there are in this river abundance of torpedos[6]
which immediately benum the arm of any man that touches
them. The Mareb rising two leagues from Debaroa, falls, after a
long course, from a rock thirty cubits in height, and sinks under
ground; but in the winter it runs through many other provinces,
and by the monastry of Alleluja, and then loses itself. The army,[7]
when they invaded these regions, dug into the sand, and found
under ground both good water and excellent fish.

The Aoaxes is not less than the Nile at its beginning, and is
encreased by the Machy and the lake Zoay, but the natives,
whose country it waters, cut the main stream into so many channels, that it is by degrees entirely lost, yet is supposed to be
convey'd by subterraneous passages into the Indian Sea.

The river Zebea, though less known, is equally considerable
with the Nile itself; it rises in Boxa, a province of the kingdom
of Narea, and, first falling eastward,[8] turns afterwards to the
north, and encompasses almost the whole country of Gingiro:
afterwards turning to the east through many barbarous and
unknown regions, disembogues it self into the Indian Sea near
Mombaza.[9]

There is no great difficulty, since we are informed of the head

---

f. Guecem *Relation*] Gulcem *1735*   g. Anguer *Relation*] Auguer *1735*   h. water
Errata] waters *1735*

---

6. "A fish which while alive, if touched
even with a long stick, benumbs the hand
that so touches it, but when dead is eaten
safely" (*Dictionary*).

7. Cf. "les Portugais" (p. 212).

8. An error: "vers le couchant"

(p. 213).

9. SJ deletes Le Grand's supporting
quotation (p. 213) from the Portuguese of
João dos Santos, *Ethiopia Oriental*, Book v,
Chap. 1.

of the Nile, and the rivers that fall into it, in giving an explication of those wonders which have perplexed both the ancients and moderns, who consulted themselves instead of the country,[1] and were bewilder'd in their own reasonings and imaginations. The circumstance which they were most in pain about, was the encrease and overflow of this river, the causes of which they were in hopes of finding by contriving imaginary systems, which are now of no other use, than to mortify the aspiring pride of man, to show how contracted is his boasted knowledge, and how vainly he reasons upon subjects which his senses have not made him acquainted with.[2]

Diodorus Siculus, having given a description of the Nile in the third chapter of his *Bibliotheca*, comes in the fourth to treat of its encrease, and collects all the opinions he had heard of those that went before him, beginning with that of Thales Milesius one of the seven sages, who tells us that the violence of the north winds, which the Greeks call Etesians, opposing the passage of the waters, forced them over their banks. But says Diodorus, if this solution were true, all the rivers that run from south to north would overflow in the same manner. Anaxagoras, and Euripides his disciple imagine, that the inundation is owing to the melting of the snow,[3] but, as he observes, there are no snows upon the mountains of Aethiopia. Besides, if the Nile were encreased by the melting of snow, the air would be colder, and the river would be hid in mists, when on the contrary, it is peculiar to the Nile, that it is not at any time covered with mists or fogs. Democritus[4] appears to have approached nearest the truth, though Diodorus confutes him like the rest, for he says, that the north-winds which blow sometime before the over-flow, bring snow with them out of colder countries, which being dissolved into rain, falls in such quantities about that time as swell the river beyond its channel.

---

1. "who consulted ... country" replaces "qu'ils cherchaient dans leur tête ce qu'ils n'y pouvaient trouver ... " (p. 213).

2. "contriving imaginary systems ... acquainted with" enlarges upon the slightly more restrained French version: " ... bâtir des systèmes; & tout ce qui a été écrit là-dessus, ne peut servir aujourd'hui qu'à confondre l'orgueil de l'homme, & à faire voir combien ses lumières sont bornées & souvent extravagantes, quand il veut rendre raison de ce qu'il ne connaît pas" (p. 213).

3. See the opening lines of Euripides' *Helen*.

4. The philosopher Democritus is said to have traveled extensively in Egypt and the east.

It has been the opinion of many that there is a subterraneous communication between the Nile and the sea, and that the inundation happens when the sea being violently agitated forces the waters into the channel of the Nile. Other accounts, even more improbable, have been invented, and very few have satisfied themselves, with the true and natural solution of this problem given of old by Strabo, St. Athanasius, and Cosmas Indoplustes who has written of Aethiopia with more accuracy than any other, and since by the Portuguese Jesuits, whose relations so well attested[5] leave us no room to doubt of the real cause, the great rains which fall at that time in Aethiopia.[6]

There is much talk of the goodness of the water of the Nile, and 'tis said, that though it is never perfectly clear, it is yet extremely light and wholesome: Galen tells us,[7] that women with child who drink of it, have easy labours, and bring often two, three, and even four children; that the sheep and goats which feed upon the banks, breed greater numbers than in any other place. Every one knows that the fertility of Egypt depends upon the over-flows of the Nile, and that the year is bad when it rises less than fourteen cubits, or more than eighteen, and that it is good when the water stands at sixteen.

There remains another doubt to be discussed, whether it be in the power of the Abyssinian emperor to turn the stream of the Nile so as to prevent it from watering Egypt. Some pretend upon the authority of Elmacin,[8] that it is not only possible, but that it has in some degree been put in execution. That the Calif Mustansir sent Michael the Patriarch of Alexandria into Abyssinia, who being received with the highest honours by the Emperor, inform'd him that the intent of his journey was to remonstrate that the Nile was sunk so low in Egypt, that the country and inhabitants suffer'd extremely; and the Emperor in respect to

---

5. "whose relations ... attested" replaces: "qui ont demeuré longtemps en ce pays-là" (p. 214).

6. A brief paragraph in the French states that snow could not cause the Nile to overflow because it does not snow in Ethiopia, and only small quantities appear on the mountain tops (p. 214).

7. Galen, the second-century physician and philosopher, was a native of Asia Minor and had studied in Alexandria. SJ

owned early editions of Galen's works (*Library*, p. 60).

8. In the *Bibliotheca Britannica*, Robert Watt calls him George Elmacinus, a native of Egypt toward the middle of the thirteenth century. Petis de la Croix refers to him as "Almakine, or Almacine, that is Alschec Almakine Georgios." He is the author of *Historiâ Saracenicâ* (1625), a chronicle of the Mohammedan Empire.

the Patriarch, order'd a mound to be broke, upon which the water encreas'd three cubits[9] in one night, the channel was soon fill'd, and the whole country laid under water, and fitted to receive the seed. The Patriarch at his return into Egypt was received with great tokens of respect by the Sultan who presented him with a long robe.

This account of Elmacin they endeavour to support by a relation of the vast and stupendous project of Alphonso d'Albuquerque, who had conceiv'd the same design of turning the Nile into a new channel, which, if we credit his son, he was upon the point of executing, when King Emanuel, at the instigation of his enemies, recall'd him. To effect this, says he, nothing more was requir'd than to dig thro' a little mountain that lies along the Nile in the country of Prester John. He had often written to his prince to send him some pioneers from the Maderas where they are accustomed to level mountains,[1] that they may water their sugar-canes. He adds, that this might be done, because Prester-John earnestly desir'd it, but did not know what measures to take. That if it had been effected, which he makes no doubt of if his father had liv'd a little longer, both the upper and lower Egypt had been laid in ruin. If the Arabs, continues he, who inhabit the desarts between Canaum and Cazuer, have been able upon any difference that arose between them and the Sultans of Egypt, to interrupt the course of the Nile, much more easily might Alphonso have done it, assisted by the power of Prester-John.

In this manner the son of Alphonso d'Albuquerque relates his father's design, but his account is not altogether satisfactory.[2] The country of Cazua may without difficulty be cut through, and, what much facilitated the enterprize of the Arabs, there is already a channel through which the Nile discharges part of its waters into the Red-Sea. Abyssinia is so far from affording any such advantages, that it is,[i] above any country in the world, fill'd

i. it is,] it, is *1735*

---

9. Cf. "trois brasses" (p. 215).

1. And "à applanir des vallées" (p. 215).

2. Cf. "Le raisonnement du fils d'Alfonse d'Albuquerque est aussi sage que l'entreprise du père l'était peu"

(p. 216). The story of the grand designs may be found in *The Commentaries of the Great Afonso Dalboquerque*, trans. Walter de Gray Birch for the Hakluyt Society (1875–1884), IV. 34, 36, and 207.

with mountains to which the Alps and Pireneans are meer hillocks. The Nile never approaches within less than an hundred leagues of the sea in any part of Abyssinia. There are several rivers between them, as the Tacaza which receives many others, and doth not join itself to the Nile, but in the twentieth degree, which is four degrees beyond the most northern part of Abyssinia.[3] The place where the Nile makes its nearest approaches to the sea, is in the twenty second degree, on this side Dancala, and even there all along the coasts extends a long chain of mountains, which ends at Rif. There is therefore no probability that the emperor of Abyssinia can divert the course of the Nile.

Mr. Ludolf nevertheless, though the impossibility of cutting a passage for the Nile into the Red-Sea through so many interposing mountains, appears from his own map, espouses the part of Alphonso's son against Father Tellez, who has demonstrated the vanity of such an undertaking, and speaks of it like a man, who considered that the enthusiasm of heroick spirits hurries them sometimes beyond the limits of prudence, and engages them in enterprizes not warrantable by right reason.[4]

As to the relation of Elmacin, to which Mr. Ludolf seems to give credit,[5] he would, I believe, have found it no easy matter to have inform'd us, what became, during the time in which the Aegyptians complain'd of famine, of the waters of the Nile; by what channel they pass'd into the Red-Sea, and by what means, and in what place, the king of Aethiopia dug this channel.[6]

Had Mr. Ludolf been sufficiently acquainted with the *History of the Patriarchs of Alexandria*, he would have found this favourite narrative loaded with more difficulties, and liable to new objec-

---

3. "which is four ... Abyssinia" grows from the statement that "La partie la plus Septentrionale de l'Abissinie est sous les seize dégrés" (p. 216).

4. "who has demonstrated ... reason" replaces a section (pp. 216–17) in which Le Grand recounts Ludolf's attack on Balthasar Telles; SJ apparently bases his comments on a long passage in Portuguese quoted from Telles (Book I, Chap. 7, p. 20). This Portuguese quotation (pp. 217–18) SJ neither translates nor epitomizes. His final statement is related to

Le Grand's conclusion about Telles: "il en a jugé comme un homme qui ne croit pas que les vues des héros soient toujours réglées par le bon sens & par la prudence" (p. 218). SJ's sympathies here, as elsewhere, are with those who reason rightly.

5. In the *Historia* (Book I, Chap. 8), Ludolf quotes and translates from the Arabic of the *Historiâ Saracenicâ*; only the English translation is offered in the *New History* (p. 41).

6. In the French this paragraph appears before the previous one (p. 216).

tions.[7] He would have discovered, that an author almost contemporary in his life of the Patriarch Michael says not a word of
this journey. That Mustansir died within a year after the ordination of Michael. And that, during that time, there was no
famine in Egypt. So that the history related by Elmacin, and by
Macrisius.[j] after him, is plainly invented only to amuse.[8]

It is observable that the kings of Abyssinia are still persuaded
that the keys of the Nile are in their hands, and that they can,
when they please, change its course, as the King Teklimanout
threatens the Bassa of Cairo, in a letter already given in the
sequel of the history; but, however they may threaten, it is
now impossible, and was no less impossible in the days of
Albuquerque.[9]

We do not pretend that a canal cannot be dug from the Nile to
the Red-Sea, but that the Abyssins cannot do it. It was attempted heretofore by Necus the son of Psammeticus and atchieved by
Darius king of Persia, who made a channel, if Herodotus be
credited, four days' sail in length, and of the breadth of two
gallies. Afterwards Ptolomy Philadelphus caus'd another to be
dug, an hundred feet in breadth, and forty in depth, which he
carried on as far as the Bitter Fountains, about thirty seven
miles, then discovering that the Red-Sea was three cubits higher
than the land, he broke off his design for fear of laying Egypt
under water. Yet the author of the cosmography written in the
consulship of Caesar and Anthony, affirms that in his time part
of the Nile ran into the Red-Sea near Ovila.

Long after, Omar the Second, who kept his ordinary residence at Medina, gave orders, in a time of famine, to Amru who
conquered Egypt, to cause a canal to be dug from Cairo to
Coltzum, which project was put in execution. But Medina
ceasing afterwards to be the residence of the califs, and being
reduced to a small number of inhabitants, the consumption of
provisions grew much less, and the canal, becoming less neces-

j. Macrisius *Relation*] Mucrisius *1735*

---

7. "he would ... objections" is less specific than the French: "il se serait plus
défié qu'il n'a fait de ce qu'Elmacin rapporte du voyage du Patriarche Michel fait
en Ethiopie par ordre de Mustansir"
(p. 217).

8. And, the French adds, "très suspecte" (p. 217).

9. At this point Le Grand presents the
long passage in Portuguese (see p. 179,
n. 4) from Telles, arguing the impossibility of diverting the Nile (pp. 217–18).

sary, was neglected, and by degrees choak'd with sand. The Arabs call that canal *Khalige Emir Al Moumenin*, or the Canal of the Calif.

A DISSERTATION[1] ON THE EASTERN SIDE OF AFRICA, FROM MELINDA TO THE STREIGHT OF BABELMANDEL

The country into which Father Jerome Lobo went in quest of a passage into Aethiopia, is so little known to us, that I cannot think it impertinent to enlarge a little upon what he hath told us.

The viceroys of the Indies have had formerly governments of very large extent subordinate to them, in which deputies were placed under the title of captain-generals. He that commanded in the isle of Ceylan stiled himself King of Malvana. The other governments were Malaca, Ormus, and Mozambique, which is the only one which the Portuguese have now left them; having lost Malaca, Ceylan, and the Spice-Islands[2] to the Dutch, and Ormus being retaken by the Persians assisted by the English.

The isle of Mozambique, with which I shall begin first,[3] lyes in fifteen degrees south. It is half a league in length, and a quarter in breadth; the citadel which defends the port, being placed at the mouth of it, is one of the best in the Indies, having four large towers, two both on the land and sea-side, and being furnished with large magazines of amunition, provision, and every thing needful for a long and vigorous defence if an enemy should attack it. Besides the unwholesomeness of the air, the inhabitants, which, to the number of about two thousand, possess this uncomfortable place, undergo great inconveniences for want of wood and water, the latter of which they are forced to fetch at three leagues' distance. The Governor hath all the trade in his own hands which consists of elephants' and sea-horses' teeth, and gold brought by his agents from the river of Sofala. This island, wretched as it is, supplies all the coast with provision,

---

1. Unnumbered in the French.
2. Cf. "ces isles d'où on tire tant d'épiceries" (pp. 221–22).
3. The idea of beginning with Moçam-

bique occurred originally in the opening paragraph of the dissertation: "Je commencerai par Moçambique" (p. 221).

cloth, and other merchandise brought thither from the Indies.

The coast of Melinda begins at the Cape del Gado which is six[4] degrees south, and runs upwards towards the Cape of Guardafui. The city of Melinda, the capital of that country, hath been accounted one of the most beautiful in all that quarter of Africa which our geographers call Zanquebar. It is situated in a spacious and agreeable plain, the houses being well built of hewn stone. When the king of Melinda goes out, he is carried upon the shoulders of the principal persons of his court, and the streets through which he passes are perfum'd, and when he enters into any city of his dominions, the most beautiful of the young virgins go out to meet him, some throwing flowers before him, some burning perfume, and others singing verses to his praise, nor do the priests on this occasion forget to sacrifice.[5]

The Portuguese lost in 1631 the isle of Mombaza, where they had built seventeen churches, and the governour of Melinda had fix'd his residence.[6] The king of this place surpris'd the fortress, and turn'd Mahometan in order to procure the assistance of the Moors.[7] Beyond the city of Melinda is the isle of Lamo which breeds great numbers of asses of a larger size than usual, but of less use. Near Lamo is the isle of Paté large and fruitful, which is governed by three kings of Paté, Sio, and Ampasa, who reside each in a city which gives the name to their territory. Ampasa was far the richest of the three.

It was formerly inhabited only by Moors, who were so haughty, so cruel, and such implacable enemies of the Christians, and particularly the Portuguese, that they were oblig'd to declare war against them. The king of Ampasa being kill'd in a battle, this city was taken, plunder'd, and burnt, and the palm-trees, which grew round it, were cut down. His head fix'd upon a lance, was carried through all the streets of Goa. The fate of the king of Lamo was even more deplorable, who being accused of having delivered Roc de Brito with about forty Portuguese to the Turks, was arrested by the captain general, whom he visited, and being carried by him to Paté, had his head cut off publickly on a scaffold, in the presence of the kings of Paté, Sio, and

---

4. An error: "dix" (p. 222).

5. "nor ... sacrifice" softens "Les prêtre[s] immolent des victimes" (p. 222).

6. "where they ... residence" appears in a marginal note (p. 222).

7. The French includes eight lines describing other islands (pp. 222–23).

Ampasa, who were obliged to be present at the melancholly[8] spectacle.

Father Jerome Lobo tells us, that after he left Paté, he travell'd along the coast part by sea, and part by land, and hath given an account of what he observed; but, as he followed the course of the shore, without daring to go far from the sea-side, he could not tell us any thing of those nations which inhabit the country a little higher. The most considerable of these are the Mossegueios who are not much less rude and uncivilized for being the allies of the Portuguese. The young people among them have a custom sufficiently barbarous and uncommon. At the age of seven or eight years, they fix upon their heads a lump of clay in form of a cap, and as the clay dries, and they grow bigger, more is added, till at last this kind of cap weighs eight or ten pounds; this they are not suffered to be without night or day, neither are they admitted to any consultation, till they have slain an enemy in battle, and brought his head to their commander.

These Mossegueios were formerly vassals and peasants[9] who revolted from their lords. They live chiefly on the milk of cows. This people having defeated and kill'd a king of Mombaza, made his kingdom tributary to the king of Melinda.

On this coast towards the north of Brava is Magadoxo.[1] After having doubled the Cape of Guardafui, the traveller meets with the ports of Methe, Micha, and Barbora; and then arrives at the kingdom of Adel, the capital of which is call'd Auca. This kingdom is call'd Zeila by the Portuguese from a port of the same name.[2] As Father Jerome Lobo[3] only passed along the coasts of Sofala, Mozambique and Melinda, he hath omitted many particulars relating to the natural history of these coun-

---

8. SJ inserts the adjective.

9. Both of these terms grow out of "des bergers" (p. 223).

1. This transitional sentence (corrected in *Errata* from "Brava and Magadoro") replaces two deleted paragraphs (p. 224): the first concerns the cities of Brava and Mogadishu on the Somali coast; the second the inland tribe of Maracates, who make the best slaves because of the care taken to emasculate the young men and to sew shut the genitals of the daughters. SJ had deleted this second point once before: see page 13, n. 2.

2. SJ omits an additional statement: "Ce fut là qu'abordèrent les glorieux martyrs François Machado & Bernard Pereira, que le roi d'Adel fit mourir ..." (p. 224).

3. By using Lobo's name SJ avoids the awkward phrasing of the French: "l'auteur que j'ai traduit ..." (p. 224).

tries which may afford some entertainment to the reader, and therefore deserve to be inserted.

This country supplies the merchants with great quantities of gold, ivory, the teeth of sea-horses, and cocos; and other things of great usefulness and curiosity are found here, nor is it easy to determine whether the sea or land be most fruitful in these extraordinary productions.

There are more sugar-canes on the banks of the Cuama and Sofala than in Brasil, but the Cafres having no art of bruising them, eat them as they are naturally produced, and make no advantage from them in traffick. Cassia is very common, and not much esteemed by the Cafres who have other purgatives of greater virtues, and prepared with less trouble. There is one wood which powder'd and taken in a glass of water, stops a flux of blood; and another which cures all kinds of sores; its qualities are such, that it clears the wound in twenty four hours of all foulness or clotted blood, and cures it in a very short time without the application of any other remedy. There is another wood in this country, which, powder'd and taken by men, brings milk into their breasts, and enables them to give suck like women.[4]

They have likewise an herb call'd by the Portuguese, *dutro*, by the Cafres, *banguini*, which has this wonderful quality[5] that taken in meat or drink, it entirely deprives a man of reason, and continues him for the space of twenty four hours in the same temper, which he was in, when he took it. He that swallow'd it in a gay humour, is entertain'd with pleasing images, and is continually bursting out into fits of laughter, and flights of merriment. But he, whom his ill fate tempts to taste it in a melancholly disposition, protracts the gloomy moments, and gives the woes of life a longer duration, nothing can he utter but sighs and complaints, or apprehend but misery and misfortune, till the force of the drug is exhausted, and he awakes from his dream of sadness. No one retains any remembrance of any thing said or done by him, while he continued thus intoxicated.[6]

---

4. "brings milk ... women" embellishes the French: "fait venir du lait aux hommes comme aux femmes" (p. 225).

5. "which has ... quality" is SJ's inserted clause.

6. "He that swallow'd ... intoxicated" imaginatively expands the French version: "on ne cesse de rire si on était gai, ni de pleurer si on était triste, & on ne se souvient nullement ni de ce qu'on a dit, ni de ce qu'on a fait pendant qu'on est en cet état" (p. 225). SJ's tale, *The Fountains*, might well be based on this idea.

Those who are so daring as to bathe in these rivers, that are infested by crocodiles, fortify their bodies, by rubbing with an herb named *miciriri*; this, as they imagine, puts these destructive animals to flight, and the notion among them is, that if the crocodile should attempt to bite them, his teeth at the touch of their bodies thus secured would become soft as wax.[7]

Four leagues from the Cape del Gada is the last[a] of the isles of Quirimba; in this island grows the tree from which manna is gather'd, which is nothing but a kind of dew congeal'd, which appears on the trunk like candied sugar, and on the leaves like pearls.

The author hath said so much already of the usefulness of the palm, that I shall not enlarge upon what has been written by him, but shall content myself with saying something of the coco[b] of the Maldives, and the tree which produces it. It is not improbable that the Maldives Islands and Ceylan have formerly been one continued tract of ground, the sea being at this day very shallow between them, in which are to be seen palm-trees procreated from those that grew there before the deluge, and which are likely to continue there for ever. These trees, which are now to be seen in the bottom of the sea, bear the same fruits which they bore formerly, for the salt water, far from being noxious to this plant, contributes to its fertility, which is the reason that those trees grow near the shore, produce a larger number of fruits, though less excellent, than those which are planted at more distance from it. When the coco is ripe, it separates from the tree, and is carried by the waves to each shore, where the inhabitants heap them up, and sell them, as an excellent antidote, at a large price.

These seas produce amber, pearls, and coral; amber grows at the bottom of the sea, and scarce ever is found but in tempestuous weather, when the violent agitation of the waves breaks it off, and drives it upon the shore, where the Cafres who come down after every storm in expectation of finding it, gather it carefully. There are three sorts of amber, the black, the brown, and the white, which is call'd ambergrise. How this substance is form'd, hath been long disputed, some maintaining that it is a

a. last (la dernière *Relation*)] least *1735*   b. coco, *1735*

---

7. According to the French, they chew the herb until they begin to feel their own   teeth softening; then they rub the juice on their bodies (p. 225).

gum which distilling from the tree is harden'd in the water, but to make this hypothesis bear any similitude of truth,[c] we ought to find trees of nearly the same species in all those countries where amber is gathered; and nature should have rais'd the same productions on the coasts of the Baltick[8] as of the Aethiopick Sea, but this doth not appear. Whales and other fishes eat amber, but do not produce it, though it is believed, that black amber, which is of little value, may be the excrement of whales, that having eaten pure amber, void it blacken'd and corrupted.[9] 'Tis reported that a little vessel bound from Mozambique to the isle of St. Laurence, anchoring all night at twenty fathoms, drew up with her anchor next morning a large piece of amber, and that other ships have had the same unexpected success. Father Dos Santos tells us, that in 1596, they found near Brava a piece of amber so high, that a man could not look over it,[1] 'tis scarce credible that pieces of such weight and bulk should be voided by any animal in the world, or should be any wax or gum harden'd in the water. Every rational man will think it much more probable,[2] that it is form'd like other minerals under the water, and that the subterraneous fires according to the different properties of the earth they act upon, produce this and other fossiles.

Coral is a plant that grows in the bottom of the sea,[3] and is so soft when first drawn up that a juice may be press'd out of it not unlike that which drops from the branch of a fig-tree newly broken off, but of a caustick nature; and by an harder pressure the pores through which it issues may be discovered; the coral by being exposed to the air grows hard. The chief fishery for it is near Tabarca in the Mediterranean, some has been found near Toulon, and likewise in the Red-Sea and in the neighbourhood of Cape del Gado.

c. truth; *1735*

---

8. "but to make ... Baltick" is an expanded and more formal rendering of: "Mais il faudrait qu'il y eût des arbres à peu près de même espece dans les différents pays où l'on trouve l'ambre, qu'il y en eût sur les côtes de la mer Baltique ..." (p. 226).

9. SJ omits one point: "L'ambre noir est peu estimé, mais le gris l'est beaucoup, & on en trouve quantité sur cette côte" (p. 227).

1. This discovery is recorded in João dos Santos, *Ethiopia Oriental*, Primeira Parte, f. 42ᵛ.

2. Cf. "N'est-il pas plus probable ..." (p. 227).

3. At this point in the French occurs the sentence that concludes this paragraph.

Though we have determined that amber is not the excrement of whales, it is not to be imagined, that we deny any whales to be in the Aethiopian Sea: there are not only whales, but another kind of fish more rare, with which the whale is always at war, and is often kill'd by her. This fish is call'd by the Portuguese *espadarte* from the sword which she has at her snout,[4] which is flat, and long, with teeth like a great saw. When the whale and *espadarte* or sword-fish encounter, they appear on the top of the water, and the sword-fish springing upwards, darts his sword strongly against the whale, and often wounds him. The whale is said to attack sometimes the *gelves*, and other little vessels which he is supposed to mistake for the sword-fish his enemy, and to overturn them if not prevented.

In this sea are likewise found great numbers[5] of tortoises of various species, who have like the whale a mortal enemy call'd the *sapi*, which persecutes them perpetually,[6] he lives among the rocks near the shore, and is about a foot long, his neck is covered with a shell three fingers broad, his skin is almost black.[7] When the fishers have taken a *sapi*, they put him into a bucket full of water, and tie a long line to his tail, then throw him[8] into any place where they expect tortoises, and if he can fasten upon any they draw them out together, for the *sapi* will not quit his hold, nor doth the tortoise if once seiz'd make any resistance.

Of the river-horse so much hath been said already, that little needs be added to the former description,[9] his teeth are more valuable than elephants', because they are whiter, and preserve their whiteness longer.[1] These creatures are found not only under the line, but even in the polar circle where they hide themselves under the ice. As to the elephant,[2] scarce a traveller who has seen the eastern parts of the world has forgot to tell us of

---

4. Le Grand adds: "Nous en avons vu" (p. 227).

5. SJ omits a reference to the many sharks found in these waters (p. 228).

6. "which persecutes them perpetually" replaces "Il leur fait la guerre, comme le furet la fait aux lapins" (p. 228).

7. SJ deletes another animal image: "s'attache aux rochers à peu près comme la sangsue" (p. 228).

8. "ce furet marin" (p. 228).

9. This statement replaces more than half a page describing the physical and emotional ("très mélancolique") characteristics of the beast (pp. 228–29).

1. According to the French, "On tient que la corne de son pied gauche est un remède souverain contre la mélancolie" (p. 229).

2. A half-page discussion of the crocodile is omitted (p. 229).

his sagacity, and therefore any thing here would be unnecessary. Although all the Portuguese writers have reckon'd the rhinoceros among the animals of Aethiopia, yet none of them affirm that they have seen him, or been eye-witnesses of the dreadful combats between him and his irreconcileable adversary the elephant.

Some of them confound him with the *abada* or *bada* of which Father John dos Santos hath written very largely. The *abada* has two horns one planted on his forehead about two feet long, of a blackish colour, smooth, and very sharp, with the point a little turn'd upward; the other on the hinder part of his head, thicker and longer, he is about the bigness of a colt of two years old. His bones powder'd and mingled with water, make a cataplasm of wonderful efficacy, which draws the poyson out of any wound, and entirely cures it.

The *zeura* is a creature peculiar to Abyssinia, his whole body is diversified with black and white streaks of an equal breadth,[3] which are as soft as silk;[d] he has a kind of wool about his feet;[e] when he runs he puts his head between his legs, and at first kicks out his heels very much. The Emperor of Abyssinia frequently accompanies an embassy with a present of this animal.

The *zeura* is often confounded with the wild ass, which is less, and hath horns, and cloven feet like a deer, with a white streak, which runs down his shoulders and thighs to his knees, his hair[f] is ash-colour'd, and very rough, his flesh tender and delicious: the Cafres call him *merus*.[4]

It has been a question a long time, whether there be such a creature as the unicorn; those who have given an account of him, have varied so much in their descriptions, and fill'd their narratives with so many fables, that they have reason on their side, who have doubted of the existence of this animal, which indeed is very rare, and found only in the kingdom of Damot, and in the province of the Agaus. He is wild, but so far from being fierce or dangerous, that he never dares trust himself but in company with other creatures. When he changes his haunt he

d. silk, *1735*   e. feet, *1735*   f. hair, *1735*

---

3. SJ omits Le Grand's useful comparison: "larges de deux doigts" (p. 230).

4. SJ deletes two sentences describing another animal with overgrown, bay-brown hair, a gentle creature with rear legs shorter than his front ones; he runs more swiftly than the stag (p. 230).

runs from one forest to another with so great celerity, that he is immediately snatch'd out of sight, which has been the occasion of so great a disagreement in the accounts of him, some affirming that he has thick and long hair, others that it is short and thin;[5] that he has a long horn in the midst of his forehead is agreed by all, but it is not so certain that this horn is an excellent antidote; whenever a horn has been found of that efficacy there is room to doubt whether it was the horn of an unicorn.

There are wild horses in Aethiopia with an head and mane like ours, and resembling them in their neighing, but with two little horns and cloven feet; the Cafres call them *empophos*.

The giraffe is the tallest creature in the world, though less bulky than the elephant;[g] his legs are so long, that a man on horseback may pass without stooping[6] under his belly. He is call'd by the Patriarch Alphonso Mendez, *struthio camelus*, as Mr. Ludolf maintains, improperly.[7]

If the *minga*[h] be not the bird of paradise, it is at least very like it, being about the bigness of a pidgeon, yellow and green, his legs are so short that they are never seen. He rests upon trees which he eats the fruit of, and when he would fly away, throws himself off, and in falling opens his wings and mounts into the air; if he should light on the ground he could not raise himself; when he drinks he skims over the surface of the water without stopping.

'Tis said that in Mexico, there is a bird call'd by the natives *cincoes*, which lives upon the dew, his plumage is of several colours, and extremely beautiful, of which the Indians make pictures with so much art and exactness, that they can be but faintly imitated by the most skillful pencil.

The *curvanes* has wings of the most beautiful black, and a belly as curiously white, a long neck, and on his head a large tuft of

---

g. elephant, *1735*   h. minga *Relation*] ninga *1735*

---

5. "which has been ... thin" effectively epitomizes a longer version: "De là vient que les uns le font plus grand, les autres plus petit, les uns d'un poil, les autres d'un autre; les uns disent qu'il a les crins longs & très fournis, les autres disent au contraire qu'il les a courts & peu fournis" (p. 231).

6. "Without stooping" is SJ's addition.

7. The comment about Ludolf is all that remains of a half page of detailed discussion quoting Mendes, Ludolf, and others about the *struthiocamelus* (pp. 231–32). Mendes's use of the term "struthio camelus" (Beccari, VIII. 38) is challenged by Ludolf in his *Commentarius*, pp. 161–62.

black feathers with a plume rising half a foot above it, his
feathers are all even, which he spreads into a kind of umbrella as
the peacock expands his tail: he is esteem'd so much by the
Cafres and Aethiopians, that they stile him the king of birds.

DISSERTATION THE FOURTH, ON PRESTER-JOHN

It hath been a long dispute whether the meaning of the word
Prester-John be Priest-John, or Precious-John; whether the
Emperor of Abyssinia were known by that name before the
Portuguese gave it him; whether the true Prester-John were not
a king in Cathay or India, and an Asiatick rather than an
African monarch.

Writers have taken much pains to assign a remote original to a
name of which the French who travelled into the Holy-Land
were certainly the inventors, as may be made appear: it may not
however be improper to examine what the Portuguese have said
on this subject.

The infant Don Henry son of John the First, king of Portugal,
made the discovery of unknown countries his particular study,
and was seconded in his inclination by the Duke of Conimbre his
nephew: this prince having read in Marco-Polo of a powerful
Christian prince in Asia call'd Prester-John, had a strong desire
of attaining some knowledge of him, and contracting a friendship with him, but dyed before he was able to accomplish his
design. King John the Second, call'd by the Portuguese the
perfect prince, had the same inclination to know somewhat
of this Prester-John, and sent in 1479, Peter Covilhan and
Alphonso Payva, with two Jews skil'd in the Arabick language,
to travel over the world in search of him. Alphonso Payva dyed
on his journey, and left some memoirs which his companion
found at Cairo, and discovered from them that the Prester-John,
whom he had been enquiring after in Asia, was the king of the
Abyssins. This news he wrote to the King his master, and passed
into Abyssinia, where he was known and confessed by Alvares.
Since which time the Portuguese having read those authors,
upon whose relations those envoys' instructions were form'd,
have been led into an opinion, that they committed the error on

purpose to impose upon their master, and that the real Prester-John was a Nestorian prince, who in ecclesiasticals[1] depended on the patriarch of Bagdat or Babylon.

John de Barros, Diego de Couto,[a] the Patriarch Alphonso Mendez, the Fathers Emanuel d'Almeida,[b] and Balthasar Telles[2] maintain together with Mr. Ludolf that the envoys were mistaken; and Mr. du Cange in his observations on the Sire de Joinville has these words,[3] "It is an old error which is now rectified, that the empire of Prester-John is the kingdom of the Abyssins in Africa, an opinion which may easily be refuted from the testimony of the Sire de Joinville, who makes it evidently appear that the kingdom of Prester-John was in Asia, and no other than the empire of the Indies, which is confirmed beyond contradiction in an epistle of Pope Alexander the Third, preserved to us by Matthew Paris and Brompton in the years 1180 and 1181, and another letter of the prior of the Order of Preaching Friars in the same Matthew Paris."[4] Mr. du Cange cites moreover the authorities of William of Tripoli and other writers.

The veneration which every man owes to the name of Mr. du Cange, to whom learning is so much indebted,[5] obliges us to give his opinion a candid examination whatever reasons there may be to differ from him.

The authority of the Sire de Joinville ought to carry great weight with it when he relates things which he was an eye-witness of, but we are not to resign up our selves implicitely to an

---

a. de Couto *Relation*] de Conto *1735*   b. d'Almeida *Relation*] d'Almerda *1735*

---

1. "who in ecclesiasticals" replaces "qui pour le spirituel" (p. 234).

2. The *Decadas de Asia* (new ed., Lisbon, 1778–88) includes the historical accounts of João de Barros and Diogo de Couto; Mendes' commentary may be found in Beccari, VIII, Almeida's in Book I, Chap. 1 of his *Historia de Ethiopia a Alta* (Beccari, V), and Telles's in *Historia*.

3. Charles du Fresne (Sieur du Cange), seventeenth-century scholar and historian, compiler of glossaries of medieval Latin and medieval Greek, edited the Sire de Joinville's *Histoire da S. Louys IX* (Paris, 1668).

4. The note by du Cange is No. 43 in his edition; an English translation (1807) of Joinville's *Memoirs* by Thomas Johnes presents Joinville's comments on I. 200 and du Cange's note on I. 361–62. John Brompton was a Cistercian abbot in Richmondshire who compiled a chronicle for the years 588 to 1198; Matthew Paris, a member of the Benedictine monastery at St. Albans, wrote a *Chronica Majora*, a history of the world from the Creation to 1259.

5. Le Grand includes a personal note: "& l'amitié dont il m'a honoré" (p. 234).

unthinking belief of what he reports upon the credit of others, especially when we have testimonies more credible than those which he depended on. It is to be considered that he wrote in his old age, a long time after the death of Saint Louis, and it is evident from the account given by him of the embassy which that king sent to the Can of Tartary, that those ambassadors are more to be esteemed for their eminent piety than their skill in geography, and that they transmitted to us, as true histories, several traditions which others would have been inclined to call in question, at least to have examined with more exactness. And, to come more closely to the point, we should willingly be informed[6] where that country lies in the farthest part of Asia, which it will take up a year to travel to from Antioch at the rate of ten leagues a day, and where that stupendous rock is to be found, which no mortal hath yet been able to pass over, which in the extreme part of the earth, with other rocks, confines the nations of Gog and Magog, who are in the last days to break forth, and come with Antichrist to destroy the rest of the world.

All that the Sire de Joinville has written on that subject relates to the defeat and death of Ung-can, and the conquests of Chingiscan or Gengizcan,[7] whom he doth not name. In his relation are found two particular circumstances, that the ambassadors found the ways fill'd with carcases and bones, and that a pretended prophet assured Chingiscan that he should subdue the whole earth. Mr. du Cange is obliged to quit his confidence in the Sire de Joinville, when he relates the election of Chingiscan by arrows. He adds, that William of Tyre who lived before the name of the Tartars was known, relates the same circumstance of the Turks or Turcomans, who entering the dominions of the king of Persia, fix'd themselves there.[8]

Mr. du Cange adds some mistakes of his own to those of his author, for he affirms, that this first Prester-John gave that name to the kings of India, and that he made seventy-two kings tributaries; this learned man confounds here the vanquisher with the vanquished: no man can pretend that Chingiscan, who subdued so many spacious kingdoms, put so many Christian princes to death, and founded the empire of the Moguls, was a

<hr/>

6. "And ... informed" freely expands "En effet" (p. 235).

7. It is SJ who adds "or Gengizcan."

8. In Joinville's *Memoirs* (1807 trans.), see Note 44, I. 363.

Christian;[9] it was he, on the contrary, that, among the rest, conquered this pretended Prester-John, as the Sire du Joinville has written.

We come now to examine the authorities by which Mr. du Cange endeavours to support his opinion;[1] the first, which he makes use of, is De Diceto an English historian, who lived in the reigns of King Richard the First, and King John.[2] This writer gives us an extract of a letter written by Pope Alexander the Third to the king of India, which same letter is found entire in Roger Hoveden, in the year 1177.[3] It cannot be determined from this letter that the prince to whom it is address'd lived in Asia rather than in Africk, or was Nestorian rather than Jacobite;[c] on the contrary, as it appears, that he demanded a church at Rome for the people of his country, and the Abyssins had formerly there the Church of Saint Stephen, considering likewise that Abyssinia is call'd by Marco Polo, the lesser India, and that the ancients have confounded the Indians with the Aethiopians, there is greater probability, that this letter was written from Abyssinia, then from any other country.

The letter of Geoffry a Dominican monk given us by Matthew Paris 1237, is more formal, and seems so directly to favour the opinion of Mr. du Cange, as to leave us without a reply. That monk gives an account of the care he had of the missions in those parts; he speaks in direct terms of Prester-John, as a prince who then reign'd towards Armenia: he mentions afterwards the Jacobites of Egypt, Nubia, and Aethiopia, and says that they have greater numbers of more dangerous errors than those of Asia. It appears by his whole letter, that he had receiv'd very exact information, and the author who has preserved it lived at the same time.

Marco Polo, whose father had been a long time at the court of Tartary, and return'd from thence in the year 1272, and who

c. Jacobite, *1735*

---

9. Joinville's *Memoirs* (1807 trans.), Note 43, I. 362.

1. "We come ... opinion" presents an idea which appears in the French immediately before the previous paragraph (p. 235).

2. Cf. "Jean Sans-terre" (pp. 235–36).

Ralph de Diceto was a twelfth-century compiler of chronicles.

3. Roger of Hoveden, a chronicler and clerk for Henry II, was another of the writers of historical Latin prose in England.

had himself been raised to high honours in the same court, and
employ'd seventeen years in important negociations, says in
positive terms, that Ung-can who was defeated by Chingiscan
was the Prester-John. And William of Tripoli, one of the
Dominicans who travel'd into Armenia, with the uncle and
father of Marco Polo, tells us, as his opinion is reported by
Gerard Mercator,[4] that in the year 1098, Coirem Can was
emperor of all the eastern Asia, that after his death, a Nestorian
priest made himself master of the province of Najam,[d] and
afterwards of the whole empire, that he was call'd Prester, or
Priest, in allusion to his profession, and John as it was his name:[5]
that after his decease, his brother Vuth, under the name of
Vuth-can succeeded him, and was attack'd by Chingis who was
a black-smith.

We shall omitt the testimonies of others[6] who cannot add any
authority to an opinion already so strongly supported, and
among those of elder date, that Mr. d'Herbelot in his *Bibliotheque
Orientale*, which was written since this book of Mr. du Cange.[7]

We are not to wonder, if upon the credit of these testimonies,
Mr. du Cange made no scruple to affirm, that the notion of the
king of Abyssinia being the Prester-John, was an old error which
is now clear'd up: yet notwithstanding the great name of so
celebrated a writer, with so strong reasons on his side, we are not
afraid to say, that this error, if it be one, is not yet so clear'd, but
it may still find those who will stand up in its defense.

It is to be observed, that the testimonies produced, are all
of them from the Latins, who have corrupted their accounts
with abundance of fables; and that Marco Polo wrote almost
an hundred years after the death of Ung-can, and I know not
for what reason he says of him that he is now generally

d. Najam *Relation*] Nujam *1735*

4. The sixteenth-century Flemish geographer, whose works included *Chronologia* (1569), *Galliae Tabulae Geographicae* (1585) and *Atlas Minor* (1610).
5. "that he was ... name" provides a fuller explanation than does the French: "qu'il fut appelé Prêtre, comme il était en effet, & Roi Jean" (p. 236).
6. Cf. the more explicit statement:

"Nous ne rapportons point les témoignages de Guillaume de Tyr, d'Alberic, de Vincent de Beauvais, de Sanudo" (p. 237).
7. Barthélemy de Herbelot de Molainville, *Bibliothèque orientale, ou dictionaire universel contenant tout ce qui regarde la connoissance des peuples de l'orient* (Paris, 1697).

call'd Prester-John, *quem hodie Presbyterum Johannem vocant.*[8] Abulfarage, a celebrated physician, almost contemporary with Chingiscan, and who hath given us a general history of the East, speaks of Ung-can in this manner.[9] In the 1514th year of the epocha of Alexander began the empire of the Moguls in this manner; Ung-can of the tribe of Certit who was call'd King John, commanded the tribes of the Oriental Turks, who profess'd the Christian religion; and had near his person a successful man of another tribe, named Tamujin, who had serv'd him with great fidelity in his infancy, and had defeated his enemies in many battles. The reputation of his valour raised him enemies, who made use of all their arts to discredit him with his prince; and never ceas'd to insinuate something to his disadvantage, till they had made Ung-can suspect him, and brought him to a resolution of seizing him. Two of the King's domesticks advertised Tamujin that a design was laid to attack him the following night. Tamujin gave orders to his people that they should go out of their tents and leave them standing, and himself lay in ambush at a little distance, with what forces he had; and when Ung-can came early in the morning to seize him, and found the tents empty, Tamujin rushing out upon him and his followers, defeated, and put them to flight. He some time afterwards in a second battle slew Ung-can, with a great part of his army, whose wife and children became a prey to the conqueror.

The same Abulfarage says moreover,[1] that while Chingis-can was making great rejoicings for the conquest of Cathay, he lost his brother Tuli, with whose death he was exceedingly afflicted, being passionately fond of him, and that in honour to his memory he decreed that his widow, the Queen Sarcutna, the daughter of Ung-can's brother, should command his armies. This princess he says, was extremely careful in the education of her children, and government of her provinces; she was prudent and faithful, and a strict observer of the precepts of

---

8. Apparently an accidental deletion: cf. "*quem hodie vulgo Presbiterum-Joannem vocant*" (p. 237).

9. Le Grand is taking the story from Edward Pockocke's Latin translation of the *Historia Compendiosa Dynastiarum* (Oxford, 1663), pp. 280–81. The account in English, differing somewhat in details,

may be found in *The Chronography of Gregory Abû'l Faraj ... commonly known as Bar Hebraeus*, trans. by Ernest A. Wallis Budge (London, 1932), I. 352.

1. See Pockocke's *Historia Compendiosa*, p. 310 or *The Chronography of ... Bar Hebraeus*, I. 398.

Christianity;[2] and she had a great respect for priests, those
dedicated to religion, and never saw them without imploring
their benediction. He concludes her character with a line of an
Arabian poet. "If the women would resemble her, the men
would lose their superiority."

Abulfarage doth not say that either Ung-can or his brother
were priests, or that either of these kings was call'd Prester-John,
though Ung-can was named King John.

Mr. de la Croix Petit, confirms in his life of Genghiscan[3] the
opinion of Abulfarage, as we shall shew in his own words, This
says he, was the same Ung-can who made so great a noise in the
Christian world, about the latter end of the eleventh century, or
rather of the twelfth, under the name of Prester-John of Asia a
title attributed to him by the Nestorians. There are yet to be seen
circulatory letters from him to the Christian princes. There is
one to Pope Alexander the Third, to the King of France, to the
Emperor of Constantinople, and to the King of Portugal. They
are all written in a very elevated stile, and the author of them has
attempted to give those to whom they are address'd, a high
opinion of the power of the prince from whom they came, as the
most mighty of all the Asiatick kings. There is in France a copy
of that which was sent to Lewis the Seventh, father of Philip
Augustus, but it doth not appear by the character to be above
three hundred years old. It begins with these words, "Prester-
John, by the grace of God, powerful above all Christian kings."

The following part of the letter is extremely pompous for a
Keraite prince, he boasts of his immense wealth, and the prodigious extent of his dominions, in which he includes the Indies,
and all the nations of Gog and Magog. He makes mention in
haughty terms of seventy tributary kings, who depend upon
him. He enlarges upon the tribute which he exacts from a king
of Israel, who has many Jewish earls, dukes, and princes, subordinate to him. He gives the King of France an invitation to
visit him, promising to put a large country into his possession,
and even to make him sovereign after his own death of all his

2. "strict observer ... Christianity"
embellishes the simple phrase: "bonne
chrétienne" (p. 238).

3. The orientalist François Pétis de la
Croix augmented and published the work
on which his father, François Pétis, had

labored for ten years: L'Histoire du grand
Genghiz-Can ... premier empereur des Mogols et
Tartares (Paris, 1710). An English trans-
lation appeared in 1722 with the title The
History of Genghizcan the Great.

dominions. He takes notice in his letter of the different nations, and of the curiosities which are found in his territories, and, in short, leaves nothing unsaid, that might contribute to the idea of his greatness. He calls himself a priest from sacrificing on the altar, and a king from administring right and justice. He speaks of St. Thomas in the end of his letter agreeably to the fabulous notions of the Indians, and concludes with desiring the King to send him some valiant knight "of the generation of France."

There is no great difficulty in discovering that these letters were suppositious and not written by Ung-can: the Nestorians who inhabited this country in great numbers, where they had establish'd themselves in the year 737 by the missionaries of Moussul and Bassora were the authors of them. They had spread a report among the Christians that they had brought Scythia over to Christianity, and that the true religion had been embraced by the greatest of its monarchs,[4] who was so entirely converted, that he had taken the priesthood upon him, and had assumed the name of John. They added these circumstances to give their fables a greater appearance of truth, and wrote those high sounding letters, to make their false zeal more applauded, and to procure the reputation of having converted so powerful a prince to Christianity.

All the assistance that these letters can furnish towards compiling an history is, that we learn from them, that it was believ'd at the time in which they were written, that this king was a powerful Christian prince, and even a priest. We have a letter of the Pope in which he is call'd a most holy priest. There is nevertheless no appearance of his being a Christian, although he allow'd Christianity in his kingdom, and part of his people who embraced it, were permitted to have bishops among them.

Thus far Mr. de la Croix Petit,[5] who cites here the very words of Rubriquis,[6] which plainly make it appear that the Nestorians imposed upon the publick[7] in those letters which they wrote

---

4. "they had brought ... monarchs" adds details and phrasing not found in the French: the report was spread "qu'ils avaient converti la plupart des peuples de la Scythie, & même le plus puissant des rois qui y régnait" (p. 239).

5. Pétis de la Croix, *History of Genghizcan the Great*, pp. 24–26.

6. Gulielmus Rubruquis, a Cordelier (a branch of the Franciscans), whose travels in the middle of the thirteenth century are recorded by Hakluyt.

7. The followers of Nestorius (d. *c.* 451) believed that two separate persons existed in the Incarnate Christ, one divine, the other human.

198 A VOYAGE TO ABYSSINIA

concerning Ung-can the pretended Prester-John. *Et vocabant eum Nestoriani Regem Johannem, & plus dicebant de ipso in decuplo quam veritas esset; sic ergo exivit magna fama de illo Rege Johane; & quando ego transivi per pascua ejus, nullus aliquid sciebat de eo nisi Nestoriani pauci.* "The Nestorians," says he, "made this prince whom they call'd King John, much talk'd of, by reporting ten times more than was true; and when I travel'd through his country, none but a few Nestorians could give any account of him." [8]

Carpin the Cordelier was sent in 1246 to the Can of Tartary by Pope Innocent the Fourth; and Rubriquis, who was likewise a Cordelier, went from St. Lewis[9] into Tartary about seven years afterwards; neither of these have given any prince of that country the title of Prester-John. Marco Polo did not travel into that country till twenty years after them, and was the first and perhaps the only writer, who has said that Ung-can's brother was a priest.[1]

After having spoken in the fifty-first chapter of Prester-John, he adds that this mighty monarch so renown'd throughout the whole world, keeps his ordinary residence in the province of Tenduch, which though it be tributary to the Grand Cans yet enjoys its own sovereigns, who are of the race of Prester-John, and that all the Grand Cans, since the death of him who dyed in battle against Chingiscan give their daughters in marriage to these kings.

The story is well told,[2] but it doth not appear that any of these princes were priests, and the kings of Abyssinia on the contrary, have almost all taken that character upon them. Severus, Bishop of Asmonine, who lived at the end of the tenth century, has left us a testimony of the religion and power of the kings of Aethiopia. Elkera, says he, was king of the Abyssins, and orthodox: this is the mighty king upon whose head the crown falls from heaven, whose dominions extend to the farthest parts of the southern world; the fourth of the monarchs of the earth, the king whose power is not to be resisted. His patron saint is[3] the evangelist St. Mark, and the authority of the Jacobite Patriarch of Egypt extends to him and to all the kings of Aethiopia and

8. There is no translation of the Latin in Le Grand (pp. 239–40).

9. Cf. "alla de la part de Saint Louis" (p. 240).

1. Marco Polo, a Venetian, travelled extensively in the east from 1272 until

1295.

2. SJ substitutes this clause for "Il n'est rien de mieux détaillé" (p. 240).

3. "His patron saint is" replace "Il relève de ..." (p. 240). The *Errata* supplies "is," which is omitted in *1735.*

Nubia: he has in his country, near his person, an orthodox bishop who is ordained metropolitan by the patriarch of Alexandria, and by him are the other bishops consecrated, and the priests ordained.

Abuselah having repeated almost the same things with Severus, adds, "All these kings are priests and offer the mysteries upon the altars, who when they are kings, kill nothing with their own hands, and he who is so unhappy as to shed blood, is for ever deprived of the office of sacrifice. When he enters the sanctuary he takes off his crown, which is the mark of his dignity, and remains standing, and bare-headed, till every one of the people have received the communion, and if he intends to communicate himself, he is the last that receives."[4] The same author, repeats the same account lower, and then tells us, "That if the king shall kill any thing, there is no pact or condition which obliges his subjects to continue their allegiance."[5]

It appears by this last circumstance how much the Abyssins reverence the priesthood; since the king though entirely absolute amongst them, and of uncontroulable authority, could not enter the sanctuary without taking orders.

The Abyssins relate that their Caleb or Elesbas, who lived in the beginning of the sixteenth[6] century, was a priest and celebrated mass forty years. It is apparent, that they had not then that strict law which absolves the subjects from their fidelity to their king, if he stains his hands with blood, for King Caleb cross'd the sea to make war upon Denawas a Jewish king of the Homerites, whose kingdom he destroy'd, and kill'd him. The Abyssins affirm likewise that Abraham, one of their kings who reign'd since Lalibala, was not only a priest, but so favour'd by Heaven[7] that two angels brought him the bread and wine which he made use of in the celebration of the sacrament.

There is therefore no room to question that many of the Abyssin princes have been priests, when at the same time, the brother of Ung-can is the only one in Asia said to have exercised that function, and even his name is not mentioned. Besides it is not very probable that this king of the Oriental Turks who,

---

4. As B. T. A. Evetts's modern edition and translation of Abû Sâlih reveals, the quotation is actually taken from a section describing Nubian rather than Abyssinian practices; see *The Churches and Monasteries of Egypt and Some Neighbouring Countries* (Oxford, 1895), p. 272.

5. Abû Sâlih, p. 286, a section specifically on Abyssinia.

6. An error: "sixième" (p. 241).

7. This favoritism is not mentioned in the French (p. 241).

being a priest, usurped the sovereign dignity in 1098, was yet living in 1177. As he therefore could not be the king to whom Alexander the Third wrote, it can probably be none but the king of Aethiopia. To this may be added, that Marco Polo who first advanced the notion, that Ung-can was the Prester-John, informs us likewise that Aethiopia was call'd the lesser India, but doth not say that the name of India was extended to the country of the Oriental Turks: it then follows from the account of Marco Polo himself that this king of India to whom Pope Alexander's letter is addressed, must be the emperor of Aethiopia; which letter as it is a valuable monument of the Church of Abyssinia, may, I hope, properly be inserted here, as it is found in Hoveden.

Epistola Alexandri Papae
Ad Johannem Regem Indorum Missa[8]

Alexander Episcopus servus servorum Dei, charissimo in Christo Filio, illustri & magnifico Indorum regi sacerdotum sanctissimo salutem, & apostolicam benedictionem. Apostolica Sedes, cui, licet immeriti, prae-

---

8. Here follows a literal transcription of the Latin (pp. 242–44).

[The Epistle of Pope Alexander Sent to John, King of the Indians

Alexander the bishop, servant of the servants of God, to his dearest son in Christ, the illustrious and magnificent king of the Indians, holiest of priests, greetings and apostolic blessing. The Apostolic See, over which we, though unworthy, preside, is the head and mistress of all who believe in Christ by the testimony of our Lord who said to the blessed Peter, whom we, though undeserving, have succeeded: "Thou art Peter, and upon this rock I will build my church." Since Christ wanted this rock to be for a foundation of the Church, which he proclaims is to be shaken by no force of winds nor by storms, therefore not undeservedly the blessed Peter, upon whom he founded the Church, deserved to receive the power of binding and loosing specially and chiefly among the Apostles, he to whom it was said by the Lord, "I will give to thee the keys of the kingdom of heaven, and the gates of hell shall not prevail against it. And whatsoever thou shalt bind upon

earth, it shall be bound also in heaven: and whatsoever thou shalt loose on earth, it shall be loosed in heaven." In particular, we had heard by what many already were reporting and by common reputation how that, since you profess the name of Christian, you wish to devote yourself ceaselessly to pious works and to turn your mind to those things which are pleasing and acceptable to God. But also our beloved son Master Philip, a physician and our friend, who declares that he conferred in those regions with many honorable men of your realm about your pious intention and purpose, reported to us constantly and earnestly that he heard clearly from these men that it is your wish and purpose to be instructed in the Catholic and Apostolic teaching and that you fervently strive for this, that you and the land committed to your highness may never see anything abide in your faith which disagrees or is discordant with the doctrine of the Apostolic See. For which certainly we

sidemus, omnium in Christo credentium caput est & magistra, Domino atestante, qui ait beato Petro, cui, licet indigni, successimus, tu es Petrus, & super hanc petram aedificabo Ecclesiam meam. Hanc siquidem petram Christus esse voluit in Ecclesiae fundamentum, quam praeconat nullis ventorum viribus nullisque tempestatibus quatiendam & ideo non immerito beatus Petrus, superquem fundavit Ecclesiam ligandi atque solvendi specialiter & precipue inter Apostolos alios meruit accipere potestatem, cui dictum est a Domino, Tibi dabo claves regni coelorum & portae inferni non praevalebunt adversus eam. Et quodcumque ligaveris super terram erit ligatum & in coelis; & quodcumque solveris super terram, erit solutum et in coelis. Audiveramus utique jampridem referentibus multis, & in fama communi, quomodo cum sis Christianum nomen proffessus, piis velis oper-ibus indesinenter intendere & circa ea tuum animum geras, quae Deo grata sunt, & accepta. Sed & dilectus filius magister Philippus medicus & familiaris noster, qui de intentione pia & proposito tuo, cum magnis & honorabilibus viris regni tui se in partibus illis verbum habuisse proponit, sicut vir providus & discretus circumspectus & prudens, constanter nobis & solicite retulit, se manifestius ab his audisse quod tuae voluntatis sit &

---

rejoice greatly with you as with a very dear son, and to him from whom proceeds every gift we pay unbounded gratitude, joining vows to vows and prayers to prayers that he who granted to you to take up the name of Christianity may inspire your mind through his unspeakable piety to be in all respects wise regarding those things which the Christian religion ought to maintain regarding all the articles of faith. For one cannot hope for salvation from his Christian profession who is not in harmony with that same profession in word and deed, for it does not suffice anyone to be called by the name of Christian who holds a different opinion than the Catholic and Apostolic teaching holds, in accordance with that which our Lord says in the Gospel: "Not everyone who says unto me 'Lord, Lord,' will enter into the kingdom of heaven, but he who does the will of my father who is in heaven." That however is added to the commendation of your virtue which Master Philip says that he heard from your people, that you long with a fervent desire to have a church in the city and some "Altar of Jerusalem" where prudent men of your realm can stay and be instructed more fully in the Apostolic teaching. Through these afterwards you and the men of your kingdom can receive and hold onto the instruction. We, moreover, who, in spite of our insufficient merits, are placed in the chair of the blessed Peter and who, following the Apostle, recognize ourselves debtors to the wise and the foolish, to the rich and the poor, are affected by every kind of concern about your salvation and that of your people and wish to call you away from those articles in which you err from the Christian and Catholic faith, and we do so readily according as we are bound by the ministry of the rule we have undertaken since the Lord himself said to the blessed Peter, whom he made chief of all the Apostles, "And thou, being once converted, confirm thy brethren." Although it might seem too hard and laborious to send someone from our side to your presence among so many difficulties and varied dangers of the places on the journey and among so many distant and unknown shores, nevertheless upon con-

propositi erudiri Catholica & Apostolica disciplina, & ad hoc ferventer intendas, ut tu et terra tuae sublimitati commissa, nihil unquam videamini in fide vestra tenere, quod à doctrina sedis Apostolicae dissentiat modo quolibet, vel discordet. Super quo sanè tibi sicut charissimo filio plurimum congaudemus & ei à quo omne donum procedit, immensas gratiarum exsoluimus actiones: vota votis et preces precibus adjungentes, ut qui dedit tibi nomen Christianitatis suscipere, menti tuae per suam ineffabilam pietatem inspiret, quòd omnino velis sapere quae super omnibus articulis fidei tenere debet religio Christiana. Non enim vere potest de Christiana professione sperare salutem, qui eidem professioni verbo et opere non concordat: quia non sufficit cuilibet nomine Christiano censeri, qui de se sentit aliud, quam Catholica & Apostolica habeat disciplina juxta illud quod Dominus in Evangelio dicit, non omnis^e qui dicit mihi Domine, Domine, intrabit in regnum coelorum, sed qui facit voluntatem patris mei, qui in coelis est. Illud autem nihilominus ad commendationem tuae virtutis accedit, quod sicut prudens magister Phillippus se a tuis asserit audisse, ferventi desiderio cuperes in urbe habere ecclesiam, & Jerosolymitanum altare aliquod, ubi

e. non omnis *Errata*] none ominis *1735*

---

sideration of the obligation of our office and upon weighing your purpose and intention, we are sending the aforementioned Philip, the physician and our friend, an absolutely discreet, circumspect, and provident man, to your greatness, trusting in Jesus Christ's mercy. But if you will be willing to persist in that purpose and intention which we understand that you have conceived by divine inspiration, being instructed in the near future through God's mercy about the articles of Christian faith in which you and your people seem to disagree with us, you will be able to have no fear at all about anything from your error which could hinder your salvation or the salvation of your people or could darken in you the name of Christianity. We ask your royal excellency, therefore, we advise and urge in the Lord that you receive this same Philip out of reverence for the blessed Peter and for us, as an honorable man, discreet and provident and sent from our side. We ask that you receive him with due kindness and that you treat him both re-

verently and devoutly. And if it is your will and purpose, as it is absolutely fitting that it be, to be instructed in the Apostolic teaching concerning these matters which the same Philip will propound to you from our part, we ask that you listen and heed and that you transmit to us with him honorable persons and a letter sealed with your seal by which we may fully learn your purpose and will. This is because to the degree that you are regarded as lofty and great and seem less inflated by your wealth and power, to that degree we will more willingly take care to admit and heed efficaciously your petitions about the granting of a church in the city and even about conferring altars in the Church of the Blessed Peter and Paul and at Jerusalem in the Church of the Holy Sepulchre since we wish to promote in every way that we can with God's help your desire about this which is worthy of much commendation and we desire to gain your soul and your people's souls for the Lord. Venice on the Rialto, September 27.]

viri prudentes de regno tuo manere possint, et Apostolicâ plenius instrui disciplinâ; per quos postmodum tu, et homines regni tui doctrinam ipsam reciperent & tenerent. Nos autem, qui licet insufficientibus meritis in beati Petri Cathedra positi, juxta Apostolum, sapientibus et insipientibus, devitibus et pauperibus, nos recognoscimus debitores, de salute tua et tuorum omnimodam solicitudinem gerimus, et vos ab his articulis, in quibus erratis a Christiana et Catholica fide, prompto animo, prout tenemur ex Suscepti ministerio regiminis, volumus revocare: cum ipse Dominus beato Petro, quem omnium Apostolorum principem fecit, dixit, et tu aliquando conversus confirma fratres tuos. Licet autem grave nimis videatur et laboriosum existere ad praesentiam tuam inter tot labores et varia itineris locorum discrimina, et inter longas et ignotas oras quemlibet a nostro latere destinare; considerato tamen officii nostri debito, et tuo proposito et intentione pensata, praefatum Philippum medicum et familiarem nostrum, virum utique discretum, circonspectum et providum, ad tuam magnitudinem mittimus de Jesu Christi misericordiâ confidentes. Quod si volueris in eo proposito et intentione persistere quam te, inspirante Domino, intelligimus concepisse; de articulis Christianae, fidei, in quibus tu et tui a nobis discordare videmini in proximo per Dei misericordiam eruditus, nihil prorsus timere poteris, quod de errore tuum vel tuorum salutem praepediat, vel in vobis nomen Christianitatis offuscet. Rogamus itaque excellentiam regiam, monemus et hortamur in Domino quatenus eundem Philippum, pro reverentia beati Petri et nostra, sicut virum honestum, discretum et providum, et a nostro latere destinatum, debita benignitate recipias, et reverenter et devote pertractes; et si tuae voluntatis est et propositi, sicut omnino decet esse, ut erudiaris Apostolica disciplina, super his, quae idem Philippus ex nostra tibi parte proponet, ipsum diligenter audias et exaudias, et personas honestas et literas tuo sigillo sigillatas, quibus propositum et voluntatem tuam possimus plene congnoscere, ad nos cum ipso transmitas: quia quanto sublimior et major haberis, et minus de divitiis et potentia tua videris inflatus, tanto libentius, tam de concessione ecclesiae in urbe, quam etiam de conferendis altaribus in Ecclesia beati Petri et Pauli, et Jerosolymis in Ecclesia Sepulchri Domini, et in aliis quae juste quaesieris, tuas curabimus petitiones admittere & efficacius exaudire, utpote qui desiderium tuum super hoc quod multa commendatione dignum extitit, modis omnibus, quibus secundum Deum possumus, volumus promovere et tuam et tuorum animas desideramus Domino lucrifacere. Data Venetiae in Rivo alto quinto Kal. Octobris.

It appears by this letter, that the king of Aethiopia was desirous of subjecting himself to the See of Rome, and requested two churches for his nation, one at Rome, the other at Jeru-

salem: at Rome the Abyssins have formerly had the Church of
St. Stephen, and another church at Jerusalem.

We have an account,[9] that in the twelfth century, the emperor
of Aethiopia was so dissatisfied with the conduct of the patriarch
of Alexandria, that he form'd a design of withdrawing himself
from his jurisdiction. This difference first arose under Gabriel
the son of Tareik the seventieth[f] patriarch of Alexandria, who
was elected about the year 1131, and was still on foot in the time
of John the son of Abugaleb the seventy fourth patriarch. The
original of this discontent was,[1] that the kings of Abyssinia
would have compelled Michael the Abuna to consecrate several
bishops, which he refused to do without the consent of the
patriarch of Alexandria, upon which the king wrote not only
to the patriarch but to the califf who not understanding the
importance of such an innovation, spoke to Gabriel about it,
and proceeded after some importunity to menaces; but being
inform'd, that if the Abyssins could obtain several bishops, they
might elect a patriarch of their own, and separate themselves
from the Church of Alexandria,[2] the califf was not only content
to drop his former demand, but commended the patriarch for
his refusal.

The same Abuna was embarrassed with other difficulties of
greater danger. There happen'd in his time a revolution in
Abyssinia, by which the legal order of succession was broken,
and the usurping prince not being able to prevail on the Abuna
to crown him, demanded of the patriarch of Alexandria that he
should nominate another, alleging that the great age of Michael
made him incapable of performing the duties of his office. John
the seventy second patriarch of Alexandria refused to comply,
and for his refusal was imprison'd by the Vizier Haly the son of
Selar,[g] whom the new king had brought over to his interest,
chusing rather to be deprived of the pleasures of liberty than to
do any thing so contrary to the canons of the Church.

These frequent debates with the patriarchs, which the kings of
Abyssinia have been embroil'd in, might easily suggest a design

f. seventieth *Errata*] seventeenth *1735*   g. Selar *Relation*] Telar *1735*

9. This clause replaces "Il paraît"   2. SJ omits the final clause: "& ne
(p. 244).   s'y plus adresser pour aucune chose"
1. "The original ... was" is SJ's   (p. 244).
addition.

of having recourse to Rome, and if Mr. Ludolf had been acquainted with these particulars, he would perhaps have been more cautious in determining, that this letter was written to the Can of Tartary, or of the Oriental Turks. It is of no great importance to know whether it was Pope Alexander the Third, who allow'd the Abyssins the Church of St. Stephen at Rome, and another at Jerusalem, that they requested such a grant is plain, and they have always obtain'd it. If the Portuguese were the first, that gave us any knowledge of Abyssinia, let the patrons of that opinion inform us, how Zara Jacob, or to speak more properly, the Abuna Nicodemus, then establish'd at Jerusalem, wrote to Pope Eugenius the Fourth. It cannot be denied that the emperor of Aethiopia is mention'd as the true Prester-John, in a letter from the Grand Master of Rhodes to King Charles the Seventh, before the Portuguese had discover'd that part of the world, and forty years before any of them had travell'd into that country; Antony Payva and Peter Covillan not being sent in search of Prester-John till the year 1477. It is easy to judge from the Grand Master's letter, whether the emperor of Aethiopia was known at that time by the name of Prester-John, which I choose to lay before the reader as it is found in page 556, of the seventh volume of the *Spicilegium*.[3]

---

3. The letter that follows is a literal transcription except where errors occur (pp. 245–46). It may also be found in the three-volume *Spicilegium sive Collectio Veterum Aliquot Scriptorum qui in Galliae Bibliothecis Delituerant* (Paris, 1723), III. 777.

[Most serene and Christian King of the French (a proper dedication being affixed on the original). Princes are always accustomed to hear gladly what occurs in foreign regions and particularly whatever has befallen to the detriment of the infidels. Recently in fact from correspondence from Constantinople, Pera, and Chios sent here to Rhodes it has become known to us that the great king of the Teucrians or Turks has prepared a great fleet and collected an army in order to attack the very city of Constantine by land and by sea. When this fleet had entered into the Danube river and many Teucrians had disembarked from it onto land, suddenly the fleet of Blanchus, by far inferior to it in number, pounced on it from a place above us and burned almost the whole fleet of the infidels. Those, however, who had sought land were slaughtered by the peoples of Blanchus. By this catastrophe and massacre administered to the Teucrians, both the imperial city itself and all the islands of the Aegean sea were freed from great fear.

Furthermore, Prester John, the Emperor of the Indians, as certain Indian priests brought here to Rhodes have said through truthful interpreters, inflicted a great massacre and carnage on the Saracens his neighbors and particularly on those who claim they are descended from the race of Muhammed, so that it can scarce be believed, for over a three

Serenissime & Christianissime Francorum Rex, debita recommendatione praemissa. Consueverunt^h semper laeto animo principes audire ea quae in exteris regionibus geruntur, & praesertim si quid est quod ad detrimentum infidelium intercesserit. Nuperrimè siquidem ex litteris ex Constantinopoli, Pera & Chio huc Rhodum missis, nobis innotuit magnum Teucrorum sive Turchorum regem classem ingentem paravisse, exercitumque coadunasse, ut terrâ marique ipsam Constantini urbem oppugnaret. Quae classis, cum in Danubium flumen esset ingressa, descendissentque Teucri plurimi ex ea in terram, repente classis Blanchi longè ea inferior numero, ex superiore ad nos parte insiluit, & ferè infidelium totam classem combussit. Illi verò qui terram petierant, à Blanchi gentibus trucidati sunt. Hoc infortunio & clade Teucris data, & imperatoria ipsa civitas, & omnes insulae Aegaei pelagi à formidine magna, Deo victoriam Christianis dante, liberati sunt.

Insuper Presbyter Johannes Indorum Imperator, ut quidam sacerdotes Indiani huc Rhodum devecti per veros interpretes dixerunt, magnam stragem & occisionem Saracenis suis finitimis, & his maximè qui ex stirpe Machometi se ortos praedicant, intulit, ut vix credatur: nam per trium dierum iter passim cadavera occisorum conspiciebantur. Destinavit praeterea oratorem is Indorum rex soldano Babyloniae cum muneribus, sicut mos Orientalium est, ei denuntians nisi ab affligendo Christianos desierit, se bellum pestiferum civitati Mechae, ubi sepulchrum Machometi esse dicitur, Aegypto, Arabiae, & Syriae, quae ditioni ipsius soldani-subjectae sunt, illaturum; flumen-que Nili totum, qui Aegyptum irrigat, & sine quo nullus illic vivere posset, surrepturum, & iter aliud illi daturum simili pacto

---

h. Consueverunt *Relation*] Consuerunt *1735*

---

days' journey the corpses of the slain were visible. This king of the Indians furthermore sent an ambassador to the Sultan of Babylon with gifts, as is the custom of Orientals, announcing to him that unless he ceased afflicting Christians he would wage a ruinous war on the city of Mecca, where the grave of Muhammed is said to be, and on ,Egypt, Arabia, and Syria which are subject to the rule of the Sultan himself, and similarly threatening that he would interrupt the whole Nile, which waters Egypt and without which no one can live there, and give it another route. The ambassador himself at first was well admitted and seen and the opportunity given him to visit the Holy Sepulchre of our Lord. When he had returned to Cairo, he was imprisoned by the Sultan himself with the intention of not releasing him unless his ambassador who had been sent to India and detained should return. These few matters are worthy of recounting and most worthy of Your Serenity, to whom we ever wish good health.

Rhodes in our convent, the third day of July in the year of our Lord one thousand four hundred forty eight. Your Serenity's Master Hospitaler of Jerusalem.]

minitans. Orator ipse primò bene admissus & visus fuit; datáque ei copia ut sanctum sepulchrum Domini nostri viseret. Qui cùm reversus ad Cayrum fuisset, ab ipso soldano carceri traditus est, hac intentione illum non relaxaturum, nisi orator suus ad Indiam missus & detentus non redierit. Haec pauca¹ sunt memoratu digna, & serenitatis⅃ vestrae dignissima, quam semper valere optamus.

Datum Rhodi in nostro conventu, die tertia Julii anno Domini millessimo quadringentesimo quadragesimo octavo. Serenitatis vestrae magister Hospitalis Jerusalem.

We are far from giving credit to every thing contained in that letter, but it is sufficient for our purpose that the emperor of Aethiopia was known in 1448 to the grand master of Rhodes under the name of Prester-John, nothing being more apparent than that the Portuguese were not the first who mentioned him by that name. Mr. Thévenot informs us that Father Jerome Lobo believed that title to have been first ascribed to him by the French who visited the Holy-Land,[4] as the reader may find in the conference related by him.

The Abyssins were much addicted to pilgrimages into the Holy-Land, and this temper prevail'd most among them at the time when the French went often into Asia to carry on their wars in those countries. It was from their conversation with the Abyssins that they learn'd the appellation of Prester or Priest-John, for those people to raise the higher idea of their monarch, added to his other offices and titles that of priesthood.

DISSERTATION THE FIFTH, ON THE KINGS OF ABYSSINIA, THEIR CORONATION, TITLES, QUEENS AND SONS. OF THEIR ARMIES, AND THE MANNER OF DISTRIBUTING JUSTICE

As the Sabaeans or Homerites were not very careful to preserve their history, the Abyssins were much less curious; so great

---

i. pauca *Relation*] *om. 1735*   j. serenitatis] serenitati *1735*

---

4. Cf. "Jérusalem" (p. 246).

has been their supiness,[1] that the very names of their kings can scarce be recover'd. The Portuguese fathers have given us the succession drawn from two different manuscripts, which, as they make no scruple to confess, scarce ever agree. They reckon an hundred kings from Meneleck the son of Solomon, and Makeda Queen of Sheba to Sultan Jassok Aduam Sagghed, but they neither tell us when their kings begun, nor when they ended their reigns. All the history they have preserved is some account of Caleb or St. Elesbas who lived in 521, of whom they relate that at the instigation of the Patriarch of Alexandria, he passed the sea with a large fleet and a very formidable army to punish Denawas, a Jewish prince who had raised a cruel persecution against the Christians; that he defeated him in two battles, and after his death, which happen'd in the last fight, made himself master of his whole kingdom, and put an end to the power of the Sabaeans or Homerites. Part of this new acquisition he dismember'd from the rest, and gave the sovereignty of it to the son of the holy martyr Aretas; the other part paid tribute to the king of Aethiopia seventy two years, till Sait Ibn di-Jazan resolving to continue no longer dependant on the Abyssins, enter'd into an alliance with the Persians; by which the kingdom of the Homerites was divided into two parties, one declaring for the Persians, the other for the Romans, with whom and the Abyssins, the Persians were at war. This debate kindled so long and destructive a war in the country, that Mahomet, finding it almost empty of men, and entirely laid waste, took possession of it with very little difficulty or opposition; since which time the Abyssins have been shut up in Africa, without having any communication with the nations of Asia and Europe, till the Portuguese having penetrated into their country made it known to the other Europeans.[2]

It is handed down by a kind of tradition, that towards the end of the tenth century, the succession of the posterity of Menilech was interrupted by the enormous wickedness of Tradda Gaboz a woman of unparalel'd impiety and cruelty, who procured the death of the whole royal family, that she might place upon the throne a son which she had by the Governor of Bugna. The

---

1. "so great ... supiness" is SJ's addition.

2. According to Le Grand, the Portu-

guese "nous l'aient fait connaître" (p. 248).

Abyssins, from the mischief she did, call her Essal that is Fire, because she destroy'd every thing about her like that devouring element. Only one prince found means to escape her malice, who conceal'd himself in the kingdom of Xaoa where his posterity continued, during the three hundred years[3] in which the family of Zague, which had usurped the government, reigned in Abyssinia.

The Abyssins who consider the princes of the house of Zague, as men who illegally seiz'd upon the kingdom, do not reckon them among their kings, for which reason, only the names of some of the most remarkable have been preserved; these, as Mr. Ludolf tells us, are Degna Michael, Newuja Christos, Lalibala, who cut so many magnificent temples out of the rocks, of which Alvarez has given us the plans, and Naaca Luabo, who as he affirms, was the last of that family, and is celebrated by the Abyssins, as a good king, a lover of peace, and favourite of heaven.[4]

The Patriarch Alphonso Mendez mentions these kings in a different order, and by different names, and says that the empire was transfer'd from the house of Israel to that of Zague in 960, and restored to the legal successor in 1300.[5]

Of all these monarchs scarce any has left the memory of his reign behind him, except Lalibala of whom the Abyssins relate many wonders, being won to an admiration of him by the happiness of a long peace which they enjoy'd in his reign, and by the great number of churches which he built of a very particular structure, being hewn out of the hard rock with pick-axes and chissels.[6]

Of these churches the most considerable is call'd after the name of the founder Lalibala,[7] who notwithstanding is buried in

---

3. Cf. "trois cents quarante ans" (p. 248).

4. "as a good . . . heaven" offers a parallelism more pronounced than it is in the French: "comme d'un prince très bien faisant, qui aima la paix & qui fut aimé de Dieu" (p. 248).

5. This paragraph epitomizes a more detailed one which notes that in 1300 Ighum Amlac came to the throne (pp. 248–49). For the passage in Mendes see Beccari, VIII. 78.

6. The French adds that Alvares and Telles have recorded the names, Alvares providing a description of the churches (p. 249). The account by Alvares appears in Chapters LIV and LV (pp. 205–28) of *The Prester John of the Indies*, ed. C. F. Beckingham and G. W. B. Huntingford, who provide plans of the various churches.

7. This statement replaces one naming the churches (p. 249).

the Church of Golgotha. He is counted among their saints,[8] and the seventh of June according to their calendar, that is the twelfth according to our computation, is kept, as a festival to his honour. Balthazar Tellez places this feast on the seventeenth, whose account of the saint whose memory is on that day celebrated, may not be unacceptable.[9]

On the seventeenth of June, says the father, died the blessed Lalibala emperor of Aethiopia, that holy admirer of the mysteries of Heaven. When that saint was born his parents determined to bring him up in the fear of God, whose care had so wonderful an effect, that when he came to the age of reason, being scourged by the command of the emperor his brother, who was enraged[a] to find that he would certainly succeed him, he was so miraculously protected that no blow would light upon him; the angel who guarded him, told him that he should build ten churches, which he did, and died in peace.

After him the crown fell again to the descendants of the house of Israel, whose names and reigns it would be superfluous and tiresome to enumerate; since their names and the number of years, for which they bore the scepter, are all that we know of them.[1]

Though the kingdom of Abyssinia be so far hereditary that only one family can sit on the throne, yet the reigning prince has the power of choosing out of the royal family whom he pleases for a successor, which, if he omits it, is done by the grandees of the kingdom, who elect him for their king whom they judge most capable of so high an office.

It was the custom formerly to keep the princes confined in the mountain Guexen,[2] where the temper and manners of each prince were diligently observed, and when they had agreed

a. enraged, *1735*

8. In the French this clause occurs in the preceding paragraph after the first reference to Lalibala (p. 249).

9. "whose account ... unacceptable" has no parallel in the French (p. 249). Telles presents the account in his *Historia*, p. 70. Almeida, from whom Telles had the story, took it from the life of Lalibala, perhaps Perruchon's *Vie de Lalibala*.

1. "whose names ... of them" is SJ's addition; thus he dismisses somewhat cav-

alierly two and a quarter pages of French which present a great deal more than names and dates of rulers: e.g., civil wars, a natural son seeking the throne, factions arising because of the pro-Catholic leanings of one ruler, and so forth (pp. 249–51).

2. This may have suggested the "Happy Valley" of *Rasselas*. See earlier note, p. 163.

upon him whom they determined to place upon the throne, the governor of Tigre went with the great men and some troops, to bring the new king. The governor left his men ranged in order at the foot of the rock, and went with the nobles to the lodging of the king elect, and fixing a ring of gold in his ear as the first mark of royalty, commanded the other princes to pay homage to their king. The princes were presently sent back to their former confinement, and the new monarch conducted to his troops at the bottom of the mountain, where the principal officers alighting from their horses paid their salutations, and conducted him to a tent prepared for his reception. There having alighted he was anointed with perfumed oyl by one of the chief ecclesiasticks, while the other priests chaunted psalms. They then dress'd him in the royal habit, put a crown on his head, and a naked sword in his hand, and placed him upon the throne, after which the grand almoner standing upon an eminence proclaims him by his name to the people, who answer with repeated acclamations, and pray for all kind of blessings upon their new monarch. This ceremony practised in the royal tent, is repeated, if it were not first performed there, in the Church of Axuma,[3] where the king enters the sanctuary after his coronation, hears mass, and receives the sacrament.

The crown of the king of Abyssinia is only a hat embroider'd with gold and silver lace, having a cross on the top, and being lined with blew velvet. The Abyssins having observed in the pictures of the coronation of their kings which adorn their churches, an angel holding a crown, have conceived an opinion that the Abyssinian crown fell from Heaven. And this opinion is so far from being of modern date, that Severus who lived near the end of the tenth century speaks of it as a thing not to be called in question.

The kings of Abyssinia having formerly had several princes tributary to them, still retain the title of Emperor or King of the Kings of Aethiopia,[4] and when their subjects speak to them in the Aethiopick[5] language they make use of the word *hatzeghe*, which answers nearly to the French word *sire*.[6]

---

3. The French includes a half page adapted from Telles describing the coronation of Susenyos in 1609 (pp. 252–53).

4. The Amharic equivalent, "Negûça nagast zaitjopja," is deleted (p. 253).

5. Cf. "Amharique" (p. 253).

6. Which, the French version adds, "nous ne nous servons que pour nos rois" (p. 253).

The emperors of Aethiopia, when they mount the throne, take an adscititious name,[7] without laying aside their former, thus David who first sent ambassadors to Portugal added the name Onag Segued,[b] Susneus that of Malec Segued, afterward Sultan Segued; Segued which is now become a kind of hereditary title signifies venerable. The escutcheon is a lion holding a cross, with this motto, "Vicit Leo de Tribu Juda."

Although for the most part the emperors of Aethiopia have a great number of wives, yet only one of them enjoys the dignity of queen, whose title is *Iteghe*. Nor is this honour confer'd any other way, than by the grant of the emperor, who when he has determined to bestow this favour upon any of his wives, orders her to be brought magnificiently dress'd from her own tent to his, where he makes her sit down by his side; upon which one of the principal men of the court proclaims aloud, that the king has made his servant queen, which puts an end to the ceremony, and the lady from that time is treated as empress. If the king her husband dies, though his successor be only her son-in-law, or even, though he be not related at all to her, he always regards her as his mother, nor can any other woman during her life take the title of queen.

No body ever eats with the emperor of Abyssinia, not even the queen her self, nor have any the honour to see him at table except his pages that wait; but the queen always eats with a great number of ladies.

Anciently the princes who had any right or pretension to the crown, were, as hath been before related, kept under a strong guard on Mount-Guexen; which custom continued for two hundred years. Naod, the father of David was the last, who was raised from that prison to the throne. As this king was playing one day with a young prince about eight years old, a counsellor that stood by observed to him, that this son was very much grown; the child immediately apprehending the meaning of his words, burst into tears, and lamented that he was grown only to be the sooner sent to Guexen. The king, touched at the return,

b. Onag Segued] Onagegued *1735*

---

7. The "hard" adjective replaces "ils en ajoutent un autre . . ." (p. 253); *adscititious*: "That which is taken in to complete some- thing else, though originally extrinsick; supplemental; additional" (*Dictionary*).

declared, that the royal off-spring should be no more confined in
that manner; thus by this accident was an end put to the slavery
of the princes of Abyssinia.[8]

As for the princesses, whom they call in this country, *ozoray*,
they had never any reason to complain of restraint, for either we
ought to disbelieve many relations of their conduct, or they
indulge themselves in a kind of libertinism, which will not easily
be made consistent with the Christianity they profess; to them
the chains of marriage are not very burthensome, for they throw
them off when they please,[9] changing their husbands according
to their own caprice, and frequently procuring their deaths. Nor
has the most insatiable ambition of monarchs either to gain or
enlarge an empire been the occasion of more broils and troubles
than the intrigues and passions of these women.[1]

Formerly the emperors of Aethiopia were never seen by their
subjects, and concern'd themselves very little in the government
of their kingdom, all the power being deposited in the hands of
two officers whom they called *bahtuded*, that is minister and
favourite. This custom is now so far changed that the king
appears in publick three or four times a year, but is never seen
at meals; and when he gives audience even to strangers, he is
always concealed behind a curtain. Instead of the *bahtuded*, there
is now a generalissimo established under the title of *ras*, or chief,
and under him two intendants of the houshold, on one of which
depend the viceroys, governors, captains and judges, and on the
other all the inferior officers of the houshold.

The king's authority is so unlimitted, that no man can in this
country be call'd with justice proprietor of any thing, nor doth
any man when he sows his field, know that he shall reap it, for
the king may bestow the fruits upon whom he pleases, and all the
satisfaction the former possessor can hope for, is that some man
be appointed to bring in the estimate of the expences he had
been at in cultivating it, in order to his reimbursement. But the
arbitrator is always favourable to the present owner, whom he

---

8. "thus by this ... Abyssinia" grows
out of the following: "& depuis ce temps
on ne les tient plus sur cette montagne"
(p. 254).

9. "to them the chains ... please" is
SJ's interpolation.

1. Compare the balanced phrases and

abstract diction of this sentence with the
French: "elles ne causent pas moins de
troubles par leurs intrigues, & pour con-
tenter leurs passions folles, que les princes
les plus ambitieux en excitent pour
monter sur le trône ou pour commander"
(p. 254).

presumes to have more interest than the person dispossessed.

Theft is so established in this country, that the head of the robbers purchases his employment, and pays tribute to the king.

With all these advantages, and this great extent of preroga- tive[2] the king of Abyssinia is by no means rich: every thing is paid in kind, and the most valuable branch of his revenue is a tythe which he takes every third year of the cattle; he receives likewise about three thousand pieces of callicoe. The governors purchase their commissions, or to speak properly their privilege of pillaging the provinces, and pay yearly a stated sum of money which arises to no great value.

The viceroyship of Tigre is the most valuable, and contains several subordinate governments, which do not pay all together above twenty five thousand livres yearly. Those of Dambia pay about fifty thousand and the rest in proportion.

The king is in possession of vast tracts of land which are put in the hands of his viceroys, who take the charge upon them of cultivating them, and giving an account of the produce. He receives no money from any of his provinces except Goiam and Narea.

As the whole revenue of the emperor consists in lands and goods, he has nothing else to pay his troops with, he therefore gives them lands, and if what he has assign'd be not sufficient, he distributes corn amongst them.

The emperor of Aethiopia is able to bring forty thousand men into the field, and among them about five thousand horse, but his forces are less formidable,[3] because they know not the use of fire-arms, of which they have but few, and less powder; they are arm'd generally with half-pikes and bucklers, instead of which some of the horsemen have coats of mail.

As they spend almost their whole lives in the camp, they order their march without much difficulty though they carry their wives and children with them, which so swells their numbers, that there are often forty thousand persons in an army of ten thousand men, who provide for themselves as they can;[c] what in some measure ballances the inconvenience of such numerous

c. can, *1735*

2. "With all ... prerogative" enlarges upon: "Avec tout cela" (p. 255).

3. "but ... formidable" is a unifying clause added by SJ.

and unserviceable attendants, is that[4] there is no nation which
can endure the extreams of heat and cold, or the hardships of
hunger and thirst and rain, with less inconvenience than the
Abyssins, who are sufficiently robust and active, but march to
action without any regularity, for they know not what a batta-
lion or squadron is, and therefore are soon disordered in a day of
battle. If the king marches with them in person he is always
attended by the flower of the nobility.

After having given an account of their wars and forces, it
would be proper to say something of their civil government and
courts of judicature, but these have been so fully clear'd in the
foregoing relation that nothing can be added, and what has
been already said, it is superfluous to repeat.[5]

DISSERTATION THE SIXTH, ON THE RED-SEA, AND THE NAVIGATION OF SOLOMON'S FLEETS

Since the Patriarch Alphonso Mendez and the Fathers
Jerome Lobo and Balthasar Tellez have written their observations on the Red-Sea, it seems proper to examine their sentiments. All three have given us a confutation of the ancient
opinions in order to establish a new one, in my opinion not
better grounded. The two former tell us that they used frequently to divert themselves upon the water,[1] and took a particular pleasure in turning the boat to those places in which any
redness appeared, where they made an Indian that waited on
them dive into the water, who always brought up with him a
plant call'd *gouesmon*, and that when this was pluck'd away the
redness always disappear'd.

That there are great quantities of *gouesmon* in the Red Sea, and
that it gives the water an appearance of redness, which it has not
naturally, is undeniable; but it is not very probable that from so

---

4. "what in ... is that" provides a connection between ideas linked in the
French only by the word "heureusement"
(p. 256).
   5. "but these ... repeat" is SJ's creation and circumvents a paragraph de-

scribing Abyssinian judicial procedures in
a murder case (p. 256).
   1. The French provides a clarifying
detail: "pendant qu'ils étaient prisonniers
à Maçua & à Suaquem" (p. 257).

trifling a cause all the nations of the earth should have agreed to give this gulph the name of the Red-Sea.

Father Balthasar Tellez remarks that tho' Moses often makes mention of the Red Sea, he never mentions it by that name; and draws this conclusion from his remark, that it was not known by it, till the Israelites went from Egypt, and Pharaoh and his whole army was swallow'd in the waters, and that it took that appellation from this great and miraculous event. He objects to his own hypothesis, that those who are drowned, do not lose much blood, and gets over it as well as he can.[2]

Mr. Bochart was the first publisher of an opinion which has been received by Mr. Ludolf, and which seems to us the most probable. We read in the 25th chapter of Genesis, that *edom* signifies red, and it is with great probability on their side, that some learned men maintain the Red-Sea to have derived its name from *edom*.[3] It is unquestionably evident from Scripture that the country of Edom bordered upon the Red-Sea, and Fuller[4] is of opinion, that the King Erythra or Erythraeus reported by the Greeks to have left his name to these waters, was no other than Esau who was called Edom after he had sold his birthright for the pottage. Nothing is more common than to give the sea a name from the neighbouring country, and we read in the first book of Kings,[5] that Solomon built his ships on the coasts of the Red-Sea in the country of Edom.

The learned Father Hardouin, believes that he has sufficient reasons for refusing to subscribe to this opinion, having discover'd in his vast reading that the Southern Ocean had the name of the Red-Sea, before it was given to the Gulph of Arabia.[6] I should agree with Vosius, says he, that the name of

2. The discussion appears in Telles, pp. 26–28.

3. Samuel Bochart, a seventeenth-century French Protestant cleric, published *Geographia Sacra, seu Phaleg et Canaan* (1675). Le Grand is discussing a section in Part 2, Book II, Chap. 16.

4. The English scholar Nicholas Fuller published *Miscellaneorum Theologicorum* ..., 3 vols. (Heidelberg, 1612) and added two new books (1622) entitled *Miscellanea Sacra*; Le Grand seems to be taking his account from Ludolf, who cites *Miscel. Sacr.*, I, Chap. 9.

5. SJ silently corrects for his Anglican audience Le Grand's reference to the third book of Kings. Le Grand's readers would know the books of Samuel as the first two books of Kings.

6. The French characterizes Hardouin as a "Jesuite d'un très profonde érudition" (p. 258). Le Grand's marginal note (p. 258) makes clear that the quotation which follows is from Hardouin's edition of Pliny (1685): "*Not. in Plin. hist. 1. 6 c. 23. n. 28.*" SJ owned Hardouin's edition (*Library*, p. 92).

the Red-Sea was derived from Idumaeus or Edom which in the Hebrew language signifies red; had it not appear'd from ancient writers, that the Southern Ocean was known by that name before it was given to the Arabian Gulph.[7] We are bold to hope for pardon from this great scholar, if we say that an appellation, common likewise to the Southern Ocean, might easily have been given to the Gulph of Arabia.

Among the reasons which Pliny sets down of this appellation, he mentions the foregoing,[8] *Irrumpit deinde, & in hac parte geminum, mare in terras quod Rubrum dixere nostri, Graeci Erythraeum, a Rege Erythrâ,*[9] relating afterwards the sentiments of those who wrote before him, without coming to any determination.[1]

It is sufficiently probable that the fleets of Solomon which sailed from the coast of Edom, made this sea so celebrated, and first gave it the name of Edom or Red, which it has retain'd for so many ages, and by which it is known by all the nations of the world.

It would perhaps be unnecessary to follow the fleets of Solomon any farther, were there not reason to believe that we should discover them on the coast of Aethiopia; nothing being more probable than that the two countries of that name supply'd them with their wealthy lading, notwithstanding it has been imagined that their voyages were much longer, since they were three years in making them.

All the learned men who have undertaken to treat of this subject have been in more care to make a pompous display of their own erudition, than a discovery of the truth. They have advanced imaginary systems to shew how well they could

---

7. "I should agree ... Arabian Gulph" is translated from the Latin quotation in Hardouin's note 28 (p. 258).

8. "he mentions the foregoing" is SJ's added transition.

9. The following translation is by Philemon Holland from *The Historie of the World: Commonly called, The Naturall Historie of C. Plinius Secundus* (London, 1601), p. 134: "the sea breaketh into the land in two armes which our countreymen are wont to call the Red Sea, and the Greekes Erythraeum, of a king named Erythras." Le Grand paraphrases part of the quotation: "ce golphe peut avait été

appelé Mer rouge, ou Erythrée du roi Erythra" (p. 258).

1. Le Grand provides the specific passage: *aut (ut alii) solis repercussu talem reddi colorem existimantes: alii ab arenà terraque, alii tali aquae ipsius natura* (p. 258). Holland's translation: "or (as some thinke) because the sea by reason of the reflection and beating of the sunne beames, seemeth of a reddish colour. There be that suppose that this rednesse is occasioned of the sand and ground which is red: and others againe, that the very water is of the owne nature so coloured" (p. 134).

defend them, and have ransack'd their memories for quotations, and their invention for arguments, to support the greatest uncertainties.[2]

Some of these writers have conjectured from the word *Parvaim*, that these ships sailed to Peru, others declare for the isle of Saint Domingo, and several for Malaca,[3] whom Mr. Bochart has examined with great diligence, and, setting a side the notion as not sufficiently supported, concludes in favour of Ceylan.[4]

I cannot but think that if these great men[5] had been acquainted with the *History of Eastern Aethiopia*, they would have taken some notice of what is said in the second book, which after having made the reader somewhat more acquainted with our author, we shall return to cite.[6]

Father John Dos-Santos, a Dominican monk, set sail from Lisbon with thirteen more of his own order in April 1586, and arriving at Mozambique in August, was employ'd in the missions of that country. His superiors directed him to keep his principal residence at Sofala, from whence he was continually travelling to all parts of that region, where he continued eleven years constantly attending these laborious duties. He made in the mean time several voyages from Sofala to Mozambique which are an hundred and sixty leagues distant, and penetrated two hundred leagues into the inland parts, passing up the river Cuamo, to Tete, where the Dominican fathers had then an establishment, which the Jesuites are now said to be in possession of. The observations which he made in his missions, were printed by him at Evora in 1609 under the title of the *Eastern Aethiopia*.[7]

---

2. The force and balance of this sentence are not apparent in the French: "Ils ont bâti des systèmes à leur fantaisie, ils les ont appuyés de diverses citations, & de raisonnements vagues & peu solides; ce qui arrive presque toujours lorsqu'on veut supposer des faits incertains" (p. 259).

3. SJ deletes some seven lines referring specifically to maps and manuscripts on this topic (p. 259).

4. See Bochart, *Geographia Sacra*, Book II, Chap. 27, p. 141.

5. This charged phrase renders "ces savants" (p. 259).

6. "which after ... cite" replaces two sentences in which Le Grand begins to discuss the work and then excuses himself to offer information about Father dos Santos (p. 259). The sailing in April and arrival in August 1586 are recorded in the opening pages of João dos Santos' book.

7. More accurately, *Ethiopia Oriental, e Varia Historia de Cousas notaveis do Oriente* (Evora, 1609). What follows in the next eleven paragraphs may be found in the Primeira Parte, fols. 6r, 44v–45r, 52v, 56v–58r. and 6or.

The fortress of Sofala, says he, is placed in thirty two degrees and an half southward, on the coast of the eastern Aethiopia near the sea, at the mouth of a river of the same name which rises in Mozambique[8] about an hundred leagues off, and runs by Zimbaoe the common residence of the *quiteve* or king of that country. The inhabitants of Sofala carry their merchandizes up this river to Manica which is sixty leagues higher in the country, where they sell their teeth,[9] and receive gold dust. Thirty leagues from Sofala, is the celebrated and wealthy river of Cuama, call'd by the Cafres, Zambese. The head of this river is undiscovered, but the tradition among the natives is, that in the midst of Aethiopia is a vast lake which gives rise to many rivers, and among them to the Cuama, which, they say, is named Zambese from a village by which it runs, not far from the lake. This river is extremely rapid, and in some places a league in breadth; at thirty leagues from the sea, it divides itself into two branches, each of which appears as large as the whole stream did before it was parted. The principal stream is call'd Luabo which divides again into two other branches, and the lesser Guilimane, or the River of Welcome-tokens, because Vasco de Gama there discovered some marks, by which he knew that he was near Mozambique, where he hoped to meet with some pilots, to guide him in the rest of his voyage to the Indies. He raised a stone pillar with a cross and the arms of Portugal, and call'd the country, the Land of Saint Raphael.

From the Guilimane rises another branch, so that this mighty river Cuama or Zambese discharges itself into the sea through five mouths; but ships can only enter at the Luabo and Guilimane, nor at the latter except in winter when the waters are high.

Vessels pass up the Luabo as far as the kingdom of Sacumbe[a] which is much higher than Tete, and there the river falls from a

a. Sacumbe *Relation*] Sicambe *1735*

---

8. Moçambique is SJ's substitution for the less well-known phrase, "les pays de Mocarangua" (p. 260).

9. "where ... teeth" may be a faulty rendering of: "ils y vendent leurs denrées" (p. 260)—their goods. Either SJ was drawing on prior knowledge—the teeth of elephants and other animals *were* valuable commodities—or a hasty glance at "denrées" suggested "dent—." *Ethiopia Oriental* also offers a general term signifying goods: "vendem suas fazendas" (Primeira Parte, f. 6r).

rock of wonderful height, beyond which the channel is so ob-
structed by rocks that it's impossible to steer a boat through it,
which impediments continue for twenty leagues as far as the
kingdom of Chicoua, where silver mines are found. This river is
called Airs from an island of the same name near its mouth,
where all the goods from Mozambique are unladed and stowed
in lighter vessels, in order to their more easy conveyance up the
river to Sene, which is sixty leagues from the coast.

The Zambese is as beneficial to the inhabitants of these countries, as the Nile was to the Aegyptians, overflowing the land in
the month of April, and giving it fatness and fertility.

The merchants of Tete come down to Sene, with great store of
gold which they fetch from Massapa in the kingdom of Monomotapa,[b] where vast quantities of that metal are always to be
had, it being in the neighbourhood of that vast mountain Fura
or Afura; on the top of which are still to be seen the ruins of
edifices built of stones and lime, a thing which is observed in no
other part of the country of the Cafres, where the kings'[c] palaces
themselves are nothing but wood and clay covered with briars.

We are inform'd by the ancient tradition of the country, that
these ruins are the remains of the magazines of the Queen of
Sheba, who, 'tis said, receiv'd all her gold from the mines in this
mountain, which was sent down the Cuama, to the Aethiopian
Sea, from whence it was transported through the Red-Sea to
that Aethiopia which lyes above Aegypt, then the empire of that
queen.

Father Dos-Santos in favour of this tradition cites the authority of Josephus, Origen, and Saint Jerome, and produces the
testimony of the Abyssins who are firmly persuaded that this
celebrated queen was of their country, where they have a village
named after her, not far from Axuma.

Others are of opinion that these magazines were erected by
Solomon, and that it was from hence that the gold was brought
which his ships were freighted with; observing in defence of their
notion, that there is no greater difference between the words
ophir and *afura*, than what the various pronunciation of several
nations might easily in so long a time have produced. In this
they all agree, that there is a large quantity of the finest gold
about that mountain, which might without the least difficulty be

b. Monomotapa *Errata*] Menomotapa *1735*   c. kings' (des rois *Relation*)] kings *1735*

convey'd down the river, as is now practised by the Portuguese, and was practised before them by the Moors of Mozambique and Guiloa, and that as it is now transported into the Indies, it might be carried anciently to Eziongeber and from thence to Jerusalem.

We have no reason, adds the same father, to wonder that the fleets of Solomon were three years in performing this voyage, for even at this day when the Cafres are better acquainted with the value of gold than they were then, the barks of Mozambique spend a whole year here, either in selling their freight, or collecting what is owing to the merchants. Navigation was in ancient times more difficult, being performed with vessels less artfully contrived, and with pilots less skilful than now; and if the pangaies be not ready to sail in the time of the monsoon they are obliged to wait for another season, so, that the vessels of Mozambique are thought sufficiently expeditious if they return within the year.

Sofala is in thirty two degrees and an half south, and Eziongeber in twenty nine and an half north, so that the whole voyage thither and back is two thousand leagues: it is likewise to be consider'd that it is impossible to sail in the Red-Sea except by day, and then almost continually with plummet in hand; that it is necessary to take the proper seasons for passing the Indian-Sea; that the stream of the Cuama is not to be surmounted without great difficulty; and that Afura stands at the distance of two hundred leagues from the sea: if we add to these obstacles the time which was spent[1] in collecting the gold and silver, we shall no longer be surprised at the time required for the voyage. As to the other lading of those fleets we find upon this coast ivory, all sorts of wood, fowls, and monkies of various kinds.

All the objection that Father Dos Santos seems to apprehend, is, that there are no peacocks in this country, though to solve this, he pretends that these fowls are to be met with farther up in the land, from whence they might have been fetch'd. It is evident that he was unacquainted with the disagreement among the interpreters about the meaning of the word *thukkijm*; some of whom imagine that it signifies paroquets, and others that the true interpretation of it is ape, though some think it to be peacocks. So that his greatest perplexity is easily avoided.

---

1. "if we add ... spent" expands "Il faut" (p. 262).

Silver is very scarce in the East, nor is it easy to discover more plentiful mines of it than in the kingdom of Chicoua which extends north eastward along the Zambese to Monomotapa. The forest of Thebe which crosses a river of the same name, is fill'd with trees of a wonderful beauty and of such vast magnitude, that of one trunk only they make boats twenty cubits long. The learned Mr. Huet,[2] is of opinion that the ivory brought into Palestine by the fleets of Solomon did not consist only of elephants' teeth, which are in great plenty to be met with in this part of Africa, but of the teeth of sea-horses on which a great value is set; these animals are as common in the rivers of Cuama and Sofala, as the elephant is in the forests and plains of Aethiopia. There is great plenty of amber on this coast, and a fishery for pearls near the islands of Bocicas; so that Solomon's fleet might have found at the mouths of the Cuama and Sofala, gold, silver, ivory, wood, and in general all that it is recorded to have brought him, except precious stones, which it went in quest of to the Gulph of Persia.

There is no less difficulty in determining the situation of Tharsis than of Ophir, the most common opinion is that Tharsis properly so call'd, is Baetica, that is, the kingdoms of Andalusia, Granada, and Murcia in Spain, but that in a more extended signification it may comprehend Africa, and perhaps in general all coasts, with the sea. Some, though but few, place Tharsis in the Indies, at or near China, and each party exert their utmost abilities to support their sentiments by a great number of authorities, in my opinion to very little purpose;[3] for since there are few writers of the age of Solomon who have treated either of geography, or the course of those voyages, it seems scarce possible to advance any thing farther than probabilities; nor do the testimonies of Strabo, Pliny, and Heliodorus, quoted with great solemnity,[4] contribute so much to clearing the truth, as displaying the authors' learning.

As these writers were neither eye-witnesses nor contemporaries, it seems best to confine our selves to the Scripture, and

---

2. Pierre Daniel Huet had written *De Navigationibus Salomonis* (1698); an English translation of *The History of the Commerce and Navigation of the Ancients* was published for Lintot and Mears in 1717.

3. This "opinion" is SJ's; it does not appear in the French (p. 263).

4. "quoted ... solemnity" is also SJ's contribution.

explain one part of it by another. To come therefore at the truth, let us compare the 71st Psalm with the 9th and 10th chapters of the first book of Kings, the 19th and 20th of the second book of Chronicles, and the 2d chapter of Judith,[5] from which it will appear that Tharsis was in Arabia. David says that, "the Aethiopians shall prostrate themselves before the Lord, and that his enemies shall lick the dust": that "the kings of Tharsis and of the isles shall bring presents, the kings of Sheba and Saba shall offer gifts." It cannot be denied that this psalm is a prophecy of the birth of Jesus Christ, and of the acknowledgement of his divinity by the Magi, who were not far distant from each other, and who appear, by their offerings of myrrh, incense, and gold, to have come from the province of Saba in Arabia; which is affirm'd by David himself. The fleets of Solomon which were fitted out at Ezion-geber sail'd to Ophir and to Tharsis either separately or together. The ships of Jehoshaphat which were lost in the port, were to have carried on the same commerce at the same places, "Jehoshaphat made ships of Tharshish to go to Ophir for gold, but they went not, for the ships were broken at Ezion-geber," I Kings xxii. 49.[6] "And he joined himself with him to make ships to go to Tharshish, and they made ships at Ezion-geber."[7] The Scripture seems to confound Tharsis and Ophir, since the same were design'd to have gone to each place; whether the squadrons separated at the mouth of the Red-Sea, at the river Sofala, or any other place,[d] they always returned together, and were therefore call'd either the fleet of Ophir or of Tharsis, as appears from the passages of the Holy Scripture, in

---

d. place; ... place, *Le Grand's punctuation (p. 264) indicates these changes.*] place, ... place; *1735*

---

5. Again SJ cites the first book of Kings rather than the third for his English readers; however, he incorrectly refers to the "19th" chapter of the second book of Chronicles: the French correctly cites "dans les Paralipomènes, chap. 9, vers. 21. chap. 20. vers. 36" (pp. 263–64). The Psalm would be 72 in the King James version.

6. "'Jehoshophat ... Ezion-geber.' I Kings xxii.49" replaces the Latin in Le

Grand (p. 264) with an exact quotation from the King James version. III Kings is changed to first, but Le Grand's incorrect citation of verse 49, instead of 48, remains.

7. "'And he ... Ezion-geber.'" replaces the Latin in Le Grand (p. 264). The King James version differs slightly from SJ's quotation: "... they made the ships in Ezion-gaber" (II Chronicles xx.36). The citation of "Paralip. lib. 2. cap. 20. vers. 36" appears in the French.

which when mention is made of the intent of those ships these two places are named indiscriminately.

When Holofernes march'd to besiege Bethulia, he found, after having passed through Cilicia, that the Jews had possessed themselves of the high mountains; taking therefore a very large compass, he plunder'd the wealthy city of Melothi, ravaged the countries of Tharsis and the Ishmaelites, and carried away the inhabitants. Tharsis therefore is in Arabia, and I am of opinion that together with Saba it made part of it, and that when David says, "They that dwell in the wilderness (or the Aethiopians) shall fall down before him, the kings, &c."[8] he speaks particular of Arabia, which, as hath already been observed was anciently known by the general name of Aethiopia, and extended along the shore of the Red-Sea to the Gulph of Ormus, where the fleet of Solomon found the precious stones, and every thing which Ophir, that is, the coast of Sofala, could not supply them with.

It is far from any appearance of probability that in an age almost entirely ignorant of the art of navigation, vessels setting sail from Ezion-geber should quit the coasts, double the Cape of Good-Hope, pass and repass the line, and visit savage and uncultivated countries, only for what might have been had near home, free from all these inconveniences, and almost without expence or danger.

None of our readers will think three years too long a time to be spent in the voyage we have been explaining,[9] if he reflects that they sail'd within sight of the shore, or very near it; that the passage is difficult; that at Sofala they conducted[e] their vessels up a river full of rocks; and that they were obliged to cut down and shape the timber which they carried away.

If an objection shall be raised that Jonas, with an intent to go to Tharsis, embarked at Joppa, now Jaffa, a port in the Mediterranean, and that, admitting our conjecture,[1] he must

e. conducted *1789*] conducted to *1735*

---

8. Cf. Le Grand's quotation: "'Les Ethiopiens se prosterneront devant lui, les rois de Tharsis, ceux de Saba, les isles lui feront des présents'" (p. 264).

9. "None ... explaining" makes personal what had been impersonal: "Le

temps de trois ans qu'on employait pour des voyages si courts ne paraîtra pas trop long ..." (p. 265).

1. SJ inserts the phrase, "admitting our conjecture."

have sail'd round Africa, 'tis hoped we may be allow'd to answer,[2] that there might have been another Tharsis, or that, supposing it the country we have endeavoured to prove it, he might have taken shipping at Joppa, with a design of going to some other place less distant from the Red-Sea. After all, as conjecture in these matters is the utmost we can arrive at, I thought these guesses which I have laid before the reader, had as fair an appearance of truth, as those reasonings which other writers have used, and continue to use every day.

DISSERTATION THE SEVENTH, ON THE QUEEN OF SHEBA

To point out the places meant by the names of Ophir and Tharsis is not more difficult, than exactly to determine the residence of the Queen of the South, so famous for the visit which she paid to Solomon, and for the encomium which she has receiv'd from the Redeemer of the World. We have already from the writings of Father Dos-Santos seen, that the wild and uncivilized nations of Africa, who are entirely unacquainted with the controversies which divide the learned world into parties, are persuaded that this celebrated princess reigned amongst them, and shew to this day the ruins of her palace, and their opinion is supported by those who have travelled into Abyssinia.

Yet however firmly this notion may be established in Africa,[1] the most learned interpreters have almost universally agreed to place her in that part of Arabia-the-Happy, known now by the name of Yemen; and as her name is not any where mention'd in the Holy Writings, and Jesus Christ only says, that "the Queen of the South shall rise up in judgment,"[2] every one is at liberty to indulge his own conjectures, and to assign her a name, and place of abode.

Father Nicholas Godigno tells us, that she is call'd Nicanta,

---

2. "'tis hoped ... answer" is more tentative than "nous répondrons" (p. 265).

1. "Yet ... Africa" is an expansion of a single word: "cependant" (p. 266).

2. The meaning of the quotation is altered: cf. "la Reine du Midi s'élèvera au jour du jugement" (p. 266).

Nitocris, Nicaula, and Makeda,[3] omitting another name, Belkis, which the Abyssins give her, who affirm that she was the daughter of Hod-Had king of the Homerites. She is likewise conformably to the Scripture call'd Nagista Azeb, that is, Queen of the South, by the Abyssinians, who agree with the Arabs in asserting that she was the wife of Solomon. Some of the interpreters who favour that opinion, imagine, that Solomon who had espoused the women of Egypt and Midian would not have refused to marry this princess, who came so far without any other motive than the reputation of his wisdom; and indeed a king who had already so many wives and concubines needed not to have made any difficulty of that matter. It is pretended farther that she return'd into her own country big with child, that she brought a son there, whom she bred up untill he was of age capable to receive advantage from the lessons of masters, and the instructions of Solomon; and then sent him to Jerusalem to be educated near his father.

At Jerusalem, as the tradition continues to inform us,[4] he pass'd several years, and was anointed and consecrated in the temple, taking the name of David in memory of his grandfather, from whence he afterwards returned, and ascending the throne, establish'd the religion of Judaea, in his native country, which gave the original to that great number of Jewish ceremonies which are still preserved among the Abyssins. This nation seems to have a particular interest in maintaining that the Queen of Sheba was of their country, for they affirm that their kings are descendants in a right line from her and Solomon, which hath been so exactly related by the Patriarch Alphonso Mendez, that I shall set down his account of it almost in his own words.[5] "The history of the country," says he,

> and a general tradition inform us, that many ages ago the Abyssins had a queen endowed with all the qualities of the greatest men. They call her Magueda otherwise Nicaula;

---

3. Nicolao Godinho (Godignus), a Portuguese Jesuit, published *De Abassinorum rebus, deque Aethiopia patriarchis Ioanne Nonio Barreto, & Andrea Oviedo* (1615). The statements on the Queen of the South are found in Book I, chap. 18, p. 114.

4. "As the tradition ... inform us" is

SJ's transition possibly suggested by the opening sentence of the long quotation that follows.

5. The Patriarch's account (all of the quoted material plus two paragraphs which follow it) may be found in Beccari, VIII. 40–43.

she is the same who from the desire she had of knowing Solomon, of whom she had heard so many wonders, went to see him in the twentieth year of her reign, in the year 2979 from the creation of the world. She carried him many presents, and was delivered in her way home of a son which she had by him, whom she called Menelech, that is, "another self." This son, after having educated him herself for some years, she sent to Solomon to be farther instructed, by whom he was taken care of, and, being consecrated in the temple, took at his consecration the name of David in memory of his grandfather. He was soon after sent back to the Queen attended by many doctors of the Law of Moses, and great men of Solomon's court, the chief of whom was Azarias the son of Zadoc the High-Priest, who stole and carried with him the Ark and one of the Tables of the Law, which are still preserved in the Church of Axuma, the chief of the Abyssinian churches.

"It is not my design," continues the father, To defend all these fictions, and in particular I am ready to give up what they relate concerning the Ark and the Table of the Law. But as, though we reject the fables that obscure the beginning of the Roman history, though we can not imagine that Romulus was the son of Mars and Rhea Silvia, or that he was suckled and fed by a wolf, we believe nevertheless that he was the founder of Rome; so though many fables may be detected in the traditions of the Abyssins, it will not be reasonable to conclude that there is nothing true in their history; that the Queen of Sheba did not reign in Aethiopia; or that she never had a son by Solomon: yet this is what the learned Pineda maintains,[6] which obliges me notwithstanding the esteem which I have for his person, and the friendship between us, to enter into a controversy with him upon this subject, since I do not see why we may not discover in this journey of the Queen of Sheba, and in her being with child by her marriage with Solomon, the same mystery which the fathers have observed in what passed between David and Bathsheba, and the birth of Solomon.

---

6. Juan de Pineda, Spanish Jesuit, orientalist, and author of *De rebus Salomonis regis* (Lyon, 1609). The relevant section is in Book v, Chap. 14.

All the objections started by Pineda amount to no more than these. That she is called the Queen of Sheba or Saba; that she was invited thither by the fame of Solomon; that her retinue was more agreeable to an Arabian than an Aethiopick princess; that she had a great number of camels; that she brought spices, gold, and precious stones; that her kingdom is call'd the Kingdom of the South; that she came from the farthest parts of the earth; that she came from Arabia, not from Abyssinia.

The name of Saba hath a meaning as undetermined as that of Aethiopia, and may as well signify Abyssinia as Arabia, since it is evident that Isaiah by that appellation has spoken of the Aethiopia that lies above Egypt, in Chap. 43d. ver. 3. and 45th, ver. 14.

Whoever will consult the texts here cited, will find that the Patriarch's warmth has made him lay hold on every thing which he imagined would be of any use in the present exigency, and that there is nothing which in those texts determines the word to a particular country.[7]

"If Solomon's fleets," continues the Patriarch,

have given him so great a reputation, and made his name famous in so many places, let a reason be given why they might not as easily have sail'd to Abyssinia as to Arabia, since there hath always been a great intercourse and affinity between the two nations, which are only separated by a streight which may without difficulty be cross'd in one day.

The grandees of Abyssinia travel with a larger train than the nobles of any other country; and the number of camels bred there is so great, that in the kingdom of Doara, we have been sometimes stopped for a whole half day by the

7. This paragraph apparently results from SJ's interpretation of the following marginal note: "Isaïe dit seulement: *Quia ego Dominus Deus tuus sanctus Israël, salvator tuus, dedi propitiationem tuam Aegyptum, Aethiopiam, & Saba pro te*, cap. 43, vers. 3. *Labor Aegypti & negotiatio Aethiopiae, & Sabaim viri sublimes ad te transibunt, & tui*

erunt. cap. [4]5. v. 14" (p. 268). [For I am the Lord thy God, the Holy One of Israel, thy Saviour: I gave Egypt for thy ransom, Ethiopia and Seba for thee.] Isaiah xliii. 3. [The labour of Egypt, and merchandise of Ethiopia and of the Sabeans, men of stature, shall come over unto thee, and they shall be thine.] Isaiah xlv. 14.

vast caravans of camels which came for salt. There is likewise incense in Abyssinia, though not in so great quantities
as in Arabia; there is excellent myrrh and abundance of
musk and civet.

As to gold, Aethiopia has an undoubted claim to the
greatest plenty of that precious metal,[8] which is found
along the banks of the Cuama and Sofala, in richer veins
than in other parts of the world. If the relations of Pliny and
some historians deserve any credit, the most valuable stones
were brought formerly from the same land. If we regard the
situation of the country, which falls next under consideration,[9] Aethiopia lyes more to the south with respect to
Jerusalem than Arabia; Idumea, 'tis true, is in the south,
but all the rest of Arabia lyes eastward, nor can any sufficient reason be assigned why the Scripture, after having
said that the Magi who came to worship Jesus Christ,
departed from the east, should call the Queen of Sheba
Queen of the South, if she came from the same place: since
therefore she is call'd the Queen of the South, it is apparent
that she was not the queen of the Homerites or Sabaeans,
who tho' their country extended to the Indian Sea, were
not so remote from Judaea,[1] as the Aethiopians whose
empire terminated at the farthest parts of Africa; which is
the reason why Isaiah speaking of those nations which live
beyond the rivers of Aethiopia, calls them, a nation beyond
which no other is to be found.

Notwithstanding it be true that no woman can now reign
in Abyssinia, it will not follow that the same custom was
then observ'd, and we are assured by the missionaries that
the women, though not formally invested with the regal
authority,[2] too often obtain the power.

The Patriarch, having thus answer'd the objections of Pineda,

---

8. SJ does not translate a marginal note
which indicates that contemporary Abyssinia has little or no gold: "L'Ethiopie
prise dans toute son étendue & telle
qu'elle pouvait être autrefois, a beaucoup
d'or; mais l'Abissinie n'en a point, ou en a
fort peu" (p. 269).

9. "which ... consideration" is SJ's inserted transitional clause.

1. SJ's added reference to Judaea clari-
fies the geography.

2. "though not ... authority" is a more
formal rendering of: "'quoiqu'elles ne règ-
nent pas ...'" (p. 269).

confesses that the Abyssins are so bigotted to the notion[3] that the
Queen of Sheba lived and reigned amongst them, that, supposing their opinion groundless, it would be dangerous to undeceive them; for the title of King of Israel, which their emperors
assume, is founded upon this persuasion. He continues to inform
us, though erroneously,[4] that the crown always descends to the
first-born, so that regal power is delivered down from father to
son in a right line;[5] and farther to confirm his sentiment,[6]
mentions two villages near Axuma, one call'd Adega David,
that is, the House of David, the other Azebo, which in the
Arabick language signifies the South, in memory of Nagista
Azeb, the Queen of the South, its ancient inhabitant; the ruins of
these houses evidently shew that they were built in the most
remote ages.

He adds, that the Abyssins still continue to retain several
names, customs and ceremonies which they received from the
Jews: they have singers or *debferas* whom they affirm to be
descendants from the Scribes, and those who kept the Taber-
nacle; and their judges or *umbares* boast loudly of their Jewish
original.[7] He omitts circumcision, the observation of the
Sabbath, the distinction of meats, the veil of the temple, the
purification of women, and innumerable other practises, anciently in use among the Jews, and now held sacred by the
Abyssins.

Although all the arguments produced by the Patriarch in
favour of his assertion, have their weight, yet they are not all
equally cogent; and the authority of Pliny will never persuade
those who are acquainted with the country, that such numbers
of precious stones were ever found in it: spices, though the soil
doth produce some, are there in small quantities.

The Jewish customs still preserved there, only prove, what

---

3. The Patriarch says merely that "les
Abissins croient si fermement ..."
(p. 269).

4. The idea that the Patriarch's view
was erroneous occurs in Le Grand's marginal gloss, which SJ otherwise ignores
(p. 269).

5. SJ omits the remainder: "& non par
la proximite du sang, jusqu'à prendre des

bâtards & même des bâtards adulterins"
(p. 269).

6. "and farther ... sentiment" is SJ's
added transition.

7. SJ deletes a definition: "Ce mot
umbar signifie également & le juge & le
siège sur lequel il est assis" (p. 270). The
earlier term, "*debferas*," was misread by Le
Grand in Mendes: it should be "*debteras*."

none will deny, that there has been a frequent intercourse between the Jews and them; which is yet more probable, if it be supposed, which no body can doubt, that the Abyssins were originally a colony from Arabia.

We read in Agatharcidas and other writers quoted by the learned Bochart, that one part of the Sabaeans applied themselves to agriculture, and the other to commerce;[8] and that they transported their spices and other fruits of their country into Aethiopia on vessels of leather, and brought back other merchandises in exchange. These ships of leather are without controversy the *gelves* of which we have so compleat a description in the former account.

The Patriarch has forgot one circumstance of more strength to support his opinion than all that hath been said. The kings of the Sabaeans were so confined, that, after their investiture with the regal dignities, they were not suffer'd to go out of their palace on pain of being stoned. A nation which would not allow their king to come out of his own palace, was not likely to have given their queen the liberty of visiting Solomon at so great a distance, unless the law[9] were made since that time, which enjoins so strict a confinement; so that if it was in force in the days of Solomon, the Queen more probably came from Abyssinia than Arabia. Josephus himself seems to be of that opinion, whose relation has been examined with great severity by the learned Bochart, and who is accused by him in plain terms of imposing upon his readers, and having given an account of the affairs transacted out of his own country with less fidelity than those of the Jews. He has, according to this critick,[1] mistaken the meaning of Herodotus, on whose testimony he depends; and Mr. Bochart observes,[a] that tho' the Aegyptians reckon eighteen Aethiopians among their kings, the only queen recorded to have reigned among them was an Aegyptian, named Nitocris not Nicaula,

---

a. Bochart observes, *1789*] Bochart, observes *1735*

---

8. The relevant section in Samuel Bochart's *Geographia Sacra* (also cited by Le Grand in the previous dissertation) is II, Chap. 27, p. 140.

9. Cf. "cette cruelle & gênante loi"

(p. 271).

1. SJ adds the reference to "this critick." The relevant section in Bochart is *Geographia Sacra*, Book II, Chap. 26, pp. 135–36.

nor was Meroe[b] ever known by the name of Saba, having received its appellation from the mother of Cambyses its founder. The ruins shown in Abyssinia prove nothing, since the Arabs show ruins of the palace of Sheba in their country with equal confidence; nor would it be less dangerous in Arabia, to affirm that Sheba was Abyssinia, than in Abyssinia, to maintain that it was Arabia.

Bochartus, in short, proves by solid and weighty arguments, that Josephus was mistaken in making the Queen of the South, Queen of Abyssinia or Aethiopia above Aegypt; and to confirm his reasonings, we may add that in the tenth chapter of the first book of Kings, she is call'd Queen of Sheba, and has no where any other name or title,[2] and in the sixth of Job, Sheba certainly signifies Arabia.[3] A great number of the fathers[4] and interpreters decide in favour of Arabia, and are supported by Philostorgus,[5] and the Nubian geographer, who place the city of Sheba in Arabia, and affirm that Belkis, the wife of Solomon, came from thence.

These opinions, so contrary in appearance, may be made consistent without great difficulty, since it is agreed that these nations have born the same name, been included in one empire, and governed by one prince. Their original is the same, the Abyssins having transplanted themselves from the land of Chus or the Sabaeans.[6] Mr. d'Herbolot says in his *Bibliotheque Orientale*,[7] that Ibrahim al Ayschram was governor of Yemen,

b. Meroe *1789*] Meroe, *1735*

---

2. SJ silently alters "third" Kings to first (p. 271) and deletes the Latin quotations from Kings x.1 and x.13: "And when the queen of Sheba heard of the fame of Solomon concerning the name of the Lord, she came to prove him with hard questions ... And king Solomon gave unto the queen of Sheba all her desire, whatsoever she asked...."

3. SJ deletes the Latin quotation from Job vi.19: "The troops of Tema looked, the companies of Sheba waited for them."

4. "a great ... fathers" is less specific than the French: "Saint Justin Martyr, Saint Cyprien, Saint Cyrille d'Alexan-

drie, enfin le plus grand nombre des Pères & des interprètes" (p. 271).

5. Philostorgius, an Arian ecclesiastical historian, wrote a church history which has survived only in fragments and in an epitome written by Photius. See p. 160, n. 3.

6. SJ deletes a line of Latin which identifies the Sabaeans as an Arab tribe ranging between the two seas and famous for their incense (p. 271).

7. Le Grand also cites the *Bibliothèque orientale* in the fourth dissertation; see p. 194, n. 7.

under the emperor of the Abyssins in the time of Abdel Mothleb grandfather of Mahomet. The punishment of this prince, who brought an army with a great number of elephants to the siege[c] of Mecca, is related in the 105 chapter of the *Alcoran*, called the Chapter of the Elephant. There came, say[d] the Arabs, a cloud of birds with the rage of thunder upon the army, each of which had a stone in his beak, which he drop'd with such violence upon the elephants that they were pierced through; nor did the vengeance end here, but pursued the emperor into his own dominions, where one of these fowls let his stone fall upon his head and kill'd him.

In the time of the Emperor Justin, Elesbas[e] or Caleb, was invited by letters from the Alexandrian patriarch to carry his arms into Arabia, in defence of those Christians, who had been put to death in great numbers, with the most exquisite tortures by Dunacras a Jewish prince. Elesbas embraced the occasion,[8] and was favour'd by God with an entire victory, which gave the Abyssins the possession of Arabia, whose authority continued there, till in the year 578 they were constrain'd, as has been before related, to raise the siege of Mecca.

What has been said seems sufficient to make appear the intercourse which has formerly subsisted between the Aethiopians of Asia and Africk, and to prove that they were anciently[9] under the same master.

DISSERTATION THE EIGHTH, UPON CIRCUMCISION

It hath appeared in the foregoing dissertation, that the Abyssins firmly adhere to a tradition long received among them, that Menelech, whom they regard as their first king was the son of Solomon, who having been educated under the care of his

c. seige *1735*   d. say *Errata*] says *1735*   e. Elesbas, *1735*

---

8. SJ adds this clause.
9. This adverb replaces: "dans des

temps beaucoup plus reculés que ceux dont nous parlons" (p. 272).

father, did, upon his return to his own kingdom, introduce the
religion of the Jews among his countrymen.

Some nevertheless maintain that this religion was long before
received in Aethiopia, and affirm, that Moses, when he fled out
of Egypt, retreated to the Aethiopians, and was their first law-
giver: this is certain, that whether they received this institution
from Menelech the son of Solomon, or from Moses, or whether
they learn'd circumcision from some descendant of Abraham,
when they chang'd their place of habitation and went out of
Asia into Africk, their firm persuasion is that they received this
practise from the Jews.

Mr. Ludolf, who never finds any thing blameable among the
Abyssins, except what they hold in common with the Catholick
Church, endeavours to insinuate, that there is no necessity of
imagining that this nation borrow'd the rite of circumcision
from the Jews, since there is no possibility of discovering its
original. These are his words in the 3d book of his Aethiopick
history. *Qui traditionem Habessinorum de Regina Maqueda admittunt,
ii fere sunt qui putant eos cognitionem veri Dei à tempore Solomonis
habuisse; ritusque Judaicos, veluti circumcisionem, abstinentiam a cibis
lege Mosaica vetitis, observationem Sabbati, conjugium leviri cum glore, &
similia, originem suam inde traxisse. Verum cum isti vel cum aliis gentibus,
vel cum Christianis primitivae ecclesiae; qui sese Judaeis accomodabant ut
infra fusius dicetur, communia habeant, haud firmiter affirmaveris, vestigia
haec esse rituum a tot saeculis ex ipsa Judaea acceptorum. Nam circumcisionem non Judaei tantum, sed etiam aliae gentes, & olim usurparunt, &
etiamnum usurpant, sine scientia originis, aut cultus alicujus sacri cogi-
tatione. Aegyptios illam primitus instituisse, vel ab Aethiopibus didicisse:
dehinc ad alias gentes, Colchos, Phoenices, Syros manasse vetustissimi
historicorum ignoratione verae originis tradiderunt. Alnajah gens
Aethiopum cultris lapideis circumcisionem peragit. Homeritas, ex quibus
nostri Habessini oriundi, inter alios expresse nominat Ephiphanius. Ut
taceamus Troglodytas, Nigritas, aliasque innumeras gentes, quae vel
causam ejus ignorant, vel munditiem praetexunt, vel circumcisionem gene-
rationi utilem esse fingunt, &c.*[1] and some lines afterwards: *Adhaec*

---

1. The translation which follows is
taken from Ludolf's *New History*, pp. 240–
41. [They that admit the tradition of the
Habessines concerning Queen Maqueda,
are of opinion, that the Abessines had the
true knowledge of God, ever since the raign of King Salomon, and that their
Judaic rites, such as circumcision, abstain-
ing from meats forbidden, observation of
the Sabboth, marriage of the brothers
wife, and the like, had their original from
thence. But in regard these things were

*permagna est inter Judaeorum & aliarum gentium circumcisionem dif-
ferentia. Hae enim genitalia tantum circumcidunt: illi vero pelliculam
etiam unguibus lacerant, ut glans plane detegatur, deciduo utrimque
praeputio.*[2] And then concludes: *Ex isto solo intelligitur Habessinos
eandem cum Judaeis circumcisionem non usurpare: neque ulla aliqua
insigni cerimonia aut commemoratione finis cujusdam notabilis peragitur,
quidquid etiam incomptus ille Tzagazaabus ineptiat; patratur enim pri-
vatim a muliercula quadam, remotis arbitris: idque ne vir quidem spectare
voluerit. Quod vero octavum diem observent, id potissimam suspicionem
Judaismi auxit. Sed omnem dubitationem tollit Claudii Aethiopiae Regis
confessio, qui, suspicionem Judaismi de se suisque amoliturus sic ait: Quod
vero attinet ad morem circumcisionis, non utique circumcidimur sicut
Judaei, quia (nos) scimus verba doctrinae Pauli fontis sapientiae, qui
dicit: Et circumcidi non prodest, & non circumcidi non juvat; sed potius
nova creatio quae est fides in Domino nostro Jesu Christo. Et iterum dicit
ad Corinthios: Qui assumpsit circumcisionem, non accipiat praeputium.
Omnes libri doctrinae Paulinae sunt apud nos, & docent nos de circum-
cisione, & de praeputio. Verum circumcisio nostra secundum consuetud-
inem regionis fit, sicut incisio faciei in Aethiopia & Nubia, & sicut
perforatio auris apud Indos. Id autem, quod facimus, non facimus ad
observandas leges Mosaicas, sed propter morem humanum.*[3]

---

commonly practis'd as well in other
nations, as among the primitive nations,
who conform'd to the Jews in several
things. It is not a thing to be easily
affirm'd, that these were the footsteps of
those ceremonies receiv'd so many ages
before from the Jews. For not onely the
Jews, but several other nations made use
of circumcision, and still so do to this day,
tho not out of any knowledge of its original, or any consideration of Divine worship. The most ancient historians tells [sic]
us, that the Aegyptians were the first that
instituted that ceremony, or else learnt it
from the Ethiopians. From thence it came
to be in use among the Colchi,
Phoenicians, and Syrians. They of
Alnajah, an Ethiopian nation, circumcise
with sharp stones. And Ephinanius ex-
presly mentions the Homerites, from
whence the Habessinians are descended,
for the same custome. We omit the

Troglodytes, Nigrytes, and other innumerable nations, which either do not
understand the cause of it, use it for cleanliness; or else pretend it to be conducible to
generation.]

2. What follows is the somewhat free
translation found in the *New History*,
p. 241. [Besides, there is a great difference
between the circumcision of the Jews and
that of other nations. For other nations
onely round the skin with the knife, but
the Jews slit the skin with their nails, till
the preputation falls down, and leaves the
nut altogether bare.]

3. Except for two inserted sentences the
following translation is taken from the *New
History*, pp. 241–42. [Whence it is easie to
find that the Habessines do not use the
same manner of circumcising with the
Jews. Neither is it performed with any
signal ceremony or commemoration. For
it is done privately by some poor woman

It was thought proper to give the reader the whole of what
Mr. Ludolf says concerning circumcision at one view. He adds
in the commentaries on his history, that he hath shewn the
difference between the circumcision of the Jews and that of the
Abyssins, and so clearly demonstrated that the Abyssins have
not received circumcision from the Jews, and that it hath been
practised for many ages among other nations, that there is no
necessity of producing any new arguments to confirm his
opinion. *Clarius est quam ut ullâ*ᵃ *probatione egeat. Dum haec scribo,
incidi in quaestionem inter quosdam viros doctos agitatam, num circumcisio
apud Judaeos an apud Aegyptios primum coeperit; vel utra gens eam ab
altera didicerit. Qui prius asserunt, pro se habent textum scripturae—qui
posterius, nituntur testimoniis profanorum autorum—cumprimis*ᵇ
Herodoti.[4] *Commen.* p. 269.

He tells us that in writing on this subject, he has fallen upon a
point, much controverted among men of learning, who are in
doubt whether circumcision was first practised among the
Aegyptians, or the Jews, and which of those two nations receiv'd
it from the other; those who attribute to the Jews the original of
this ceremony have the authority of Scripture on their side, and
those who espouse the part of the Aegyptians are supported by
the credit of Herodotus, and other prophane writers.

See here[5] Moses on one side, and Herodotus on the other! See
here the sacred writings, the inspirations of the Almighty,

---

a. ullâ *Relation*] nullâ *1735*   b. cumprimis *Relation*] imprimis *1735*

---

or other, without any standers by, not so
much as the father himself. ⟨The fact that
they observe the eighth day particularly
raises suspicion of Judaizing.⟩ But the
confession of Claudius king of Ethiopia,
takes away all doubt, who to clear himself and his people from all suspicion of
Judaisme, says thus.

"But as to the custome of circumcision,
we do not circumcise like the Jews, for we
understand the words of St. Paul, the
fountain of wisdom, who saith, It profits
not to be circumcis'd, nor doth circumcision avail: but rather the new Creation,
which is faith in our Lord Jesus Christ.
And then to the Corinthians he sayes,

again, who hath taken upon him circumcision, let him not keep his preputium. All
the books of St. Paul's learning are among
us, and tell us of circumcision and the
preputium; but our circumcision is done
according to the custom of the countrey,
like incisions of the face in Ethiopia and
Nubia, and boaring the ears among the
Indians." ⟨Moreover, what we do, we do
not do for observing the Mosaic laws but
because of human custom.⟩]

4. The quotation is closely paraphrased
in Le Grand's (and SJ's) next paragraph.

5. Cf. "Ainsi voilà" (p. 275). "Voilà"
becomes "See here!" throughout this
passage.

thrown into the balance against the fables of heathen history! See here their authority supposed of equal weight, and their testimonies cited with equal confidence! All that Mr. Ludolf finds to object to the relation of Herodotus, is, that he has not determined the precise time of the fact, so that the matter is to remain undecided, till mankind is come to an agreement about the Aegyptian computation. *Quia Herodotus nullum tempus determinat, vana sunt caetera argumenta.* A little more positiveness had turned[c] the scale in favour of Herodotus.[6]

Grotius, that name so justly celebrated,[7] was sufficiently apprised how much this way of reasoning turn'd to the advantage of infidelity, and therefore opposed it with all the power of his learning, and was so successful in this laudable attempt,[8] that he has made plain from a multitude of different authors, what religion teaches us to believe, that God in commanding Abraham to use the rite of circumcision, meant it a mark of covenant between his posterity and the Creator, and that every other nation that hath practised circumcision learn'd it from him or his descendants.[9]

Mr. Ludolf who has told us all he knew on this point, has been in care to overlook this testimony of Grotius, which entirely overthrows the reasonings of Marsham and his followers. To answer Grotius, it is necessary to prove that some nation was circumcised before Abraham, to find some author either contemporary with Moses, or of equal authority, and when he is

---

c. turned *1789*] turn *1735*

---

6. Compare this sentence with the French: "Il ne manquoit donc à Hérodote qu'un peu plus de hardiesse pour avoir plus de crédit & d'autorité" (p. 275).

7. SJ adds the laudatory parenthetical remark. Hugo Grotius, born at Delft and educated at Leiden, was widely known as a statesman, diplomat, theologian, and scholar. SJ owned a copy of *De jure belli et pacis* (*Library*, p. 63).

8. "and was so ... attempt" is another addition. SJ's favorable opinion of Grotius is clear enough in the comments he made to Boswell: "'As to the Christian religion, Sir, besides the strong evidence which we have for it, there is a balance in its favour from the number of great men who have been convinced of its truth, after a serious consideration of the question. Grotius was an acute man, a lawyer, a man accustomed to examine evidence, and he was convinced. Grotius was not a recluse, but a man of the world, who certainly had no bias to the side of religion'" (*Life*, I. 454).

9. See Book 5, Section XI of Hugo Grotius, *The Truth of the Christian Religion*, trans. John Clarke, 4th ed. (London, 1743), pp. 232–33.

found it will be proper to examine whether such a testimony deserves more regard than the tradition, which is still preserved among the Abyssins, that they practise circumcision in memory of their King Menelech, the son of Solomon.

It is true, that in the confession of faith given by the Emperor Claudius, otherwise Asnaf Segued, 'tis said that their circumcision is of a nature different from that of the Jews, and that it is continued amongst them, not because it is directed by the Law of Moses, but in compliance with an ancient custom. To which may be added the declaration of Eben-Assal.[1] Circumcision, says he, is still retain'd among the Cophtes and Abyssins, not as a rite directed by Heaven, but only as a custom. The Law anciently directed that it should be done on the eighth day, and circumcision performed at any other time, was reckon'd invalid; which is the reason that those who have received the new Law, and yet are circumcised, do not do it on the eighth day, and are of opinion that it is not allow'd to make use of that day to this purpose. Circumcision is, upon the whole, a thing which may either be done or omitted among us, so that they who continue to use it, do it not as a thing imposed by law. Tecla Mariam says nearly the same thing in his answer to the questions put to him by the cardinals.

Circumcision gave room in the infancy of the Church to a great number of disputes, but the decision of the first Council of Jerusalem is well known. 'Tis well known likewise, that there was a controversy on this account between St. Peter and St. Paul; and that St. Paul made no scruple of circumcising Timothy his disciple, after he had declared that it was lawful to circumcise, or not to circumcise. The first bishops of Jerusalem continued to be circumcised, but when it was observ'd, that the Jews made so bad an use of this complaisance toward them, that they insisted on circumcision as an essential rite, great endeavours were used to undeceive them, as appears from Justin Martyr's dialogue with Tryphon, in which having owned that he thought a Jew converted to Christianity and living agreeably

1. *The Encyclopedia of Islam* notes that the name, Ibn al-Assāl, applied to three brothers in this Coptic family; all wrote on medieval Christian Arabic literature. Both Wansleben's *Histoire de l'eglise* *d'Alexandrie* (Paris, 1677) and Eusèbe Renaudot's *Historia patriarcharum Alexandrinorum Jacobitarum* (Paris, 1713) make use of Ibn Assal and could have been Le Grand's source.

to its precepts, though he should still retain his veneration for the
Law of Moses, in a state of salvation, provided he did not oblige
others to follow his example; he says, that no communion ought
to be allow'd with those, who, while they make profession of the
religion of Jesus, compel all those gentiles who have embraced
the same faith to follow the Law of Moses.[2]

This testimony of Justin Martyr plainly shews the conduct of
the primitive Church towards the Jews; but when the Jews
contended for circumcision as a necessary institution, it was
entirely laid aside.

The bishops who from the time of the apostles, governed
the Church of Alexandria never were circumcised, so that
Frumentius who was sent by St. Athanasius to preach the
Christian faith in Abyssinia was certainly uncircumcised: nor is
there any probability that, when he converted them, he permitted them to retain the use of circumcision which was practised
amongst the Christians of Egypt. Ibn Assal says justly, that the
Cophtes and Abyssins were circumcised, but makes no mention
of the other Christians in Egypt, which makes it thought that the
Cophtes, having by the favour of the Turks, continued masters
of the Church of Alexandria, might receive the custom of
circumcision in complaisance to their protectors; that at first
every one was at liberty to use it, and afterwards every one was
obliged.

About the year 836 James the fiftieth patriarch of Alexandria
consecrated John metropolitan of Aethiopia, and sent him into
that empire, where he had the charge of the Church, which he
held for some time, till a knot of the nobility cabal'd against him,
and, having brought others over to their party, drove him out of
the country. About the same time Aethiopia groan'd under the
complicated miseries[3] of war, pestilence, and famine, their
armies were routed and put to flight whenever they came in
sight of the enemy. The Abyssins were easily persuaded that the
violence and indignities offered to their metropolitan had

---

2. "in which having owned ... Moses"
epitomizes in the third person three quarters of a page of dialogue (pp. 276–77)
translated into French by Le Grand from
the dialogue of Justin Martyr with
Trypho, the Jew. SJ owned Thirlby's
1722 edition of Justin Martyr, which in-

cluded the dialogue with Trypho (*Library*,
p. 74).

3. The passage is more emotional than
its French counterpart: "L'Ethiopie fut en
même temps affligée de toutes sortes de
fléaux" (p. 278).

brought these evils upon them, and therefore recall'd and re-establish'd him. But the queen, whose malice was not yet satis-fied, raised new persecutions against the Abuna, and left him only the choice of being circumcised, or leaving the kingdom. John chose to undergo circumcision, and being strip'd, had upon him by a singular miracle, say the Cophtes and Abyssins, evident tokens that he had been circumcised on the eighth day.

Two patriarchs of Alexandria, Mark the son of Zara, and John the son of Abagaleb, who presided over that church at the end of the twelfth and the beginning of the thirteenth centuries, would have establish'd an opinion that circumcision was ab-solutely necessary to salvation, and publish'd many writings in defense of their sentiments; which were answer'd by Mark the son of Elcumbar, who proved that circumcision was one of those superstitions which ought to be laid aside. It was at length determined, after a long and warm dispute, that circumcision was a thing indifferent, and left to every man's choice, but that those who continued the practise, should perform it without ceremony, and never in the church, and that none after having received baptism should be circumcised. It is observed by Alvarez, that the Abyssins in his time conformed to that decree, circumcision being a thing of choice and practised without formality, though they alleged that it was commanded by God.[4]

He relates one account which, if it were true, would be no less wonderful than what hath been already related of John the Abuna.[5] A priest affirm'd to him, that not having been suffer'd by his father, who was a Frank to be circumcised, he had lain down one night after his father's death, with a strong desire of doing now, what had been so long forbidden him; and when he rose in the morning found the marks of circumcision upon him, which, said he, is a plain indication that the practise is approved by God, who otherwise would not have wrought a miracle to countenance it. He was answer'd by Alvarez, that he must have no mean opinion of himself to imagine that God wrought a special miracle to bring him from an imperfect condition to a

---

4. Alvares makes the observation in Chap. XXII of *Prester John*, p. 109.

5. The French contains additional in-formation: when a priest, remarking that Christ was circumcised, asked why the Franks were not, Alvares replied, "que Jésus Christ ne s'était fait circoncire que pour accomplir la loi, que cette loi avait cessé depuis que nous n'y étions plus soumis" (p. 278). This account may be found in Chap. XCVII of *Prester John*, p. 349.

state of perfection; and that there was reason to fear that it was rather an illusion of the Devil, than a miracle of God.

It appears from all these stories how much the Abyssins are prejudiced in favour of circumcision, and although by the constitutions of their church, every one is at liberty,[6] yet there are times in which they enforce the practise of it upon others, as is clear from the excommunication issued out against them on the 12th of February 1559, by[d] Andrew Oviedo then Bishop of Hierapolis, and co-adjutor to the Patriarch John Nugnez Barretto. This excommunication imports among other things that the Abyssins refuse to submit themselves to the Pope, and to acknowledge the power of the Roman See; that they observe the Sabbath, which is lately crept in amongst them, that they practise circumcision, and make their slaves and those who are converted to Christianity, be circumcised, often making violence, where they cannot obtain a compliance; that they esteem it a sin to eat swine's flesh; that they hold the man criminal who having conversed with his wife, shall enter a church the same day. It is not probable that this father would have excommunicated the Abyssins had not these faults been certainly proved upon them.

The Patriarch Alphonso Mendez confirms the foregoing account, and adds,[7] that the Abyssins in excuse of their zeal for circumcision, affirm, that they do not practise it in obedience to the Law of Moses, but for the same reason that they cut their hair and nails, for the sake of cleanliness; St. Paul having shewn by circumcising his disciple Timothy, that it was nothing criminal or forbidden. They nevertheless look on uncircumcision as a mark of infamy, nor do they think any term of reproach more severe than *cofa*, that is uncircumcised. Such a man they will not allow to eat with them, but break all the cups which he had made use of, and call in the priests with their ritual to purify the vessels which he has polluted by eating or drinking in them.

What still more evidently shows their zealous adherence to this rite, is, that after they had driven the Jesuites, and with

d. by *Errata*] but *1735*

---

6. "although by ... liberty" renders: "quoi qu'on prouve que la circoncision est libri parmi eux ... " (p. 279).

7. Deleted is a reference to circumcision of females. The added material from Mendes appears in Beccari, VIII. 62.

them the Catholick religion out of Aethiopia, a decree was issued out, commanding all the young people who during the confusion of religious affairs[8] had not been circumcised, to conform immediately to the ancient custom, and if a rude soldier met with any that had not the marks of circumcision upon him, he gave him a stroke upon the part with his lance, to serve him instead of it.

But however rigidly the Abyssins may retain circumcision, they are still more zealous in observing the Sabbath, though perhaps this practise is not more ancient than the former, for their present rigorous exactness was not in use till the time of the Emperor Zara Jacob. There is in the monastry of Byzen a monument of one Abba Philip whom the Abyssins reverence as a saint, observing his festival yearly in July. The most important and celebrated action of his life was, that once when the emperor of Abyssinia would have obliged his subjects to work on Saturday, he represented to him that God had commanded that day to be kept holy, in such strong and moving terms, that the edict was revoked.

Mr. Ludolf however, endeavouring every where to apologize for the Abyssins, produces an excuse for them here from the Emperor Asnaf Segued's declaration or profession of faith, where it is alleged that they do not sanctify the Sabbath after the way of the Jews, and that they observe Sunday in a manner very different. The Abba Gregory assured him that on Saturday they only refrain'd from more laborious employments.

Quod vero attinet ad celebrationem nostram, prisci Sabbati diei; non sane celebramus illud sicut Judaei; qui crucifixerunt Christum, dicentes: sanguis ejus super nos & super liberos nostros. Quia illi Judaei neque hauriunt aquam, neque accendunt ignem, neque coquunt ferculum, neque pinsunt panem, neque migrant de domo, in domum. Nos autem ita celebramus illud, ut administremus in eo sacram coenam & exhibeamus in eo agapas (idest convivia charitatis pauperibus vel viduis dari solita) sicut praeceperunt nobis patres nostri Apostoli in Didascalia. Non celebramus illud ita sicut Sabbatum[e] i.e. feriae primae, quae dies est nova, de qua David ait, haec est dies quam fecit Dominus, exultemus & laetemur in eâ: quia in eâ resurrexit Dominus noster Jesus Christus & in eâ descendit spiritus sanctus super

e. ita sicut Sabbatum *Relation*] ita Sabbatum *1735*

8. "during ... affairs" is SJ's creation.

Apostolos in Coenaculo Sionis, & in ea veniet iterum[f] *ad remunerationem justorum & ultionem peccatorum.*[9]

We cannot but make two remarks, that Mr. Ludolf affects to translate by *Sacra Coena* what we call the Sacrifice of the Altar, and that he uses the word *agape* for those charities distributed to the poor in those great communions, where meat and drink is given: nor can we omit observing that the emperor makes use of an extraordinary way of reasoning to prove that they do not sanctify the Saturday,[1] when he affirms that they celebrate mass and distribute alms on that day, as if that was not sanctifying it.

Mr. Ludolf cannot but know, that when in the time of Sultan Segued, an insurrection in the kingdom of Damot was suppress'd by Rassela Christos, one of the severest punishments inflicted by him on the rebellious people was, that he obliged them to labour on a Saturday: nor is he ignorant that in the collection of canons reverenced by the Abyssins in the same degree with the Gospel, the observation of the Sabbath is forbidden, and that the twenty ninth canon of the Council of Laodicea[g] directs to work on Saturday.

The Abyssins eat no kind of flesh forbidden by the Law, and one of the means used to inspire into the people an implacable hatred of the missionaries, was to tell them, that the fathers did eat swine's and hare's flesh, and mingled it with the consecrated wafers. In vain is it urged against them that the use of these meats is indifferent, that the Banians eat nothing that hath life, and that the Tartars eat the flesh of camels and horses con-

---

f. iterum *Relation*] interum *1735*   g. Laodicea (Laodicée *Relation*)] Laadicca *1735*

---

9. The Latin quotation appears in *Commentarius*, p. 239. [As concerns our celebration of the old Sabbath day, we do not celebrate it like the Jews, who crucified Jesus saying, "His blood be on us and on our children." Those Jews, you see, neither drink water nor kindle fire nor cook a meal nor knead bread nor travel from house to house. We, however, celebrate it so that on that day we administer the Sacred Supper ⟨sacram coenam⟩ and hold Feasts of Love ⟨agapas⟩ (that is, charitable banquets customarily provided paupers and widows) as our fathers, the Apostles, taught us in the *Didascalia*. We do not celebrate the old Sabbath as the new Sabbath, i.e., the first day of the week, which is a new day about which David said, "This is the day which the Lord hath made. Let us be glad and rejoice therein," because on it our Lord Jesus Christ arose and on it the Holy Spirit descended on the Apostles in the upper room of Zion and on it He will come again to reward the just and punish sinners.]

1. SJ deletes the clause: "comme faisaient les Juifs" (p. 281).

formably to a custom long established in their country;[2] that to eat horses and camels is not forbidden by any precept of religion, and that the Banians do not profess Christianity.

The Jewish rites are in many other instances observed by the Abyssins; one brother takes the wife of another; the men do not enter a church the day after they have conversed with their wives;[3] nor do the women come to the divine worship after childbirth, till the days of their purification are over, which for a girl are twenty four.[4] They fast thrice in February in commemoration of the penitence of the Ninivites: their manner of chaunting the psalms has a great conformity with that of the Jews: and indeed in so many things do they agree, that it would not be easy to determine whether the Abyssins are more Jews or Christians.

DISSERTATION THE NINTH,
ON THE CONVERSION OF THE ABYSSINS

After the ascension of our Saviour Jesus Christ into Heaven, his Apostles divided themselves, and went to carry the light of his Gospel into various countries: Saint Bartholomew preached to the Arabs; St. Thomas travelled into Parthia; and St. Matthew applied himself to the conversion of the Nubians, where he found his work facilitated, and the nation disposed for the reception of Christianity[1] by Philip the eunuch of Queen Candace,[2] who had already sown the first seeds of religion,

---

2. "conformably ... country" expands the phrase, "accommodée à leur manière" (p. 281).

3. "after they ... wives" is SJ's substitution for: "lorsqu'ils ont rendu les devoirs du mariage" (p. 281).

4. "nor do the women ... twenty four" represents SJ's solution to the problem created by a missing line of type. His quarto edition of Le Grand reads: "les femmes de même n'en approchent point, lorsqu'elles / te jours à se purifier, lorsqu'elles sont acouchées d'un garçon, & quatre-vingt, si elles ont eu une fille" (pp. 281–82). Le Grand's manuscript (BN

MS 9094, f. 392v) and the two-volume Amsterdam edition (II, 12) supply the missing line: "... n'en approchent point, lorsqu'elles [ont les incommodités à quoi elles sont sujettes; elles sont quaran]te jours ...". SJ errs in translating "quatre-vingt."

1. "St. Matthew ... Christianity" expands: "Saint Matthieu alla en Nubie. Ce dernier trouva déjà la matière préparée" (p. 283).

2. SJ seems to be combining some facts: "L'eunuque de la Reine Candace, que le diacre Philippe avait baptisé ..." (p. 283).

which St. Matthew cultivated and raised to fruit: he did not however travel far up into the country, the conversion of the Abyssins being reserved for the age of St. Athanasius Patriarch of Alexandria; which great event is thus related by Rufinus.[3]

Meropius, the philosopher, a native of Tyr,[a] took a resolution to travel, either that he might enjoy the conversation of other philosophers,[4] or for the sake of traffick, which was not thought inconsistent with the profession of philosophy; the Abyssins themselves give him no higher title than that of merchant. This man after having wandred over all India, determined at length to return home with two young men, his kinsmen, and the companions of his travels; and touching at an island in the Red-Sea, the rude inhabitants, unaccustom'd to the sight of strangers[5] fell upon him and cut him in pieces.[6] This story is told by the Abyssins in a different manner, that Meropius fell sick and died upon this island, and that the people seized on Frumentius, and Edesius his companions, that they might present them to the king, who gave them a kind reception, placed them near his person, and advanced them. Finding in Frumentius a greater capacity, he made him his treasurer, and Edesius his butler, in which post each behaved himself with so great applause, that some time after when the king died and left his son under the guardianship of the queen, she would not grant either of them the permission they desired of leaving the kingdom, but left the management of publick affairs entirely to Frumentius; who made use of this new authority to bring the people under his inspection to the knowledge of Jesus Christ. Then he inform'd himself whether there were not some Christian merchants in Abyssinia; and whether some did not come to that island, and finding that they did, he contracted a nearer acquaintance with them, granting them great privileges, and places to assemble in a publick manner; and soon after accustomed the Abyssins, to our ceremonies, and excited in them a great desire of being instructed in our mysteries, and in short

a. Tyr Relation] Tigre 1735

---

3. Rufinus, presbyter of Aquilèia in northern Italy, traveled to Alexandria and Jerusalem. His account is found in Historia ecclesiastica, I. 9.

4. Cf. "soit pour voir d'autres philo-

sophes ..." (p. 283).

5. SJ deletes a further explanation: "se jetont les incommodités à quoi elles sont sujettes" (p. 283).

6. Cf. "le massacrèrent" (p. 284).

prepared them so well to receive the Gospel, that nothing but labourers were wanting to compleat what he had happily begun.

Neither distance of place, nor length of time, nor the honours to which they had been raised could efface in Frumentius and Edesius, the love which every one so naturally feels for his native country; so when the young king was of age to take the government into his own hands, they implor'd and obtained leave to visit their kindred. Edesius went to Tyre, and Frumentius to Alexandria, where he found St. Athanasius newly made bishop of that great city; and applying himself to him, gave him an account of his voyages, and told him with how little difficulty all Abyssinia might be brought over to Christianity.

We need only recollect the warmth of zeal with which St. Athanasius defended the divinity of Jesus Christ, to apprehend how great was his transport at meeting with an opportunity to extend the Christian name;[7] he spent no time in deliberating whom he should delegate to this important charge, but consecrated Frumentius bishop, and sent him into Abyssinia, where the progress he made, surpass'd the utmost hopes which had been form'd either by himself or St. Athanasius. Never did any nation embrace Christianity with greater ardour or defend it with more courage than the Abyssins; their bishop had gained their affections, and as they were prepossessed in his favour, were easily persuaded that the religion which he came to preach, was the only true one.

Constantius the emperor, a great enemy to consubstantiality, who look'd on the defenders of it as innovators and corrupters of the Christian religion, made use of many expedients to introduce Arianism into Aethiopia, by sending ambassadors, and writing to the Kings Abra and Asba, to prevail upon them that Frumentius the Bishop of Axuma might be put into the hands of George, lately made Patriarch of Alexandria by the Arians, in the place of Athanasius whom they had forced to quit the see, and retire to a place of obscurity; the letter is preserved down to us by Athanasius himself in his apology addressed to Constantius.

All these endeavours were ineffectual, the Abyssins continued

---

7. "to extend ... name" replaces "d'étendre le royaume de Dieu" (p. 284).

to hold the faith uncorrupted, and, though Philostorgus[8] erro-
niously affirms that an Arian bishop was hearken'd to at
Axuma, and established his notions there, they refused to deliver
up Frumentius, and adhered to his doctrine and person with the
same unshaken resolution. Such was the care of the holy bishop,
that no schism or heresy rais'd its head, or disturbed the peace of
his Church; and so mild and amiable was his conduct,[9] that the
nation, which was charm'd with it, gave him according to their
custom a new name, Abba Salama, the pacifick father.

As the Church of Abyssinia acknowledges the Church of
Alexandria as its mother, it is subject to it in a particular
manner, not having the liberty enjoy'd by other churches of
electing her own bishop; this subjection is as ancient as their
conversion to Christianity, and confirm'd by that book of
canons which the Abyssins hold in equal esteem with the sacred
writings.

This canon is the 36th of Turrien's collection, and the 42d of
the version of Abraham Ecchellensis:[1] I give it as it appears in
each of those books, without intending to write a formal criticism upon that collection, thought by some learned men to be
nothing more than a bad translation of the *Codex Canonum
Universalis*, to which the translator has made what additions he
pleased.

*Ut non possint Aethiopes creare nec eligere patriarcham, quin potius
eorum praelatus sub potestate ejus sit qui tenet sedem Alexandria, sit tamen
apud eos loco patriarchae & appelletur catholicus. Non tamen jus habeat
constituendi archiepiscopos, ut habet patriarcha; siquidem non habet patriarchae honorem & potestatem. Quod si acciderit ut concilium in Graecia
habeatur, fueritque praesens hic prelatus Aethiopum habeat septimum
locum post praelatum Seleuciae; & quando facta fuerit ei potestas con-*

---

8. Le Grand has already cited Philostorgius, an Arian church historian, in the
second and seventh dissertations.

9. Neither his mildness nor his ami-
ability is mentioned in the French
(p. 285).

1. The sixteenth-century Spanish
Jesuit Francisco Torres (Turrianus) published many works on church practices
and church history, including *De Ecclesia*

et ordinationibus ministrorum Ecclesiae
(Cologne, 1578). Abraham Ecchellensis
was "a learned Maronite" (*Catholic
Encyclopedia*) born in Hekel or Ecchel on
Mount Lebanon; in addition to teaching
at Rome and Paris, he published a
number of works on religious topics, including a collection of the canons of the
Council of Nicaea (Paris, 1641).

stituendi archiepiscopos in provincia sua, non licebit illi constituere aliquem ex illis.[2] We don't understand the last words, *non licebit illi constituere aliquem ex illis.*

This canon is thus translated by Abraham Ecchellensis: *Ne patriarcham sibi constituant Aethiopes ex suis doctoribus, neque propria electione, quia patriarcha ipsorum est constitutus sub Alexandrini potestate, cujus est ipsis ordinare & praeficere catholicum, qui inferior patriarcha est; cui praefato in patriarcham constituto, nomine catholici, non licebit metropolitanos constituere, sicut constituunt patriarchae; etenim honor nominis patriarchatus illi defertur tantummodo, non vero potestas, porro si acciderit, ut congregetur synodus in terra Romanorum, & adfuerit iste sedeat loco octavo, post dominum, Seleuciae qua est Almo-Dajoint nempe Babilonia Harac; quoniam isti facta est potestas constituendi episcopos suae provinciae, prohibitumque fuit ne ullus eorum ipsum constituat.*[3]

Many remarks might be made upon this canon, from which it appears that the Abyssins have not the power of electing their patriarch; that when they had the power of electing him, they might not pitch upon an Abyssin; that he is so far subordinate to the patriarch of Alexandria, that none but the patriarch can elect and consecrate him; which shews either the insincerity or ignorance of Zaga-Zabo, who said the Abyssin religious at Jerusalem chose their patriarch; that though he is honour'd with title of patriarch he is not invested with the authority, yet he

---

2. [Granted that the Ethiopians cannot elect a patriarch, but rather their prelate is under the power of the one who holds the See of Alexandria, yet he is in place of a patriarch among them and is called "catholicus." He does not, however, have the right of appointing archbishops as the patriarch does have, since he has neither the rank nor the power of patriarch. But if it should happen that a council be held in Greece and this prelate of the Ethiopians be present, he would have the seventh place after the prelate of Seleucia, and whereas the power of appointing archbishops is afforded this latter in his province, it will not be permitted the former to appoint any of them.]

3. [Let not the Ethiopians appoint for themselves a patriarch from their doctors nor by their own election, for their pat-

riarch is appointed under the power of the one at Alexandria, whose right it is to order and install a catholicus, who is less than a patriarch. When this person aforementioned has been appointed as patriarch, under the name of catholicus, he cannot appoint metropolitans as patriarchs appoint, for only the honor of the name of the patriarchate is conferred on him, not in reality the power. Accordingly, if it should happen that a synod be assembled in the land of the Romans and he should be present, he would sit in the eighth place after the lord of Seleucia where Almo-Dajoint is, that is, Babylonian Harac, since to the latter the power is granted of appointing bishops for his province, and it is forbidden that any of them appoint him.]

bears the title of Catholick, and has the next seat to the bishop of Seleucia;[4] that Catholick like patriarch is no more than an empty title without the power, since all other bishops so distinguished may constitute archbishops and metropolitans, which the patriarch of Abyssinia cannot do.

As this canon is one of the most important relating to the government of the Church of Abyssinia, it might be of use to examine at what time and on what occasion it was made. It is not known that the patriarch of Abyssinia ever assisted at any council, so that the rank he had held there could not by any prescription influence this regulation, nor is there any probability that any care was taken about adjusting his rank since his separation from the Catholick Church. The Jacobites never conven'd any council: these canons never appeared in Greek, nor were ever cited by any of the Greek writers, which makes the conjecture probable that it was made at Alexandria before the Arabs made themselves masters of it, and was afterwards adopted by the Church of Antioch. The Abyssins are so bigotted to the Church of Alexandria,[5] that they account it a great sin to doubt of the authority of her canons, nor have ever thought of withdrawing their necks from the yoke how heavy soever they have found it. This is without doubt one of the principal causes of that ignorance[6] which prevails among them;[7] for that part of this celebrated canon which forbids their metropolitan to be a native has always been exactly observed by the Alexandrian patriarchs, so that perhaps no Abuna was ever capable of conversing with his flock, which certainly must much hinder him from forming a judgment of capacities of those ordain'd by him. The offices are performed, and the sacraments administred in the ancient language of the country, which is not now understood, and must be learned as a foreign tongue; nor is the Abuna ordinarily more skill'd in this than in the common speech.[8]

---

4. "and has ... Seleucia" renders part of the French: "il aura séance après celui de Seleucie & avant tous les autres métropolitains" (p. 286).

5. "so bigotted" is SJ's charged rendering of "La respectent si fort ..." (p. 287).

6. SJ omits the rest of the critical comment: "& des erreurs où ils sont tombés" (p. 287).

7. An important consideration is de-

leted: "comment des peuples peuvent-ils être instruits lorsqu'ils ne sauraient entendre leur pasteur, ni se faire entendre de lui?" (p. 287).

8. SJ deletes a sentence pointing out the fact that the Abyssinian Church has been able to preserve the purity of its faith only to the extent that the Alexandrian Church has preserved hers (p. 287).

Mr. Ludolf has erroneously[9] asserted that the Abyssins were always Jacobites,[1] though he doth not deny that they receiv'd the faith in the time of Athanasius: a contradiction unpardonable![2] the names of Jacobite and Eutychian were not then known in the world; and Frumentius the delegate of Athanasius could not teach the heresy before the author of it was born. The Abyssins therefore were not Jacobites in the sixth century. Nor was the King Caleb or Elesbas of that sect, if we may give any credit to the acts of the martyr Saint Aretas which was known to Mr. Ludolf, who tells us that the Aethiopian manuscripts agree with the Latin writings.

Quis celebris iste rex fuerit nunc demum recte cognitum est, postquam Alph. Mendezius Patriarcha Lusitanus in Aethiopia, relationem suam edidit, ex qua B. Tellez sequentia exscripsit.[b] *Iste Rex Elesbas, Aethiopibus Calebus dictus, valde sanctus vir fuit & pro tali celebratur ab Ecclesia Romana in cujus martyrologio reperitur die 16. Octob. Vitam illius descripsit*[c] *Simeon Metaphrastes, &c. Eadem historia Aethiopicè verbo tenus reddita reperitur in Synaxariis Aethiopum, quae*[d] *sunt quasi illorum flos sanctorum.*[3] And somewhat lower, *Alphonsus Mendez supra dictus, qui hanc historiam cum libris Aethiopum contulit, referente Tellezio, ait, stupenda est conformitas quae reperitur inter libros Latinos & Aethiopicos.*[e] *quos contuli exactissima diligentia. Illi enim verbo tenus cum nostris conveniunt in verbis, quae habent Surius & Baronius.*[4] Ludolf's *Comment.* p. 232.

b. excripsit *Relation*] excripit *1735*
c. descripsit *Relation*] descritit *1735*   d. quae *Relation*] que *1735*   e. inter . . .
Aethiopicos *Relation*] in libris Latinis & Aethiopicis *1735*

9. SJ adds this adverb.

1. Ludolf's arguments, drawn from Book III, Chap. 2 of his *Historia Aethiopica*, as well as Le Grand's statement that he contradicts himself are omitted (pp. 287–88).

2. This interjection seems to grow out of the material SJ has omitted.

3. [Who that celebrated king was now at last has been correctly ascertained after Afonso Mendes, the Portuguese patriarch in Ethiopia, published his report, from which B. Telles transcribed the following. That king, Elesbas, called Caleb by the Ethiopians, was an exceedingly holy man and is celebrated as such by the Roman Church in whose martyrology he is found on October 16. Simeon Metaphrastes wrote his biography, etc. The same history in Ethiopian *verbatim* is found in the *Synaxaria* of the Ethiopians, which are, as it were, the flower of their saints.]

4. [The aforementioned Afonso Mendes, who compared this history with the books of the Ethiopians, by Telles' account, says that the agreement is astonishing which is found in the Latin and Ethiopian books which I compared with the most exacting diligence. They agree *verbatim* with our books in the words which Surius and Baronius have.]

After these incontestable evidences that Elesbas was a Catholick, Mr. Ludolf is pleas'd to make a question of it,[5] and it appears by his decision that the Roman Church has put in the number of her saints a prince who disown'd the Council of Chalcedon, and anathematised Pope Leo, and that the Jesuites, so firmly attach'd to the Court of Rome, wrote the encomium of an heretical king.[6] Absurdities which will hardly be credited![7] But since the Patriarch Alphonso Mendez is the original upon which Balthazar Tellez has built his history, let us hear that author's own words. *Ex historia regis Caleb, Tacenae[f] fillij, quem nostri Elesbaan dicunt, & ad diem 27. Octobris sanctorum catalogo apponunt indubitatum evadit, novem illos monachos inter septuagesimum vel octogesimum quinti saeculi annum in Aethiopiam penetrasse. Nam anno quingentesimo vigesimo secundo, qui fuit quintus Justini Imperatoris, rex ille piissimus, ipsius & Asterii Patriarchae Alexandrini hortatu, expeditionem adversus Hunan Judaeum Homeritarum tyrannum & sanctorum martyrum Aretae & sociorum tercentum & quadraginta interfectorem suscepit; consulto prius monacho, qui ante quadraginta & quinque annos in vicinam Auxumae turrim se intulerat, à quo totius belli eventum anticipato est edoctus; cujus nomen nostri annales silentio supprimunt, sed Aethiopici & omnium in ea regione linguae unanimi consensu & traditione Pantaleonem, unum ex illis sanctis novem monachis, fuisse conspirant.*[8]

f. Tacenae *Relation*] Facenae *1735*

5. Le Grand prints the question: *Sed hic non levis suboritur quaestio cui religioni addictus fuerit ille Elesbaas sive Calebus, Melchitarumne an Jacobitarum?* [But here a question by no means frivolous arises as to which religion that Elesbas or Caleb followed, the one of the Melchites or the Jacobites.] Le Grand goes on to quote another comment by Ludolf: since the Council of Chalcedon, "les Ethiopiens ont reconnu Dioscore & ses successeurs pour leurs véritables patriarches" (p. 288).
6. Cf. "un roi hérétique & schismatique" (p. 288).
7. This forthright opinion has no parallel in the French (p. 288).
8. [From the history of King Caleb, son of Tacena, whom our writers call Elesbas and whom they place in the catalogue of

saints on the 27th of October, it is proved beyond doubt that those nine monks between the seventieth and eightieth years of the fifth century penetrated into Ethiopia. For in the year 522, which was the fifth of the Emperor Justin, that most pious king, Caleb, at the urging of the emperor himself and of Asterius, the Patriarch of Alexandria, undertook an expedition against Hunas the Jew, tyrant of the Homerites and slayer of the holy martyrs Areta and her three hundred forty companions. He first consulted a monk who forty five years before had betaken himself to a tower near Axum. By him he was informed of the outcome of the whole war in advance. Our annals suppress his name in silence, but the Ethiopians both by the consensus of tongue of all in that region

The Abyssins received the faith from an apostle truly orthodox and preserved it in its purity,[9] till the Arabs, getting possession of Alexandria, espoused the party of the Jacobites, who had
been engaged in contention for superiority, and now being
supported by the power of the conquerors dispossessed the
Melchites of their churches, sent an Abuna of their sect into
Aethiopia, and propagated their opinion in the East with little
opposition.[1]

It doth not appear that in those calamitous times or in any
other the Abyssins ever apply'd to Rome; the letter of Pope
Alexander the Third[2] cannot be proved to have been written to
the king of Aethiopia, and that of the Abba Nicodemus[3] to Pope
Eugene the Fourth carries more evident marks of forgery: nor
can any certain proof be produced of an intercourse between the
Popes and the Abyssins.[4]

Francis Alvarez a Portuguese priest is the first who has given
us any account of this country that can be depended on. He
travel'd thither in the train of Rodriguez de Lima the king of
Portugal's ambassador, as chaplain to the embassy, and has
given an exact relation, which has stood the test of examination,
nor have any cavilling objections lessen'd its reputation.[5] From
this account we learn, that the Empress Helena grand-mother

---

and by their tradition unanimously agree
that he was Pantaleon, one of those nine
holy monks.] The discrepancy in the
dates—16 and 27 October—for the
saint's day is found in Le Grand's sources.
SJ omits Le Grand's comment that
there is no point in saying that the Greeks
do not number Caleb or Elesbas among
the saints, and Le Grand's question,
"Siméon Metaphraste: est-il Grec ou
Latin?" (p. 289). The quotation from
Mendes may be found in Beccari, VIII.
70–71.

9. SJ deletes a quarter page explaining
the Abyssinian descent into schism and
heresy (p. 289).

1. "till the Arabs ... opposition" epitomizes one third of a page on the Jacobites
and the difficulties of the Melchites (pp.
289–90).

2. SJ omits the remark that the letter

provides the first evidence "que les papes
aient eu connaissance de l'Abissinie"
(p. 290).

3. SJ omits his title: "Supérieur des
Religieux de Jérusalem" (p. 290).

4. "nor can ... Abyssins" epitomizes a
passage expressing doubts that a people in
schism for several centuries, without dealings with Rome, should express such veneration for the Pope that they kiss the feet
of all who come from Rome. The letter, it
is suggested, was composed at Jerusalem
and merely signed by Nicodemus, who
wished to pay his respect to Pope Eugene
(p. 290).

5. "nor have ... reputation" replaces
more specific phrasing: "Les reproches
que lui font les pères Almeida & Tellez, &
après eux Mr. Ludolf n'ont rien diminué
de sa réputation" (p. 290).

and governess of the Emperor David, finding herself attack'd on all sides, implored the assistance of the king of Portugal, and sent on that message an envoy named Matthew, who was received by Don Emanuel with great joy. This prince already reckoning Abyssinia among the kingdoms which he had subjected to the Catholick Church, fix'd upon Edward Galvan, whose abilities had been try'd in many important negociations, for his ambassador to the emperor of Aethiopia, and fitted out a considerable fleet to transport him thither, of which he entrusted the command to Lopez Alvarez. This fleet set sail, and met with a prosperous passage, but the ambassador, being of a great age, dyed in the isle of Camaran. The designs of Don Emanuel were retarded by this unfortunate accident four years, and what was still worse, Rodriguez de Lima who was named to succeed in the embassy, neither had the wisdom nor the experience of his predecessor, being capricious, insolent and haughty in the last degree. He arrived at Abyssinia in April 1520.

The ambassador was accompanied by Matthew the empress's envoy and a numerous train. Matthew fell sick when he entred Abyssinia, and dyed in a house belonging to the monastry of Bisan. I do not here relate all that happen'd remarkable in this embassy, of which Alvarez's ample account may be consulted, but content my self with giving an extract.[6] Don Rodriguez continued in that country six years, not coming away till 1526. He left with the Emperor John Bermudes his physician, who was afterwards patriarch of Aethiopia, and brought away Christopher Licanate,[g] more known by the name of Zagazabo, with the title of Ambassador to the King of Portugal, and Francis Alvarez, who was now dignified with the office of Ambassador from the Emperor to Pope Clement the Seventh. The fleet which carried all these ambassadors left Goa in the beginning of January 1527, and cast anchor in the Tagus on the 25th of July; but as they were going to land they received information that the plague raged at Lisbon, and were therefore obliged to pass forward to Santaren two leagues higher,[7] where the three ambassadors landing, went to Conimbre to pay their compliments

g. Licanate *Relation*] Licanare *1735*

6. "but content ... extract" is SJ's comment. The full account may be found in *Prester John.*

7. An error: "dix lieues au-dessus" (p. 291).

to the king of Portugal being preceded by all the prelates and
persons of quality; the Marquis de Villareal conducted the
ambassador of Portugal[8] to the king, who favour'd him with a
gracious audience.

Zagazabo did not go to Rome, but continued in Portugal,
where John de Barros the famous historian who has written so
admirable an account of the affairs of the Indies, and Damian
Goez asked him what questions they imagined necessary to a
knowledge of the state of Aethiopia,[9] and committed to writing
the informations they received from him, which, however, are
not much to be depended upon,[1] his answers being generally
filled with exaggerations, and even with direct falshoods. Father
Nicholas Godigno a Jesuit speaks of them in the following severe
terms.[2]

*Multa sunt ab iisdem Abassinis magnifice narrata vulgo credita, & à
quibusdam ex nostris memoriae tradita, quae falsa esse certo postea de-
prehendimus. Inde factum, ut Damianus Goez & Joannes Barrius aliique
alioquin diligentes, & amantes veritatis auctores non pauca hoc de genere
scripserint, quae longe à vero distare, nullus fere Lusitanorum ignorat.
Damianum & alios ea tempestate fefellit Zagazabus, quem ad Joannem
Regem Abissinus Imperator oratorem misit. Hic enim non contentus res
suas nimium exaggerare & in majus attollere, plurima insuper commentus
est, quae homines sinceri ac minime mali cum à veritate abhorrere ne
suspicari quidem possent, pro veris accepta posteritati commendarunt. Sed
cujusmodi illa essent, anni insequentes patefecerunt. Itaque & si ab eo, quo
dixi, tempore, aliquam habere coepimus Abassini imperii cognitionem; id
tamen non ante nobis probe cognitum, quom & Joannes Bermondius patriarcha, de quo postea non nihil referam, à Romano Pontifice ex Italia
missus, illuc iisset; & Stephanus Gama dux Lusitanus cum armatâ
militum manu ad easdem terras ex India trajecisset; & multi postea ex
nostris diu ibidem commorantes per se paulatim singula fuissent experti. Ab
anno quidem nati Christi 1560 quo religiosi Societatis Jesu in Abassiam
sunt ingressi, sic omnia Lusitanis patere, ut non secus ea quam propria &
domestica norint; adeoque res constant, ut siquis nunc de Abassinorum
imperio scribat quid quam, aut proferat quod vel leviter à vero deflectat,*

8. Cf. "l'Ambassadeur d'Ethiopie"
(p. 291).

9. "asked ... Aethiopia" expands the
terse phrase: "l'interrogèrent" (p. 291).

1. "which, however ... upon" is SJ's

addition.

2. "severe terms" is also an addition.
Le Grand draws the Latin quotation that
follows from Godignus, *De Abassinorum
rebus*, Book I, Chap. 1, pp. 2–3.

illico coargui possit falsitatis.[3] And in page 241. *Non me latet Zagazabum illum, de quo saepius memini, multos Abassinorum suorum excusasse errores; cumque negare rem ipsam utpote nostris notissimam, non posset, legalem animum negasse. Sed jam monui ab illo Damianum Goez, & alios per idem tempus historicos fuisse deceptos, multaque ex ejus narratione mandasse litteris, quae falsa fuisse deprehensum postea est. Scio enim Teclam Mariam Abassinum monachum, de quo dicam infra, in recensendis suorum erroribus sic à Zagazabo discrepasse, adeoque in hâc re male inter se convenire Abassinos, qui apud nos sunt, ut Thomas à Jesu in Thesauro suo de Abissinis agens, eorumque ex variis autoribus ritus referens, merito dicat difficile esse hisce de rebus certum aliquid definire.*[4]

Alvarez had scarce breath'd the air of Portugal, before he

---

3. [Many things told magnificently by those same Abyssinians were commonly believed and recorded by certain of our people, which things we have since discovered for certain to be false. Then it happened that Damian Goez and John de Barros and others, diligent and truthloving writers in other respects, wrote down many things of this sort. Almost no Portuguese is unaware that they are far from true. Zagazabo, whom the Abyssinian emperor sent to King John as ambassador, deceived Damian and others at that time. For this man, not content with exaggerating his history excessively and elevating it, fabricated much in addition, which fabrications sincere men, by no means base, commended to posterity what they had accepted as true since they could not even suspect that it veered from the truth. But the following years revealed what sort of things these were. Therefore even if from the time I spoke of we began to have some knowledge of the Abyssinian empire, yet this was not thoroughly known to us before the time that John Bermudes the patriarch, about whom I shall relate something later, sent by the Roman pontiff, went there, and Stephen da Gama, the Portuguese general, with an armed band of soldiers crossed from India to those same lands and many of our people staying there for some time found

out various things on their own. From the year A.D. 1560, at any rate, when religious of the Society of Jesus entered Abyssinia, everything opened up to the Portuguese so that they knew them no differently than their own domestic affairs. The subject is so well agreed upon that if someone writes or makes public anything that varies from the truth ever so slightly, he can directly be refuted.]

4. SJ's reference to page 241 may simply be a transposition: Le Grand correctly cites page 214 in Godignus. [I am not unaware that Zagazabo, whom I have often recalled, excused many errors of his Abyssinians, since a law-abiding mind cannot deny this very thing as being well known to our people. But I have already warned that Damian Goez and other historians of that same time were deceived by him and entrusted to writing many things that he told which afterward proved false. For I know that Tecla Mariam, an Abyssinian monk about whom I shall speak later, in reviewing the errors of his people, so disagreed with Zagazabo and that the Abyssinians who are with us so ill agree on this subject that Thomas à Jesu, dealing with the Abyssinians in his *Thesaurus* and reporting their rites from various authors rightly says that it is difficult to assert anything for certain about these matters.]

burn'd with impatience to throw himself at the feet of the Pope with his new commission; but the king, who likewise design'd an embassy to his Holiness, could not fix upon a proper person; at length he determined to invest Don Martin his nephew with that character, who set out accompanied by Alvarez. In January 1533 they entred Bologna, where the Pope, and Charles the Fifth, who was to receive the crown from the hands of his Holiness, then resided. It may easily be imagined what a confluence of persons of all ranks were drawn together by the expectation of seeing this august ceremony performed. Alvarez who had left Portugal only as chaplain to the ambassador of Portugal, had the pleasure of appearing before this grand assembly in the character of ambassador from Aethiopia. He kiss'd the feet of his Holiness in the name of David king of Abyssinia, presented him with letters from that prince, and made an harangue.

About this time a Moorish prince surnamed Grane or the Left-handed, made an irruption with fire and sword into Aethiopia, and conquered great part of it without the least resistance. David alarmed by the rapidity of his conquests, sent John Bermudes to demand succours from the Christian princes; he, to make the greater haste cross'd the Red-Sea, and travel'd through Palestine, being persuaded that he should with most certainty, and in the shortest time arrive at Rome by that way.[5] Never had ambassador greater success in his negociation, he was made patriarch of Abyssinia, and coming to Lisbon invested with his new dignity, obtain'd of King John the succours he requested, returning from thence to the Indies, and taking Zagazabo with him. Stephen de Gama fitted out a numerous fleet, entred the Red-Sea, and landed in Abyssinia four hundred Portuguese soldiers under the command of his brother Don Christopher de Gama; which handful of men preserved Abyssinia from ruin, and fixed the crown on the head of Claudius the eldest son of David; a great service, very ill acknowledged and requited. The young emperor forced the Patriarch Bermudes out of his dominions, dispersing the Portuguese into different provinces, contrary to the promise he had made of putting them in possession of the third part of his territories if they would deliver him from the victorious armies of

---

5. Pope Clement VII had died and had been succeeded by Paul III (p. 293).

his enemy. Pope Julius and the king of Portugal having received information of all that had passed in Abyssinia, came to a resolution of sending another patriarch and two bishops. The person chosen for the patriarchate was John Nugnez Barretto[h] a man more venerable for his sanctity than his learning, though he had the reputation of being the greatest scholar of the Society. The two bishops were Melchior Carneyro of Conimbre who was made Bishop of Nice, and Andrew Oviedo who was dignified with the title of Bishop of Hierapolis.[6]

Though these prelates were nominated in the time of Julius the Third, the Patriarch and Bishop of Hierapolis did not set out till 1556, taking with them ten Jesuits. The Viceroy Petro Mascarenas had sent James Dias into Abyssinia with the title of ambassador, to discover the disposition of King Claudius, giving him Father Gonzalez Rodriguez a Jesuit for his companion. The precaution was just; the ambassador met with a kind reception, but when he came to tell the subject of his embassy, was soon given to understand that the emperor was by no means pleased that the Pope and the king of Portugal should be so forward to intermeddle with the affairs of his conscience and his empire. Father Rodriguez returned to the Indies, where it was determined upon the information which he brought, that the Patriarch should continue at Goa, and that the Bishop of Hierapolis should go to Abyssinia. He took with him five companions,[7] and had a voyage doubly prosperous, landing in Abyssinia five days before the Turks got possession of Mazua and Arkiko, the two places of easiest entrance into that country. Their success however, was not agreeable to these prosperous beginnings.

The king of Abyssinia valued himself upon understanding his own religion better than any other person, and therefore would voluntarily engage in frequent disputations, by which, as he always thought himself victorious, he was made more arrogant and obstinate. The most fallacious arguments were received from his mouth with loud applause, while his opponent could not make himself heard, or if he was listened to, all he said was

h. Barretto] Barretti *1735*

6. The French briefly describes their consecrations (p. 293).

7. Their names appear in the French (p. 294).

turned to ridicule, and answer'd by reproaches. The Bishop of Hierapolis attack'd him more than once without quitting the contest, but finding that no good was to be expected from personal conferences,[8] resolved to write: the king read the book and spoke with some contempt of the arguments which it contain'd, telling him at the same time that nothing should oblige him to forsake the religion of his ancestors, and submit himself to the Bishop of Rome; this he spoke in a tone which gave the Bishop sufficient reason to believe that he should never make any great advances in his business at court, and that it would be prudent to remove from it; whereupon he withdrew into the provinces, where God pour'd out His blessing upon the labours of these new apostles, who had made a much greater harvest had the province been at peace; though they were not without receiving some advantage from the tumults of those times,[9] for it is probable that the king, who saw with uneasiness the progress made by the Jesuits, would have come to the last extremities had he not been hindred by the war in which he was engaged.

Nur the king of Adel laid all the country waste, and penetrated into the very center of Abyssinia, and Claudius marching against him lost the battle together with his life, being succeeded, because he had no children by his brother Adam; a prince who had all the bad qualities of his brother, without any of the good:[1] 'tis said, that being a long time prisoner among the Arabs, he embraced their religion, which he did not abjure till he was ransomed by his brother. He received favourably enough the compliments paid him by the missionaries on his accession to the throne, but was no sooner inform'd of the numerous converts made by them, than he call'd the Bishop of Hierapolis before him, and with an air of fierceness and cruelty forbid him on pain of death to continue to preach the doctrines of the Church of Rome. He was answer'd by the Bishop, that his menaces should not affright him from his duty, and that nothing could happen to him more welcome than an opportunity of dying for the faith he came to preach, that he might take off his head or expose him to wild beasts, but should never hinder his labours for the salvation of souls. With these words, he let his robe fall, presented his head,

---

8. Cf. "ces disputes" (p. 294).

9. "though they ... times" is SJ's addition.

1. "a prince ... good" occurs in the French at the end of the sentence (p. 295).

and with his hands and eyes raised towards Heaven, besought the Almighty that he might be thought worthy of martyrdom. The king unable to bear the freedom of speech used by this generous prelate, fell upon him in a rage, tore his cloaths, and with blows forced him out of his presence, commanding soon after that Francis Lobo and he should be taken to an uninhabited mountain, frequented only by wild beasts. They were indeed recall'd some time after from this dismal habitation, but that calm was of short continuance, and the tempest of persecution raged again, involving in distress not only the missionaries, but likewise such of the Abyssins as had been persuaded by their preaching to embrace the Roman religion. Thus pass'd the whole reign of Adam Segued, banishment, imprisonment, and favour alternately succeeding each other.

The Turks and Bharnagash uniting their forces against Adam Segued routed him entirely, and so much shatter'd his army that, being no longer able to keep the field, he was compel'd to retire, and abscond in the mountains where he led an unhappy restless life till he died in the year following, that is in 1563.

About the same time arrived an account of the death of the patriarch in the Indies,[2] and Don Sebastian, in despair of ever being able to unite Abyssinia to the Church of Rome, entreated the Pope that he would recall the missionaries, and send them into China, Japan, and other places where their labours might be more effectual: the Pope in compliance with this proposal,[3] issued out a brief, enjoining Father Oviedo[4] and the Jesuits to leave Abyssinia, and to repair to other places. The Bishop answer'd that he was ready to obey, but that, the Turks being now in possession of the ports he could not by any means transport himself to any other place, because no vessels now put in on that coast; adding that it would be more proper to send them assistance than to recall them, and that if he could obtain only five hundred Portuguese soldiers, he could not only bring back the Abyssins into the pale of the Church, but subdue many idolatrous nations; that there were on the coasts of Mozambique

---

2. SJ omits an important detail: "Le père André Oviedo fut fait patriarche" (p. 295).

3. "in compliance ... proposal" is SJ's added transition.

4. The fact of Oviedo's elevation to the patriarchate, deleted earlier, would have made this point clearer. "The Bishop" in the following sentence is SJ's substitution for "Oviedo" (pp. 295–96).

and Sofala, many gentiles that only wanted to be instructed; that a neighbouring prince related to the king of Abyssinia had testified a great desire of embracing Christianity; that the Turks began to put the whole empire of Aethiopia in danger, who if they should get possession of it, would give them great disturbance in their Indian acquisitions, which they would find great difficulty in maintaining; that all these dangers, greater than he was able to express, would be obviated by sending the troops which he still continued to request and hope for; that Melac Segued, a prince without judgment or experience, had nothing but the name of emperor; that he was already embarrass'd with the old enemies of his father; that peace was the general wish of the people, who were persuaded that they should soon enjoy it, if the Church of Rome were once acknowledged; that though the greatest part of the religious opposed them, yet all were not so strongly prejudiced, and that many were hindred from declaring in their favour, by the fear of losing their preferments and employs, or of some severer punishment; that nothing could be of greater advantage to the Church, or contribute more to the security of the Portuguese than to make Abyssinia a Catholick kingdom; that, setting aside so glorious a prospect he could but reflect that he was accountable for all the souls that should perish through his abandoning them; that he had collected two hundred and thirty Catholicks, who would be driven to and fro, destitute of all spiritual assistance, living then in huts which they had built, where they were instructed, and pass'd their lives in a frequent celebration of the sacraments, and in other exemplary virtues; that this number encreased every day by the arrival of others who came from different places to be instructed and converted; that to conclude, the conversion of the Abyssins was the great work to which he was called by God, and to which he was devoted and consecrated; if after what had been said, his Holiness should determine him to any other place, he was ready with the humblest obedience, to go to China, Japan, or the most barbarous nations, being prepared to resign his life for the glory of God.

A greater warmth of zeal is hardly to be met with, which it is to be wish'd had been more regulated by the precepts of the Gospel; the patriarch had deserved greater encomiums had he always remembred that the holy Apostles were sent as "sheep among wolves," and that his mission was designed not for soldiers but preachers, whose only security was not resistance

but flight; that it is the virtue of a Christian, and more particularly of a missionary to bear persecution patiently for the
Kingdom of God: but these are lessons which the Portuguese
missionaries are not very well qualified to hear, and less to
practise. The patriarch prepossess'd with an opinion that the
Abyssins would never submit themselves without compulsion to
the Church of Rome, made this loud demand for troops, which
he continued to repeat till his death, in 1577. Of the five Jesuits
that were with him not one returned to the Indies,[5] the last of
them was Father Francis Lobo who was alive in 1596.[6]

Melac Segued died in 1596, leaving only a natural son very
young, who was acknowledged as king by the grandees, that
hoped to have the management of affairs during the minority;
but when he came to take the government upon himself, they all
revolted, and having dethroned and banished him into the
province of Narea, set the crown upon Zadenghel, his cousin,
grandson of King David. Father Peter Pays,[7] a Jesuit, who
without attempting any thing went into Aethiopia, was
favourably received, conceived great hopes that the Catholick
religion might be now successfully propagated, but the time was
yet to come, in which the authority of St. Peter's successors
should again be acknowledged in Abyssinia. The virtue of Zadenghel made him formidable to those who had exalted him to the
throne, and the dissatisfaction still encreasing united his enemies
in a conspiracy, which grew to that height, that he was surprised
and killed. Jacob was then recalled, but was opposed by Socinios
grandson of King Basilides, and consequently the next heir,
who, after a contest of three years with various fortune, gave
Jacob at last a total defeat, and took possession of the empire,
calling himself Sultan Segued.[8]

There never appeared a fairer prospect of making Abyssinia
subject to the See of Rome: four Jesuits[9] who had made their
way into that empire, being but a day's journey from the place
where the king won the victory which established him on the

---

5. The French provides a brief account
of how each died (p. 297).

6. SJ omits Francis Lobo's prediction
that other missionaries would come, the
arrival of Father de Silva, and an account
of his work until 1602 (p. 297).

7. SJ has added a first name. He may
have been drawing on his memory, or he

may have mistaken "Le père Paez" for
"Peter Pays."

8. "who, after ... Segued" epitomizes a
more detailed account of the struggle for
the throne (p. 298).

9. They are named in the French
(p. 298).

throne, went to congratulate him; he received them with great
benevolence, provided immediately for their subsistance, and
furnished them with wine from his own table, then enquiring
after Father Payz,[1] he commanded them to send for him, and
upon his arrival, permitted him to dine in the royal tent, with
only a curtain between them; instances of so great an honour are
very uncommon in Abyssinia. After dinner they had a long
conference, in which the new king inform'd Payz that he much
desired some Portuguese forces, which the father told him might
easily be obtain'd by renouncing the errours of the Church of
Alexandria, and embracing the religion of Rome: the condition
was accepted by the emperor, and the father wrote immediately
to the Pope, the king of Portugal, and the viceroy of the Indies;
the three letters being signed by Sultan Segued, who six years
afterwards wrote others with his own hand.

The new king had four brothers by the mother, but of different fathers,[2] to whom he committed some of the most important trusts in his empire,[3] and indeed he had need of some, whose
fidelity and diligence he might depend on, for in the two first
years of his reign there was nothing but civil wars, factions, and
revolts; the greatest danger was threatned on the side of Bagameder, where one of his disobedient subjects had call'd in the
Galles to his assistance and put himself at their head. Sela
Christos the Governor of Bagameder,[4] was not without reason
distrustful of his troops, and was forced to have recourse to a
stratagem to make them march against that war-like people
who have almost always been the terror of the Abyssins;[5] at
length falling unexpected upon his enemies he made so great a
slaughter, that those who were left were glad to purchase their
peace[6] by bringing the head of the revolted chief.[7]

1. This is *Gaspar* Pays: "il leur demanda
des nouvelles du père Gaspar Paez leur
témoignant qu'il leur savait très bon gré
de l'attachement qu'il avait eu pour le feu
roi Zadenghel" (p. 298).

2. The French includes the marital history of the sultan's mother and an account of the various children born to her,
including Sela Christos, a martyr for
Catholicism (p. 299); the name appears
also as Rassela Christos.

3. SJ deletes a catalogue of some newly
promoted relatives (p. 299).

4. The appositive draws on a fact from
the omitted catalogue.

5. In the French this description of the
Gallas appears in the preceding sentence
(p. 299).

6. They were "trop heureux de
pouvoir se sauver" *and* to purchase peace
"à ce prix" (p. 299).

7. A brief paragraph in the French recounts a simultaneous uprising in Tigre
(p. 299).

The year following there was an insurrection in the kingdom of Tigre, procured by one who pretended to be King Jacob, and to have escaped out of the battle in which he was believed to have perished. This man retreating to the mountains of Bisan between Debaroa and the Red-Sea, made a descent from thence into the level countries, destroying or carrying off all that was found in his way, so that commerce was interrupted, and the rebellious troops enriching themselves with plunder grew every day more formidable. At length Sela Christos was order'd to march against them, Ala Christos in the mean time having the charge of the province of Bagameder. But unhappily the remedy of one misfortune was the cause of another, for the Galles who were restrain'd by the fear of Sela Christos, seizing the opportunity of his absence, broke into the province in so great numbers, that the king was obliged to march against them with the greatest part of his forces, and was unhappily defeated in two battles; the report which made his loss greater than it really was, raised the hopes of his enemies[8] whom Sela Christos was hardly in a condition to resist. In this extremity he wrote to the king, that he should repair to Axuma, and being there solemnly crowned, assemble all the forces of his empire. The king had already revenged his former losses, having, when he received those letters gain'd a compleat victory over the Galles, after which he led his army to Axuma, where he was consecrated and crown'd by Simeon the Abuna on the 24th of March in the year 1609. Then taking the road to Debaroa he struck such a terror into his adversaries, that their chief abandoning those whom he had seduced by counterfeiting Jacob the late emperor, retreated alone,[9] and hid himself with such caution that he could not be found while the emperor continued in those parts. But no sooner was one sedition suppress'd than another was raised; Melchisedec a slave of the late King Melac Segued coming down from the mountains of Amhara joined Arsou[i] who pretended to be the brother of Zadenghel, and entring the province of Dambea was with his companion, received and supported by the inhabitants. Emana Christos the king's brother arrived soon enough to

i. Arsou *Relation*] Arson *1735*

---

8. The French is more explicit: rather than raising the hopes of his enemies, the rumor "rendit le faux Jacob plus audacieux" (p. 300).

9. "he struck ... alone" expands and explains the original idea: "Jacob le sentant approcher abandonna ceux qu'il avait séduit; il se sauva seulement ... " (p. 300).

oppose them, and Melchisedec thinking himself strong enough
to hazzard a battle lost his life; Arsou[j] being taken prisoner was
carried to the king, who commanded his head to be struck off.
Ras Sela Christos followed the king, and the government of
Tigre was confer'd upon Ampsala Christos. The counterfeit
Jacob imagining that he had now nothing to fear, the king being
at a great distance, appear'd again, having once more got some
troops together. He was join'd by two of the grandees,[1] though
they knew he imposed upon his followers, and was encouraged
by the viceroy's slackness to attack him. Ampsala Christos was
informed of their design, and determined to meet them with
what forces he had, but was dissuaded from it by a Portuguese,
who advised him to plant some musketeers in ambush near the
road, and to fall upon them when they were in a consternation at
the noise of the fire-arms. The stratagem was so successful,[2] that
the two grandees were prisoners at the viceroy's mercy, who sent
Father Payz to pray for them; the head of the counterfeit Jacob
was cut off and sent to the viceroy.

In all these wars there was not any thing of religion made use
of as a pretence. Although the Jesuits had already advanced
themselves to great credit with Sultan Segued, it was some time
before any more were sent into Aethiopia, till in 1618, and the
five following years nine of the Society arrived in that empire,[3] a
succour very necessary to repair the loss which the mission of
Abyssinia had suffered by the death of Laurentio Romano,
which was followed by that of Peter Payz, who had the pleasure
to receive Sultan Segued's renunciation and administer to him
the Sacrament of Penance, and when by that last action he had
compleated the duties of his mission, he rendred up his soul in
May 1622.

The emperor publish'd some time after a declaration, shewing the motives of his conversion in which he animadverted with
great severity[4] on the scandalous conduct of the late Abunas,
and set out their vices in very lively colours. The design of Sultan
Segued in this declaration was to prepare the nation for a

j. Arsou *Relation*] Arson *1735*

1. "He ... grandees" epitomizes the
more detailed discussion (p. 300).
2. The French notes merely that "Ce
conseil fut suivi" (p. 301).

3. The French names the priests who
arrived in 1618, 1622, and 1623.
4. "in which ... severity" is SJ's
addition.

reception of the Patriarch Alp. Mendez, that none might be surprised at the extraordinary honours which were intended him, and were afterwards paid him, a particular account of whose mission has already been given in the foregoing relation of Father Jerome Lobo. It is to be wish'd that the patriarch, a man without controversy[5] possess'd of many great and excellent endowments, had loaded himself with less business, and been more cautious in the exercise of his authority, which he carried to the same height in Abyssinia, as in a country subject to the Inquisition; turning by these violent measures, the whole world against[6] the missionaries, and raising such a detestation of the Jesuits, as continues in the country to this day.

DISSERTATION THE TENTH, ON THE ERRORS OF THE ABYSSINS RELATING TO THE INCARNATION

The greater numbers of those who have written on the religion of the Abyssins have fallen into one of these extreams, either they have affirm'd that it is so corrupted with Jewish superstitions that its professors retain only the name of Christians, or they have pretended that the primitive purity is only preserved in Abyssinia, and that no error or corruption can be charged upon them; that they have abandoned the Eutichian heresy; that the schisms supposed to be kept up in the East, are only continued because the different parties do not sufficiently understand each other; and that the controversies between them and the Catholick Church are only disputes about words.

Neither of these opinions is exactly agreeable to truth;[1] it has appeared in the foregoing dissertations by what far-fetch'd arguments[2] the Aethiopians endeavour to defend themselves against the charge of Judaism; and perhaps they might clear themselves if a single custom only was insisted on, but whoever

---

5. "A man without controversy" is SJ's creation and seems at odds with the remainder of the sentence (p. 302).

6. "turning ... against" renders literally, "Il révolta tout le monde ..." and alters what appears to be the sense of the passage: everyone *in Abyssinia* turned against them.

1. Cf. "On peut dire que les uns & les autres se trompent" (p. 303).

2. Le Grand says only "de quelle manière" (p. 303).

shall take into one view such an assemblage of practises
borrow'd from the ancient Law, as is found in their religion, will
be easily convinced that the Jewish worship has much infected
their Christianity.

When we shall speak of their errors in regard of the use of the
sacraments, we shall prove at the same time that they are not so
numerous, as those generally imagine, who being unacquainted
with the state of the Eastern Church, condemn a little too
inconsiderately every thing that is not agreeable to the customs
of their own country. Men of this turn of mind,[3] have made it a
crime in the Abyssins to fast on a Wednesday rather than on
Saturday: to confirm infants when they baptize them; and to
admit them to the communion at the same time. Though these
are ancient customs retained by the Eastern Church to this day.
It is not over-politick to talk in so high a strain of the Sovereign
Pontiff's authority, to princes jealous of their power, and who
are ready to suspect that a lord is going to be set over them.
David, king of Abyssinia, weary with hearing of nothing but the
Pope, could not forbear asking Alvarez one question, which
threw him into such a perplexity that he had nothing to say.

The Abyssins pretend that they are not Eutychians,[4] and,
indeed, they confess that Jesus Christ is truly God and man, and
that the divine and the human nature were united without
mixture or confusion; they treat Eutyches as an heretick, and
pronounce the anathema against him, but then they place
Dioscorus that warm defender of the Eutychians in the number
of their saints, and reject the letter of Leo to Flavian esteeming it
unclean, and terming the Council of Chalcedon an assembly of
foolish and factious men, who in compliance with the Emperor
Marcian betrayed the truth. They give those who receive that
council the name of imperialists or Melchites, and confound
them with the Nestorians.[5] They avoid making use of the word

3. "Men ... mind" is SJ's free rendering of: "Ne doit-on pas, par exemple, être
surpris ..." (p. 304).

4. SJ deletes the remainder of the sentence: "ce qui est démenti par leur profession de foi" (p. 304).

5. For a discussion of the divisive religious issues touched upon in this paragraph, see the Introduction, pp. xxvii,
xxx–xxxi. The Council of Chalcedon
(Kadiköy, near Istanbul), convened by

the Emperor Marcian in 451, specifically
repudiated the errors of Eutyches (the
human nature of Christ lost in the divine)
and of Nestorius (two separate Persons in
the Incarnate Christ, one divine and one
human) to affirm the doctrine of the single
Person with two natures (divine and
human) of the Incarnate Christ. The
letter or *Tome* of Leo I to Flavian (449),
attacking Eutyches, was also reaffirmed at
Chalcedon.

nature, and when they do admit it, they say Jesus Christ was composed of two natures, but had not two natures. *Ex duabus, sed non in duabus Naturis.*

Sanutius the fifty fifth Jacobite patriarch of Alexandria, has explain'd himself thus in a letter which he wrote the second year after his election.

Credimus etiam quod in fine temporis, Deus cum dignatus est salvare genus nostrum a servitute, misit filium suum unigenitum in mundum, qui incarnatus est, similis nobis in omnibus factus, ex spiritu sancto & ex Maria Virgine, assumpto corpore perfecto absque peccato: corpore, inquam, anima praedito modo incomprehensibili, fecitque corpus illud unum suum, seu univit illud sibi, absque alteratione, commixtione aut divisione; ita tamen ut una natura fuerit, suppositum unum, persona una: passus est in corpore propter nos, mortuus est & surrexit a mortuis secundum Scripturas, & ascendit in coelum, sedetque ad dexteram Patris. Cum vero dicimus Deum passum esse pro nobis & mortuum, secundum fidem intelligimus eum pro nobis passum esse in corpore, cum ipse sit impassibilis, Deusque ille unus, quemadmodum docuerunt nos patres ecclesiae sanctae. Quicumque vero per blasphemiam eum dividens, asseruerit Deum Verbum neque passioni neque morti esse obnoxium, sed hominem ipsum esse qui passus & mortuus fuerit, atque ita diviserit illum in duo, Deum Verbum ex una parte, & hominem ex altera; ita ut in duabus naturis, aut duabus personis constare eum existimet, quarum utraque operetur, quae naturae suae consentanea sunt, ejusmodi homines ita introducere moliuntur fidem[a] impuram Nestorii: Conciliique profani & obscoeni Chalcedonensis, contra fidem Ortodoxam. Illos anathematisat Ecclesia universalis Apostolica; illos fugimus & execramur; anathematisamusque eos qui confitentur quod Deus Verbum post unionem incomprehensibilem duas naturas habeat. Nos vero recte confitemur quod Deus Verbum suscepit in se voluntarie passiones in corpore: neque enim dubium est, unionem omnino & in omnibus unam esse. Quippe naturae quae primum unitae[b] sunt, nulla omnino ratione separantur, Verbo ita dispensante, cum sint inseparabiles, etiam in ipso passionis tempore, quam in corpore suo suscepit. Alioquin incideremus in errorem similem Photini & Sabellii, qui impie asseruerunt divinitatem recessisse, humanitatem vero cruci affixam fuisse: quos, et sententias eorum impias, anathematisamus, eorum anthropolatreien fugientes.[6]

---

a. fidem *Relation*] sidem *1735*   b. unitae *Relation*] unita *1735*

---

6. [We also believe that at the end of time, when God deigned to save our race from slavery, he sent his only-begotten son into the world who became flesh, like to us

The confession of faith by Mina or Mennasbi[c] patriarch of
Alexandria, is conformable to the letter.

*Confitemur naturam unam et personam unam perfectam, ex duabus per
unionem, absque alterutrius destructione, commixtione et corruptione unius
verbi incarnatam. Testatur etiam Cyrillus in eadem sententia fuisse patres
antiquos, et recentiores eadem comparatione uti solitos, animae scilicet et
corporis. Credimus igitur et affirmamus quod unus est Christus Filius Dei
ex duabus naturis et personis divinitatis et humanitatis perfectis; quodque
factus est natura una, persona una verbi incarnati et inhumanati: neque
omnino dicimus post unionem naturas duas, personas duas, voluntates duas
et operationes diversas; qui enim eam sententiam tenet excommunicatus est
et damnatus a sanctis patribus, praeclarisque ecclesiae doctoribus, ut supe-
rius ostendimus; atque haec est Nestorii sectatorumque ejus sententia.*[7]

c. Mennasbi *Relation*] Mennasti *1735*

in all respects, by the Holy Spirit and the
Virgin Mary, assuming a perfect and sin-
less body, the body, I say, being endowed
with soul in an incomprehensible way,
and he made it his one body or united it to
himself apart from any alteration, mixture, or division in such a way that it was
one nature, one substance, and one
person. He suffered for us in the body, was
dead, and rose again from the dead according to the Scriptures and ascended
into heaven and sits at the right hand of
the Father. But when we say that God
suffered for us and died, according to faith
we understand that he suffered for us in
the body, although he himself cannot
suffer, and God is one, as the fathers of the
holy church taught us. But whoever blas-
phemously dividing him shall assert that
God the Word is subject neither to suffering nor death but that it was the man
himself who suffered and died and shall
thus divide him into two, into God the
Word on one hand and man on the other,
in such a way that he regards him as consisting of two natures or two persons, of
which each operates as is consistent with
its nature—such men contrive to introduce in this way the impure faith of
Nestorius and of the profane and obscene

Council of Chalcedon against the Orthodox faith. The universal, apostolic church
anathematizes them, we flee and curse
them, and we anathematize those who
confess that God the Word after the
incomprehensible union has two natures.
We, however, confess correctly that God
the Word took upon himself voluntarily
sufferings in the body, for there is no doubt
that the union was altogether and in all
respects one. To be sure, natures which
have once been united can be separated in
no way by the dispensation of the Word,
since they are inseparable even at the very
time of the passion which he undertook in
his own body. Otherwise we would fall
into an error like that of Photinus and
Sabellius who impiously asserted that the
divinity withdrew but that humanity was
fastened to the cross. We anathematize
them along with their impious opinions
avoiding their anthropolatry.]

7. [We acknowledge one nature and
one perfect person incarnate out of two by
means of union, apart from the destruction of either one or the mingling and
corruption of the one Word. Even Cyril
testifies that the ancient fathers were of the
same opinion and that the more recent
were accustomed to employ the same

Every man who has the least sense of humanity must lament the miseries which are the constant attendants on heresy and schism, but no man that makes profession of a religion can censure a council the decrees of which his church receiv'd, or not condemn those errors which that assembly hath condemned: yet this is what Mr. Ludolf has made no scruple of doing. He ascribes the loss of Egypt to the irreconcileable[8] hatred subsisting between the Melchites and the Jacobites, to the severities of the governors, and to the violences used to the Jacobites by the Greek emperors; and relates on this occasion a fact which ought not to be forgotten, from an Abyssin manuscript of the Abbe Samuel.[9]

The emperor (apparently Heraclius) sent two hundred soldiers to seize all the bishops. The Abbe Paul who had fled into the desert was arrested by the peasants and brought home. Maxirien who was entrusted with the execution of the emperor's orders, having assembled the monks, presented to them a confession of faith,[1] drawn up, with these words *Credite in id quod scriptum est in hoc codice.*[2] This form was full of blasphemies. They all stood silent, but plainly show'd by the dejection of their looks that they did not receive it; upon which the officer enraged, ordered them to be scourged in a cruel manner, and continued to threaten them with greater severities,[3] till Abbe Samuel rose up, and being ready to die for the sake of truth, told him that they neither admitted that corrupt confession, nor the Council of Chalcedon, nor owned any other patriarch than the Abba Benjamin their master and pastor, adding, "I affirm that the

comparison, namely of the soul and the body. We believe therefore and affirm that Christ the Son of God is one from two perfect natures of divinity and humanity and that he was made one nature, one person of the Word incarnate and made man. Nor do we say at all that after the union there are two natures, two persons, two wills, and diverse operations. He who holds that opinion is excommunicated and condemned by the holy fathers and the illustrious doctors of the Church, as we have shown previously, and this is the opinion of Nestorius and of his sectarians.]

8. SJ adds the adjective. The passage in

Ludolf to which Le Grand is referring is in Book III, Chap. 8 (pp. 310–11 of the *New History*).

9. See *Commentarius*, p. 463.

1. And, according to Le Grand, "leur commanda de l'accepter" (p. 306).

2. [Believe in that which is written in this book.]

3. "and continued ... severities" epitomizes the dialogue: "'Moines rebelles, leur disait-il, pensez-vous que, je veuille vous épargner, & que je n'ose répandre votre sang? pourquoi ne me répondez-vous pas?'" (p. 306).

Roman Emperor is heretical, I here pronounce an anathema against the book which you present me, and against the Council of Chalcedon, and those that receive it." Then tearing the book he threw it before the door of the church.[4]

The Council of Chalcedon is acknowledged orthodox by the Lutherans and Calvinists as well as by the Catholicks, yet Mr. Ludolf not only excuses instead of censuring the Abyssins, but likewise all the Jacobites; he attacks the Council itself and gives his opinion that in treating with the Abyssins on religious subjects, it would be proper not to mention it,[5] but, omitting the words *nature* and *person*, to comprise the doctrine in other terms, to which, says he, "I am persuaded the Abyssins would readily subscribe." An admirable expedient, and truly worthy of its author! thus were we to reconcile an Arian, no mention is to be made of consubstantiality or the Council of Nice, or of the Virgin Mother of God[6] in the conversion of a Nestorian; as in discoursing with the Abyssins, no notice is to be taken that in other terms we teach the same doctrine with the Council of Chalcedon.[7]

It is yet more necessary for the Abyssins to acknowledge the Council of Chalcedon, and the letter of Saint Leo to Flavian, because, as we are told by Mr. Ludolf,[8] the words by which *substance*, *person*, and *nature* are expressed in their language are very equivocal, and capable of acceptations which may easily be confounded, so that to clear their belief of all ambiguities which might for ever give occasion to disputes among them, they can propose no other expedient than to speak, as the Church speaks in the Council of Chalcedon. But this they are so far from

---

4. Ludolf's conclusion, presented in French and in Latin, is deleted: the Ethiopians and all the Jacobites reject the Council of Chalcedon (p. 307).

5. SJ deletes a half-page quotation in Latin drawn from p. 459 of Ludolf's *Commentarius*.

6. SJ deletes another clause: "ni faire mention du Concile d'Ephèse?" (p. 307).

7. "as in discoursing ... Chalcedon" epitomizes the French: "On prêche les Jacobites, il faut éviter avec soin de prononcer le terme des deux natures; il ne faut pas leur laisser entendre qu'avec le change-

ment de ces termes on ait tiré du Concile de Chalcedoine le Canon qu'on leur rapporte; ainsi plus de précision dans les articles de notre foi" (pp. 307–08). A deleted paragraph suggests that the loaded question caused his informant to say what Ludolf wanted, and also that the missionaries must have used deceit and trickery against the Abyssinians to mask what the Church believes about the causes of the schism (p. 308).

8. *New History*, Book III, Chap. 8, p. 315.

approving, that to confirm themselves in their errors they have recourse to forged miracles; and contrive to utter voices from tombs, which pronounce Leo a wicked destroyer of souls, and his book polluted and impure, and declare the Emperor Marcian[d] and Pulcheria accursed, together with the Council of Chalcedon, the bishops who were assembled at it, and all who believe that since the incarnation two natures subsist in our Saviour Jesus Christ.[9].

After such anathemas as these, pronounced in this manner, and authorized by pretended miracles, we ought, if we follow Mr. Ludolf's advice, to disguise and dissemble our opinion, to avoid the mention either of two natures or of the Council of Chalcedon: one would imagine it scarce possible that he should carry his indifference with regard to so important a point of religion so far, unless he were some Latitudinarian, or patron of toleration.

The Patriarch Alphonso Mendez whose knowledge was equal to Mr. Ludolf's ignorance of divinity, though our author would doubtless have favour'd him with the same excellent advice, seems by no means inclin'd to have follow'd it; that prelate who had spent ten years in endeavouring the conversion of the Abyssins, speaks of their notions concerning the incarnation of our Saviour[1] Jesus Christ, in these words.

Sed plures & obstinatiores illorum sunt in Dominicam Incarnationem positiones. In primis enim duplicem Christi naturam cum Eutychete diffitentur: unam vero, eamque solam divinam ex duabus factam, ut in hominibus fit ex corpore & anima, cum Monophysitis, & unam voluntatem, & naturalem operationem, cum Monothelitis, tuentur: et eodem modo cum Nestorianis unam personam ex duabus conglobatam, inter naturam & personam nihil discriminis agnoscentes; personam vero rentur ipsam esse corporaturam, nec illam solis substantiis rationalibus, sed etiam inanimis, ut navibus, arboribus, & montibus assignant. Divinitatem & humanitatem ex aequo componunt, illam natam, vinctam, & mortuam; istam omnipotentem & omnia loca pervadentem, stulte buccinantes; Eutychitem ob levi uscula sensa haereticis, Dioscorum ipsius in omnibus patronum doctoribus & martyribus apponunt; divum Leonem & Con-

---

d. Marcian *Errata*] Marcians *1735*

---

9. After inserting "our Saviour" SJ deletes the Latin sentence of anathema (p. 308) for which Le Grand cites *Historia*

patriarcharum Alexandrinorum Jacobitarum, p. 120.

1. SJ again inserts "our Saviour."

cilium Chalcedonense paribus probris & diris insectantur, & impuris cantionibus proscindunt.[2]

Eutyches was accused of having embraced the heresy of the Apollinarians, and was in that point abandon'd by Dioscorus, and the Abyssins after his example pronounce him accursed; but as they follow him in the rest of his errors, rejecting the Pope's letter and the Council of Chalcedon, they are no less chargeable with heresy and schism. The Eutychians have met the same fate with the rest who have separated from the Church, being divided, as they are not restrained by any authority, in different sects. Timotheus a priest of Constantinople has enumerated the various parties of Eutychians, and given us the characteristick by which each is distinguish'd from the rest, and having compared the efforts of the Eutychians against the Council of Chalcedon, with those of the Arians against the Council of Nice, he concludes with a triumphant exclamation.[3]

DISSERTATION THE ELEVENTH, CONCERNING THE SACRAMENTS, PARTICULARLY THOSE OF BAPTISM AND CONFIRMATION

We have shown in the ninth dissertation that the Abyssins have admitted many Jewish ceremonies into their religion; and in the tenth that they are Jacobites, and that M. Ludolf's

---

2. The Latin quotation from Mendes appears in Beccari, VIII. 61–62. [But more numerous and more stubborn are their positions on the incarnation of our Lord. Particularly, they deny with Eutyches the dual nature of Christ. They regard it as one, sole, divine nature made from two as happens in men with the body and the soul, together with the Monophysites, and one will and natural operation, together with the Monothelites, and in the same way with the Nestorians, one person united out of two, recognizing no difference between nature and person. Person, however, they consider the same as body, and they assign it not only to rational substances but even to inanimate, such

as ships, trees, and mountains. They put together equally divinity and humanity, the latter born, bound, and dead, and the former omnipotent and omni-present, trumpeting stupidly as they do so. They assign Eutyches for some of his minor opinions among the heretics, Dioscorus, his patron in all respects, among the doctors and martyrs. The divine Leo and the Council of Chalcedon they hound with utterances equally insulting and dire, and they satirize them with foul songs.]

3. "he concludes ... exclamation" replaces the actual quotation (pp. 309–10) for which Le Grand cites *Monumenta Ecclesiae Graecae*, III. 419.

defense of their errors is insufficient. It is now our intention to give an account of their belief concerning the sacraments.

The Catholick friends of Mr. Ludolf made complaints of the captious questions put by him to Gregory the Abyssin, which we shall not repeat, contenting our selves with proving that the Abyssins like us believe seven sacraments, though they differ from us in the manner of administration. Their definition of a sacrament is sufficiently conformable to ours. We hold that a sacrament is an outward[1] visible sign of an invisible grace, which God implants in our minds at the time when the sacrament is confer'd; and indeed all the eastern Christians, of what church soever, hold a sacrament to be a divine and holy institution, perform'd by the ministry of a priest, and which by things material, corporeal, and sensible, manifests and sets forth the spiritual grace which God communicates by the means of that sacrament to those who worthily receive it. They except baptism, because, in case of necessity, that may be administred by a layman, or even by a nurse. Joseph Abudacni, in his *History of the Jacobites*, printed at Oxford in 1675,[2] says expressly, that they have seven sacraments like the Papists, Greeks, and Armenians. Mr. Ludolf did not think it convenient to confine himself to printed books, or to consult the liturgies that lay by him, but introducing this Abyssin upon the stage, by his manner of asking questions makes him say what he assures us he did, and what is entirely contrary to the truth.

It cannot however be denied that in some instances, the accounts given by the Jesuits are not to be depended on, for either through ignorance, or to make their mission seem of more importance, they have accused the Abyssins of errors which are not to be found among them.

Father Nicholas Godigno speaking of the Dominican of Valencia[3] who has made himself famous for the lyes and imperti-

---

1. SJ adds the adjective.

2. *Historia Jacobitarum seu Coptorum in Egypto, Lybia, Nubia, Aethiopia tota* ... (Oxon., 1675); an English edition by Sir Edward Sadler was published in London, 1692.

3. Identified by name in the French (p. 312), Luis de Urreta published his book at Valencia (1610) under the title: *Historia Ecclesiastica Politica, Natural, y Moral de los Grandes y Remotos Reynos de la Etiopia, Monarchia del Emperador llamado Preste Iuan de las Indias*. There is an abstract of this work in Purchas, but Donald M. Lockhart thinks SJ might have relied on the original for some elements in *Rasselas*; see "'The Fourth Son of the Mighty Emperour': The Ethiopian Background of Johnson's *Rasselas*," *PMLA*, LXXVIII (1963), 520–23.

nences which he publish'd about the kingdom of Prester John;
together with Father Balthasar Tellez and Mr. Ludolf affirm
that confirmation and extreme unction are not in use among the
Abyssins.[4]

We will set against the testimony of one missionary and Jesuit
the testimony of another, and oppose these Portuguese Jesuits,
men zealous indeed, but too much prejudiced, and who had
little other knowledge than the learning of their schools, with a
French Jesuit, grown old in the missions of Egypt, and that
wanted neither time nor opportunity to make himself fully
acquainted with the religion of the Cophtes or Jacobites,
profess'd by the Abyssins. This Jesuit is Father du Bernat who in
his letter to Father Fleuriau[a] superintendant of those missions
gives an account of the care he has taken to understand the
opinions of those people. The letter is dated at Cairo the 26th of
July 1711, from which we shall extract the most important
passages.[5]

"I have," says he,

> apply'd my self with all possible diligence, to the consider-
> ation of the sacraments as administred by the Cophtes, not
> only having laid hold on every occasion of seeing them
> celebrated, but consulted likewise the most learned among
> them and read their rituals and other ecclesiastical books.
>
> It is not to be expected from the Cophtes that when they
> are asked[b] the number of the sacraments, they should
> immediately answer like the children among us, that they
> are seven; I have observed already that they want cate-
> chisms among them. Whoever desires to know their senti-
> ments on this point,[6] must go through all the sacraments,
> asking them concerning each, whether it be a visible sign of

a. Fleuriau *Relation*] Fleurian *1735*   b. are asked *Errata*] asked *1735*

4. "affirm that ... Abyssins" epitomizes twelve lines quoting Godignus,
Telles, and Ludolf (p. 312). The statements may be found in Godignus, p. 215,
Telles, p. 91, and Ludolf (*New History*),
pp. 274–75.

5. "from which ... passages" expands
the French phrase, "écoutons-le," yet
little of the material is omitted (p. 313). At

the end of the seventeenth century it was
Father du Bernat, posing as a domestic
named "Matthieu," who accompanied
Poncet. Father Thomas-Charles Fleuriau
edited and published the correspondence
and memoirs of the Jesuit missionaries.

6. SJ substitutes this long introductory
clause for the conjunction "mais"
(p. 313).

an invisible grace, and whether it be a sacrament;[c] they will immediately answer that they believe it to be a sacrament, nor do they make the least hesitation about any one of them. If you proceed to ask them whether all the sacraments are of divine institution, they do not understand the question, but if you explain it upon each sacrament singly they agree with you in confessing that Jesus Christ has instituted them, and commanded them all to be used in his Church. Such confessions as these are what every one ought to be satisfy'd with from a people that have no schools of divinity among them,[7] who are perplex'd at first about the meaning of a question, and cannot express themselves clearly concerning it. I could wish that your doctors who determine so positively upon the belief of the Cophtes, had more regard to what I have mention'd, or were upon the spot to converse with them.

I am afraid you will not be able to understand what I have to say, unless I first explain to you the meaning of the words *meiron*, and *galilaeum*. The first is the holy chrism so named from the Greek *myron*, the other is the consecrated oyl. The consecration of the *meiron* is performed with great expence and many ceremonies by the patriarch himself assisted by the bishop; so that it had not been renewed in twenty four years, when in the year 1703 before Easter, many bishops, priests and deacons assembled themselves here in order to the consecration of the *meiron*, which is composed not only of oyl of olives and balm, but of many other precious and odoriferous druggs, which it is the business of the patriarch together with the bishop to mix and prepare. This ceremony must be performed in the church with singing of psalms, and continues almost all the day. I was inform'd that beside the prayers proper on this occasion, they repeat or sing over all the books of the Old and New Testament, which I cannot comprehend unless it be understood of particular parts of each book, or the priests divided into different choirs take different books, but this I

c. sacrament, *1735*

7. And, the French adds, "c'est leur imposer que de leur attribuer d'autres sentiments" (p. 313).

pass over, as of no great consequence. The patriarch on Holy Tuesday consecrates the *meiron*;[8] on Easter Sunday and the two following days, he throws what remain'd of the old, into the vessels of the new, and distributes to each bishop, the quantity which he has occasion for in his diocess. When he consecrates an archbishop of Aethiopia, he gives him some of this *meiron*, which is not sent into that country on any other occasion; so that it was esteem'd a signal mark of favour, when I was intrusted with a bottle to carry to the archbishop. I was, for my sins, hindred from executing this honourable commission, being, when I came to the frontiers of Aethiopia, forbidden to enter that kingdom. I shall add to this account that the emperor of Aethiopia is anointed at his coronation with this *meiron*, and that the expences of the last consecration amounted to a thousand crowns.

The *galilaeum* is not so costly, being nothing more than the oyl which having been used in washing the vessels that held the *meiron*, is made holy by the drops of that liquor which are mingled with it; of this kind of oyl, if there be not a sufficient quantity, the priest consecrates more.

I come now to the administration of the sacrament of baptism.[9] The mother dress'd in the neatest manner possible presents herself at the gate of the church with the infant, which is likewise dress'd with equal care, there the bishop or the priest whose office it is, repeats some long prayers over them, first beginning with the mother;[d] then taking them into the church, he anoints the infant six times with a holy oyl, by way of exorcism; and afterwards thirty six times with the *galilaeum* upon so many parts of his body; then he blesses the font throwing twice into it the holy oyl,

---

d. the mother *1789*] mother *1735*

---

8. "or the priests . . . *meiron*" differs from the French in punctuation and consequently in meaning: "'. . . ou que les prêtres divisés en plusieurs choeurs, prennent des livres différents. Quoiqu'il en soit de ce point qui n'est pas de conséquence, le jeudi saint à la messe le patriarche bénit le *meiron*'" (p. 314). The error may have occurred in the dictation, Hector misunderstanding the phrasing. Also misleading is the translation of "Jeudi Saint" as Holy Tuesday.

9. This sentence replaces an awkward transitional sentence: "'Cette espèce de prélude m'a paru nécessaire, & je passe à la pratique des Coptes dans l'administration des sacrements: Voici celle du baptême'" (p. 314).

and making each time three signs of the Cross with the *meiron*, all which is accompanied with long prayers. Having thus ended the benediction of the font, he dips the infant three times: at the first as far as the third part of his body, with these words, "I baptise thee in the name of the Father"; at the second, two thirds of his body, saying, "I baptise thee in the name of the Son"; at the third time he puts in his whole body, repeating, "I baptise thee in the name of the Holy Ghost." He then administers the Euchar-ist to the newly baptised infant with only the element of wine, having first confer'd confirmation upon him. He dips his finger in the chalice, and so touches the child's mouth.[1] It is to be observed that the mother doth not appear out of her own house for forty days after having brought a son, and twenty four after a daughter;[2] so that baptism is defer'd for that space. There is likewise another reason for delaying it, that the mother may have time to procure proper dresses; so that on some of these accounts they often spend six or seven months before the child is brought to baptism, and if during that interval any distemper attacks the child so as to threaten its life, it is carried to the church and laid on a carpet near the font, in which the priest dips his hands, and rubbing the body over at three times, repeats[e] the form of baptism[3] already recited. If this baptism be performed in the evening or at any hour in which mass is not allow'd to be said, the priest must stay with the mother and the child in the church till the morrow, that the child may be admit-ted to the communion. The foundation of this custom, is, that among the Cophtes baptism can only be performed in a church, and by the hands of the bishop or priest. This abuse[4] is attended with this deplorable consequence, that if the infant be not in a condition to be carried to church, the

e. repeats *Errata*] repeating *1735*

1. SJ omits the following sentence: "Comme les Coptes ne réservent point l'eucharistie, ils celebrent le baptême avant la messe, & á la fin ils communient l'enfant baptisé" (p. 315).

2. Once again SJ's translation of "quatre-vingt" as "twenty four" misrep-resents the required eighty days of purifi-cation after the birth of a female child.

3. "in which ... baptism" epitomizes a more specific six-line description of the ritual (p. 315).

4. SJ deletes a disapproving sentence: "Abus dangereux & mêlé d'erreurs touch-ant la validité de ce sacrement, conféré en tout lieu & par toute personne" (p. 316).

priest comes to the house, and having repeated the prayers for the mother, and perform'd the six unctions on the child, he asks thrice whether the child believes in three persons[5] and being answer'd, "Yes," by the godfather and godmother, he goes on with other prayers, pronounces the benediction, and goes away. If they are reproached with suffering a soul to perish, they produce this canon in their defence: "If any infant after the last unction, or even after the first, dies, be not afflicted, but be assured that the unction is to him instead of baptism, and that he shall be saved by that baptism."

Thus far Father Bernat: as to the objections which may be drawn from this canon against the necessity of baptism; the reader may find them obviated in the 5th volume of the Abbe Renaudot's *Perpetuity of the Faith*, who cites other canons, plainly proving that the necessity of that sacrament is maintained by the Eastern churches.[6]

Alvarez has, in my opinion, committed many mistakes in his account of the Abyssinian manner of baptising; for he affirms that they have no fonts, and that the priest pours water on the infant as it is held in the godfather's arms, pronouncing at the same time these words, "I baptise thee, &c."[7] The ceremony is performed in a manner entirely different. The font is filled with water which the priest blesses, throwing into it salt and oyl, having first sung with the other clergy some hymns, and repeated several prayers, and read the Epistle and Gospel. Then the godfather leaving the women at the gate, carries in the child, which, after the lamps are lighted, is, upon the godfather's declaring his desire to have him baptised, received by the priest,[8] and immersed in the water three times, with the form of baptism.[9] The priest then, having dried his body with a linnen

---

5. The priest asks, "s'il croit en un seul Dieu en trois Personnes" (p. 316).

6. "the reader ... churches" epitomizes three quarters of a page of discussion (pp. 316–317) drawn from Eusèbe Renaudot, *La perpétuité de la foy de l'eglise catholique*, Volume v (1713). Specifically, Le Grand is using material from Book II, Chap. 2, which is headed: "Que tous les chrétiens Orientaux croient la nécessité absolue du baptême, comme elle est en-

seignée dans l'Eglise Catholique." Chapter 3 offers objections which might be made to the arguments of Chapter 2.

7. Alvares's account may be found in Chapter XXII of *Prester John*, pp. 109–10.

8. SJ deletes a clause: "Alors le prêtre fait les exorcismes, & les autres cérémonies" (p. 317).

9. The priest says: "'Je te baptise, au nom du père, &c.'" (p. 317).

cloath, confirms him, and anoints all his joints with oyl, then proceeding to say mass, admits him to the communion. 'Tis pretended by Father du Bernat that the priest only touches his mouth with his finger dip'd in the chalice, but others affirm that he gives him part of the Host. Notwithstanding all these ceremonies, the Jesuits pretended that the priests erred in the form of baptism,[1] saying instead of "I baptise thee in the name, &c. I baptise thee in the waters of Jordan"; and that others made use of forms different from that commanded by Jesus Christ; upon this supposition whether true or false, they rebaptised great numbers of Abyssins, which, though done with the proviso, if they were not lawfully baptised before, highly offended the whole nation, and was one of the injuries which King Basilides complain'd of to the Patriarch Alphonso Mendez, when he drove the Jesuits out of his dominions.[2]

Of the repetition of baptism practis'd by the Abyssins, though Mr. Ludolf denies it, we have unanswerable proofs;[3] and the ceremony is described by Alvarez in a manner so plain and simple, that I believe the reader will not be displeased with an account extracted from him.[4]

On the fourth of January 1521 the Portuguese were commanded to carry their tents to the place at which Prester-John was to be baptised, according to their custom, on the Feast of Epiphany, where being asked if they would be baptised, they answer'd by Alvarez, that they had received baptism already

---

1. "the Jesuits ... Baptism" is a milder version of the criticism: "les pères jésuites prétendirent que les prêtres par ignorance péchaient dans la forme" (p. 317).

2. SJ omits the complaint: *Illud nostris ante coetera injuriosum & odiosum quod illis à vestris sit indictum, ut baptismum (quasi ethnici aut publicani essent) secundo baptismo extruderent; cum hac de re inter nostros & Romanos levis sit disceptatio* (p. 318). [That in particular is unjust and hateful which was declared by your people to ours, that they would set aside their baptism by a second baptism (as though they were heathens or tax gatherers), since there is a slight disagreement on this matter between our people and the Romans.] The passage may be found in *New History*, Book III, Chap. 6, esp. pp. 288–91, and the letter

from the Emperor to Patriarch Mendes appears in Beccari, IX. 29–32; the specific passage is on p. 31.

3. "Of the repetition ... proofs" epitomizes a short paragraph rebutting Ludolf's conclusion that the Abyssinians condemn a repetition of Baptism. Ludolf "ne prend pas garde que le Roi Basilides se plaint comme d'une chose injurieuse & odieuse que les missionnaires aient douté de la validité du baptême des Abissins, & qu'ils les aient rebaptisés comme s'ils étaient des païens" (p. 318). There are, the paragraph concludes, irrefutable proofs of rebaptism among the Abyssinians.

4. The account may be found in Chapter XCVI of *Prester John*, pp. 343–47.

and could not repeat it. There was a pit dug for this purpose, into which they descended by six steps,[5] where an old man who had been preceptor to Prester-John, standing up to the shoulders in the water immersed the heads of those who presented themselves, repeating at the same time, "I baptise thee in the name of the Father, of the Son, and of the Holy Ghost." The king ordering the Portuguese to be call'd, desired Alvarez to give his opinion of that ceremony, whose answer was, that nothing could make it innocent or excusable except the good intention, that we are taught by the Council of Nice "to acknowledge one baptism for the remission of sins";[6] and that the Council of Nice was acknowledged as well by the Abyssins as by the Romans. But, answer'd the king, you ought to propose some means by which those who having apostatised are again returned to the Church, may be reconciled.[7] As for apostates, returned the Portuguese, we ought to instruct them, and to pray for them, and if they continue obstinate to burn them; but if they with humble contrition and sorrow beg for pardon and pity, the Abuna ought to absolve them, imposing upon them such pennance as he shall judge convenient, unless he shall choose rather to refer them to the Pope, in whom the whole power of the Church resides. Alvarez repeated a second time that if apostates would not be converted they ought to be burnt as the custom is in the Roman Church.

This discourse was approved by the king, who inform'd him that his grandfather had, by the advice of many learned and able men, directed this baptism, lest those great numbers that had fallen off from the Church, should perish for want of means of recovery.

This repetition of baptism is then an error introduced about sixty years before the arrival of the Portuguese. It is something more than a meer ceremony in commemoration of the Baptism of our Saviour Jesus Christ,[8] for they have entertain'd so firm a persuasion, that by being baptised again only their sins are

---

5. "On the fourth . . . steps" compresses a much longer first-person description of the ceremony (pp. 318–19).

6. SJ omits the Latin equivalent (p. 319).

7. SJ ignores Alvares's apt comment: "*Qui crediderit*, répondit le Portugais, &

baptisatus fuerit, salvus erit; qui vero non crediderit, condemnabitur" (p. 319). ["He who believes and is baptized will be saved. But he who does not believe will be condemned."]

8. "our Saviour" is SJ's inserted phrase.

forgiven them,[9] that, when they had abolish'd the Roman religion, and driven the Jesuits out of their empire, a general rebaptisation was commanded, "in order," says the patriarch, "to wash away the filth which they imagined they had contracted, by receiving the orthodox faith."[1]

It is hard to comprehend how Mr. Ludolf after testimonies so authentick should dare to produce the accounts of Gregory L. 3. C. 6. *Relata a Gregorio refero, Alvarez aliter, & tanquam verum baptismum, virosque cum foeminis promiscue rebaptisatos narrat. An tum temporis ita fecerint, & an Alvarezius verba baptisantis recte intellexerit, equidem dubito.*[2]

Did Alvarez only tell what he had seen, had not he had a conference with the king on that subject, in short had the whole affair depended on his single testimony, others might here have suspended their opinion no less than Mr. Ludolf: but his narration is confirmed by all the Jesuits who have been since his time in Abyssinia. Father Nicholas Godigno whose *History of Abyssinia* is collected from the letters of Gonsalvo Rodriguez and Antonio Fernandes, upon this very article contradicts Urreta, that Dominican who has made himself so much talked of by the impostures he has been the author of about Abyssinia; who, though censured no less by Mr. Ludolf than by other learned men, had affirmed before him, that this celebration of baptism was only a ceremony instituted in commemoration of the baptism of Jesus.

Quotannis ipso Sancto Epiphaniae die, in memoriam ac reverentiam baptisati Christi, corpora in lacubus aut fluminibus sole re abluere, mystis praesentibus, & preces quasdam recitantibus. Inde ait occasionem aliquos accepisse falso existimandi, solere Abassinos baptisma iterare. Haec ille, sed jam suprâ ostensum est Abassinos baptismum modis pluribus repetere, & hunc cum aliis tenere errorem.[3] The same author afterwards writes

---

9. The French would suggest a reading of: "only by being baptized again ..." Cf.: "ce n'est qu'en se faisant rebaptiser que leurs péchés leur sont remis" (p. 319).

1. The Patriarch's comment is translated from Latin (p. 319). The full passage may be found in Beccari, VIII. 376.

2. From *New History*, p. 291: [All this I relate from Gregorie's own lips. The relation of Alvarez is quite different, as if it were a real baptism, and that the men and women were at that time promiscuously rebaptiz'd. Whether they did so, or whether Alvarez rightly understood the words of the baptizer, I very much question.]

3. Quoted from Godignus, *De Abassinorum rebus*, Book I, Chap. 35, p. 213. [Annually, on the holy day of Epiphany, in memory of and out of reverence for Christ at his baptism, they are accus-

thus, *Apud antiquiores historicos reperio, ex veterum imperatorem in-stituto, esse apud hanc gentem positum in more, baptisati pueruli in fronte quaedam inurere stigmata.*[4]

Alvarez speaks of these stigmata or marks in these terms. "As to the marks which appear on the face above the nose, or on the eyebrows of black slaves, they are not made with fire, nor on any account relating to religion as it has been falsely presumed."[5]

Some ancient authors have written, 'tis true, that the Nubians baptised by fire, but they were ill informed of that country and of the religion which then prevail'd and still prevails there, which we should even at this time be very ignorant of but for the Portuguese Jesuits; neither the knowledge nor the veracity of the Abyssins is to be depended on, those who have been in Europe having given such various accounts of their religion, that it is impossible to know which deserves the most credit.

Scio, says Father Godigno, *Teclam Mariam Abassinum mona-chum, de quo dicam infra, in recensendis suorum erroribus sic à Zagazabo discrepasse, adeoque in hac re male inter se convenire Abassinos qui apud nos sunt, ut Thomas a Jesu in Thesauro suo de Abassinis agens, eorumque ex variis autoribus ritus referens, merito dicat difficile esse hisce de rebus certum aliquid definire; idem ego jure possem dicere, nisi quae hic propono ex ipsis patrum nostrorunt, qui in Abassina[f] degunt, omniaque perspecta habent, cognovissem litteris.*[6]

f. Abassia *1735*

---

tomed to wash their bodies in lakes and rivers in the presence of clergy who recite certain prayers. From that some have used the occasion to conclude falsely that the Abyssinians are accustomed to repeat baptism. So he says, but we have shown previously that the Abyssinians repeat baptism in several ways and that they hold this error along with others.]

4. Quoted from Godignus, Book I, Chap. 35, p. 213. [Among the more ancient historians I find that by the practice of the old emperors it had been established as custom in this nation to brand marks on the brow of a baptized child.]

5. Alvares discusses the practice in Chapter XXII of *Prester John*, pp. 110–11.

6. Quoted from Godignus, Book I, Chap. 35, pp. 214–15. [I know that Tecla Mariam, an Abyssinian monk about whom I shall speak later, in reviewing the errors of his people so disagreed with Zagazabo, and that the Abyssinians who are with us so ill agree on this subject that Thomas à Jesu, dealing with the Abyssinians in his *Thesaurus* and reporting their rites from various authors, rightly says that it is difficult to assert anything definite about these matters. I would rightly be able to say the same thing except that what I put forward here I learned from the very letters of our fathers who dwell in Abyssinia and have thoroughly looked into everything.]

The world has been more acquainted with Abyssinia since the Father Balthasar Tellez has written the history of it. Had that father, or those who furnish'd him with his memoirs, been more acquainted with the Eastern Church, they had not by their mistakes accused the Abyssins of errors which they are free from, or furnish'd the enemies of the Roman Church with arms against it.[7]

Mr. Ludolf affirms from the testimony of Father Tellez, to which he might have added those of all the Portuguese Jesuits, that confirmation is not known to the Abyssins,[8] to whom I shall not scruple to oppose the single relation of the same Father Bernat.

Baptism says he, writing to Father Fleuriau,[g] is immediately followed by confirmation, which is administred by the same priest in this manner; after long prayers he repeats thirty six unctions on the body of the infant, which are performed with the *meiron*, saying at the anointing of the forehead and eyes, "The ointment of grace and of the Holy Spirit"; of the nose and mouth, "the ointment, the pledge of the Kingdom of Heaven"; of the ears, "the ointment of communion of everlasting life"; of the hands within and without, "the holy unction to Christ our Lord, and the indelible character"; upon the heart, "the perfection of grace and of the Holy Spirit";[9] at the knees and hands,[1] "I have anointed you with the holy ointment, in the name of the Father, of the Son, and of the Holy Ghost."

The Abbe Renaudot had long since written the same thing in his memoirs[2] of the Church of Abyssinia, which he has been pleased to communicate to us, which may be farther illustrated[3] by what he says, in his fifth volume of the *Perpetuity of the Faith*, concerning the baptism of the Aethiopians.[4] This learned abbè

g. Fleuriau *Relation*] Fleurian *1735*

---

7. "furnished ... against it" adds a flourish to the French: "fourni des armes aux hérétiques" (p. 321).

8. Ludolf's statement is unequivocal: "They are utterly ignorant of *Confirmation* and *Extreme Unction*" (*New History*, pp. 274–75). Ludolf is referring to Telles, p. 91.

9. And, the French adds, "'bouclier de la vraie foi'" (p. 321).

1. SJ's mistranslation of "coudes" (p. 321).

2. Cf. "Mémoires manuscrits" (p. 321).

3. "which ... illustrated" is SJ's transitional clause.

4. The French (p. 322) includes a twelve-line description of the ceremony taken from Renaudot's *Perpétuité de la foy*, v, Bk. II, Chap. 11.

tells us in the same work, that confirmation is called *meiron*, or the holy ointment, from the ointment used in the administration of this sacrament, by the Greeks, Syrians, Cophtes, and Aethiopians. These proofs are in my opinion sufficient to make it clear that the Abyssins receive confirmation as a sacrament, of which whoever desires a more perfect knowledge, may consult the authors already cited.

DISSERTATION THE TWELFTH, ON THE EUCHARIST AND PENNANCE

The Abbe Renaudot has so well explain'd the belief of the Abyssins concerning the mystery of the Eucharist in the fourth and fifth tome of *The Perpetuity of the Faith*, that we cannot do better than refer the reader thither, where he will observe the irresistible[a] force with which he opposes and confutes the errors of Mr. Ludolf, and confirms the truth of that adorable mystery. Wansleb had before treated on the same subject, though with less learning, yet in such a manner as obliged Mr. Ludolf either to examine it more nicely, or explain himself with more circumspection. All the learned were scandalized at his affectation of expressing the sacrament celebrated on our altars by the term *Sacra Coena*[1] the Holy Supper, and his declining the use of any other. The Abbe Renaudot,[2] after having refuted him in his *Perpetuity of the Faith*, was obliged to engage him again in his defence of the history of the patriarchs of Alexandria, in which he writes thus.[3]

> Mr. Ludolf who wrote for all the world, and not for the Protestants alone, ought to make use of such expressions as are known to the churches of which he speaks. Those which he translates by *Sacra Coena*, are rendred in the dictionaries of Protestants themselves by the words *Eucharist* and *liturgy*;

a. irrestible *1735*

1. SJ adds the Latin term.
2. Contrary to his general practice SJ here introduces a name to avoid the periphrasis of the French: "L'illustre & savant abbé que nous venons de citer"

(p. 323).

3. The quotation that follows does not appear to be translated from Renaudot's *Historia patriarcharum*, as Le Grand suggests.

and although Castellus copied Mr. Ludolf's dictionary,[4] he hath yet explain'd the word, *korban* by Eucharist, which Mr. Ludolf had not done, having rendred it *panem & vinum benedictum in Sancta Coena*.[5] 'Tis so call'd by the Aethiopians and Arabick Christians before the consecration, but after it, 'tis term'd "the body and blood of Jesus Christ." The verb from which that noun is derived he renders *sacramcoenam distribuit minister*,[6] using a barbarous expression unknown equally to prophane and ecclesiastical Latin writers, for the sake of giving a false and equivocal interpretation. It is false, because he restrains the word which signifies the whole action or ceremony of administring the sacrament, which the Orientals call the mystical oblation, "anaphora," "kadas," and "the sacrifice," to the single act of distribution. He has left his readers to guess whom he means by "minister," whether he be such a person as the greatest part of Protestants mean by ministers, or whether he be a deacon, subdeacon, or one of an inferior order. He likewise in his translation of *korban*,[7] confounds the oblation that is first blessed by the prayers, with that which is made after the consecration. If in the history of Alexandria, I had translated those words, which are as much Arabick as Aethiopian, after the dictionary of Mr. Ludolf, and speaking of a solemn office, had said that the Patriarch celebrated the "Supper" in such a church, or that the minister "at the Supper," distributed the blessed bread and wine to the people, the translation would be no less ridiculous than if speaking of what pass'd in a Calvinist church, I should say, "the priest said mass." Grotius with reason ridiculed the editors of the memoirs of Philip de Comines at Geneva, who inserted the word "supper," instead of "mass," and it is no less improper for Mr. Ludolf to introduce into his account of the ceremonies of religion, forms of speech never known before.

---

4. Edmund Castell, *Lexicon heptaglotton, Hebraicum, Chaldaicum, Syriacum, Samaritanum, Aethiopicum, Arabicum conjunctim* (London, 1669).

5. [bread and wine blessed in the Holy Supper.]

6. [the minister distributed the Holy Supper.]

7. The French repeats Ludolf's translation of *korban: panem & vinum benedictum in sacra coena* (p. 324).

Mr. Ludolf after having given us these prayers, "Convert this bread that it may become thy pure body, which is joined with this cup of thy precious blood.—Let the Holy Spirit descend, and come and shine upon this bread, that it may be made the body of Christ our God, and let the taste of this cup be changed, that it may become the blood of Christ our God";[8] after having related these prayers with some others, he asks Gregory the meaning of the words "convert" and "change," and whether the Abyssins believe transubstantiation, a word certainly much less intelligible to the Abyssinian, than the other which are sufficiently plain and determinate. Gregory, who certainly did not understand him, answers that the Abyssins know nothing of transubstantiation, and do not trouble themselves with scruples about such difficult questions, that the bread and wine were in his opinion converted from common food into the holy[b] and mysterious representative of the body and blood of Jesus Christ,[9] and that from prophane it becomes sacred, so as to represent to the communicants the body and blood of Jesus Christ.

It would not be improper to demand of Mr. Ludolf his reason for asking Gregory, on account of the words "change" and "convert," if he did not believe that the bread and wine[1] were changed into the[2] body and blood of Jesus Christ. The answer of Gregory, *sibi videri*, that it is his opinion, is not the answer of a man thoroughly instructed in his religion, and the *mysteriosum* and *representativum* seem rather the expressions of some Zuinglian, than of that Abyssin.

As for the testimony of Father Balthasar Tellez he shall make

b. common ... holy *1789*] common into *1735*; common into holy *Errata*

---

8. "'Convert this bread ... God'" is translated from Ludolf's Latin quoted in Le Grand (pp. 324–25). The passage in Ludolf occurs in Book III, Chap. 5 (pp. 275–76 in *New History*).

9. "that the bread ... Jesus Christ" creates difficulties as SJ translates Le Grand's version of Ludolf: "'qu'il lui paraissait néanmoins que le pain & le vin vulgaire sont convertis dans le mystérieux, & le représentatif du corps & du sang de Jésus Christ ...'" (p. 325). The problem seems to be caused by Le Grand's translation of the following: "sibi tamen videri panem & vinum vulgare converti in mys-

teriosum & repraesentativum corporis & sanguinis Jesu Christi ..." (Ludolf, *Historia*, Book III, Chap. 5). Compare the English translation: "Nevertheless it seem'd to him probable and like, that the vulgar bread and wine was chang'd into the mysterious representation of the body and blood of Jesus Christ" (*New History*, p. 276).

1. SJ deletes an essential term (italics mine): "la *substance* du pain & du vin" (p. 325).

2. Again "la *substance* du corps & du sang ..." (p. 325).

all the use of it he can; it is agreed that that father doubts of the validity of their consecration, because of some defect in the form, but our dispute is not about validity of their consecration, but about their belief, and it appears from the Aethiopian liturgies[3] which have been transmitted hither, that they are fully persuaded of the real presence.

Let any man read the history of the Church of Alexandria, and consider the purity required of the priest when he says mass, and the laity when they communicate, and consider whether all this is required only for a symbol which has nothing in it of reality.[4] But if even that should be affirmed, let him consider what can be objected to the acclamation and profession of faith made by the people, when the officiating priest pronounces these words, "This is my body which is broken for you for the remission of sins"; at which all cry out, "Amen, Amen, Amen. We praise thee, Lord God, this is truly thy body, and so we believe."[5]

The priest having likewise said over the cup, "This is the cup of my blood which shall be shed for you, for remission, and for the redemption of many"; the people answer, "Amen, this is truly thy blood; we believe." The priest continues, "You shall do this, you shall do this in remembrance of *Me*"; the people answer, "We declare thy death, *O Lord*, and believe thy holy Resurrection, Ascension, and thy Second Coming. We call upon thee *O Lord* our *God*; we believe that it is truly so." After the priest has said the prayer at the breaking of the bread, the people reply; "The armies of the angels of the Saviour of the World stand before him, and surround the body and blood of our Lord and Saviour Jesus Christ; let us come before his face, and with faith worship Jesus Christ." After the prayer of repentance or absolution, when the priest has communicated, he gives the Communion to the people with these words, "This is the bread

---

3. "that father doubts ... liturgies" epitomizes the following passage: "... qu'il doute beaucoup de leur consécration, d'autant qu'au lieu de dire sur le corps de Jésus Christ, 'Ceci est mon corps,' ils disent, 'Ce pain est mon corps,' & sur le sang, 'Ce calice est mon sang.' Il s'agit ici de la créance, & non de la validité de la consécration; on laisse aux théologiens à juger, si 'Hic panis est corpus meum' pour 'Hoc est corpus meum,' empêche la con-

sécration, & le changement du pain au corps de Jésus Christ. Il est toujours constant partout ce qui nous reste de liturgies, qui sont en usage chez les Ethiopiens ..." (p. 325).

4. See Wansleben's chapters on the mass and on communion in his *Histoire de l'eglise d'Alexandrie*, pp. 93–98.

5. Throughout this section SJ omits the Latin equivalents (pp. 326–27).

of life, descended from Heaven, verily the precious body of Emanuel our God. Amen." The communicant then answers, "Amen." The deacon who presents the cup, says, "This is the cup of life descended from Heaven, which is the precious blood of Jesus Christ." He who receives it, says, "Amen, Amen." At the giving thanks, the priest says, "My King, and my God, I will sing thy praises, and will bless thy name for ever and ever. Our Father which art in Heaven, lead us not into temptation, since we have been made partakers of thy holy body, and precious blood; and we give thee thanks that we have been thought worthy to communicate in the mystery of glory and holiness,[6] which surpasses all understanding. I will bless thee, and praise thy name for ever and ever."

It is not easily to be believed by one who reads these prayers taken out of the common Aethiopian liturgy, that these people do not believe the real presence. Nor is it unjustly observed by the learned abbe who has publish'd those liturgies, that Mr. Ludolf's writings either from his prejudices in favour of his own religion, or from his ignorance of the Alexandrian Church, only serve to confound and obscure the little knowledge we might have of the Abyssinian religion.[7] The Patriarch Alphonso Mendez pretends to doubt whether the priests do really consecrate the elements, because the material part is defective, and he imagines the priests not rightly ordained. As to the matter, he remarks, that they make use of leavened bread, and that it is not really wine, which they use as wine.[8] The patriarch was a man of a very extensive knowledge, but very little acquainted with the customs of the Eastern churches.

It was never objected to the Greeks that they made use of leavened bread, which has been long in use in the West. And the prayers, piety, and solemnity with which the Orientals prepare the korban, are decencies which the Latins would not do amiss to imitate in the making of their Hosts.[9]

6. For "glory and holiness" the French offers the single phrase "sainteté." Here SJ uses the Latin equivalent which reads misterio gloriae & sanctitatis (p. 327).

7. SJ omits a comment concerning Ludolf's reliance on Telles: "Il est vrai qu'il l'appuie sur le témoignage du père Balthazar Tellez, qui dit que ces peuples

qui prétendent communier sous les deux espèces, ne communient pas sous une" (p. 327).

8. Mendes discusses these matters at some length (Beccari, VIII. 65–66).

9. This comment about the preparation of the korban should be compared with the French: "On n'observe rien de tout

As for wine, there is little of it in Aethiopia and it is scarce possible to keep it there; to remedy this inconvenience they keep raisins in the sacristy, which they steep for some days in water, and having dried them a little in the sun, express the juice, which is forbidden to be kept in any other vessels, than those dedicated to that use, which are laid up in the sacristy. Which is thus explained in their rituals. *Observet quoque sacerdos diligenter vinum, ne in acetum versum fuerit, aut saporem suum amiserit.*c *In necessitate autem sumatur uvarum succus, aut ex uvis passis liquor expressus, modo expers sit ignis aut alterius hujus modi excoctionis, cum enim vinum bonum deest, cum isto liturgia celebrari potest. Non oportet omnino sacerdotem ad altare deferre vinum in eo vase quod fidelis quisque laicus vir aut foemina attulerit, sed deferet illud in vase quod in ecclesia, peculiariter ad hunc usum destinatum sit.*[1]

The Father du Bernat, being design'd for the mission of Aethiopia, was at a loss how to say mass there, and consulting Mr. Poncet who had been there, was assured by him that the water penetrating the raisin restor'd it to its natural juice, and that, consequently what was express'd was true and natural wine, that it was the same thing whether the water entred through the skin of the raisin, or at the root of the vine; but this reasoning gave little satisfaction to Father du Bernat.

It is true that the orientals do not elevate the Host, or, to use their term, the *Isbadicon*, immediately after the consecration, but just before the Communion. Then the deacon cries out *Attendamus*, and the priest, *Sancta Sanctis.*[2] At the time of the elevation the deacons lift up the tapers and crosses, and the people bowing and uncovering their heads cry out, "Verily so it is, O Lord have

---

c. amiserit *Relation*] amisecrit *1735*

---

cela parmi les Latins, quand on fait les hosties. La manière avec laquelle ils le préparent a beaucoup plus de décence que la nôtre" (p. 328).

1. In Le Grand this Latin quotation appears after the next paragraph; SJ deletes a paraphrase which appears at this point (p. 328). [Let the priest also diligently observe the wine so that it does not turn to vinegar or lose its flavor. If necessary, however, let grape juice be used or the liquid extracted from raisins, provided

that it not have been treated with fire or another form of cooking of this sort, for when good wine is not available, the liturgy may be celebrated with this. But the priest ought not at all bring the wine to the altar in that vessel which some faithful layman or laywoman has brought, but let him bear it in a vessel which is intended especially for this use in the church.]

2. [Let us give heed], and the priest, [Holy unto the Holy.]

mercy on us." On Sunday the people only nod with their heads bare, but on other days they bow down their faces towards the earth.

He that celebrates having first received the sacrament himself, presents it to his assistants, and afterwards to the people in this manner. If he has dip'd the body of our Lord in the blood, he says, "Here is verily the body and blood of Emanuel our God." If it be not dip'd, he only says, "Here is verily the body of Emanuel our God. Amen." The communicant answers, "Amen." And in some churches, "We believe and confess it to the last breath of our lives." Those who have communicated retire without turning their backs to the altar. If the priest shall by misfortune let one particle of the body,[3] or one drop of the blood fall to the ground, he is neither permitted to administer nor to receive the sacrament for forty days, being obliged to abstain during that space from the use of fat meats, to rise and make fifty prostrations every night.

That they receive the Communion in two kinds is not denied; this custom continued many ages among us, and was allow'd the Bohemians by the Council of Basile; the Patriarch Alphonso Mendez wrote to the King Basilides, that he was ready to indulge the Abyssins in it[4] but was answer'd that his concession came too late.

It is owned, that however free the Abyssins may be from any conformity in their notions of the Eucharist with the enemies of the Roman Church,[5] yet with regard to confession, they are guilty of some errors. Three patriarchs who succeeded each other,[6] endeavoured to abolish confession, and gave Mark the son of Alkonbari who appear'd with great zeal in the defense of it, abundance of trouble, he through his behaviour which was not the most regular, gave his adversaries great advantages over him in the controversy, yet had his followers, and confessed

---

3. Cf. "du Corps de Jésus Christ" (p. 329).

4. According to the French, the Patriarch was ready "de le rétablir" (p. 329).

5. "It is owned ... Church" epitomizes a paragraph of French: "Peut-on croire, après ce que nous venons de rapporter, & qui est extrait ou des liturgies ou des rituels de l'Eglise d'Alexandrie, ou des histoires d'Ethiopie, que les Abissins ne croient pas la présence réelle, ou qu'ils n'aient pas autant & plus de vénération que nous pour le sacré corps & le précieux sang de Jésus Christ, que nous adorons dans le Saint Sacrement de l'autel" (p. 329).

6. The French names them (p. 329).

great numbers. They had found out a very extraordinary method of supplying the defect of this part of pennance; the priest after having burnt incense upon the altar, went round the church and perfumed the people, who imagined that they sufficiently confessed their sins by crying out, "I have sinned, I have sinned." The priest on his part repeated some prayers, which were a kind of absolution. When corruptions crept in amongst them, and the priests began to abuse their power, complaints were made not only of the rigour of the penances which they imposed, but likewise of their indiscretion. Whereupon confession being found too heavy a yoke, was neglected, and instead of throwing themselves at the feet of a priest, they had recourse to the expedient of throwing incense into a censer with other perfumes, and murmuring a few words with their mouths in the smoke, and crying out "I have sinned," believing themselves absolved by that ceremony from all their faults. This superstition was called the Confession of the Censer.

Mark the son of Alkonbari preached against so strange a manner of confession, he blamed the mixture of spices, affirming that frankincense only was to be used in churches because it was offer'd by the Magi to Jesus Christ. The preaching of Mark had a good effect upon his audience and himself. He discover'd, and detested the errours of the Jacobites, and became a convert together with his auditors. This corruption, great as it was, continued under John the son of Abulserah and the two patriarchs his immediate successors,[7] but was afterwards rectified, and the missionaries, who have often exagerated the errors of the Abyssins, say nothing of this. They confess themselves seldom indeed, and instead of the penitent[d] accusing himself as among us, the priest there examines him upon every article, imposing the pennance prescribed by the canons, which is commonly sufficiently severe. The priest then repeats several prayers over the penitent to implore God's pardon for him, and to obtain the spirit of compunction to be sent down upon him with a fervour and zeal necessary to perform the pennance injoined him. The Abyssins being of opinion that satisfaction is an essential part of

d. penitent *1789*] penitents *1735*

7. After previously deleting the names, SJ here inserts one; cf. "sous ces trois patriarches qu'on a nommés" (p. 330).

this sacrament, the priest doth not give an entire absolution till the pennance is performed, or at least the greatest part of it. A priest who has been guilty of any considerable fault cannot say mass till he has confessed, and is guilty of sacrilege, if he acts contrary to this precept; the pennance imposed is generally twice as severe as that prescribed to a layman for the same fault.

The use of confession may have been interrupted by a corruption not less ancient than the Jacobite Church, of which we may discover as satisfactory proof in the ninth century. The Patriarch Sanutius or Cheneuda had the weakness to absolve from excommunication a deacon of a disorderly life, and being reproached with it by his secretary, made this answer, "You do not know, my son, that he had the confidence to partake of the Holy Communion without first confessing his sin to God, imagining that by approaching that holy table he was reconciled to the Church, and become a perfect Christian, and that by receiving the sacrament his sins were forgiven him, depending on those words, 'This is my body, eat it, that your sins may be forgiven you'; his crime on the contrary was much greater."

The learned abbe who hath given the world the history of the patriarchs of Alexandria, affirms that the Cophtes never proceeded so far as to make any doubt of the necessity of confession and pennance.

Severus bishop of Aschmunein, who lived in the tenth century has written a treatise on the method of making an efficacious confession: Wansleb[8] who affirms that the Cophtes do not all agree in this point, cites some of those who have written against him. Michael bishop of Damiete,[e] who lived when this dispute was carried on with the greatest heat, was one of the most violent against confession; Abulbaracat quotes several treatises written since on preparation for confession. Wansleb adds, that he knows certainly that they do confess, though but rarely, not from contempt of the sacrament, but, some from ignorance and stupidity not knowing how they ought to confess, others for fear of the long and severe pennances imposed upon them.

We are told by Francis Alvarez, that Peter Covilhan never

e. Damiete *Relation*] Damiesa *1735*

8. All of the information in this paragraph is found in Wansleben's *Histoire de l'eglise d'Alexandrie*, pp. 136–37.

confessed to the Abyssin priests, because he had no opinion either of their discretion or their secrecy, and knew that they revealed the confessions made to them; and he tells us in another place, that they confess and communicate standing.[9]

Father Tellez relates,[1] that though the Abyssins hold confession to a priest necessary to obtain forgiveness of their sins committed after baptism, they are yet under many errors concerning it. For they do not confess till they are twenty five years old, imagining themselves till then in the age of innocence, and they speak of one that dies at sixteen or seventeen years, as we speak of an infant. When they confess, they content themselves with saying in general, "I have sinned, I intreat you to give me absolution." And if they are pressed by the priest to particularise their faults, they desire him to examine them, and are asked by him whether they have committed murder or theft, and whether they have broken the fifth commandment, as if these were the only sins mankind was obnoxious to.[2] And what is yet worse, the priest doth not give them absolution in the manner of the Latin Church, but having repeated some words strikes the penitent with an olive branch,[3] of which they take care never to be without great plenty, that absolution may not be difficult to obtain. This last circumstance on which Mr. Ludolf has display'd his erudition by quoting the Roman poets,[4] wherever Father Tellez learned it, is not mention'd by the patriarch with whose words we here present the reader.[5]

---

9. Covilhã's views on Confession may be found in *Prester John*, p. 369; the Abyssinian practice of standing during Confession is mentioned in Alvares's responses to the Archbishop of Braga (*Prester John*, p. 511).

1. All but the final sentence of this paragraph is taken from Telles, p. 92.

2. "as if ... obnoxious to" is SJ's version of "comme s'ils ne reconnaissaient point d'autres péchés que ceux-là" (p. 332).

3. SJ deletes some of the criticism: "ne devrait-on pas punir un confesseur qui s'acquitte si mal de son ministère, & renvoyer ou du moins instruire un pénitent qui ne sait pas mieux se confesser" (p. 332).

4. The French names them: Plautus, Persius, Juvenal, and Claudian (p. 332). Ludolf's note (No. LVI) may be found in his *Commentarius*, p. 375.

5. Le Grand takes the Latin quotation that follows from Mendes's *Expeditionis Aethiopicae*, Book I, Chap. 6; it may be found in Beccari, VIII. 64–65.

[Not slight are the errors that mar their practice of the sacrament of penance, for few of them set forth the types and number of their sins but say generally, "I have sinned, absolve me," and the absolution accords with the confession. However, an unusually alert confessor would sometimes ask the penitent what it was from which he was going to absolve him. But he would reply, "I have lied, I have violated

Sacramenti poenitentiae usum non exigui errores lacerabant, paucis peccatorum species & numerum exponentibus, generatimque dicentibus, peccavi, me absolve; & confessioni solutio congruebat. Attentior tamen confessarius aliquando rogabat à quibus accedentem esset exsoluturus. Ille vero addebat, mentitus sum, alienam famam vel uxorem violavi. Tunc ipsum injuncta mulcta liberum abire jubebat; sed nemo, antequam illam penitus persolveret, sacro Eucharistiae epulo accumbebat, cum nonnum- quam unum vel duos annos jejunare, & singulis diebus quinquaginta, vel centum vel omnes Davidis Psalmos recitare juberetur. Unde ortum, ne moribundis eadem synaxis praebeatur; cum putent nihil ipsis profuturam confessionem, si desit tempus ad satisfactionis cumulum addendum. Illâ nemo, ante vicesimum quintum aetatis annum, quem innocentiae terminum credebant, animi sordes eluebat. Tales vero tantum rebantur mechari, occidere & aliena furari, nec tamen ulla cuiquam redhibitio imponebatur; sed novi apud eos juris regula vigebat; ut non dimitteretur peccatum, quin restitueretur ablatum. Cum solutâ scortari adeo erat innoxium, ut cum duo

---

another's reputation or his wife." Then, having enjoined penance, he would bid him go away free. But no one, until he had thoroughly performed the penance, would kneel at the holy supper of the Eucharist, since he would be ordered sometimes to fast for a year or two and daily recite fifty or a hundred or all the Psalms of David. Whence it happens that this rite is not offered to the dying since they think that confession will avail them nothing if there is no time for completing it by giving satisfaction. No one would remove the stains on his soul by that means before the age of twenty-five, which they regard as the end of innocence. But they reckon as such stains only adultery, killing, and stealing what is another's. Yet no restitution at law would be imposed on anyone, but rather a ruling of strange legality prevailed among them that a sin was not forgiven without restor- ing what had been taken away. Upon absolution it was regarded as so harmless to indulge in promiscuity that when a couple had agreed to indulge themselves for a whole winter or a summer, they would go to a clergyman so that he would bind them, on pain of anathema, that the

man not depart to another woman nor the woman to another man, and a husband going off to battle would ask his wife to assign him for his soldier's bed any one of her attendants or maids she wished with whom it was supposed to be no sin in God's eyes to fornicate nor even was it considered a marginal offense that would keep him from being refreshed by the angelic bread on Sundays as was the case with those mentioned previously Many were unaware of the true form of this sacrament. Two more common methods took the form of a prayer. Only one exhi- bited the form of a judicial pronounce- ment. The former were: N., servant of God, may Jesus Christ remit your sin and may he remit it for you by the mouth of Peter and Paul and may he render you free from its bond. N., servant of God, may the Paraclete, bestower of pardon, wipe out all your sins. The latter: May your sin be forgiven you by the mouth of our Lord Jesus Christ and of Saints Peter and Paul and of the three-hundred eighteen fathers who were orthodox. No one will doubt that the first two forms were trifles nor whether the third will afford controversy for theologians.]

pacti essent per totam hyemen vel aestatem congregari, clericum adirent, ut interposito anathemate, vetaret ne ille ad alteram, vel illa ad alterum abiret, & maritus ad praelium discedens uxorem praecaretur, ut quam vellet ex pedissequis, vel ancillis, sibi in militarem thorum[f] *designaret, cum qua libidinari nihil erat ante Deum piaculi, vel in vicinia offensionis, quo minus singulis diebus Dominicis angelorum pane, ut & praedicti reficeretur; plerosque vera hujus sacramenti forma latebat, duae communiores precationem, una tantum aliquam judicialis sententiae formam exhibebat. Illae erant: N. serve Dei, mittat te peccatum, illudque tibi Jesus Christus Petri & Pauli ore dimittat; teque ab illius vinculo liberum reddat. N. serve Dei, Paracletus, veniae*[g] *largitor, omnia tua peccata deleat. Ista: Solvatur tibi peccatum tuum ore Domini Nostri Jesus Christi, Sanctorum Petri & Pauli; & tercentum decem & octo patrum qui rectae fidei fuerunt. Duas priores formas nugaces fuisse, nemo dubitabit, num tertia probanda sit theologis controversum.*

It is easy to discover from this account of the patriarch, that, though some corruptions with respect to the sacrament of pennance have been introduced, yet auricular confession is practised among the Aethiopians, that there are some among them skilful enough to distinguish the circumstances of sins, *peccatorum species,* and that they consider the number, *et numerum;* that there are confessors who examine their penitents about other sins, than murder, theft, and adultery, who demand whether they have been guilty of lies, and calumny; and that they impose severe and long pennances, agreeable to the canons observed among them.

Father du Bernat tells us, that with regard to the sacrament of pennance, there is an exact conformity of belief between the Cophtes and the Romanists,[6] with a difference of ceremony and custom. As to belief[7] they hold themselves obliged to confess to the priest their particular sins, with the number of them, after which the confessor repeats a form of prayer to implore pardon and remission of sins, and a second prayer[8] answerable to that said by us after the absolution. What he terms the difference of ceremony is the precatory form made use of by the Cophtes and

f. thorum *Relation*] morem *1735*   g. veniae *Relation*] venia *1735*

6. "between the Cophtes ... Romanists" expands the phrase "avec nous" to clarify it for an English reading public (p. 333).

7. SJ adds the transition.

8. SJ deletes a clarifying clause: "qu'ils nomment bénédiction" (p. 334).

Greeks in giving the absolution. He adds, that he[9] endeavoured
to give himself farther satisfaction by enquiring of the priests,
whether in the administration of this sacrament they express'd
nothing in positive terms; and was inform'd that the penitent
before he goes away, says, "I have sinned, my father, give me
absolution," and is answer'd by the priest, "Be thou absolved
from thy sins."

The same father having complained of the indulgence of the
confessors, owns that in[1] scandalous sins, they are more severe,
and oblige them to perform the pennance enjoined, at least in
part, before they give them absolution, but this is a case that
rarely happens; they act in the same manner with those who are
enemies to each other, and compel them to a reconciliation.

Alvarez relates that he knew one in Aethiopia named Ababitay,[h] who had been several years excluded from the sacraments for having three wives, that he discarded two, and kept
the third, being thereupon admitted into the church, as a par-
taker of the sacraments, as if he had never had above one wife.[2]

In short, what ever Mr. Ludolf may say with all his Aethiopick learning, the Abyssins like us,[3] hold the sacrament of pennance, and auricular confession, which is part of it. They believe
with us that Jesus Christ[i] is really and essentially present in the
Eucharist which they adore and receive like us, but in two kinds.
The insnaring questions of Mr. Ludolf to Gregory prove nothing
but his insincerity; and Gregory answers nothing but his
ignorance.

DISSERTATION THE THIRTEENTH, ON EXTREME UNCTION, ORDINATION AND MARRIAGE

The Cophtes, the Syrian Jacobites, the Nestorians or
Melchites,[1] call what the Greeks term *euchelaion* and the extreme

h. Ababitay *Relation*] Ababitag *1735*   i. Christ *Errata*] Church *1735*

---

9. The French provides a first-person
account (p. 334).

1. The verb "owns" avoids the wordi-
ness of "puis il dit: 'Il faut portant avouer
qu'à l'égard des ...'" (p. 334).

2. Alvares adds that he was told that
Ababitay "had had seven wives and thirty
sons by them" (*Prester John*, p. 105).

3. SJ adds the comparison.

1. A diverse group: the Copts and the

unction, *kandil* or *zeis el katidil*, that is the lamp or oyl of the lamp. An account of the manner in which this sacrament is administred among them will be a sufficient explanation of the name. Several priests take the oyl of a lamp of seven branches, over which they have repeated some psalms and prayers, and anoint the sick with it, not in his bed, or at home, but in the church, to which he is carried before he comes to the last extremity.

All the Orientals say that this practise was instituted by Christ himself, when he sent out his Apostles, by two and two to preach the Gospel, giving them power over unclean spirits. The Apostles drove out the unclean spirits, and anointing the sick with oyl cured them. That in conformity with that practise the Apostle St. James, Chap. v. ver. 14. says, "Is any sick among you? let him call for the elders[2] of the church, and let them pray over him, anointing him with oyl in the name of the Lord, and the prayer of faith shall save the sick, and the Lord shall raise him up, and if he have committed sins, they shall be forgiven him." The ritual of Gabriel patriarch of the Jacobites, prescribes the manner of the administration of this sacrament.[3]

A lamp of seven branches, filled with good oyl of Palestine is set near the image of the Blessed Virgin, and the Gospel and cross are placed near it: the priests assemble to the number of seven (though the number is of no strict importance) and the eldest of them begins the thanksgiving in the liturgy of St. Basil, and burns incense before the reading of the Epistle of St. Paul; then they all repeat *Kyrie eleeson*, the Lord's Prayer, the 31st Psalm, the prayer that is in the liturgy for the sick, and the others set down in the office of extreme unction. These being ended, he lights one of the branches, making the sign of the cross upon the oyl, and in the mean time the others sing psalms. After he has ended the prayers for the diseased, and read a lesson out of

Syrian Jacobites adhered to the monophysite doctrine of the single Divine nature in the Incarnate Christ rather than a double nature—Divine and human—after the Incarnation; the Nestorians believed in the doctrine that there were two separate persons in the Incarnate Christ—the Divine and the human; the Melchites were Eastern Christians who adhered to the orthodox faith and who accepted the deliberations of Ephesus and Chalcedon: the name "Melchite" itself refers to their accepting the religion of the ruler.

2. Cf. "les prêtres" (p. 335).

3. The quotation which follows is translated from Renaudot's *La perpétuité de la foy*, v. 338–39.

the epistle general of St. James, with the *Sanctus, Gloria Patri*, and the prayer of the Gospel, he says a psalm alternately with another priest, and then reads a Gospel, the three prayers that follow in the liturgy, one to the Father, another for peace, another general; then the Nicene Creed and the Prayer that follows it.

Then the second priest begins the benediction of his branch, and lights it, making the sign of the cross, then says the Lord's Prayer and three others of the liturgy, reading a lesson from St. Paul, and one from the Gospel, with a psalm and a particular prayer for the sick. The same prayers are repeated by the other priests in their order, so that in this ceremony, as the author of *Ecclesiastick Science* observes,[4] they read seven lessons from the epistles, seven from the Gospels, seven psalms, and seven particular prayers, besides those set down in the liturgy.

When all this is ended, he on whose account the lamp is blessed, if his strength will permit, approaches, and sits down with his face turned toward the east. The priests, putting the Gospel and the cross upon his head, lay their hands on him. The eldest priest having said the proper prayers, makes the sick stand up, and with the Book of the Gospels gives him his benediction, and then the Lord's Prayer is repeated. Afterwards the Book is open'd and the passage read to him which first occurs. They rehearse the creed, and three prayers, after which they raise the cross over the head of the sick, and pronounce the general absolution out of the liturgy. If the time will allow, they afterwards say other prayers and make a procession in the church, with the blessed lamp and lighted tapers, to implore God to cure the sick by the intercession of the martyrs and other saints. If the sick be not in a condition to be

---

4. Le Grand is quoting Renaudot (v. 339), who makes clear elsewhere in *La perpétuité de la foy* that he is referring to Abusebah, "auteur d'un traité de la science ecclesiastique." Renaudot may have been using a version of *La perle précieuse traitant des sciences ecclésiastiques* by Ibn Sabâ, a thirteenth-century Jacobite who wrote about the liturgy. An Arabic text was published in Cairo in 1618. The translation by Jean Périer in *Patrologia orientalis*, 16 (Paris, 1922), 591–760, presents related materials but does not describe the specific practices Le Grand cites. Abu (the father of) and Ibn (the son of) could be confused.

brought himself near the altar, another is substituted in his place. After the procession the priests anoint the sick, and each other; the assistants likewise receive an unction, but performed in a different manner from that on the sick.

Wansleb gives the same account in his history of the Church of Alexandria, except that he says nothing of the procession or that which follows, but affirms that they anoint the sick seven days; a practise formerly in use among the Latins, as appears from the Sacramentary of St. Gregory, and the notes of the learned Benedictine Hugh Menard.

It is nevertheless probable from the letter of Father du Bernat that either the avarice or ignorance of the priests has introduced some abuses with regard to this sacrament; that learned and pious missionary's[a] account of it is in general this.[5]

The sacrament which we call the extreme unction is called by them the holy unction or *kandil*, that is the lamp, which being commanded by St. James to be used to the sick, is, by means of a distinction of the sick, into the sick of diseases, of sins, and of afflictions, applyed by them, as by the Greeks, to all sorts of persons. Their manner of administring it is this; the priest assisted by the deacon,[b] having pronounced the absolution to the sick, burns the incense, and taking a lamp blesses the oyl, and lights the wick, then says seven prayers, between each of which the deacon reads a lesson taken from the Epistle of St. James and other parts of Scripture. Then the priest taking the holy oyl from the lamp, anoints the forehead of the diseased,[6] with these words, "God heal you in the name of the Father, of the Son, and of the Holy Ghost." Nor is this all, for an unction is likewise performed on the assistants, lest, say they, the Evil Spirit might enter into one of them; so great is their ignorance.

---

a. missionary's *1789*] missionaries *1735*   b. deacon; *1735*

---

5. "In general" is SJ's addition and suggests the epitomizing that follows. He deletes the opening of Father du Bernat's account: "'Ce n'est pas qu'ici les confesseurs aient à se plaindre d'être accablés d'une foule de pénitents; un seul penitent leur est ordinairement une pénible & longue occupation; est-ce pour le mieux disposer, l'instruire, l'interroger, l'exhorter? Non, c'est pour lui donner en même temps le sacrement ...'" (p. 337).

6. SJ inserts "Of the diseased" for clarity.

According to the ritual this ceremony is performed by seven priests, each of which lights his wick. If there be a bishop present with six priests, it belongs to his office to light the seven wicks, and say seven prayers, the priests only reading the lessons. The same rites are observed whether the sacrament be administred in the church after confession or in the house of the sick.

Father Goar, that learned Dominican, who, after having resided so long among the Greeks, has favour'd the world with so many excellent works,[7] has observ'd in his notes on the euchology that the sick were not always carried to church to receive extreme unction, and that it was sometimes administred to them at home and in their bed. He doth not condemn the custom among the priests of anointing each other and the assistants, after having administred the extreme unction, with the same oyl. But he, and Arcudius,[8] together with the Abbe Renaudot, maintain that neither the priests nor the others imagine that they by that means receive extreme unction, and that what they do with so much devotion is only to show their respect to the holy oyl: so that neither Mr. Ludolf nor any other Protestant can conclude that the Greeks and Orientals do not reckon extreme unction among their sacraments.

Mr. Ludolf 'tis true supports his opinion by the testimonies of Father Godigno and the Patriarch Alphonso Mendez,[9] but he had at the same time the contrary account of Wansleb his scholar before his eyes, who had been, as he knew, in Egypt, and had visited the chief monastries there, had read many manuscripts, held long conferences with the Cophtes, and written his history of their Church under the immediate inspection of the patriarch. He ought certainly in this case to have distrusted the missionaries whose relations he professes in other cases to depend so little on. He ought to have consulted their rituals and catechisms or at least his Gregory;[c] instead of this caution he resigns himself with the most implicit credulity to the accounts of the patriarch, and the Fathers Tellez and Godigno. *Comment.*

c. Gregory, *1735*

7. Jacques Goar, a French Dominican, published his *Εὐχολόγιον sive Rituale Graecorum* at Paris in 1647.

8. Petrus Arcudius, a Greek ecclesiastic, published *De Concordia Ecclesiae occiden-*talis et orientalis in septem sacramentorum ad-*ministratione* (Paris, 1626).

9. In Book III, Chap. 5 (p. 271 in *New History*) Ludolf cites Godignus but not Mendes.

p. 267.[1] So that it seems the missionaries are only to be believed when they favour the Lutherans and Calvinists.[2]

The opinion of the Cophtes or Jacobites concerning marriage cannot be better explain'd, than by the account of Father du Bernat; which I here give from his own letter.

What now remains, Reverend Father, is to give you an account of what relates to their marriages. The single reading of the ritual, sufficiently proves that the Cophtes hold marriage to be a real sacrament; mention being made in all the prayers of the grace of Jesus Christ confer'd in it. When two persons have agreed to enter into this state, the priest going to their house examines whether there be any impediments, and betroths them by repeating several prayers. The pair then go to church, where they are confessed by the priest, who after long prayers, asks whether they are agreed to accept each other;[d] consent being given on each side, they hear mass and communicate.

See here a sacrament celebrated with much solemnity; to which it were to be wish'd the Cophtes had somewhat more regard, and that either they understood with more exactness that binding obligation, or rather that they would confine themselves to the observation of it. For not only in case of adultery, but even of long sickness; or upon casual aversions, or quarrels about domestick affairs, and often upon some disgust they cut the sacred marriage knot, a liberty taken by the wife no less than the husband. The party which attempts the dissolution of the marriage, first applies to the patriarch, or to the bishop to desire it, who, after trying some persuasions to the contrary, consents. The same party then comes again for a permission to contract a second marriage which is easily obtain'd. If it should at any time fall out that the reasons alleged for a separation are too frivolous to be allow'd, if they can prevail on any priest to

d. other, *1735*

---

1. At this point the *Commentarius* cites Telles, Bk. I, Chap. 37, Godignus, Bk. I, Chap. 35, p. 215, and Mendes in Epist. Calend. Junii 1626.

2. "instead of ... Calvinists" epitomizes a quarter page of criticism concluding with the question of whether the missionaries are no longer to be believed "lorsqu'ils ont des opinions qui ne peuvent s'accorder avec les erreurs de ces hérétiques?" (p. 339).

be so complaisant as to marry them, they are excused by being excluded some time from the sacraments.

This is the French missionary whom we oppose to those of Portugal, when they affirm that the marriages of the Abyssins cannot be call'd marriages, since the bride and bridegroom seldom come together without an intention of parting upon the first opportunity. The ceremony of marriage is not performed in secret but publickly, they receive the Communion when they are married, and believe that by communicating they are made one body; if the marriage be not solemnized before a priest it is to be declared void.

Alvarez hath describ'd the ceremony of a marriage at which he assisted.[3] It was performed by the Abuna or patriarch. The man and woman were at the door of the church, where a kind of bed was prepared on which the Abuna made them sit down, going round them in procession with the cross and censer, then laying his hands on their heads, he told them that as they were now become one flesh, they ought to be of one heart and one mind, and after having made a short exhortation to the same purpose, proceeded to say mass, being assisted by the bridegroom and bride, who afterwards received the nuptial benediction. These marriages are firm and binding, nor to be dissolved but upon strong reasons; nor do the meaner people often indulge themselves in those scandalous separations too frequent among persons of quality.

The easy dissolution of marriages and polygamy too frequent among these nations, are probably Jewish superstitions, which the Jacobite Church doth not appear to approve, since she denies the sacrament to those persons who have more wives than one. The Jacobites have the same notions with us of the essentiality of a priest to the solemnization of marriage, and agreeable to our usage, say mass, and give the Communion.[4]

They have likewise another custom of crowning the bridegroom and bride, the crowns being placed on their heads with great ceremony by the priest, are worn eight days, and then

3. See Chapter XXI in *Prester John*, pp. 106–107.

4. This sentence epitomizes a more detailed account but omits entirely the comment that the Jacobites "croient que le mariage est indissoluble; & si on tolère le divorce, on peut dire qu'on se rend à la dureté de leur coeur, comme Jésus Christ l'a dit des Juifs" (p. 341).

taken off with equal ceremony and as many prayers. From this practise the sacrament of marriage is called by Greeks and all the Orientals, "the coronation," and the unlawful marriages are termed "marriages without a coronation"; a proof that they look on the ministry of the priest as necessary to that sacrament.

It now remains that we speak of the sacrament of ordination. Though the Abyssins thro' their servile dependance on the patriarch of Alexandria, have been almost whole ages without an Abuna, yet there is no reason to think that the succession has been interrupted, unless in the patriarchs themselves. The Abuna, who is ordained and sent into Aethiopia by the authority only of that patriarch, is the only person who confers orders, and makes readers, deacons, or priests. The manner of conferring orders has been so little spoken of by the missionaries,[5] that Father Tellez was obliged to refer us to. the writings of Alvarez.

We are inform'd by Alvarez, that he assisted at the ordination of two thousand three hundred fifty six persons,[6] and that it was less numerous than usual, because the coming of the Abuna had not been sufficiently publish'd, and generally five or six thousand were ordain'd at one time. A white tent was fitted up, and the Abuna came with a great number of attendants upon his mule, upon which he sat while he made a short harangue in Arabick, that if any of those who came to receive orders had more than one wife, he should retire on pain of excommunication, after which he alighted and sat down by his tent, while some of the priests placed those who came for ordination in three rows, examining them at the same time only whether they could read by presenting them a book, and marking them according to their approbation of them, upon the arm; those that were so mark'd ranged themselves together. The examination being over, the Abuna entred his tent,[7] and laid his hand upon the head of each, repeating in the Coptick language this prayer, *Gratia divina quae infirma sanat, &c.* After each particular priest had been ordained in this manner, the Abuna said many pray-

---

5. Cf. the French: "Les missionnaires ... se sont si peu ou si mal expliqués touchant la manière ..." (p. 341).

6. Alvares describes this mass ordination (he actually writes 2357) in Chap.

XCVII of *Prester John*, pp. 349–51.

7. SJ deletes a needed detail: "qu'on faisait défiler ceux qui avaient été admis" (p. 342).

ers, and gave many benedictions with a little iron cross; the priest read the Epistle and Gospel, and the Abuna saying mass gave the Communion to all the priests.

Alvarez objected to the king[8] that they dishonoured the priesthood by admitting the blind and lame, and that they were guilty of the highest offence against decency, in suffering the candidates for orders to stand intirely naked, without even covering that which modesty requires to be conceal'd.

The same Alvarez writes, that they confer the sub-deaconship and inferiour orders without any examination, and even on infants at the breast, and on children at any time to the age of fifteen.[9] They must be unmarried to be made clerks, but they take wives before they assume the priesthood, because a priest cannot marry.

They who would be ordained clerks or sub-deacons pass in a row before the Abuna as he sits in a chair in the midst of the church. He crops their hair, makes them touch the church-keys, puts a napkin on their heads, and the vessels used at the Communion[1] in their hands, as a token that they are to serve at the altar: this ceremony ended, the Abuna says mass, and admits those whom he has ordained to the Communion.

This account is sufficiently conformable to the answers of Tecla Mariam, when he was examined at Rome concerning this ordination. "I was fifteen years old," said he, "when the archbishop gave me the first orders, he crop'd my hair in five places in form of a cross, repeating in the Coptick language some prayers which I did not understand, anointed my forehead with oyl, and then said mass." Tecla Mariam, not being able to give a satisfactory answer to all the questions which were put to him, was re-ordain'd.

This re-ordination was not approved by those who understood the state of the Eastern-Church. The Abyssins, no less than the Cophtes and Greeks, give nearly the same definition of ordination as we, agreeing that it is a sacred mark, accompanied with many solemn ceremonies, with which the bishop, by the

---

8. SJ's terse clause replaces the following: "Alvarés témoigna au Roi qu'il n'était pas édifié de ce qu'il avait vu" (p. 342). The complete set of objections may be found in *Prester John*, pp. 352–53.

9. The description on which Le Grand bases this comment appears in *Prester John*, pp. 354–55.

1. "vessels ... Communion" explains the single word "burettes" (p. 343).

imposition of hands, confers on the persons ordained a portion of grace convenient for the ecclesiastical office to which they are raised.

They believe with us that episcopacy, the priesthood and deaconship were instituted by Jesus Christ, and deliver'd down to us by the Apostles and their successors; that this sacrament is necessary for supplying the Church with ministers; that a man not ordained according to that institution cannot consecrate the Eucharist,[2] or perform any office of a priest. If the priests have ever been obliged in Abyssinia to perform the offices of bishops, it hath proceeded from ignorance or indiscreet zeal. Their canons direct that the priest shall be sound in all his limbs, a man of learning, of a good character, and reputable family; neither slaves, nor bastards, nor even those born of a second marriage can be admitted to orders.

The Abuna is charged with confering the priesthood on unworthy persons, and not only of neglecting to observe a proper distance of time between the different orders, but of confering several at one time, a practise contrary to all discipline ancient and modern.

Whatever the missionaries and after them Father Balthasar Tellez may say, there is no denying the validity of the orders confer'd by the Abuna according to the practise of the Eastern Christians; and there is reason to wish that the Patriarch Alphonso Mendez had, before he repeated baptism and holy orders consulted on that subject some wise and learned persons, versed in the knowledge of antiquity, and the practise of the Eastern Church.

DISSERTATION THE FOURTEENTH, ON THE INVOCATION OF SAINTS, MIRACLES, PRAYERS FOR THE DEAD, FASTS, IMAGES, AND RELIQUES

Having shown the conformity of the Abyssinian belief concerning the sacraments with ours, it remains that to compleat

---

2. "Eucharist" is an added clarifying term; the French has only "ne peut ni consacrer..." (p. 343).

our undertaking, we prove that Mr. Ludolf has dealt unfairly on other points of controversy, by showing the sentiments of the Abyssins and their practise, with regard to prayer for the dead, invocation of saints, miracles, reliques, the distinction of meats, and fasts, and tradition, all which are points on which we reproach the Protestants with errors.[1]

Mr. Ludolf who had so many liturgies in his hands which he ought to have made publick, could not be unacquainted with the prayers which they use for the dead.

In the mass attributed to St. Basil, the priest after the commemoration of the saints goes on. "Remember likewise, O Lord, the priests and laymen, grant Lord, that their souls may repose in the bosom of the Saints Abraham, Isaac, and Jacob, send them into that happy place, where refreshing waters may be found, into that paradise of delights, from whence are banished all sighs, sadness and sorrow of heart, and where they may rejoice in the light of thy saints. Remember, O Lord, our fathers and our brethren who have dyed in the true Faith, give them rest with thy saints, and with those whom we have now commemorated; give rest to sinners,[2] and remember those who have made these offerings, and those for whom they are made. Remember, O Lord, those who have dyed in the true faith of our fathers and our brethren, grant that their souls may rest with the saints and the just; conduct them, and assemble them in a pleasant place near cool and living water, in a paradise of delight, and with those whose names we have now repeated."

Alvarez, who satisfies himself with telling what he was an eye-witness of, speaking of the obsequies in use among the Abyssins, says, that when they have brought the body into the church, they throw it immediately into the grave, without singing, saying any thing of our office for the dead, or celebrating any mass for the sinner;[3] that they sanctify[4] themselves with sprinkling the body with holy water, perfuming it with incense, and reading the Gospel of St. John.[5]

The Abyssins have no particular masses for the dead and do

---

1. SJ has reversed the meaning of this passage: according to Le Grand, these "sont autant de sujets de reproches que nous font les Protestants" (p. 345).

2. Cf. "aux trépassés" (p. 346).

3. Cf. "le trépassé" (p. 346).

4. "sanctify" may be an aural error for "satisfy"; cf. "qu'ils se contentent" (p. 346).

5. Alvares presents this account in *Prester John*, p. 111.

not change the order of their service, but they always use prayers and commemorations for the dead, and in the collection of canons which they pretend to have been extracted from the Constitution of St. Clement, it is directed, that sacrifice shall be offer'd, and prayers said for the dead on the third and seventh days, and at the end of the month, and of the year. And in the statutes of the Patriarch Christodulus, who lived about the middle of the eleventh century, 'tis order'd that on Palm-Sunday after mass shall be read a lesson out of the epistles of St. Paul, the Gospel, and the prayers for the dead.[6]

He then adds, "It is neither convenient nor allowable for Christians to lament or wear mourning for the dead on Sundays, but the litanies and mass shall be used for them, and prayers shall be said, and alms given that God may have mercy on the souls of the deceased."[7]

Though the Abyssins do not entirely agree among themselves about the state of the soul after its separation from the body, they yet all acquiesce in this opinion, that to enjoy eternal felicity the divine justice must first be satisfied, and that the prayers said and good works done, for the dead, supply the defect of what they had omitted in their lives, provided they have not made themselves unworthy of them.

Those who read the answers given by the Abyssin Gregory to Mr. Ludolf's questions B. 3d. will hardly entertain any high opinion of his genius or capacity. Mr. Ludolf doth not allow that the Abyssins pray to the saints, but ascribes the notions which prevail among them in this point, to the pathetick discourses of their bishops, who, by a rhetorical apostrophe address themselves to the saints, and introduce them speaking, and thus, according to Mr. Ludolf, the corrupt custom of invoking the saints was introduced among the Abyssins.[8]

Mr. Ludolf, when he wrote this, had his mind intent upon somewhat else, or did not know that the Abyssins have only one metropolitan, and no other bishops, that this metropolitan is a foreigner, who either doth not understand the language, or at

---

6. Renaudot, *Historia patriarcharum*, p. 422.

7. Having rendered "trépassés" as "sinners," SJ here accurately translates "des défunts" as "the deceased." Apparently "trépassés" suggested "tres-

passers," hence "sinners." Renaudot's Latin (p. 422) would indicate that "the deceased" is appropriate in all instances.

8. *New History*, Book III, Chap. 5, p. 279.

least understands it very imperfectly, and never preaches:[9] the invocation of saints, if it be a corruption, is a corruption of long continuance, since we hold it in common with nations, which have been near twelve hundred years in a state of separation from the Church of Rome.

The same may be said of miracles, of images, and the veneration paid to reliques. Their books are filled with histories of miracles; they repair to the tombs of their saints,[1] and consult them, and receive answers from them.

They set down in their kalendar, the feasts of the translation of the bodies of saints, for which I appeal to Mr. Ludolf; and to the kalendar which he has given us.[2]

The 1st of January St. Stephen, the first martyr. The Cophtes make this day the feast of the discovery of his body, and place the feast of his martyrdom on the nineteenth of September; about this my Abyssin owns there is a dispute.[3]

The 22d of the same month, "The translation of the body of Timothy," which the Alexandrians affirm to have been carried to the Church of the Holy Apostles at Constantinople.

The 28th, "The translation of the body of Ephraim the Syrian."[4]

The 30th, "The translation of the bones of forty nine martyrs."

The 31st, "The emersion of the body of Hippolytus out of the sea."

In the month of February, "The translation of the body of Joseph. The translation of the body of Marcian. The discovery of the head of St. John."

If we should go through the rest of the kalendar, we should find more days set apart for the commemoration of these translations than in ours.

As for miracles Mr. Ludolf will not deny that they can supply us with an endless number. "But of their saints" says he, *Hist.*

---

9. SJ omits three points (all attributed in Le Grand to the *Hist. patriarch. Alex.*): "que les sermons sont très rares en ce pays-là, que ces peuples s'en tiennent à leur catéchisme, & qu'un Abuna n'oserait entreprendre d'introduire aucune nouveauté" (p. 347).

1. "of their saints" is a rendering of "de

ceux qui sont morts en odeur de sainteté" (p. 347).

2. The material that follows is taken from *Commentarius*, pp. 403-09.

3. The Latin quotation from Ludolf is deleted (p. 347).

4. SJ translates all of the quoted entries from Latin (p. 348).

B. 3d. "they relate most astonishing miracles; it being little more than common among them to have mountains removed, the tempestuous ocean quieted, the dead raised, water drawn by a stroke from the rock, and rivers pass'd over without being wet."[5] He thereupon makes this beautiful remark in his commentaries, "The wiser doctors of the Church of Rome acknowledge that miracles without sound doctrine are not sufficient to prove the truth of any church or religion."[6]

In that we are agreed, but that is not our present business, which is to know whether the Abyssins, like us, believe that God sometimes works miracles to make the glory of his saints manifest, and to show that he doth not disapprove the worship paid to them.

They have no carv'd images, but their churches are full of pictures, among which there is a picture pretended by them[7] to have been sent by Jesus Christ to King Abgarus, and one of the Blessed Virgin drawn by St. Luke.

Father du Bernat speaking of the Jacobites, says, "They have, without comparison, more respect for images than we, they prostrate themselves before them, and after having touched them respectfully with their hand, rub their eyes and face with it. I shall remark by the way that these people did not probably borrow the veneration paid by them to images, from the Greeks, from whom they have so much aversion, and that it is consequently very ancient in the Church of Alexandria. They have indeed none but pictures, but I never found any among them who condemned the use of images, or was not willing to pay them the same honour."

Alvarez in his description of the monastry of Bisan, assures us that it is full of painting, and that the church is hung round with the figures of the Patriarchs and Apostles, and that of St. George on horseback, which is to be seen in almost every church; that there is in this a great piece of satin, on which is drawn a crucifix, the Virgin, the patriarchs, prophets and Apostles; and that many other pictures are preserved there, which are never ex-

---

5. "'they relate ... being wet'" is translated by SJ from Latin (p. 348); the passage may be found in *New History*, p. 256.

6. "'The wiser ... religion'" is also translated from the Latin (p. 348).

7. "among which ... by them" weakens the comment: "Ils ont plus de foi que nous à l'image qu'on prétend ..." (p. 348).

posed but on festivals.[8] These pictures, says Wansleb, are never shown till they are blessed, and are all extremely modest.

Some examples may be of force to convince the most incredulous Protestant, of the respect, which the Abyssins, so long separated from the Church of Rome, have for images. Asaba the eldest son of Abdel-Aziz the Governor going into the Church of Holovan, spit in contempt upon a picture of the Blessed Virgin holding our Saviour in her arms;[a] the night after, he had a dreadful vision, in which he thought[b] himself carried before a judge seated on a throne, and encompassed with soldiers cloathed in white, where Jesus Christ came and demanded justice for the insult offered him by Asaba, upon which one of the soldiers stab'd him with a lance. When he awaked he found himself in a high fever, and died immediately. A Mahometan having pierced a crucifix with his lance, imagined that he had received the blow and was fix'd to the crucifix, nor could he be recovered till he had promised to become a Christian. Stranger stories than these are not to be met with in our legends.

'Tis well known what stories the Abyssins have believed, and even what continue to believe about the Ark and the rod of Moses, which they imagine are preserved amongst them.

As the kings of Nubia and Abyssinia encamp or travel with their whole family, they have obtained from the patriarch of Alexandria to have a moveable altar, that they may not wherever they are, be without the celebration of the mass. This altar is carried with great ceremony agreeably to the genius and custom of the people who have a great veneration for every thing made use of for the service of the altar, as sufficiently appears, by the solemnity with which the *korban* or consecrated bread is made. None enter the church otherwise than with their feet bare. The sanctuary is not open to any except the priests and deacons, who would think themselves guilty of a great sin, if they should spit in it.[9]

Mr. Ludolf, who loses no opportunity of displaying his vast learning, has taken care to tell us, that in the first dawn of

a. arms, *1735*   b. which he thought *1789*] which thought *1735*

8. The description of the monastery appears in *Prester John*, p. 87.
9. "The sanctuary ... spit in it" provides a logical reversal of the original order: "ils croiraient commettre un grand péché s'ils crachaient dans le sanctuaire, il n'est même permis qu'aux prêtres & aux diacres d'y entrer" (p. 349).

Christianity, when the Church mourn'd under the oppression of heathen emperors, the divine mysteries were distributed on tables placed in the burying-yards and made in the shape of a coffin which they filled with the bones of dead Christians, from whence proceeded the veneration for reliques. He was so enamour'd of this thought that he has procured this coffin to be engraved,[1] and imagines that from hence the Abyssins call the altars which they carry with them by the name of Arks. It is, methinks,[2] more natural to suppose that this nation being firmly persuaded that they have had the Ark of the Covenant from time immemorial in their Church of Axuma, and having for their moveable altars a veneration not very different from that of the Jews for their Ark, have given the same name *Tabout*.

There hath yet appeared no great conformity between the religion of the Abyssins and Protestants, nor will there appear more in what we have to add. Anciently the Abyssins went in large troops to visit the holy places, and Alvarez assures us that in his time there was a great conflux of people at the tombs of Aba Licanos, and Aba Gariman:[3] there is no country in the world in which there are so many churches and monastries, or such numbers of religious.[4] The monks are confined to the observance of the strictest rules. Fasting and abstinence is carried here to the greatest height, even so far that 'tis not easy to believe what Alvarez has written on that subject.[5] During the great Lent, they neither eat butter nor milk, nor any thing that has had life. They fast all the Holy Week upon bread and water; every Wednesday and Friday of Lent, many of the religious as well women as men spend the night in the frozen pools up to the neck in water; they always wear the hair-cloath and iron-chains, which often enter so deep into the skin that they cannot be seen: they eat only every other day. Thus Lent is observed throughout

---

1. In *New History*, Book III, Chap. 6, the discussion covers pages 294–97, and the illustration of "a marble coffin" appears opposite p. 296.

2. This archaism replaces "ce semble" (p. 350).

3. On the feast day of Abbagarima, says Alvares, "there were here more than 3000 cripples, blind men, and lepers" (*Prester John*, p. 166).

4. The French text distinguishes between canons and monks: "Les chanoines se marient comme les autres prêtres, & souvent leurs enfants héritent de leurs prébendes; ce qui est très contraire aux canons. Les moines ne se marient jamais" (p. 350).

5. Alvares devotes three chapters (CX–CXII) to Abyssinian practices during Lent (*Prester John*, pp. 389–404).

Abyssinia, men, women, and children fasting with great exactness; so that the king being once encamped near his enemies in Lent, his soldiers were so weaken'd and macerated by the severities of that season, that they were unable to defend themselves. Mass is never celebrated on those days till evening, and they who communicate generally do it fasting; the Lent lasts there fifty days. They fast in Advent with almost the same rigour as in Lent, and the life of a religious among them is a perpetual abstinence.

The missionaries notwithstanding never left declaiming with very little prudence against the corrupt lives of the monks, even going so far as to declare that they spent more time with the women than in their convents; they confounded the good with the bad, and by their undistinguishing reproaches, and severe reflexions[6] made all the religious rise against them, who brought upon them the general detestation of the whole empire.

Alvarez is more sparing of his reprehensions, and has been just in giving those monks who lived a life of true penitence their due commendations, but had the corruption been greater and more universal even than the missionaries pretended, the rules of the orders still continued the same, and by those rules they ought to have judged of their profession. When the monastick life was first introduced into Abyssinia is not known; some are of opinion that Frumentius the Apostle and first bishop of the Abyssins might have brought with him into that kingdom some disciples of the great Saint Antony, that solitary saint whose name is held in great veneration there. Others imagine that it was first practised in this empire in the reign of Amiamid, supporting their notion by the Chronicle of Axuma, which relates, that in his time great numbers of monks[7] from Greece and Egypt spread themselves over all the empire, that nine of them fix'd in the kingdom of Tigre, where each built a church.[8]

In the time of the Patriarch Benjamin a new colony of monks, entirely Jacobites, was sent thither, and by their means it was that the sect so soon prevail'd over all the country,[9] they had

---

6. "undistinguishing ... reflexions" is SJ's expansion of "la manière dure & offensante" with which they spoke of the monks (p. 351).

7. Cf. "plusieurs moines" (p. 351).

8. The French names all nine monks (p. 351).

9. "the sect ... country" is SJ's milder version of: "le poison de l'hérésie se répandit si promptement dans tout le pays" (p. 351).

at their head Tecla-Hemanot, who was esteemed a saint among them. It is not probable that the Abyssins have ever since that time received any Catholick monk, whatever may be said on that subject by the Fathers Lewis de Angelis, Augustin, Francis,[1] John Dos-Sanctos, and lastly by Wansleb.

DISSERTATION THE FIFTEENTH, ON THE HIERARCHY OR GOVERNMENT OF THE CHURCH OF AETHIOPIA

Whoever reads Mr. Ludolf's *History of Aethiopia*, will discover that it is undertaken with no other intention than to show on one side the difference between the Roman Church and the Alexandrian, and on the other, the conformity of the Alexandrian with the Protestant churches. We are told by him, B. 2. C. 9. that the emperor of Aethiopia has an unlimited authority as well in religious as civil matters, over the church no less than the state; and he endeavours to prove his assertion by reminding us of what Sultan Segued did *for* and *against* the Jesuits, whom he call'd into his empire, and banish'd out of it, without consulting the patriarch of Alexandria. That prince, continues he, has, notwithstanding the patriarch, the whole ecclesiastical jurisdiction in his own hands, and assembles the councils or synods of his kingdom.[1] "It may be proper," says Mr. Ludolf, B. 3. C. 7. "to examine here in what manner the Church of Abyssinia is governed: we have said already that the king is vested with all the ecclesiastical authority, and that the judges appointed by him take cognisance of all sorts of affairs, and that none are exempt from their examination, except some trifling causes; ecclesiastical immunities are unknown in that country, and neither the clergy nor the monks have any privilege of exemption: the canon *Siquis suadente Diabolo*, was never heard of here, nor does any thing hinder their being punish'd by secular judges; they are often treated injuriously without any dread of excommunication."[2] For this Mr. Ludolf quotes the testimony of Father

---

1. SJ appears to have split into three persons a single French Augustan priest: "Louis des Anges Augustin, François ..." (p. 351).

1. *New History*, pp. 198–99.
2. SJ is translating from Le Grand's French (p. 353) but cf. *New History*, pp. 305–06.

Balthasar Tellez.[3] He knows not to what lengths the immunity of ecclesiasticks has been carried in Spain and Portugal where it has scarcely been heard of, that a priest or monk has suffer'd death even for the most enormous crimes. A priest bred in these prejudices looks upon the punishment of an ecclesiastick as a violation of all laws divine and human, and calls that injury and violence which was done by a severe and exact administration of justice, for the preservation of tranquillity and the publick welfare. The Patriarch Alphonso Mendez was extremely offended, at what the emperor thought he had no right to complain of,[4] that the prince had by his own authority order'd the interment of the general of[a] Saint Anthony's order, who had relapsed before his death. His remonstrances on this occasion were the original of those quarrels which produced consequences so fatal to the mission and missionaries.

There is not in the world a monarch more absolute than the emperor of Aethiopia, who hath nevertheless no authority in ecclesiastical affairs; nor has any right so much as to enter the sanctuary unless he be invested with holy orders. 'Tis for this reason that the emperors of Aethiopia are generally made deacons, and some of them priests. The Church of Abyssinia is governed by the metropolitan whom they call Abuna, that is, our father; and this metropolitan has no other bishop subordinate to him. He is named and consecrated by the patriarch of Alexandria who to keep this church in a more absolute dependance never gives them a prelate of their own country, so that, the Abuna, neither understanding the language, nor being able to make himself understood, it may easily be conceived how the Church is governed, and with what justice the pastor may say, "I know my sheep, and my sheep know me." Yet ignorant and unacquainted as he was with the people, he has formerly had so much power, that no man was acknowledged as king till he had been consecrated by the hands of the Abuna. So essential was this once thought[5] that the Abuna has sometimes made use

---

a. general of *Errata*] general *1735*

---

3. See *Commentarius*, p. 441, for the reference to Telles. The discussion of ecclesiastical immunity appears in Telles, p. 96.

4. "at what ... complain of" goes beyond what the French suggests: "de ce que l'Empereur Sultan Segued n'approuvait pas ..." (p. 353).

5. SJ adds this opening clause.

of this power to exclude usurpers and preserve the regal dignity to the true prince, a proof of which we have in the *History of the Patriarchs of Alexandria*, which was neither known to Father Tellez nor Mr. Ludolf.

In the life of John the seventy second patriarch of Alexandria, it is related,[6] that a prince of the house of Zague being refused consecration by the Abuna, demanded of the patriarch of Alexandria another metropolitan, he whom they then had being so old that he could not any longer execute the duties of his office. The patriarch who was acquainted with his intention, answer'd, that it was not allow'd by the canons to ordain a bishop for any place without the consent of him who was then in possession of the see, and chose rather to undergo a long and severe imprisonment from the grand vizier, who the emperor of Aethiopia had gain'd over to him, than to act contrary to his duty. Another king pressing the Metropolitan Michael to consecrate more than seven bishops, and being answer'd by him, that he could not do it without the consent of the patriarch of Alexandria, wrote on that affair to the patriarch and sultan, and not being able to obtain what he demanded, persecuted and banished the metropolitan: but the disapprobation of Heaven was soon visible in the many calamities with which the kingdom was afflicted[7] without ceasing, till the king acknowledged his fault, renounced his pretensions, and implored pardon of the Alexandrian patriarch.

The Abuna Kilus, having made himself notoriously infamous by many crimes,[8] Lalibala one of the most virtuous kings that the Abyssins ever enjoy'd, could not bear that they should go unchastised, and demanded of the patriarch of Alexandria that he should punish him. Kilus went into Egypt to clear himself of the crimes alledged against him, but his pleas being found insufficient, he was deposed with great ceremony, at Cairo. The patriarch consecrated Isaac who was received in Aethiopia, with greater honours than had ever been paid to any Abuna.

No one can imagine that if the kings of Abyssinia had an

---

6. Renaudot, *Historia patriarcharum*, p. 525.

7. "but the disapprobation ... afflicted" embellishes the French: "mais Dieu n'approuva pas la conduite de ce roi, il affligea son royaume de plusieurs fleaux ..." (p. 354).

8. SJ presents a darker villain than does Le Grand: "L'Abuna Kilus était tombé dans plusieurs crimes" (p. 354).

absolute power in ecclesiastical affairs and over their clergy, they would have recourse to a foreign power to punish their Abuna, when he stood charged with notorious crimes; or that they would remain so many ages in a mean and troublesome dependance on the patriarchs of Alexandria, especially when they have been almost whole ages without an Abuna, and consequently without priests and all kinds of spiritual assistances.

When they call councils or assemble synods, they do no more than was done by the Emperors Constantine and Theodosius,[9] and is done at this day by Christian princes, when they call their clergy together upon any necessity of the church or state; who yet are not said to lay their hands on the censer, or to have the same power over the church as the state.

The Abuna is in possession of a large extent of lands which yield him a considerable revenue, and the more because in this country where every man is in a state of servitude, his farmers are exempt from tribute, or pay it only to him, except in some lands which he holds in the kingdom of Tigre by paying a rent of five hundred crowns to the king, a tax laid upon him by King Theodore, and called *Eda Abuna*, or the Abuna's acknowledgment. They still make a collection for him of salt and linnen-cloth which rises to a considerable value. In spiritual matters he owns no other superior than the patriarch of Alexandria, and has little correspondence even with him after he is ordained. He is named first after him in all the publick prayers, and is honour'd with the seventh or eighth seat in the Arabick collection of canons called the Canons of Nice. His dignity tho' he has not a single bishop under him, places him above the metropolitans; and probably when this rank was first assigned him, regard was had to the extent of his diocess. Dispensations are only granted by him, and several have been so avaricious, that they have carried that power much farther than is allowed by the canons.

The Abuna is in some respects a patriarch, in others he is not; nor can we better inform the reader of the extent of his authority, or of his rank, than by referring him to the canon already set down in the ninth dissertation.

We have shown, in the explication of those canons the melan-

9. Cf. "Constantin, Théodose, Marien" (p. 354).

cholly and vexatious dependance of the Abyssinian Church, and the abuses and corruptions which are in some degree the necessary consequences of such a state, which the princes certainly, had they any power over their clergy, or did they believe it lawful for them to intermeddle in ecclesiastical affairs, would not have born so long. This servitude is nevertheless as ancient as the church of Abyssinia, and hath continued from the time they were first blessed with the light of the Gospel.

The Abuna therefore acknowledges the patriarch of Alexandria as his superior in these affairs, and acknowledges none but him.

The prelates which are sent thither are incapable of instructing the people, since they neither understand the language nor the customs of the country. Their whole office is to ordain priests yet more ignorant than themselves, and often of corrupt morals; from hence proceed all those errors and abuses with which we so justly reproach the Abyssins.

The *komos* or *hegumenos*[b] are the first ecclesiastical order after the bishops, and as there are no bishops in Aethiopia, the *komos* acknowledge no order above themselves, and precede all the other priests. *Hegumenus ejusdem ordinis est atque*[c] *archipapas sacerdotum seu archipresbyter, atque*[d] *adeo jus habet pronunciandi orationem absolutionis super sacerdotem celebrantem, ut etiam adolendi incensum post eum, & communionem accipiendi post eum, ante*[e] *omnes alios. Quando simul adest, episcopus accipit ab eo thuribulum.*[1] A priest cannot be ordained a bishop among the Cophtes, unless he be first a *komos* or *hegumenos*, which is not the same with the sub-presbyter, affirm'd by Mr. Ludolf to be the priest or the deacon: this sub-presbyter, is the same with what we call assisting priests when mass is celebrated with greater solemnity.

Low masses or particular masses are not known in Abyssinia, where mass is celebrated only in one manner by the priest accompanied with many priests and deacons. Alvarez writes,

b. hegumos *1735*   c. atque *1789*] atq: *1735*   d. atque *1789*] atq; *1735*   e. post eum, ante *Relation*] ab eo, unte *1735*

---

1. Renaudot, *Historia patriarcharum*, p. 585. [An hegumenus is of the same rank of priests as an archipapas or an archipresbyter and in the same way has the right of pronouncing absolution over the priest who is celebrant as well as of lighting incense after him and of receiving communion from him before all others. When a bishop is present, the bishop receives the thurible from him.]

that the Abyssins although they did not absolutely condemn our practise, were astonish'd at the manner in which the Portuguese celebrated the divine mysteries, and were particularly surprised to find that they did not go barefoot to the church, and that they spit in it.[2] The monks never marry. 'Tis pretended that there are two sorts of them, one of which forms a congregation under their general who resided anciently at Debra-Libanos, but that monastry being much exposed to the incursions of the Galles, he left it to establish himself and his monks in the kingdom of Bagameder. The others have the same common rule, but their monastries have no dependance on each other. They are for the most part in great credit, and monks are often employ'd in the most important affairs of state. The former ascribe their institution to the famous Tecla Haimanout, whose feast they celebrate with much solemnity on the 24th of August and the 24th of December, and in the month of May they commemorate the translation of his reliques. He is believed by the Abyssins to have work'd a great number of miracles. The other monks claim Eustathius for their founder, to whose honour in July they celebrate a festival.

There are likewise two sorts of hermits; some who choose that kind of life that they may, in some measure, be more at liberty; and others who quit their convents with the leave of their superiors to lead a life of greater austerity in solitude.

There is no doubt that the monks make vows though they do not always keep them with sufficient exactness.

The Patriarch Alphonso Mendez relates that he enquired of Azage Tixo, secretary to the king of Aethiopia, who had been a monk, if the religious made any vows; and that he was told by the secretary a man of gay temper, that the religious, lying prostrate on the ground, promise their superior aloud, to preserve their chastity, adding in a low voice, "as you preserve yours"; and that they make all the other vows with the same restriction.[3]

We may say nevertheless that in Abyssinia, as in every other place, there are pious and wicked monks to be found; and that the pious part of their monks carry austerities and mortification much farther than the most rigorous of our hermits.

F I N I S

2. SJ again deletes a reference to Abyssinian canons: "Les chanoines se marient, & souvent leurs canonicats passent à leurs enfants" (p. 356).

3. See Beccari, VIII. 74.

INDEX

Most place names have been indexed in their modern form as found in *The Times Atlas of the World,* with the name as spelled in the *Voyage* indicated in parentheses. If the spelling of a name in the *Voyage* is very different from the modern spelling, the name is indexed separately, with a cross reference. Some older forms—for example, Constantinople—have been left, and the modern equivalent (Istanbul) placed in parentheses. Ethiopian locations can often be found on the Carte d'Abissinie reproduced on the endpapers in this volume. Although this map, a redrawn version of Ludolf's somewhat inaccurate one of 1674, should not be relied upon in lieu of a modern map, it does provide a useful tool for readers of this volume. Ethiopian locations listed in the index have been keyed to the latitudes and longitudes listed on the edges of that map. A sample entry will look like this: Beilul, Red Sea port (Carte, 13/72); where the name on the Carte differs significantly from the spelling in the text, the entry will look like this: Gingiro (Carte: Zendero, 8–8/½/65). The appearance of the Hakluyt Society Lobo (*The Itinerário of Jerónimo Lobo,* 1984) just before this index went to press has made possible some identifications and some guesses at locations; these are attributed to *Hakluyt.*

Individuals are indexed under modern spellings of their names except for a few better known to readers of Le Grand or Johnson in one form (e.g., Sultan Segued rather than Susenyos). Cross references are provided.

The abbreviation Ab. is used to designate Abyssinian.

Aaron, angry at Moses, 159
Ababitay, an Abyssin excluded from sacraments because he had three wives, 296
Abada, or *bada*, two-horned animal, 188
Abagaleb. *See* Abugaleb
Aba-Garima (Abbagarima, Aba Gariman), monastery inhabited by a devil, 77; tomb of, 311
Abagnes, naked king of, 13 n.1
Aba Licanos, tomb of, 311
Abargale, Ab. province (Carte, 14½/67−68), 162, 163
Abasseni, "a nation of Arabia," 160 n.5
Abavi, Father of Waters (Nile), 81, 171
Abbott, John Lawrence, xlix−1, li, liii n. 7
Abdel-Aziz, 310
Abgarus, King, 309
Abra, King, 246
Abraham (Bible), 234, 237
Abraham, Ab. king, 199
Abrim, country traversed by Nile, 173
Abudacnus, Joseph, teacher of Arabic at Oxford (c. *1600*), *Historia Jacobitarum seu Coptorum*, 273
Abugaleb (Abagaleb), father of John the patriarch, 204, 240
Abu'l Baracat (Abulbaracat), quotes treatises on confession, 292
Abû'l Faraj, Gregory (Abulfarage) or Bar Hebraeus *(1226−86);* prelate and historical writer: *Historia compendiosa dynastiarum*, on Chingiscan, 195−96
Abulfeda. *See* Assiouthi
Abuna, head of Ab. church: appointed by patriarch of Alexandria, 314; cannot be an Ab., 249; horse trader appoints self as, 120; powers of, 316
Abû Sâlih (Abuselah): *Churches and Monasteries of Egypt and Some Neighbouring Countries*, 199
Abusebah. *See* Ibn Sabâ
Abuselah. *See* Abû Sâlih
Abyssinia or Aethiopia (Ethiopia): dissertation on, 159−68
  Abyssins: C. da Gama's troops have no confidence in, 66; credulity of, 76−77; physical characteristics of, 161; as spectators at battle between Grañ and Portuguese, 65

Christianity in: conversion of Abyssins, dissertation on, 244−65; corrupted, 43; idiosyncratic beliefs, xxxi−xxxii
church of: Alexandrian church, relationship with, 247−49; beliefs of, 52−55; no bishops in, 317; Claudius and Oviedo argue about, 257−58; Council of Chalcedon rejected by, xxvii; emperor suggests submission to Rome, xxix; Franciscans given mission by, 139; Geddes praises, xlv; and heresies, Eutychian and Nestorian, 266−72; hierarchy of, 313−15; Incarnation, dissertation on church errors relating to, 265−72; Jacobites of, 157, 193; Jesuits banished by, xxxiv; Ludolf "misrepresents," 157; Mendes' concern for, 131; Mendes' interest in, SJ's view of, liii; Renaudot's memoirs of, 283; Roman Catholic church, conflicts with, xliii, 5; Roman Catholic missionaries, no security for, 97; Roman Catholics persecuted by, 118−19; Roman Catholics' plight in, 115; sacraments of, 273; saints in, 55, 308; turmoil in, 120. *See also* Johnson, Samuel
description and geography of: xxvi-xxvii, 21, 42, 162−67; climate, 44, 55−56, 168; crops, 44−45; farm revenues, 61−62; Gondar listed as capital, 138; mountains, 35, 38, 166−67, 178−79; natural resources, 168; rainy season related to Nile floods, 89; snow as possible cause of floods, 88, 176
history of, 40−41; called the lesser India by Marco Polo, 193; Lobo an early authority on, xxxvi; Portuguese first gave knowledge of, 205
kings of: additional names of, 212; no authority over ecclesiastical affairs, 314; belief they hold keys of Nile, 180; coronation of, 211; dissertation on, 207−15; military might of, 214; pedigree of, 41; power of, 213−14; mentioned, 203, 204, 205
legends of: Prester John, xxvii, dissertation on, 190−207; Queen

322

338

INDEX

Lobo da Gama *(continued)*
Jerónimo, xxxii
Lockhart, Donald M., translator of
Hakluyt *Itinerário*, xxxvi, xxxviii n.,
xl n.3, 163 n., 273 n.3
London Evening-Post, advertisement
for *Voyage* at reduced price, xxvi
Louis VII *(1120–80)*, king of France,
196
Louis XIV *(1638–1715)*, king of
France, xlv
Loyola, Ignatius, St. *(1491–1556)*,
Spanish founder of Society of
Jesus, suggests Oviedo to lead first
Jesuit mission to Ethiopia, xxix
Luabo River, Moçambique, 219
Lucan *(38–65)*, Roman epic poet,
Pharsalia, 169
Ludolf, Hiob *(1624–1704)*, scholar
and writer on Ethiopia: on Ab.
reverence for Sabbath, 242–43;
believes Al-Makīn about possibility
of diverting the Nile, 179–80;
Basilides' quiet reign, attempts to
defend, 129, 133; Catholics and
missionaries, his criticism of,
xliii–xliv, 5, 153; on circumcision,
234–35, 236; contempt for
Wansleben, 158; criticized xliv, 133,
237, 270–71, 284–85, 288, 296,
306, 307; dissertation on his history
of Abyssinia, 151–59; *gondar* or
guender identified by him as
meaning only *camp*, 138; Gregory
made famous in his history, 130; SJ
praised him, xliv; Murat answers
him in *New Account*, 155–56;
quarrels with Piques, 153–55;
quoted, 160 n.; his reliance on
Gregory criticized, 152, 157, 281;
his scholarship, 151; song of
rejoicing on expulsion of Jesuits
quoted by, xxxi; on
transubstantiation, 286
Commentarius, 236, 243 n., 250, 269
n.9, 270 n.5, 293 n.4, 300, 301
n.1, 308 n.2, 314 n.3
Historia Aethiopica, xxvii n.2,
234–35, 250, 286 n.9, 308 n.3,
313
New History, 269 n.8, 270 n.8, 279
n.2, 281 n.2, 286 n.9, 300, 307
n.8, 309 n.5, 311 n.1, 313
*New Account of the Present State of
Aethiopia*, 137, 155–56
mentioned or cited: 163, 164, 166,

171, 173, 189, 191, 205, 209,
216, 243, 251, 252 n.5, 269, 272,
273, 274, 279, 283, 285, 293,
308, 310, 315, 317
Luke, St., supposed to have drawn
picture of Blessed Virgin, 309
Lutheranism, Peter Heyling attempts
to spread in Ethiopia, 122 n.1;
Ludolf represents Abyssins as
Lutherans, 157, 158
Lynan, Edward, ed., *Richard Hakluyt
and His Successors*, xxxix n.1

Maccabees, Books of, canonical but
omitted from Ab. scriptures, 53
Macé, interpreter for du Roule, 144
Machado, Father François, martyred
by king of Adal, 183 n.2
Macheda. *See* Makeda
Machy River (Carte: Matshi,
9½/69–70), tributary of Awash,
175
Macrisius, 180
Maçua. *See* Massawa
Madeiras Islands, Portugal, 178
Madrid, xxxiv, 101, 116
Maegoga. *See* Maigoga
Magadoxo. *See* Mogadishu
Magalotti, Lorenzo *(1637–1712)*,
Italian philosopher, translates
Wyche version of Lobo, xxxvi
Magi, the, 223, 229, 291
Magueda. *See* Makeda
Mahomet (c. *570–632*), the Prophet,
233
Mahomet Gragné. *See* Grañ, Ahmad
ibn Ibrahim al-Ghazi
Maigoga, ancient name for Fremona,
55, 57, 163
Mait (Methe), Somalia, 183
Makeda (Macheda, Magueda,
Maqueda), Queen of Sheba, Queen
of the South, 41, 208, 226, 234
Malabar, Indian cape, 8, 9; barks of
feared by Jesuits, 114
Malacca, Malaysian trading port, 181,
218
Maldives Islands, Indian Ocean, 185
Maleck River (Melecca), White Nile
(Carte, 9½–15/62–65), 166, 175
Malec Segued III, added name for
Sultan Segued, 212
Malindi (Melinda), Kenya, an entry
point for Abyssinia, inhabited by
Gallas, 10, 14, 23, 69, 182, 183
Malvana, Sri Lanka, king of, 181

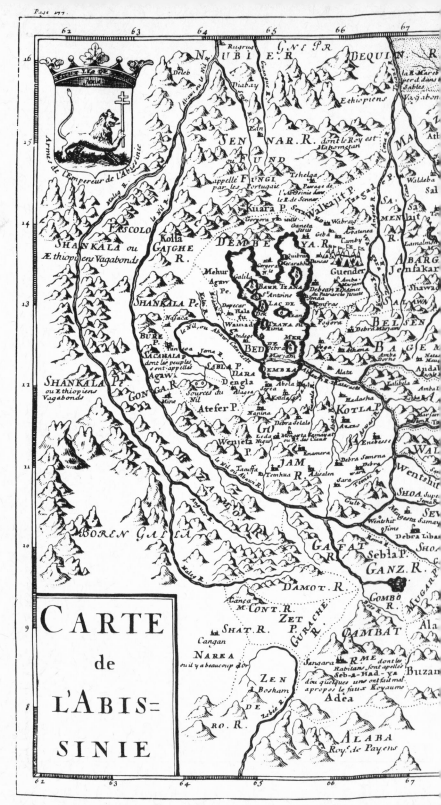

Abyssinia, from a map (redrawn from Ludolf's earlier map) in Le Grand's French translation of